Praise for *Flight*

'An adventure story that encapsulates both a physical and spiritual journey… interesting and original with some startling contrasts between the ordinary and the extraordinary.'

Bookseller & Publisher

'Dub writes evocatively about a beautiful landscape but, in the end it is the touching love story between Fern and Adam that truly compels.'

Sydney Morning Herald

'A mesmerising tale of the real, unreal and surreal…'

Weekend Gold Coast Bulletin

'*Flight* contains all the elements of a Gothic romance: the villain the persecuted heroine, the damaged hero and the forbidding mansion. Dub has a firm handle on action and pacing but in the end the realistic details of this novel: the Tasmanian wilderness, the shambles of Fern's mother's house… enable Flight to take off on what proves to be an enjoyable voyage.'

The Sunday Australian

'The sharp depiction and the emotional force of the narrative are impressive. Still more striking is Dub's ability to maintain the reader's fondness for her eccentric characters… *Flight* is an effective, well-written and glimmering novel with well-drawn characters, a good sense of place and a satisfying number of twists along the way.'

Flinders Indaily.

'This tightly written contemporary gothic tale grips readers from the first page…'

Busselton Dunsborough Times

'*Flight* is propelled by passion and sincerity as well as the rapid trajectory of the story line. It's a novel that will speak particularly to those who find themselves troubled by a sense of powerlessness over their lives.'

Tasmanian Times

Other Works by Rosie Dub

Fiction

Gathering Storm
*Between Worlds (*sequel to *Flight)*

Dr Rosie Dub is the author of the novels, *Gathering Storm*, *Fligh*t and *Between Worlds* (a standalone sequel to *Flight*). Her PhD explored the nature of story and its role as a developmental tool for individuals and cultures. Rosie shares her research in her *Alchemy of Story* newsletter on substack and the *Alchemy of Story* workshop series she runs in Australia and the UK.

Alchemy of Story

Rosie Dub
https://rosiedub.com/

Flight

Rosie Dub

First published in Australia by HarperCollins Fourth Estate, 2012.
Second edition, published by New Mill, 2017
Third edition published by Alchemy of Story, 2025

'Green Ears' by Jalal al-Din Rumi from The Essential Rumi, translated by Coleman Barks, published by Harper San Francisco, a division of HarperCollins, 2004. Text reprinted with kind permission from Coleman Barks.

Cover design by Jason Anscomb
Formatting by Streetlight Graphics

ISBN: 978-0-6481227-2-2

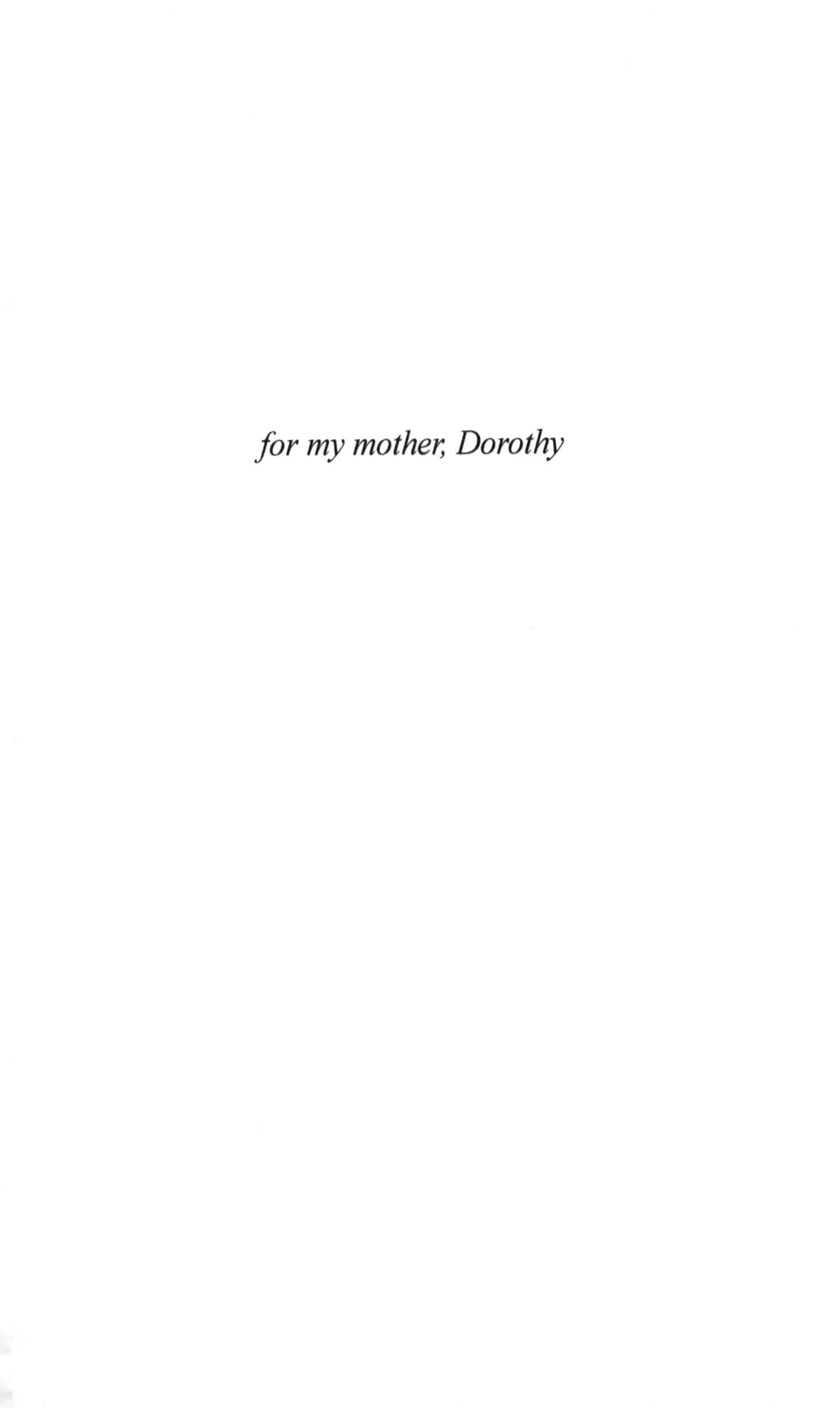

for my mother, Dorothy

The way of love is
not a subtle argument.

The door there
is devastation.

Birds make great sky-circles
of their freedom.
How do they learn it?

They fall, and falling,
they're given wings.

Rumi

Prologue

I came early, slithering into the outside world and into safety, or so I hoped. But this was to be the first of many hopes, all dashed against the brutally sharp edges of reality.

As in all great myths, my birth was accompanied by a prophecy. I, it seemed, would be the death of my father. How this was to come about no one could say. But the prophecy was there; it escaped from the mouth of Simple Simon, the old gardener at the Botanic Gardens in Adelaide where my mother often went to sit in her lunch hour.

On this particular day she was waiting to meet my father. He was late and the pregnant girl felt a persistent nagging worry. There was something big hovering around the edges of things, a sense that life had woken up that morning slightly askew. Nothing she could put her finger on, but it was enough to make her nervous. And then there were the contradictions: worry that he would come, worry that he would not. Fear and love tugging her between them until all she could feel was a tearing anxiety. You see, my father was a strong-willed man, older than her, but still too young, he said, to be tied down like this. He would have walked away but he was snared by his desire for my mother. She was beautiful and fragile and needy, easy to bully but also detached in a way that he could never put a finger on. This detachment was what kept him there, waiting, wanting her to surrender completely.

It was summer but there was an unexpected chill in the air. The wind was a fresh south easterly, not the usual hot northerly that stirred up dust and discomforts, and the sky was clear enough to make everyone's heart lift. Even my mother's, the seventeen-year-old girl with the rounded belly who sat on a bench chewing a devilled-egg sandwich and watching Simon methodically plant a row of violets, a flurry of chattering birds surrounding him.

When a magpie greedily pecked Simon's finger, perhaps thinking it a fat juicy worm, my mother forgot her troubles for a moment and laughed. Simon looked up, directly at her, and her laughter quickly turned into a shudder. Where one eye should have been there was a socket, dark and deep. One eye looking out, the other inwards – perhaps this was the secret of his second sight. Or then again, it might have been the snakebite all those years ago which had left him hovering between life and death for weeks on end. When he finally woke, he knew things other people didn't, but he had forgotten how to live in this world. No one knew how old Simple Simon was or how long he'd been working in the Botanic Gardens. He was a fixture, like the giant oak under which my mother sat.

Simon stood up straight, wincing as he stretched, one hand massaging the small of his back, the other leaning on his spade. 'Ah,' he said, shaking his head. 'That one will be the death of her father.' Wincing again at the creaking in his swollen joints, he walked over to my mother and poked his finger into her tight belly. 'Mark my words, the death of him.' Then while she sat staring at him, open-mouthed, he went back to his planting, still shaking his head, but with a gleam in his eye.

At that moment I moved. Well, bounced really. Did a somersault in a small space, causing my mother to double over in pain and think her time had come. It hadn't. I wasn't going anywhere. Safety, I thought, lay in the warm fluids that contained me. And I didn't want to kill anyone, especially my own father, though even then I wasn't exactly fond of him. Already there'd been words, accompanied by white knuckles and fists, sending me curling up into a tighter self-protective ball. My father didn't love me. Even then I knew that. And he didn't love my mother. Like me, she stood between him and his plans. He wanted only to conquer her, in the same way he planned to conquer the world. You see, my father had big ideas swirling inside his head. Even then he loved power more than people. Even then he would let nothing stand in his way.

My mother loved my father but for all the wrong reasons. Love, hate and fear were woven tightly within her. She was young and weak and couldn't distinguish between these things. She wanted me and she didn't. She was afraid. It's not unusual. And Simon's prophecy had filled her throat with the burning need to tell. So when my father arrived a few minutes later, she laughed a kind of brittle nervous laugh and repeated what Simon had said. It was a big mistake, because more than anything my father wanted to live. He was a rational man, or so he claimed, but underneath that rationality lay a deep-rooted superstition. Underneath everything, he knew the power of shadow.

At first he tried to laugh it off but my mother could see the discomfort in his eyes and the tension in his fingers, already bunching up into fists.

'You should have got rid of it,' he hissed. 'I told you.' Then he hit my mother hard in the belly, the shock and pain spreading through her thin skin and into me.

At that moment I decided it was safer out than in. I fled, bursting the bag that contained me, sending the warm liquid pouring down my mother's legs, soaking her pants and forming a puddle on the ground under where she sat, her heart beating in terror from the attack, her breath coming in quick panting bursts. Her fear spread quickly into me. In a panic I bounced my head again and again, pushing at her uterus, sending out waves of contractions. She ran, out of the gardens and onto the footpath, winding her way through pedestrians, doubling over with the pain as another contraction hit, then running again, away from him, away from the agony that was me and that was tearing her neatly down the middle.

It was lunch hour in the city and there were a lot of people about. She could see the concern in their eyes but her terror didn't allow her to respond. Like a panicked horse she bolted, not noticing where she was. It took a Don't Walk sign to bring her to her senses. Perhaps it was some instinct for survival, or the need to protect me. Perhaps it was fate, for the prophecy had been written in the stars and spoken aloud by Simple Simon, setting it in motion. Or perhaps someone reached out their hand and grabbed her arm or dress, yanking her to a halt. It could have been any of these things that made her stop, only a half-second away from the truck that muscled across the intersection, dangerously close to the kerb, making everyone step back and brushing the wind through her hair just as my head burst free of the birth canal, only to find itself imprisoned in her underpants as she slid, moaning, to the ground. And all the time my father stood back in the crowd, watching me emerge and wanting to stamp the life out of me but unable to come forward. Yet.

He was biding his time. My father wasn't an evil man but he had already done wrong, and this deed had set in motion others. Then it was only a matter of time, as the prophecy ate away at him, turning him into its slave. Perhaps the seeds of madness had already been planted deep in his heart, in this life or another. Or perhaps they were sown later; I am not sure, for it is hard to see the beginnings of things.

People always say that children can't remember. That babies have no language and therefore no memories. That an abandoned baby can't be traumatised. They're wrong. There are many ways of knowing. The memories we carry in our consciousness are not the only ones. There are others, ones we can't relate in words, and yet their scar tissue builds up so that we live every day of our lives in reaction to them. I have learned first-hand that we carry memory in our cells. Unresolved trauma acts like a cancer, scarring, mutating, warping the cells that contain it until they become sick. Remembering is implicit in the decision to enter the labyrinth, to look inside ourselves, at our wounds and our carefully buried strengths. It's there in the patterns we identify in our lives. And there too in the truths we discover and recognise as having always known. I know these things because I have looked deeply into myself and seen what needed seeing.

I was born in Adelaide on the second of January, 1989. From the beginning, life for me was a serious matter of survival, but it was also something I did not relish at all. There's a contradiction in this, I know, and one that tugged me this way and that, making me strong, yet fearful; determined, yet too ready to give up. A contradiction that for many years trapped me in a half-life, a twilight world of muted colours. A prison I didn't even know I was in until I made my escape.

I entered this world wearing my mother's blood and carrying the marks of my father's fist on my back. Within minutes of my birth an ambulance arrived, its siren sending my heart thumping too fast all over again. There were danger signals everywhere and I could no longer distinguish between what was safe and what was not. But I was a tiny baby, born a month early, and the hands of those men were gentle as they carried me to the relative safety of the hospital.

He tried one more time, in the hospital ward, his large hand grabbing me by the leg and swinging me up and out of the plastic crib and head first into the wall. One swing, but he hadn't built up momentum yet. My mother's loyalties were torn, but for that one crucial moment the hormones swilling through her body put her on my side. She screamed. Just once, but there was a tone in it, enough to bring people running. Before the next swing a nurse appeared in the doorway and, reading the madness in my father's eyes, pressed the alarm.

Already a master of disguise, my father recovered quickly, cradling me in his arms, uttering comforting baby noises while I stared mutely up into his eyes, my heart thudding in my chest.

'I slipped,' he told the nurse. 'I almost dropped her. My God, they're so fragile.' Then, as a nurse took her from him, 'She's alright, isn't she?'

Uncertain now, the nurse looked at my mother lying there in the crisp white hospital bed, wearing a white hospital gown because there'd been no time to pack, sobbing, milk leaking from her nipples.

My mother looked at each of us in turn, seeing the threat in my father's eyes, the bewildered fear in mine and the question in the nurse's. Then, stony-faced, she turned away from us all. She had made a decision.

'It was an accident,' she said. 'He slipped.'

But she did sign the adoption forms. To keep me safe.

Then she wrapped me tightly in a white blanket, placed me back in the plastic see-through hospital-issue crib and wheeled me into a room full of other howling cribs, setting me loose into a sea of indifference with no anchor and no oars, with only the sun, the moon and the stars to navigate by, and no lessons to help me decipher them.

On my original birth certificate there is a blank space next to *Father*. My mother's name is listed as Joan Childe. My name is listed as Erica. On my second birth certificate my father's name is listed as Richard Parsons, my mother's as Grace Parsons My adopted parents called me Fernanda after an evangelical missionary they favoured at the time. I called myself Fern.

More than anything I wanted to fly. But in order to fly, one must first be willing to fall. And fall I did. This is the story of my journey, following the clues back through the twists and turns that made me into what I was, searching for the moments of definition: the overheard sentence, the intention in another's eyes, a boy seducing a girl, a fist, a beating and a mother turning away. I had to go deep into the underworld and enter the labyrinth, with no guarantee of return, seeking the threads that I could weave into a rope thick enough to haul me out again.

In my story there are those gifted and cursed with the power of prophecy. There's a young man haunted by the past and an old man haunted by the future. There's death and corruption and injustice. There's love and passion and hatred, all carried across lifetimes. Occasionally there's compassion. But more often, as in real life, there is fear.

I'm there too. Haunted and hollow. An outline, waiting to be filled in. Poised trembling before the entrance to the labyrinth. A shadow of the self I should have been. A shadow of who I am now as I sit here looking for a beginning when there isn't one, when there never is, because life is simply not neat, and one story hardly ever ends before another begins. Instead they span time and space, reaching back into a past that extends beyond our first breath and into a future that extends beyond our last, through a multitude of lives and tied only by the threads of souls and their patterns.

In the absence of a clear beginning, I will draw an artificial line through time and begin on that stiflingly hot afternoon, in the attic room of a run-down terrace in the inner suburbs of Sydney…

Chapter One

It had been days, possibly weeks, since Fern had ventured out of her attic. Her house mates had tried everything they could think of to get her to open the door: banged, shouted and cajoled, but they'd stopped short of breaking it down. After all, it was her choice. Then they'd begged her to come out, telling Fern that it made them uncomfortable to have her pacing back and forth above them. They didn't say it, but she knew what they were holding on the tips of their tongues. She could hear the unspoken words as clearly as the sirens that pierced the night.

Today was hot, a humid, smothering kind of heat. Though it was midday it seemed more like dusk with the dark clouds brooding above the smoky orange haze. It was as if the world was paused, waiting for something to break. She felt it inside herself too, the tautness that comes when a rubber band is stretched too far. It made her anxious, this waiting. With the smoke and the pollution clinging to the wet air it was hard to breathe. It had been this way for weeks, and now everything was damp: green powdery mould clung to her shoes and bags, and in the drawers, her limp clothes smelled sickly sweet. Even the fan gave little relief, only pushing warm air around the room. She'd become used to its constant whirring and the swish of air in her face as it passed, ruffling her hair for a second, the papers on her desk lifting and falling, her mosquito net billowing in gentle rippling curves. To some extent the fan was useful, keeping the mosquitoes at bay, exiling them into dark corners among her clothes and under her desk.

Suddenly Fern felt she would suffocate if she didn't get some air. Panicking, she threw herself at the window, struggling with the lock but the wood, swollen by the damp, had stuck. She tugged, feeling the desperation rising inside her, and at the very moment she opened her mouth to scream with frustration, the window suddenly gave, making her lose balance and almost fall through. Leaning out of the window as far as she could, she breathed deeply, the hot air catching in her throat and sending her into a spasm of coughing. Perhaps it was a fraction cooler outside but the pollution was worse and the atmosphere thick with smoke. She felt it settle on her skin, tickling her nose and making her sneeze.

The traffic noise was so loud: three lanes one way, almost constant, like a slow-flowing river. Everyone was going somewhere, doing something yet Fern had nothing to do. How did I get here? she asked herself. To this room, this afternoon, this state of mind? It wasn't sudden or dramatic - just a series of decisions she guessed - though she couldn't follow the maths. How one day off college had turned into two. How one skipped shift at the pub and one missed date had multiplied into many. Until here she was, unable to rouse herself from the torpor she'd sunk into. Depression, Claire called it. 'Simple,' she'd said. 'Just get some pills.' But Claire was wrong. It wasn't simple at all.

A siren started up in the distance, then another and another, rising into a frightening crescendo. It seemed as if the city was spiralling towards chaos, the air filled with smoke and sirens and the nervous tension of millions of people running one step ahead of themselves. Or perhaps chaos had already arrived, an unwelcome guest slipping in through a back door when no one was watching. And by the time anyone did notice it would be too late.

Flakes of ash were floating in through the window. They looked like snow, weightless and aimless, leaving gracefully curving trails. Fern watched them settle on her skin, landing so gently she could only imagine a sensation. She touched one and ran her finger down her arm, leaving a dark smudge on her skin. Then she drew a line with another until if formed a pattern. For some time she stood looking at the ash spiral on her arm, wondering.

Leaving the window open, Fern climbed back onto her bed. The fractionally cooler air was worth it, even with the smoke, but the mosquitoes were buzzing around her legs and her ears, looking for blood. She pulled the mosquito net across the bed and lay watching the frustrated insects fly around and around, sometimes settling on the white mesh as if they might chew a way through. In the strange pre-storm light her room looked whiter than ever. Almost glowing. White walls, white floors, the mosquito net a white sail.

Downstairs, Pete and Claire were still moving around. Their busy activity had been going on for two days and Fern's initial alarm had dulled. Instead she was irritated and bored. She supposed it was ironic that she felt trapped up here; after all, she'd chosen to stay in her room. But usually the others left early each day and then Fern would come out of her room, safe from questions and expectant faces. She would wash up a few things and wander about the house, even go down the street for supplies if necessary. Today was a weekday, probably Tuesday, and yet they were still here filling up the house with noise and breaking all the rules: clomping up and down the narrow staircase, negotiating furniture through doorways, issuing orders, laughing, moving on, leaving her behind.

It would be so easy to stand up, walk over to the door, unlock it, walk down the stairs, smile, speak … So easy, but she couldn't do it. She hardly spoke anymore, except to buy milk and bread and coffee when she needed it, though even then she could get away with barely a word. She just piled what she needed into a basket and paid at the counter. People almost never bothered with please and thank you in Sydney. They looked through you. She was used to it now, used to the contradictions it created inside her: an exhilarating sense of liberation and a howling loneliness that threatened to engulf her.

Fern tensed at the sound of footsteps on the stairs up to her room. A few seconds later someone knocked on her door.

'Fern, are you there? It's me, Claire.'

Fern didn't move. Claire meant well. She wasn't angry like Pete was. Sometimes she even left things outside the door: a hot meal, flowers, a book. At first Fern had spoken to Claire, even let her in. But Claire wanted answers to questions that had no answers. She wanted to fix everything, as if there were solutions. It made Fern feel like a stupid rebellious schoolgirl. In the end she had stopped letting her in and now she didn't even answer when Claire tried to talk to her.

Claire knocked again and tried the door. 'Fern, you've got to listen to me. We're leaving … The house is empty. You have to come out. Don't you understand? You can't just stay here. The landlord will find you.'

Fern felt the panic rising from deep inside her belly. She held her breath, waiting for Claire to give up and go. If she kept still enough maybe they would all leave her alone.

Claire sighed. 'Your mum rang again last night. She's worried. I told her, Fern. I'm sorry but I can't cover for you anymore. It's gone too far.' Claire tried the door handle. 'Please come out,' she pleaded. 'I don't know what to do. I don't even know if you're alive.'

There were more footsteps and then a new, heavier banging on the door. 'Fern, open this fucking door.'

'Maybe we should force it open, Pete.'

'Yeah right, so we break the door down and kiss goodbye to any hope of our bond. We need the fucking money.'

'But she might be sick or dead.'

'She's probably moved out.'

'She's in there, I know it. Fern, please let us in.'

'Leave it, Claire, there's nothing we can do. She's bloody bonkers anyway. Let them come and take her away.'

Fern lay quite still, listening to their footsteps going back down the stairs, one flight and then the next. Her heart was racing, her chest and throat cluttered with unspoken words. Pete was right, she was bonkers. It was only a matter of time before someone came and knowing this was all tangled up with relief and dread.

Sometime later, Fern heard Claire's footsteps again and then a gentle knock.

'Here's some mail for you.' There was a pause, as if Claire were listening, then she slipped some envelopes under the door. 'I've got to go now. We don't know how long we'll be at the new place, but if you need anything, any help, or somewhere to sleep, let me know. Look after yourself, Fern,' she added, and then quietly, 'I miss you.'

As Claire's footsteps receded, Fern glanced at her clock. It was 1.03 pm. She was all alone. Abandoned. Fern felt a surge of anger at the world. It wasn't her fault. She hadn't chosen this shadow life, instead it had crept up on her from behind. More tears came as she lay on the bed wishing she could turn back time and engage with the world again, the way she used to. Life had once been full of possibilities. There had been joy too, not always, but sometimes it had taken her over and life had seemed so good. Wistfully, she remembered how she and her house-mates had laughed together over long dinners of lentils and cheap red wine, had sunny afternoon picnics in Centennial Park, sat up nights moaning over assignments and woken in the mornings eager to step into a new day.

Downstairs the back door slammed and a few minutes later a truck started up in the alley. The house was suddenly quiet. Fern waited five minutes, then another five, just to be safe, before unlocking her door and peering down the stairs. She listened, her ears alert to the slightest noise, afraid that it was a trick and someone would be lying in wait for her. But there were no human noises, only the familiar creaks and sighs of the terrace house below. After another few minutes, Fern crept down the stairs to the first floor, then down another flight to the ground floor. The house was completely empty. Her footsteps echoed loudly, the sound bouncing off the bare walls; even her breathing was louder, now there was nothing to absorb the noise. Already the house had taken on an empty smell, something indefinable, like the taste of water, more an absence than anything else: no wafting perfumes or ripening peaches, no floating trails of breath or burning toast. Only vacant spaces were left, waiting for new definitions.

Fern walked from one room to the next, amazed at how quickly life can go from a place. There were square white patches on the walls where pictures had hung, rectangles and semicircles of dust on the floor where furniture had sat, stained patches on carpets marking red wine spills, mould on the windows which curtains had once hidden. It was too light now, too quiet and too loud. Every tiny sound made her jump until finally a sudden creak sent her flying back up the stairs, two at a time.

With the door locked behind her, Fern stood in the centre of her room, catching her breath. She could feel the great space of the house underneath her, stretching, yawning into the distance as if she were standing at the top of the tallest tower. It made her dizzy. But it also made her feel safer, to be so far from everyone.

On the floor were the three letters and a folded piece of paper that Claire had slipped under the door. On the paper Claire had written her new address and phone number. Fern put it in her wallet. There was a letter from the college, one from Grace, and one with 'card only' written in the corner. Fern ripped it open. A Christmas card from Auntie Alma, with a five-dollar note. Better than the oversized undies she used to give Fern each year. But surely it was too early for Christmas cards. Fern could hardly believe she'd lost so much time.

The letter from the college confirmed what she already knew. She had failed. Non-attendance, not handing in assignments … She had never got around to withdrawing, so now she was faced with a huge debt. For nothing. What had she learned? That she didn't want to be a fashion designer after all. How could she justify designing clothes when there were so many more important things to do? There were people starving and tortured, left without homes; environments stripped and poisoned; corrupt governments. Fern had a sense of something she needed to do and an urgency within her to get on with it but she didn't know what or how or where to start and she felt powerless to make any difference. The result was this strange paralysis that had trapped her in a shadowy half-life.

Fern picked up the letter from Grace and sighed. This would be the most difficult to read. Already she could feel her mother's disappointment weighing her down. And the 'I told you so's', because her father had never wanted her to do fashion design. Perhaps she should have heeded his advice and got a job in the bank, though even now she shuddered at the thought. The tedium of doing the same thing day after day, under fluorescent lights, gagging on customers' perfume and pretending the world was just as it should be.

It was a short letter, only a single page.

Dear Fernanda,

I don't know what's happening to you but I'm terribly worried. I've been ringing but you won't answer. Claire has told me that you haven't been to college or work and that you won't come out of your room anymore. What's wrong with you? What has happened? Would you like me to come to Sydney? Or if it isn't working out for you, come back to Adelaide. You'll always be welcome here.

Please ring me, I'm so worried.

Love from Mum

PS See a doctor, perhaps it's chronic fatigue.

Fern laughed out loud at this. See a doctor. What doctor could she see for a sickness of the spirit? A priest? No, she thought, I want nothing more to do with that hypocritical crap.

Perhaps she should go home … It would be good to see her mother. She could move back into her old bedroom, let her mother fuss over her, cook her meals, do the washing. But Grace would insist on calling her Fernanda and her father would be there, angry and afraid and controlling everything with his illness. He'd call her a bum and a failure, sigh and hold his heart, grind his teeth, suffer in his room for days on end - all because of her. No, she couldn't go back, couldn't let him drain her life away anymore.

Fern slapped at the skin of her legs, hit herself on the cheek, the ear, the neck. The mosquitoes were having a feeding frenzy and even the fan wasn't helping. She climbed back into bed and lay watching the numbers change on the digital clock. Her stomach was growling with hunger, but she ignored it. Tomorrow she would deal with food; today she would savour the lightness of an empty stomach.

At 3.59 pm the numbers on the clock disappeared and the fan stopped its whirring. Someone had switched off the electricity.

Fern stayed in bed, trying to calm herself and breathe through the panic as her world closed down around her. Just before dark she got up to look for her torch but the batteries were flat and she didn't have any spare ones. Defeated, she lay down once more and waited.

As dusk was drawing the last of the light from her room there was a flash of lightning followed by a distant rumble of thunder. The possibility of a storm drew Fern out of bed and over to the window. Outside, the air was unnaturally still as the sky deepened into night. Fern stood in the sultry heat, watching the flashes, mainly sheet lightning, with the occasional fork shattering the sky. Looking up she noticed the silhouettes of fruit bats flying overhead in their nightly ritual. There were thousands of them, all heading in the same direction, encased in an eerie silence as their wings moved in unison.

Suddenly there was a blinding flash, followed immediately by a sharp angry clap of thunder. A gust of wind blew in the window, sending the white curtains into a horizontal dance. The rain began, slowly at first, heavy drops beating on the roof just above Fern's head. Then a deafening roar as sheets of water bucketed down from the sky, lit by flashes of lightning and accompanied by rumbling thunder.

Fern leaned out as far as she could, letting the rain pummel her head. The air was fresh, washed clean already and dazzled by forks of lightning. She loved it, loved the noise and the power of it. It made her feel alive again, as if she were waking from a deep sleep. Quickly the gutters began to run, then, blocked by debris, they spilled onto the road, until the cars were swishing through deepening puddles.

In the flashing light of the storm, Fern suddenly thought she saw a man standing in the shadows on the other side of the road. Her heart beat faster as she strained to see him through the pelting rain. His hair, shoes, trousers, shirt, even the raincoat hanging loose from his shoulders, were all black, making it hard to distinguish him from the shadows. He was wearing dark glasses and his face was very white, almost glowing, as if a torch were hidden behind those glasses.

Fern watched transfixed as the man turned his head upwards and directed his gaze at her, then lifted the dark glasses away from his face, revealing white-blue eyes, their piercing light staring into her, pinning her to the spot. The light grew until it was burning her retinas, pouring through her head and into her body. The pressure was intense but painless. Fern knew she should have been afraid - should have been tearing herself free of those eyes - yet all she could do was surrender. It was as if there were two Ferns, one succumbing to the experience, another detached and watching. Neither were frightened. She wondered vaguely if she was having a stroke, but it didn't matter. If she were to die, it would be worth it for this. A feeling of great joy spread through her, almost unbearable in its intensity, and she wanted it to go on forever.

Too soon, the man covered his eyes once more with the dark glasses. Immediately the pressure ceased and Fern's joy drained away, leaving only a faint echo of itself. As she watched, he raised his hand and gave her a small wave. Instinctively she lifted hers to wave back then left it there, hanging uncertainly. The gesture seemed both too much and too little. It was strange that though streams of traffic were passing, their headlights didn't seem to illuminate him, nor did the streetlight two doors down. Still, Fern felt no fear, only a sense of inevitability and a stirring excitement. Feeling the sting of a mosquito on her leg, she looked down briefly. When she looked back the shadow man had gone.

Filled with a new energy, Fern paced the room, her thoughts chattering incessantly, trying and failing to make sense of what had just happened, who this man was and what he wanted from her. It was hours before she could settle and when she finally lay down in bed and closed her eyes, her pupils darted back and forth as if she were dreaming. The darkness behind her eyelids was filled with colour, an array of patterns kaleidoscoping into space. For hours more she watched, entranced, not noticing the passing of time.

When Fern finally slept, she found herself slipping in and out of dreams through which a golden snake slithered silently. Fear and desire pulled her between them as she ran from the snake. Then, realising it was faster than her, she stopped and let it settle on her foot only to wake with a gasp when it bit her, the poison seeping slowly into her bloodstream. Almost immediately sleep tugged Fern back under and she felt a hand caressing her brow before tracing a finger along the outline of her cheek and neck. The fingers were thick, coarse-skinned and speckled with pale hairs, but sensual too, and they stirred something inside of her that had been dormant for too long. She woke again, burning with desire, trying to clasp onto the hand but it had disappeared. Whose hand was it, she wondered, realising with a fleeting disappointment that it could not be the dark-haired shadow man's.

Without the fan the humidity had seeped into everything. Fern was wet through and the sheets were damp and limp, but despite this she felt better than she had in many months. She thought about summer in Adelaide, its oven-dry heat so different from this stickiness. Remembered turning the pillow over and over looking for a cool patch, laying wet flannels on her face, sleeping on the bathroom floor, its tiles cool underneath her. And sometimes the exquisite joy of sleeping outside under the stars.

Disturbed by the heat and the incessant buzz of mosquitoes outside her net, Fern threw off her sheet and imagined herself back there in the city of her childhood, staring up at the Milky Way and savouring the gentle night breezes. After a time she slept again, undisturbed by the shadow man who hovered just outside her dreams. Waiting.

Chapter Two

They came for her the next afternoon. It was almost a relief. Fern was standing at the window watching the clouds build up in the north, and the sun fade once again beneath a pall of smoke, the surge of hope she'd felt that morning fading with it.

When she'd woken, the air had been fresh and the light had felt like an old friend, the sun streaking through the window and across her bed for the first time in days. Feeling full of the possibilities of life, Fern had ventured out, walking through the streets with a light step and sending tentative half-smiles to the people she passed. In the Botanic Gardens she'd found a sunny spot looking out over the harbour and sat on the damp grass, breathing in the fresh breeze mixed with the pungent smell of seaweed and watching the ferries plough back and forth, leaving temporary road maps in their wake. Filled with hope, Fern had made a promise to herself: I will start again, she'd vowed. I'll find my own way. Somehow.

Yet now here she was, back in her attic; nothing had changed, she was no closer to finding a way out of her situation and her promise had a hollow ring to it. Even the strangeness of last night's experience was receding, albeit slowly. The waterfall of light that had poured through her seemed less real, though every time she shut her eyes, colours still flashed behind her lid, and despite her growing doubts a tiny residue of joy still clung obstinately to her.

Fern froze as the front door suddenly opened, the noise echoing through the empty house. There were voices, at least one man and two or three women. At some point she identified Grace's voice. Her mother, maybe a social worker, almost certainly the landlord. Their voices grew louder as they approached, up one flight of stairs, then another until Fern could hear them on the other side of the door, puffing and panting.

'Fernanda, dear, it's your mother. Are you in there?'

There was a pause while they waited for a response. Fern held her breath, resisting the desire to call out to her mother. The words were going around inside her head, a kind of pleading neediness. *Mum. Oh Mum.*

'Please open the door, Fernanda.' She sounded hesitant and self-conscious, an actor uncertain of her audience. 'You're not well, darling. You need help. Do come out.'

Fern felt tears welling up in her eyes. She had intended to submit, to let her mother hug her, bring her down from her attic, soothe her and sort her out. But remembering her promise to herself that morning, Fern knew with absolute certainty that she had to seek her own way, that she mustn't let herself be rescued like this. In order to find herself she had to escape. She'd already tried once: fleeing her childhood home, coming to Sydney and studying. But then it has all unravelled and she'd retreated to this attic, fleeing life, her body on automatic, a machine with no feeling. Instead of escape she'd ended up trapping herself in another box. A resounding failure but nevertheless she had to try again.

They were talking quietly now amongst themselves. Fern could only hear the hum of their voices not their words but she knew what they would do next. She had to get out. Forcing herself to move slowly and quietly she pushed the window up to its highest point, grasped the frame and pulled herself through, then pushed it down gently behind her. Just then she heard a loud thud, followed by another. Panicking, she climbed onto the ledge above the window, making herself as small as possible. Looking down she felt the dizziness begin, a wave of vertigo bringing the ground spinning up close and then away again, back and forth. Fern froze as the ground below suddenly disappeared and for a moment she felt herself poised at the edge of a sheer cliff, the rocks below sharp and hard, waiting to crush her.

Just as she felt herself slipping over the edge something dragged her gaze from the ground, breaking the spell. Perched above the neighbour's attic window was a giant bird - a white eagle, one fierce eye fixed on her. It was the first time she'd ever been so close to such a powerful bird and it was magnificent. But surely eagles wouldn't come into the city like this; perhaps it was fleeing the fires.

Behind her there was a splintering sound as the door burst open. They were through. Any minute now they would find her. She had to move. A single glance downwards sent her spiralling into fear once more and a sob burst out of her as she imagined herself falling, her body splattering on the pavement below. With an effort she dragged her gaze upwards and fixing it on the eagle began to crawl across the roof. Momentarily forgetting her pursuers, Fern paused and watched as with a whoosh of its powerful wings the bird rose into the air. Mesmerised by the bird's beauty, she followed it with her eyes as it flew higher and higher, until, catching an air current, it stilled its wings and soared out of sight. As it disappeared, a single white feather floated gently down, landing outside her neighbour's window.

Fern finished crossing the steep roof as quietly as possible, wincing at every creak and trying not to imagine how easily she could slide off. It felt in some way as if the eagle had lent her its wings; she could feel them working in her shoulder blades, balancing and counterbalancing as she crawled, giving her the confidence to keep moving. But even so she'd never be able to get down off the roof. Her only chance was her neighbour's window. She picked up the feather and tucked it into her bra, then turned to the window, which like her own, faced onto the street. It was open a fraction and her heart lifted in hope. She tugged at the frame, afraid that it would be locked in position, but it shifted just enough for her to squeeze through. A few metres away she could hear her own attic window sliding open and then voices, louder this time. 'She must be out here.'

Carefully pushing the window down, Fern locked it behind her then looked around the cluttered room. Hearing footsteps on the roof, she quickly hid herself behind a pile of boxes and peered out just as her landlord's face appeared at the window, his greedy eyes searching for her in the gloom. She held her breath as he tried the window but it didn't budge and Fern felt her body sink in relief as his footsteps made their way back across the roof.

Exhausted, Fern stayed in her dark, safe spot behind the boxes, waiting for her heart to slow down and wondering what she could do next. She couldn't face the roof again so she would have to get out through her neighbour's house without being seen. That was hard enough. But what then? she wondered, badly needing a plan, something to keep the panic at bay.

She strained her ears, listening for sounds that would tell her if the neighbours were home. If they were, then Fern had little chance of sneaking out and even less chance of explaining her presence if she were caught. She didn't even know their names. The wife was mad - Fern had seen her before, standing on a milk crate in Taylor Square, an elderly woman ranting about the end of the world. Once she'd pointed her finger at Fern and told her that she had the power to change the course of history. Embarrassed, Fern had scowled, and walked away, wondering if the woman's husband knew what was happening to his wife. She was certain he wouldn't approve.

The husband wore a suit. Fern used to watch him stop outside the front gate each morning, set down his briefcase and straighten his tie before picking up his briefcase again and striding off down the street. Her housemates used to laugh and think he was a pompous arse, but Fern always thought it was a little ritual, a way of shifting him from one world into another, like a duck shaking its feathers when it stepped out of the water.

It could have been ten minutes or an hour that Fern sat there among the dusty boxes, before the shuffle of footsteps on the stairs brought her back to her senses. The door opened and quiet feet walked purposefully in. As they passed her hiding place, Fern caught a glance of lime green thongs and livid, thickened ankles, before a friendly woman's voice, said, 'Would you like a cup of tea?'

Shocked, Fern stayed motionless, hoping the woman would go away.

'Come on now, I know you're there.' There was a pause. 'It's alright, I don't mind. It's quite exciting really, harbouring a fugitive. Do come out, you're making me talk to myself and we all know that's not a good sign.'

Despite herself, Fern nearly laughed out loud as a face peered around the boxes. There was no trace of the ferocious, desperate creature who'd singled out Fern in Taylor's Square. This was a different woman, with kindly eyes and a smile that made Fern relax.

'Ah, there you are. Come on out, it's perfectly safe.'

Fern stood up awkwardly, pins and needles rushing up and down her legs. 'I'm sorry,' she said. 'How did you find me?'

'Well, that's a hard one to answer. Let's just say I knew you were coming though I didn't expect you quite so soon. She frowned. 'These days, with time speeding up the way it is, anything can happen. It's just so hard to keep up.'

A look of weariness settled on her face and for a moment she seemed ancient Then she drew herself up again, looking at the ceiling as if she was calling in energy from somewhere up there. As Fern watched, her face came to life again and it was obvious that once she would have been beautiful.

'Still, in the end it was easy. Someone rapped on the door looking for you so I knew you must be up here.' Seeing Fern's face, the woman quickly added, 'Don't worry, I told her I kept that window locked for fear of burglars and no one could have possibly climbed in.' She laughed. 'I also said I thought I heard someone shimmying down the drainpipe and was just about to ring the police. That should put her off a bit.'

'Thanks,' said Fern, wondering why this woman had helped her.

'Don't mention it.' The woman held out her hand. 'My name's Cassandra. Though Cassie's what everyone calls me.'

'I'm Fern.'

As they shook hands, Fern's attention was caught by the gleam of Cassie's rings: all silver, one woven into a Celtic knot, another displaying a rich purple amethyst, and another a chunk of golden amber. Around Cassie's neck hung a large blue stone, threaded with gold. Fern couldn't take her eyes off it.

'Come on then,' said Cassie. 'Now we know each other, let's have that cup of tea.'

Fern followed Cassie down a flight of stairs. It was strange to be in a house the mirror image of her own; she felt as if she'd stepped into the looking glass. Nothing was where it should be, especially the kitchen: a long thin strip of closed-in balcony which leaned precariously over the front of the house. It made Fern dizzy, as if she were perched on the roof once again, about to slide down to the road.

'You get used to the funny angles. Strange cooking in a crooked oven, though: cakes come out thick at one end and thin at the other. There's a real art to getting it right.'

Fern stared at the open umbrella suspended above the stove and then looked back at Cassie, a question in her eyes.

'Ah, that. It does look a bit strange, I guess, but there are some awful leaks in here and it stops the rain plopping in the dinner.' She sighed. 'You can't get landlords to do anything these days. And Hector's worse than useless.'

'Is that your husband?'

'Oh no, Hector's my brother. Completely mad, if you ask me. Goes off to work in that office every day and sits there staring at a computer screen. Then he comes home and does the same thing.' She shook her head. 'Can't be good for you.'

'So you're not married?'

'Heavens no! Good Lord, what would I do with a husband? … Mind you, I was attractive in my time. There were plenty of men who wanted me.' She looked sad for a moment. 'Trouble was, I didn't want any of them.' Cassie rummaged through a shelf cluttered with various sized jars full of dead leaves. 'Ah, here we are. How does chamomile sound? Nice and calming. And while we're at it, a dose of Rescue Remedy wouldn't go astray after what you've been through,' Cassie said, searching through what was obviously her medicine drawer, though there wasn't a Panadol or bandaid in sight. Instead, there were ointments and salves and tiny dropper bottles, one of which Cassie handed to Fern. 'Here, a couple of drops of that under your tongue should set you straight.'

Wondering how she could be rescued by a drop, Fern nevertheless did as she was told.

'No, no, you keep it,' said Cassie when Fern offered it back. 'I've a feeling you'll need it. Just a few drops anytime you've had a scare.'

'Thanks.' Still sceptical, Fern slipped the remedy into her pocket. But as she stood watching Cassie prepare the tea, she felt the tension in her shoulders gradually soften and wondered if there was something in it after all. She thought of Claire, who was studying medicine. Would she approve of Cassie? Probably not.

Tea in hand, Fern followed Cassie into the dining room. There were a couple of faded lounge chairs with brightly coloured throws across their backs. A raggedy woven mat covered part of the floor and the rest was floorboards. Bunches of drying herbs were strung from the ceiling, along with ropes of garlic and onions. It was a comfortable room, welcoming and calm. They sat down at a rough wooden table, its surface thick with wax from two dripping candle holders that had become a permanent fixture in the centre.

'Here,' Cassie said, handing a biscuit tin to Fern. 'Have one of these. They're date and walnut. I made them myself.'

Fern eyed Cassie across the table as they ate. She seemed so calm, a million miles away from the madwoman Fern had seen predicting the end of the world.

'I saw you.' Fern hesitated, not sure whether to go on, but Cassie was looking at her quizzically so she had to. 'Down on the corner of Oxford Street … You were-'

'On my soapbox. That's right.' Cassie sniffed. 'Oh dear, now I'm going to cry.'

Alarmed, Fern watched as Cassie's eyes filled with tears.

'I can't help it,' she said between sobs. 'I know things. They just come to me out of the blue and it wouldn't be right to keep them to myself. I have to tell. It's the least I can do, don't you think?'

'Yes,' said Fern, nodding sympathetically, not sure how to react to this strange woman unashamedly crying on the other side of the table. It had been so long since she'd had a conversation with anyone that she'd almost forgotten how to do it and now she couldn't think of the right words to comfort Cassie. Thinking perhaps a hug would do, Fern half stood up, but she'd never been good at that sort of thing so she sat down again and waited helplessly for the crying to stop.

After a while Cassie sighed and wiped her eyes. 'I'm not mad,' she said, 'though sometimes I wish I was. Unfortunately, it's my fate to be excruciatingly sane. It's the rest of the world that's mad.' Cassie munched sadly on another biscuit. 'Oh well, enough of that. Let's have a look at you,' she said, leaning across the table and staring into Fern's eyes.

Fern felt more and more uncomfortable as Cassie stared into one eye and then the other, her sweet date breath mingling with the chamomile and coming in little rasps as she concentrated.

'Ah, I knew it … I knew it.' She drew away, a triumphant gleam in her eyes.

'What?' asked Fern.

'You're an old soul. You have the power to make things happen. Remember that - *the power to make things happen.* But you need to take the time to find out who you are.'

Confused, Fern pondered Cassie's words, trying to uncover the meaning behind them. What power did she have? None, she thought bitterly. Things happen to me and I let them. I don't have any control. I never have. Fern couldn't imagine taking control of her life and yet just the previous day she'd promised herself that she would do just that. A promise she'd already broken. Or had she? Running away like that wasn't necessarily a defeat. Rather it was a way of making a space for change. For the briefest of moments Fern sensed the potential of that idea as it planted itself within her.

And what did Cassie mean about taking the time to find out who she was? Did this carry hidden depths too or was it more clear cut? Perhaps she simply needed to find out who her birth parents were, something she'd toyed with on and off for a few years now. She knew her birth mother's name and that she lived in Katoomba, in the Blue Mountains; Fern had even spent the weekend up there once. It had felt odd, knowing her birth mother was in the same town. But she had never done anything more. It was cowardice, she knew, but she'd made up all sorts of justifications, telling herself that on balance it was better not to pursue it, that just knowing her mother's name was enough. She didn't want another mother because she already had one who loved her with a touching loyalty. Fern loved Grace too and didn't want to hurt her.

Fern's thoughts were interrupted as Cassie took her hand and began studying her palm.

'Mmm,' the older woman said at last, 'a messy hand, especially when it comes to relationships. You'll be hurt, girl, over and over. A strong fate line though, which might help keep you on track. But I can tell you one thing, there's travel there, and it's soon.'

'I'm not going anywhere,' said Fern, pulling her hand away abruptly.

Cassie looked up sympathetically. 'Dear, whether you like it or not, there's a big journey ahead of you. And I can tell you now, it's not going to be easy. Though at least you won't be alone.'

Fern had a fleeting glimpse of a face, of tousled fair hair and eyes she couldn't read. For a second she felt the stirring of desire and remembered the fingers that had stroked her neck in her dream. 'No,' she said without thinking. 'Not him.'

Cassie looked at her curiously. 'Ah, so you know your companion?'

'No,' said Fern, blushing. 'I mean … ' She searched for the words she needed. 'I don't want to be with anyone. It's better that way.'

Cassie smiled gently. 'In my experience it's better not to deny fate. Now, you'll need a few things,' she added, rummaging about in the medicine drawer again. 'Ah, here it is, some Dragon's Blood to stem any infections. And let's see … Aconite for when the fear of death comes over you … Arnica for bruising … and Apis, that will have to do – for bites.' Cassie handed Fern some tiny bottles with neatly written labels. 'Here, put them in this,' she said offering Fern a small velvet drawstring pouch.

'Thank you,' said Fern, slipping the bottles into the pouch and then into her pocket, the weight tugging at her shorts and making them lopsided.

'Use them wisely, they're hard to find these days and getting harder. The government wants to ban the lot of them. Too much like bloody magic they say. You can't see it, you can't measure it, so it doesn't exist. More likely they're worried people will stop buying their drugs.' Cassie took a deep breath. 'I'm sorry, I shouldn't be shouting, you're frightened enough as it is. I just get so wound up when I think of it. How could they ban healing? Not again. We all know what happened last time. You picked a herb or helped a baby out into the world and they burnt you at the stake.'

Alarmed, Fern stepped back quickly, feeling a surge of dizzying nausea as a fierce heat seared her skin, its intensity agonising before it just as suddenly disappeared.

'Here,' said Cassie undoing her necklace. 'You'll need this too.'

'I can't take that,' protested Fern.

'You must. It's lapis lazuli, a protective stone with the power to reverse curses. It'll open you up so the guardians can contact you.'

'The *what*?' asked Fern incredulously as Cassie hung the necklace around Fern's neck.

'What's that?' asked Cassie, ignoring Fern's question and pointing at the tip of the white feather sticking out of her shirt.

'Just a feather.' Fern pulled it out and handed it to Cassie, who held it reverently.

'Where did you find this?'

Fern briefly described the eagle on the roof, omitting the part where she'd felt the balancing strength of its wings above her, and her awe at the majesty of the bird. As she spoke, Fern was all too aware of the flatness of her words, the tone that said nothing special had happened, as if she were too urbane to appreciate beauty, a tone she'd perfected over the years and now found she couldn't escape. Despite this, the excitement shone in Cassie's face.

'A gift from an eagle! That's incredible. Things have moved faster than I thought.' She reluctantly handed the feather back to Fern. 'This is a gift of great power - you mustn't lose it.'

Fern held the feather close, feeling its softness stroking her face. It was just a feather, and yet …

Cassie's eyes took on a faraway look and her voice changed. 'You'll find out in your own time. But I will tell you this, even though you might not want to listen. This feather will grant you greater perception and the ability to walk between worlds, with all the responsibilities that entails.'

Cassie stopped, her eyes refocusing, her face slightly bewildered as if she were stepping back into herself. Fern felt more confused than ever. She liked Cassie and wanted to trust her, but she couldn't understand what was going on. She'd left magic behind her a long time ago but now here it was being forced down her throat: dragon's blood, fortune telling, powerful feathers, stones that opened pathways for guardians. None of it could possibly be real yet there was something stirring about it. It felt as if she'd stepped into a story, equipped with all the tools and weapons for a journey. But I can't be the heroine of any story, she thought. If anything, I'm the damsel in the tower, waiting to be rescued.

Cassie, went over to the window and peered down the street. 'They've gone. You'd better be going too.'

Fern felt her shoulders tensing up at the prospect of going out there again, but she knew there was no choice.

'Hurry now,' said Cassie, ushering her out of the room.

Fern followed Cassie down another flight of stairs to the ground floor. She didn't understand anything but she did trust this eccentric woman. Her unanswered questions were spinning around in her head but the trust was centred peacefully in her heart.

'This is Hector's bit,' said Cassie. 'Look at it, machines everywhere. How can he live amongst all that?'

It was almost as if the house was divided neatly in two: the top half organic, the bottom half high-tech, though both were fraying around the edges, with peeling paint and dusty broken blinds.

'Wouldn't believe we were twins, would you?' said Cassie. 'There's nothing identical about us, I can tell you. Still, we need each other … And his heart's in the right place.'

Unlike Fern's, Cassie's tiny backyard was lush and green. She'd planted every patch of dirt with herbs, and the concrete courtyard was cluttered with pots. Bees clustered on the flowers and the dusk smells were intense: lavender and oregano, thyme and mint, and jasmine climbing the fence. Loath to leave this sanctuary, Fern hesitated. The world outside seemed dangerous and uncertain.

Cassie took Fern's hand. 'I can't ask you to stay, dear, though I'd like to. It's not your path. You can't hide away any more, it's time to face life.'

'Thank you,' said Fern, recognising the truth in Cassie's words. 'Thank you for everything.'

'Oh, don't be silly, it was the least I could do. Everyone needs help sometimes. You'll find other helpers, but there'll be enemies too, and it won't always be clear which is which.' She patted Fern on the stomach. 'Trust your gut feelings girl, they're the thread that will lead you through.' Cassie pulled Fern in close, giving her a bear hug that brought tears to Fern's eyes. 'Look after yourself … And watch out for traps, dear.'

Cassie had spoken lightly, like a mother reminding her child to take a handkerchief, but Fern felt a shiver run down her spine as she extricated herself from Cassie's arms and turned towards the darkening alley.

Chapter Three

The house felt sullied somehow, the intruders' lingering intent caught in the atmosphere. Fern slipped off her shoes and quietly climbed the steps, expertly avoiding every creak. When she reached the attic she cautiously stuck her head around the door, but no one was there. Her room looked the same but was somehow completely different. It was no longer hers. She had no choice but to quickly gather a few things and get out before they came back and caught her.

On the desk was a scribbled note from her mother: *Dear Fernanda, please ring me,* with a phone number she didn't recognise. Her mother must have finally bowed to the times and bought herself a mobile phone. Fern stuffed the note into her wallet, then turned to packing, quickly realising how little she could realistically take. A suitcase would be impractical to haul around, so instead she emptied out her daypack, the one she'd used for college. It was like stepping back in time, she thought, pulling out notebooks and watercolour paints, an overdue library book, material samples, her good scissors and half a rotten sandwich.

Fern hurried around the room, starting at every sound and barely able to think. Quickly she pulled on a fresh t-shirt, one of the offerings Claire had left at the door. She packed some loose silk pyjama pants that she loved to wear because they were big and loose and the silk felt sensuous on her skin, then a pair of shorts and a couple of skirts, light things that would crush but took up hardly any room. She stuffed in some extra t-shirts, retrieved from the dirty washing basket, then grabbed a few pairs of undies and a spare bra, some sandals and a lightweight cardigan - her favourite one, with the pearl buttons. It was too hot to imagine it would ever be cold again, but even so she put in a pashmina shawl that looked good with her skirts.

Her bag already bulging, Fern stared wildly around the room, chewing nervously at her nails. Spotting her tin pipe, she slid it into the backpack. It had been months since she'd played it but even so she couldn't imagine life without at least the possibility of making music. Next, Fern stuffed in her knitting gear, transferred Cassie's pouch of remedies to her pack and slipped the eagle's feather into the top pocket. Then she zipped up her pack and tied her favourite hat onto one of the straps. It was cone-shaped and made of bamboo, its brim so wide that it kept the sun off her shoulders too.

Fern hauled the heavy bag over her shoulders and took one last lingering look around her room, wondering anxiously what would happen to her belongings before realising with a shock that she didn't care. There was something appealing about the prospect of starting again. Quietly she closed the door behind her and, with it, the part of her life which this room had encompassed. Creeping down the stairs she felt vulnerable, like a soft-skinned creature emerging from its shell.

On the street, Fern paused for a second, wondering which direction to go then realising with another shock how free she was to choose. She'd never been any good at making decisions; every choice closed doors, yet not choosing was itself a choice, shutting more doors than ever. She hesitated for just a moment longer, then turned towards the city, wanting to be near the safety of people and bright lights.

The unfamiliar weight of the pack tugged on her back, its loose straps slipping one at a time over her shoulders as she walked past row after row of terrace houses, three storeys high, warm yellow light finding its way out through curtain cracks and slicing through blinds and metal bars. The basement flats had windows below the footpath; most had their curtains drawn against the earth which threatened to engulf them. Fern wondered what it would be like to live underground like that, the lights on even during the sunniest part of the day, looking up at the footpath through a barred window and seeing only the legs of passers-by. How long before you developed your other senses: whiskers twitching, ears tuned to the slightest sound, sniffing your way around? And if it rained too much and the drains blocked, the place would flood and you'd drown.

One window was naked behind its bars, a light burning brightly through it. Looking down as she passed, Fern briefly glimpsed a hand, the thick fingers clasping a glass filled with an amber liquid.

It's amazing what you can read in the pattern of feet, thought Adam, taking a sip of his bourbon. Catching sight of Fern's feet, encased in soft gold slippers, he saw that she didn't know where she was going, saw that she was in no hurry, and then lost interest in her. Adam took another, bigger mouthful from his glass, feeling the liquid burning its way down his throat as he watched a man's feet now, moving purposefully. Too fast and quiet. He wondered briefly when the girl would realise she was being followed, but the wonder was not strong enough to become more than a passing thought. He took another gulp, draining the glass and continued his vigil, staring up at the street above, his mind trapped in its own private concerns.

After a while Adam put his empty glass down but he misjudged the distance and it landed too hard on the table, startling him with its loud crack. Swearing, he pushed himself out of his seat, gathered his keys and wallet, fumbled with the buttons of his crumpled shirt and ran his fingers through his messy fair hair. Then he climbed up the stairs and stepped out into the night, resigned to another evening at the Underworld, obliterating himself.

Fern was only a couple of blocks from Oxford Street when suddenly and for no good reason she knew she was being followed. She had seen and heard nothing out of the ordinary but could feel prickles of fear working their way up her spine. Forcing herself to stop briefly, she casually looked behind, as if uncertain of her way. There were a few people littering the footpaths and she couldn't, in that small moment, separate her tracker from the others. She crossed the road and glanced back again, noting a thin man in a white shirt but she was unable to identify anything more to distinguish him. Fern fought her instinct to run, sensing it would be better if she pretended that she hadn't noticed. With this pack weighing her down she couldn't run anyway and she didn't have the strength to confront him. Instead she would have to use her wits.

On Oxford Street she felt safer. Dinner crowds were forming on the footpaths and the road was lined with traffic. Fern wove her way quickly through the pedestrians, hoping to lose the man this way, all the time sifting through the films she'd seen, the stories she'd read, trying to remember how characters shook off the people following them.

Fern stepped into a bookshop, welcoming the blast of cold air that evaporated the sweat and panic on her skin. She positioned herself near the window, partly hidden by a shelf of books, and surreptitiously watched the passers-by. The first two thin men in white shirts she dismissed. One was walking too intently, as if he had somewhere to go and the other was with a friend. But the third man was clearly looking for someone, his eyes scanning the crowds on the pavement. He paused outside the bookshop window and looked in. Heart thudding, Fern bent quickly, snatched up a book on golfing techniques from a lower shelf and began blindly flicking through its pages. At least now she knew what he looked like: pointed face, sharp nose and thin lips, but with long jowls that suggested he was older than he wanted to look. He reminded her of a bloodhound, the way he seemed to be sniffing the air for her scent. He had thinning brown hair too, and tight jeans sitting below a pot belly. Not someone who stood out in a crowd.

When Fern cautiously peered over the bookshelf, he was gone. The relief she felt was quickly overtaken by anxiety. Her instinct was to get away from here as fast as she could, but she was hungry and tired and common sense told her there was no point running without a destination. She needed to sit down somewhere and try to think through everything that had happened. And she needed to eat. Her stomach was empty, and when she was hungry, she couldn't think at all.

Cautiously, Fern slipped out of the bookshop, into the stream of people and then into the nearest cafe. Finding an empty table in a corner, she slid off her backpack and pushed it under the table, then chose the bench seat so she could sit with her back to the wall. The bloodhound man couldn't exactly confront her in here, unless he was an assassin, but even then he'd want to do it secretly, she imagined; a sachet of poison dropped into her glass, or perhaps a gun with a silencer, so he could just stroll past and casually pull the trigger. She'd fold quietly onto the table and everyone would think she was drunk or asleep and look away, embarrassed. No one would realise until the blood formed a pool on the floor and someone stepped in it.

Fern's thoughts were interrupted by a bottle of water and a glass being placed on the table. A waiter was standing over her expectantly with a pad and pencil.

'A latte and …' Quickly she glanced at the blackboard on the wall, scanning it for something relatively cheap that would fill her up. 'Nachos, please.'

As the waiter stalked away to the kitchen, Fern berated herself sternly. She needed to pull herself together and stop her imagination running in ridiculous directions; clearly she'd seen too many films. But her fear had taken her over and now her legs felt like jelly and her whole body was trembling, inside and out. She poured a glass of water and drank it in one gulp, then a second. Feeling a little better she leaned back and let the velvety cushions comfort her. Dimly lit, the cafe had peaceful ambient music playing, real pot plants and just enough people to make a buzz in the atmosphere without feeling closed-in and deafening.

When the coffee came, Fern sipped it gratefully, feeling the caffeine jolt her brain back into action. She went over everything that had happened, trying to arrange all the elements into a pattern that made sense, but no matter how hard she tried it all seemed absurd. Claire had been right, Fern couldn't stay hidden away in her attic forever, but she'd never imagined how serious it would get, with people forcing her door in and her mother here in Sydney looking for her. Perhaps Grace had called the police in to look for her, or a private detective - might that explain the man who was following her? But surely they wouldn't be interested: she wasn't even a missing person.

And then there was the eagle. Her thoughts kept returning to that enormous, majestic bird. It had bewitched her somehow, lent her its wings. Even now she could feel the tug of muscles that had never been used. At least not in this life, she thought suddenly, then stopped herself. There was only one life. Of that she was certain. We are born and we die. There's nothing else except dust and oblivion, no heaven, and no hell, except on this earth. But even so, her thought left her troubled, as if something within her had been dislodged a fraction. Perhaps she was going mad.

Thinking about Cassie, with her garbled warnings and blessings, Fern wondered who got to draw the line between normal and mad. Sometimes it seemed to her that the conventions of normality were like the walls of a prison keeping people in order. Yet the world seemed mad to her, madder each day. Fern could see it, even here on Oxford Street with people staring past each other, faces wrinkled with worry, bodies moving too fast, caught up in the pace of things. Everyone wanting, wanting and never filled. Better then to ask what sanity was.

The nachos were good. Crunchy and spicy, with plenty of melted cheese and sour cream, every mouthful helping Fern's mind focus again. She pulled out her notebook and pen, scooped up some guacamole with a corn chip and began a list of certainties.

1. The man I saw on the street outside my attic is not the same man who is following me.
2. The man who is following me is not my landlord.
3. Cassie is mad, but she seems saner than everyone else.

Fern read it over, shocked at how few certainties she could find. And even these were filled with unanswered questions. Neither 1 nor 2 actually helped identify the man who was following Fern, or the other one who had stared up at her from the pavement with eyes that had drained the fear from her. And 3 was completely unhelpful.

As she finished the last of the nachos it all suddenly became clear in her head. There was an explanation for everything: the bird was simply lost, or had flown into the city to escape the bush fires; Cassie was just an eccentric old woman, kindly but crazy; and the bloodhound man was someone her mother had hired to find her. None of these things were connected. There was no mystery after all.

Fern was surprised to feel a growing sense of disappointment as she successfully reasoned away the events of the past few hours. Something about the magic of it had made everything seem fresh to her, the way life had been when she was a child. A world full of possibilities and wildness, with the prospect of adventure. Then just as the last of the magic drained from her, Fern remembered the shadow man outside her window – his eyes and that liquid light pouring into her. She hadn't imagined him or what he'd done to her and she couldn't explain him away.

For the time being though, she would have to put him aside and focus instead on practicalities. She drained the last of her coffee and began another list:

Who do I trust?

1. Mum

Fern paused a moment, considering, then reluctantly crossed it out. She did trust her mother's love but not the conventions within which she lived. Grace was hardly ever strong enough to stand up to her husband, who was a control freak, and Richard would go to any lengths to make Grace and Fern conform to his narrow church-bound world.

She tried again.

1. Cassie

But mad or sane, Cassie had told Fern she couldn't help her now. Fern thought for a while longer, chewing the end of the pen, her sense of isolation increasing by the minute. There were friends in Adelaide, but she needed someone here. Jeff? No, she couldn't ask her ex-boyfriend for help. Then she remembered the piece of paper Claire had given her and the invitation: *If you ever need somewhere to stay...* Well, now she did.

Claire's address was in her wallet, along with her mother's phone number. Looking at her mother's note again, Fern felt the familiar tug. Resisting the temptation, she returned it to her wallet and instead looked at Claire's address: 53 Kent Street, Stanmore. She would be able to catch a train from Central. It would be polite to ring first, but her phone was flat and a quick search revealed that she'd left her charger behind. There was no point looking for a public phone as no one used them anymore; they'd become museum pieces, dotted around the city, smashed up and scribbled on, targets for vandals, symbols of another era.

Fern tucked Claire's address in her pocket, heaved the pack onto her back and wearily made her way up to the counter to pay the bill. Out on the pavement she looked around nervously, scanning the crowd for the Bloodhound but there was no sign of him. Perhaps she'd misinterpreted the incident; it might have been coincidence that he'd crossed the street behind her.

She turned towards the station and began weaving her way through the crowds. After the quiet peace of the cafe, Oxford Street seemed madder than ever: too many people, walking fast, looking through each other, talking loudly on phones, oblivious, or strolling together, pausing in front of restaurants to read the menus; music blasting out of shops and cars; endless streams of headlights; shop windows filled with flashing lights and Christmas decorations … It didn't help that the clouds had built up again, shutting out the night sky and shutting in the heat. Now it was hot and damp, the atmosphere rippling with lightning and tight with expectation, claps of thunder adding to the tension. Fern felt trapped, a prisoner in a 3D movie. Every part of her ached to return to her attic, to the quiet and peace of her white world. If only she could shut the door on noise and colours and lights, but mostly on all these people.

She was only a few blocks away from the station when the rain started. It was slow at first, a few gigantic drops, their size an indication of what was to come. Then all at once the clouds let down their load and the air liquified, the street steaming and sending out fog and the scent of hot bitumen. Soon the rain was so thick Fern could hardly see in front of her. She could just make out the blurry outline of lights as her feet swished through puddles. There was no point trying to stay dry. The rain soaked through everything. Her sodden clothes hung heavily on her and the water ran in thick rivulets down her face, turning neon lights into sorry, faded beacons. It muffled sound, muting the music that burst through club doors and turning the swish of tyres into the distant roar of a river. It sent the restaurant and garbage smells pouring down the gutter and filled her mouth with the smoky acid tang of city rain.

Then through the rush of the downpour came a sharp sense of impending danger. Pausing, Fern turned and stared behind her but could see nothing. Even so, she was certain the Bloodhound was there. She could sense his nearness in her spine, in the tingling of her scalp, and in her gut.

The crowded street had been emptied by the rain, so aside from a few scurrying people, Fern was practically alone with him. She picked up pace, trying to run with her heavy pack, knowing he was getting closer and not sure now where she was going. Trapped and lost, going round and round in the wilderness of the city.

Then she saw him behind her, walking fast, not running but Fern's pack was slowing her down and he was gaining on her. Every time she glanced behind her the space between them was smaller. Please help me, please help me, the words a refrain in her mind, playing over and over. He was so close she could hear his feet thudding, imagine his panting dog breath coming in little bursts and his hand reaching out …

Panicking, Fern veered to the side, plunged through the nearest door and into a small foyer with a set of stairs leading down into the basement. Half blinded by the rain in her eyes and the sudden bright lights, Fern couldn't stop herself in time. Her feet slipped from under her and she felt herself fall, bumping from one step to the next, before sinking into darkness.

Chapter Four

The first thing Fern noticed was the music, a kind of fusion band maybe: an indigenous Australian rhythm with a hint of something else. At its centre was the sound of drums, their hypnotic rhythm reverberating within her. Then there were the smells: a carpet wearing a history of spilled drinks and sweat, a rich leathery scent and a pungent perfume she couldn't identify.

Fern tried to call out but her mouth wouldn't open and she could make no sound in her throat. She tried to open her eyes but it felt as if they were glued shut. There was light here though, she could feel it on her eyelids and she wanted so much to stay near it but the rich beat of the drums vibrated through her, drawing her down with them into a tunnel of darkness.

At some point Fern managed to prise her eyes open. It was too dark to see anything, but when she reached out her hands she felt a smooth cold surface on both sides. A part of her was afraid, trying to hold on to something, reason perhaps, even though the rest of her was falling. Despite her fears the fall went on and on, until Fern thought it would never end. After a time the fear left her and soon after that she landed on the ground with a gentle bump.

It was still dark, but cold now too. As her eyes became used to the darkness she could see enough to learn she was in a stone room of some sort, lying on thick slabs of rock. The cold seeping into her back forced her to move and she sat up, then stood, wincing at the stiffness of her muscles. There was a large lump on the side of her head which she assumed came from falling down those stairs, moments or hours ago, she had no idea. Her head throbbed in a rhythm with the drums she could still hear in the distance.

A faint light was coming in under the door, providing a little illumination. Fern scanned the room for clues but it was entirely empty and there were no windows to help her decipher where she was. The door was made of heavy wood. Certain it would be locked, she reached out and grasped its dark wooden bolt. To her surprise it opened at her touch. Outside was a dimly lit hallway with ornate black metal candle holders studded along the walls at intervals, each holding a lit candle. They flickered as she moved past them, stirring the cold air in her wake and making her shiver.

The hallway went on and on, past a great number of identical doors, all closed. After a time Fern could no longer restrain her curiosity. She paused in front of one of the doors, listened carefully, then hearing nothing she pulled it open and gaped in amazement. The room inside was large and plushly furnished, the floors covered by colourful rugs, and the walls with tapestries; one depicted a fierce dragon breathing fire, another, a lady in a long gown, with two unicorns kneeling at her feet. From the ceiling hung a wide circle of black metal, holding at least twenty flickering candles. On the far wall was a fireplace so large she could have stepped into it, and a fire blazing within. In front of the fireplace stood a long wooden couch, softened with cushions. Fern was so cold she walked quickly towards the fire, and so taken by this medieval room and its furnishings that she didn't notice the gigantic black bear asleep on the hearth rug until she was almost upon it.

Fear surged through Fern freezing her to the spot as the bear lazily opened one eye and then the other. She watched helplessly as it fixed both eyes on her and raised its head a little, studying her as if deciding how to respond. Finally instinct overcame Fern and she shrank away from the creature, taking backward steps towards the door. Instantly the bear leapt up with a roar, baring its teeth and charging at her. She screamed and ran back out of the room just in time, pushing the door shut behind her, but before she could click the lock into place the bear fell against the other side. Using all her strength she tried to hold the door in place but the bear was stronger and fraction by fraction the door opened.

Sobbing, Fern called for help, even though she knew it was hopeless.

'You called?' said a voice.

Startled, Fern turned to see a man standing beside her, his face framed by long blond hair. His dark eyes were staring steadily at Fern but she couldn't take her gaze from his cloak with its colours that never settled but shifted as he moved, shimmering through the warm golden colours of autumn.

'Allow me,' said the man, and Fern watched in amazement as he opened the door, stepped into the room with the bear and closed the door behind him.

Fern waited, wondering what was going on inside the room. Eventually, after her heart had settled back into an even rhythm again and her legs regained their strength, Fern's curiosity overcame her fear and she risked opening the door a crack. What she saw made her gasp, for the man and the bear were sitting calmly side by side on the wooden couch. She stared in disbelief: how could he sit fearlessly next to an animal that could rip him apart in a moment?

'You can come in now,' he said, turning to look at Fern, his lips forming a hint of a smile.

'Is it safe?' Fern called, her voice wobbling uncertainly. 'It doesn't look safe.'

'It's never safe, but please don't let that stop you.'

Cautiously Fern opened the door further and stepped into the room, forcing her feet to take one step after another towards the strange pair. The man gazed at her steadily but the bear ignored her and Fern felt suddenly ashamed, as if she had failed a crucial test. She stopped just out of reach of the bear's claws and in front of the man with the shimmering cloak and calm voice.

'Thank you,' she said.

'You're welcome.'

'Who are you?' Fern asked, and the question sounded like an accusation.

'I am the Bear Handler.' His eyes sought hers and Fern saw a clarity in them that made her ashamed all over again. She turned her gaze away.

'Where am I?'

'You are in the underworld.' Before Fern could ask what he meant, the Bear Handler spoke again. 'You can stroke this bear, she will allow it now.'

His voice was gentle but firm, leaving Fern with no choice. Cautiously she reached out her hand to touch the bear's fur. Her fingers sank into its softness and she was surprised at how thick it was. So warm. She felt a strength filling her and kept her hand there, wanting to reach in deeper, wanting to step inside the bear's skin, to be worthy of this creature that no longer deigned to notice her.

'The bear is yours now, you must live with her always,' said the Bear Handler. 'If you risk her danger then she will help you find treasure … Remember that all worthwhile things hold danger.'

Then he was gone and the bear was gone and the warm fire-drenched room was gone. Instead Fern was back in the empty room, stumbling across the stone slabs before they too were gone and she was ascending the tunnel, not flying but not walking either. It felt as if she were floating outside of gravity, only something was pulling her upwards - the drums, perhaps; their volume was increasing again. They were a powerful magnet and she the iron filing being drawn from a great distance, until finally she found herself lying on a soft surface, her head thumping as if her brain had taken on a life of its own and was trying to push its way through her skull.

The drums stopped and in their place Fern could hear the hum of voices in the distance, the clinking of glasses, and the breathing of someone very close to her. She became aware that a hand was lying gently on her forehead, its comforting warmth dulling the pain. Opening her eyes, she found herself lying on a leather couch, looking up at the shadow man who had stood gazing at her window the previous night.

His hair was dark and thick, falling in waves across his face. His jaw was strong and square, his mouth full, his nose chiselled – a classic face from an ancient statue. He was beautiful. There was nothing to suggest how old he was, no traces of dye in his hair, no wrinkles. He looked old and young at once. Then there were his eyes. All she could do was wonder at them. Up close they were even more alluring. They glowed, as if there were tiny globes behind each pupil, and the blue was so hypnotic that she found herself slipping into it, her whole self pouring into his eyes. As it did so a calmness spread through her, relaxing her adrenalin-charged muscles.

It could only have been a matter of seconds before he put on his dark glasses and the spell was broken. Fern's rational self quickly took charge again, sending doubts and fears surging through her. Where was she? What was happening to her? She forced herself to take stock, to concentrate on one thing at a time rather than succumb to the flood of sensations that was threatening to overwhelm her. The room was dark, with a small bar in the corner, a few low tables, couches and large cushions scattered around. Wall lights glowed dimly behind shades in a variety of colours – purple and red, blue and yellow – casting deep shadows in the room. It felt intimate - even more so with this man's hand still resting on her head – and so different from the strange medieval place she'd just been.

She must have been hallucinating - had someone slipped a drug into her drink? But she couldn't remember actually having a drink. No doubt there was a simple explanation after all - nothing supernatural, no magic or kidnappings and no drugs. She'd been chased by some pervert, burst in the door, lost her footing, slipped down the steps and knocked herself out. The rest was all a dream.

Abruptly Fern pushed the man's hand away and sat up. She had to clutch the edges of the couch for a few moments as the blood rushed from her head and the room seemed to spin wildly, before settling again into the right place.

'Ah, Fern, you're back.' When the man smiled his face became even more beautiful, taking Fern's breath away and most of her fears. Still, she resisted smiling back.

'Who are you?' she asked. 'And how do you know my name?'

'I am the barman,' he said, laughing, and his laughter made her want to laugh too, as if this was a great joke, despite the fact that he hadn't answered her second question.

'What's your name?' she asked, determined to get the answers she needed.

'You have called me Shadowman and in your wisdom you were right, for I am that too. But my name is Shamesh.'

'It's not very polite to hang around people's windows.'

'No, and I apologise, but it was necessary to watch over you.' Shamesh smiled again. 'I think you already know that I am not the one you should fear.'

Fern shivered, remembering the Bloodhound. 'There was a man following me …'

'He will not bother you again tonight.'

'But who is he?'

'The man is only a servant, but one you must eventually face.'

'Why? Who does he work for?'

'That you will discover for yourself.' Shamesh glanced at his watch. 'We have a great deal to discuss, though much of it will have to wait.' He stood up. 'Come, you probably need a drink.'

Fern couldn't take her eyes off him. The way he moved, so lithe and graceful, as if he were weightless and the air provided no resistance. He wore pale blue jeans and a t-shirt, casual, but expensive-looking with an image on the back, a golden disc with wings.

Fern followed him to the bar and perched on a stool, watching as he opened fridges and helped himself to their contents as if he owned the place. Perhaps he did. There was an air of authority about him, a confidence that came with money. There might be other ways to gain that kind of confidence, but Fern didn't know them.

'Champagne, I think … or would you prefer coffee?'

'Champagne, please,' said Fern, marvelling at how calm she felt and amazed that she would even consider drinking champagne at a time like this. She watched carefully as he produced glasses and a bottle.

'Bollinger? Yes?'

Fern nodded as he deftly removed the cork, allowing only a little trail of vapour to rise. It had been a long time since she had drunk anything but the cheapest bubbly.

Shamesh filled the glasses and handed one to Fern. As he did so she noticed a ring on his middle finger: silver with a large stone set in it. A sunstone, sparkling seductively as it captured the light.

'Cheers,' he said, clinking his glass with hers. 'It's not every day you embark on a journey.'

Fern was startled. Cassie had said the same thing. 'What do you mean, a journey?'

He raised an eyebrow as if she should know the answer. 'The journey you must take to pursue your life's purpose.'

Fern felt a sudden twinge of excitement. Wasn't that what she'd been looking for? A reason to move forward. A direction of some sort. Anything to pull her out of the rut she'd become trapped in. But almost immediately the excitement was stifled by a familiar heaviness and her mind filled with an anticipatory disappointment. What was the point of a journey? she asked herself. It wouldn't work. Nothing ever did.

She took a large gulp of champagne, savouring the feel of the icy bubbles burning their way down. 'Where is this journey supposed to take me?' she asked, mustering her most cynical voice.

'That I can't tell you.'

'What if I don't go?'

'It's simple. If you refuse this call, then you will die,' he said, sending a shiver up Fern's spine. 'The call of the soul is not something to take lightly. And when you have been chosen there is no choice. You cannot change your mind.'

'But I don't want to go on a journey. Why me, anyway? I didn't ask for this.'

'Yes you did. Every day that you've been imprisoned in your attic, this is what you have been asking for. Your true self that is, not the thing you call you.' He finished his glass and poured another. 'Everyone comes to earth with a lesson to learn and with a task, a creative path they must follow. There is a need within each person to remember why they are here but most won't recognise this need and few find the path. It requires great courage to take this journey. To do so you must follow your heart and live without fear.

'Without fear! The world's a terrifying place,' said Fern.

Shamesh smiled. 'It doesn't have to be so.'

Fern stared at him, unable to imagine a world without fear yet sensing his own fearlessness. 'What's your path?' she asked eventually.

Shamesh smiled but there was a great sadness in his voice. 'I stand as a witness on the side, teaching those who will listen to become flames that pierce the darkness … '

'That's a tough job.' said Fern.

'Indeed it is,' said Shamesh, clearly amused.

Fern was in two minds. Part of her was intrigued by this man but the other was beginning to suspect he was some sort of religious fanatic and that she should get out of here as quickly as possible. But first there were questions to which she needed answers.

'What happened before? I fell down the stairs and hit my head. Was I unconscious?'

'You needed to go down into the underworld to find your power animal.'

Shamesh's answer left Fern even more confused. 'But where is this underworld?'

'That is difficult to explain. It's a parallel reality, if you like, one that exists both within and alongside this world.'

The bear had seemed so real. Fern could still feel the sensation of her hand sinking into the depths of its fur. And when she shut her eyes it now felt, strangely, as if she was sitting inside the skin of the bear. She could see its black fur around the edges of her vision, feel its incredible strength. It made her want to roar.

'So you have met the bear,' he said, pouring more champagne into their glasses.

Fern glanced quickly at him. She hadn't mentioned the bear. The alcohol was mixing with Fern's weariness, she could feel it creeping up her legs, making them weak. She could also feel herself slipping away from the certainties she'd always lived with, and instead diving deep into the realm of the impossible. If it were true that Shamesh could read her mind, then she would have to be careful with her thoughts. She blushed. Perhaps he already knew she'd thought him beautiful. Fern felt as if she was becoming public property – her innermost thoughts scooped up and laid out for everyone to see, like useless trinkets at a market.

'The man said the bear was mine.'

'Yes, you have been given a great gift. But it is not yours in the literal sense. The bear is autonomous but will help when you are in need.'

'How am I supposed to call on a figment of my imagination for help?' asked Fern, trying to summon up enough of her normal cynicism to keep these possibilities at bay.

'Animals have qualities, symbolic powers if you like. On one level the bear is strong and loyal, but also playful. On another level it is a symbol of the unconscious. It hibernates, but only for a few months through the winter. Like the bear you need to enter the cave so as to awaken your power and then you must bring this power out into the open. Both of these aspects of the bear are part of your journey.'

Fern shook her head, unable to take it all in. 'There was a man,' she said hesitantly. 'The Bear Handler he called himself.'

'Yes, you are very lucky. He is your guide in the spirit world. Not everyone will meet their guide so soon.'

'What's so special about me? Why do I get a guide?'

'Whenever there is a genuine call for help that is drawn from a great need, then helpers will arrive,' said Shamesh. 'That is the law.'

Fern looked at him, searching his face for a sign that he was having her on. 'I'm going mad,' she said, draining her glass.

He smiled. 'Perhaps. Or perhaps you are only just beginning to find sanity. We'll see. These are risks you must take.'

'Why? Who says I have to take any risks? Isn't it my decision?'

Shamesh smiled. 'A decision you've already made.' His face became serious. 'A great part of you has already been taken. So much in fact, that if you do nothing you will die, or at least become catatonic - a state you will soon see first hand … Your journey is to retrieve yourself and become fully human.'

Fern couldn't understand his words, though she recognised something in them. For a long time she'd felt as if there was hardly any of her left, as if she was hanging onto her body by the finest of threads.

'What am I then if I'm not human?' she asked, suddenly hurt by the insinuation.

'I will answer your question with another. Do you believe being human is a birthright or something that must be earned?'

'We're the human race. We're born that way,' said Fern.

'Perhaps.' Shamesh smiled and then abruptly changed the subject. 'That's enough for now. Come, I want to introduce you to someone before you go to your friend.'

As Fern followed Shamesh she was puzzling over how he knew about Claire, but when he opened the door, waves of noise burst through, hitting Fern like a solid force and scattering her thoughts. The temporary peace she'd felt fled in the face of this chaos. Surprisingly there was no live band in sight, though the instruments were set up on a small stage in the corner. Instead, recorded music was blaring out from loudspeakers. Normally the rhythm would inspire Fern to move, tapping and jiggling until she would have to dance, but tonight it was a shouting chaos that quickly became trapped in her head, banging angrily around the walls of her skull.

Still following Shamesh, she wound her way between tables, mostly empty. There were a couple of solitary drinkers at the bar, and one girl was dancing, swaying hypnotically to the rhythm, lost in her own world. There was no sign of the Bloodhound.

'It's just picking up,' said Shamesh. 'When the pubs shut in an hour or so it will really get going.'

Once again Fern could feel doubts slipping into her mind. Talking to Shamesh in the quiet of the other bar she'd almost believed him about the underworld and journeys and power animals. Back there she'd felt his power. But here, none of it seemed likely. Shamesh was simply a good-looking bar manager with delusions of grandeur.

'Here we are,' said Shamesh, stopping abruptly.

Fern was puzzled to see a young man slumped across a table littered with empty glasses, his shirt untucked and strands of messy blond hair sitting limply in a puddle of spilt beer. She couldn't imagine why Shamesh would want her to meet this snoring man who smelled of alcohol and something worse.

Adam was dreaming. In his dream a boy was looking at him with holes where his eyes had once been. Birds who cackled like old women, swooped down on him with hooked beaks, and red painted claws. He ducked and dived for cover but they kept coming and he knew they wouldn't stop until they got him. 'A life for a life,' they shrieked. 'A life …' but then one had him by the arm, shaking him, and Adam jumped up, fists clenched, ready to fight. In an instant the birdwomen disappeared and instead Shamesh was standing there with those glasses that hid eyes Adam could never look into; alongside him was a girl with a tough expression and eyes full of fear.

Adam sank back down onto his chair. He couldn't help it, his head wanted to rest on the table and his eyes kept shutting despite the terror that awaited him in his dream world.

'Wake up, Adam. I want to introduce you to someone.'

'Yeah, what?' said Adam, his eyes struggling with a room that wouldn't stay still around him. With an effort he fixed them on the girl who standing next to Shamesh. She looked about twelve and like an elf, he thought, so bloody fragile. He looked at her feet and wanted to laugh at those sparkling gold shoes. He knew them from somewhere but the effort to remember made his head hurt. Her legs looked good though, thin but there was shape to them. But he couldn't make out her edges, they were blurred. Trying desperately to focus, he searched her face again. She looked haunted, like someone with nowhere to go - like him.

'Adam, this is Fern,' said Shamesh. 'Fern, Adam.'

Adam stood up shakily. 'Hey,' he said, reaching out his hand.

'Hi,' said Fern dismissively, ignoring his hand and looking instead at Shamesh with a question in her eyes.

'You two are going on a trip together,' said Shamesh.

'With him!' the girl said before Adam could even digest Shamesh's words.

With an appalled expression on her face she looked him up and down, her eyes resting for just a fraction too long on his groin, and all at once he could feel the wetness there, already spread in a dark patch across his jeans. The colour rose in his face. He stammered something about spilling his beer, but he was only making it worse and even as he spoke he could smell the warm piss. Suddenly he hated her. His fists were clenched and he felt an intense urge to smash her face. He tried to hold himself back but the anger was surging up and blinding him. When he couldn't bear it anymore he swept one arm across the table top, sending glasses crashing to the ground.

Fern flinched. 'I'm not going anywhere with him,' she shouted, and weaving through tables and chairs, she ran out of the door.

Chapter Five

Almost without realising what she was doing, Fern had run up the stairs, onto the street and along the pavement for a few blocks as if all the forces of evil were behind her. She'd given no thought to direction, wanting only to put as much space as possible between herself and the madness of that place. The rain had stopped, though the gutters were still full and the roads had become mini rivers. Oblivious, she splashed through the dirty, ankle-deep water with its floating litter: cigarette butts, plastic wrappers and soggy food. She slipped once and fell, soaking her clothes and scraping her knee. A sharp pain shot through her ankle as it twisted under her. Flooded with adrenalin, she ignored it, leaping up again and running on.

Finally, out of breath, with her heart racing, Fern found herself near Central Station and stopped. She looked around for the first time, scanning the street for signs of the Bloodhound. It was still steamy hot but Fern was shaking with a mix of weariness and shock. The atmosphere on the streets had changed: after-dinner crowds and groups of staggering drunks charged it with a sense of menace. If she could just get to Claire's then everything would be okay. She'd be off the streets and safe - no more freaks or stalkers and no more talk of journeys or spirit guides.

As she turned into Central Station and headed for the suburban trains, Fern realised with horror that she was not carrying her backpack. She considered retracing her steps but the thought of going back to that bar was simply too much. It would have to stay there until tomorrow.

Fern searched her pockets for the change from the cafe and found enough to buy a train ticket. As she tried to find the right platform, people veered around her, leaving a space. Standing there, dirty and soaked through, Fern caught their disgusted glances before they looked quickly away. In the space of a few hours she had turned into one of the people she used to avoid.

At Stanmore, Fern got off the train and realised she had no idea how to get to Claire's house. She hesitated, not wanting to engage anyone in conversation, then, with her ankle beginning to throb, she limped to the nearest convenience store and asked the old man behind the counter for directions.

It had been months since Fern had ventured out of central Sydney and into the suburbs; away from the main street it seemed almost too quiet, with only the distant sound of sirens, the occasional flash of a television through a window and, just once, the roar of a plane filling the sky overhead. Walking along the deserted streets, Fern was nervous, starting at shadows, her heart thumping at the rustle of the wind in a tree, the sudden bark of a dog. She was at the end of her tether and just wanted to lie down on the pavement and rest. It was only the fear that kept her going, following the old man's directions, limping along the street for two blocks, turning left and then right, past house after house of people locked inside behind security doors and metal-barred windows, safe from the night.

At the house, Fern picked her way through a mess of discarded shoes on the verandah and rang the doorbell, then waited. A light came on and a girl Fern didn't recognise opened the door and stared hard at her.

'Is Claire home?'

'Yeah, I think she's in bed though,' said the girl suspiciously. 'It's late.'

'Could you tell her that Fern's here?' Fern's voice was small and cracked, full of unshed tears. On the edge. The girl recognised it and nodded, but she didn't ask her in.

'Hang on a minute,' she said and shut the door in Fern's face.

When Claire appeared she was bleary eyed and yawning, but anxious. 'My God, Fern! What's happened?'

But Fern couldn't speak; her throat had filled with a lump she couldn't swallow away and her eyes with tears, which soon overflowed. Claire's pity had pushed her over the edge.

'It's okay … You'll be fine,' Claire said, pulling Fern inside. 'You're safe … You're here now.'

Fern's breath came in big sobbing gasps, the shaking, grasping fear that had dogged her all night, released at last. Her legs gave way beneath her and both girls sat on the floor in the hallway, hugging each other. Eventually Fern stopped crying, though she continued to gasp intermittently.

'I'm sorry, I didn't mean to do that,' she said, throwing Claire a half-smile.

'It's okay. Now let's get you fixed up,' Claire said, sounding bright and efficient. 'You'll feel better after a shower. I'll get you something to change into.'

Fern let the hot water wash the night from her and some of the tension. I'm safe, she thought. At least for now. She didn't want to think of the future, just bask in this temporary reprieve.

Dressed in Claire's pyjamas, Fern limped down the hallway. Hearing raised voices in the kitchen, she stopped uncertainly at the door.

'If you help her out now we'll never get rid of her.'

Claire replied quietly, 'She's my friend, Pete. In my world friendship stands for something.'

'And what's that supposed to mean?'

Fern gathered her courage and stepped into the kitchen, trying to look as if she'd not heard when they both knew she had.

'I'm going to bed,' said Pete, brushing angrily past her and slamming the door behind him.

'I'm sorry, Claire, it's just for tonight. I don't want to cause any trouble.' Fern sat down uncertainly on a chair.

'It's okay. Don't worry about it. Pete's not as bad as he sounds. He thinks I'm too kind-hearted.' Claire frowned and pulled out the first-aid kit from under the sink. 'Your ankle looks a bit swollen, I'll wrap it up.'

'No, it's fine.'

'Are you sure? It'll swell up overnight and you won't be able to walk tomorrow.'

'No really, it's fine,' said Fern tucking her feet under the chair.

Claire seemed disappointed. She'd always been a good fix-it person, Fern recalled. She loved wrapping and mending, finding practical solutions to emergencies. But what had happened to Fern over the last twenty-four hours was far from practical and she doubted Claire would be able to understand, accept or fix any of it.

'So, what happened?' asked Claire, handing Fern a mug of hot chocolate. 'Did the landlord find you?'

Fern nodded. 'He came with my mother and someone else. I had to climb out the window.'

'Why?'

Fern looked at Claire and suddenly the whole thing seemed absurd. Claire would never have climbed out the window. She would never have locked herself in her room in the first place. 'I didn't want them to find me,' said Fern, wishing that would be enough of an explanation but knowing it would not. She sighed and began telling Claire her story but leaving out so many bits that in the end there wasn't any thread to it and none of what was left sounded remotely plausible. When she finished, the story hung suspended in the air, released in part, but not delivered, because Claire didn't believe her. Why would she? thought Fern. Her behaviour had been strange for months now and Claire had already been more patient than she needed to be.

Claire finished her hot chocolate, a sad expression on her face. 'I don't know what to say, Fern. It all sounds so strange. Are you sure you didn't imagine it? Why would anyone follow you? And this club - it sounds as if you've had some sort of hallucination. Did someone drug your drink?'

'No,' said Fern. 'Oh, I don't know. Maybe I imagined it all.'

'Look, it's nearly one o'clock,' said Claire. 'Why don't you get some sleep? We'll work it all out in the morning. I've made up a bed for you on the couch.'

Fern followed Claire into the living room where they stood facing each other awkwardly. Fern's story had come between them and neither knew how to step across the divide.

Claire turned away first. 'I'll shut these doors so the others don't disturb you in the morning.'

'Thanks, Claire. I'm really grateful.'

Claire looked at Fern, a worried frown on her face. 'It's okay. I just hope you can find your way out of this. You need to engage with the world again, Fern - the real one.'

Fern lay down on the couch and threw the blanket over her. It had been the longest day of her life. She was exhausted and needed to sleep. But she also needed to think. For a moment Fern fervently wished she'd told Claire less. But the next moment she was drifting into sleep, accompanied by the crash of glass and the memory of a golden-haired man, with dark eyes that saw too much. Fern hazily recalled the instant she'd laid eyes on Adam. She'd had a wild urge to run. He mattered somehow in her life; she could feel his importance. She didn't recognise him, but somehow she knew him, and she knew those hands. With that recognition had come a surge of desire, swiftly followed by the certainty that she mustn't let him get close to her. Having reminded herself of that, Fern turned onto her side and slipped into a deep sleep on Claire's lumpy couch.

In the morning Fern woke with a start to the sound of voices, the clatter of cups and the rich aroma of brewing coffee mingling with the smell of toast. Other people's lives. She was always on the outside, curious but detached, unable to connect. Once again Fern yearned to be back up in her attic, floating on a sea of white, locked up and away from everyone.

The remnants of her dream flitted in and out of her consciousness, the swish of fabric, a hooded cloak, empty of everything but shadows and disquiet. Standing up, she felt an acute pain in her ankle that made her gasp. Claire had been right: this morning her ankle was twice its size and a deep purple all over. Unable to put any weight on it, Fern hopped to the kitchen, wincing with pain.

Claire turned around, flashing a bright smile. 'Hi, did you sleep well? … Oh Fern, that looks terrible. You should have let me wrap it up last night.' She took some frozen peas out of the freezer. 'Here, put these on. It's a bit late, but it might help.'

'Thanks.' Fern sat on a chair and put her foot up, holding the peas in place. The cold etched its way greedily into her ankle, sending a fresh ache into the bone. 'Where are the others?'

'Pete just headed out cycling and Kate's not up yet.' Claire poured herself a bowl of muesli. 'Breakfast?' she asked.

Fern shook her head. She wasn't hungry. The anxiety she felt wasn't leaving room for anything else. Tomorrow had come and it hadn't brought any answers. 'A coffee would be good though.'

'Sure, I'll brew up some more.'

While they waited for the coffee to bubble on the stove, Claire bandaged Fern's ankle and Fern used Claire's phone to google The Underworld.

'It's not there,' she finally admitted, a fresh wave of anxiety surging through her at the prospect of losing her backpack.

'Never mind, you have to go back anyway,' said Claire, digging a safety pin out of the first-aid kit. 'It shouldn't be hard to find … There. How's that? It should be tight, but not tight enough to cut off your circulation.'

'That's great, Claire. Thanks.'

Fern watched Claire pour out the coffees. She envied her friend all those certainties which mapped out life in the clearest possible way. There didn't seem to be any murky areas in Claire's world, no swamps or quicksand, and no tightropes to balance on. In contrast there were few certainties in Fern's life. She would drink her coffee, borrow a few dollars and then go back into the city and retrace her steps. After that? She didn't want to think. She couldn't keep running forever. Perhaps she should just let them get her, whoever 'they' were.

'Let's sit out the back,' said Claire. The courtyard's nice and sunny. Here, I'll carry your coffee - you'll spill it if you hop like that.'

The courtyard was small and private, surrounded by tall fences, and in one corner a glorious eucalypt, its branches swaying in the breeze. They sat on intricate white lacework chairs, the metal already hot in the morning sun. The matching table wobbled on pavers which had lifted and subsided over the years with the shifting roots of the tree.

Fern sipped her coffee, savouring the surge of energy and clarity it brought. She lifted her face to the sun, loving the feel of it on her skin. Sitting here, she could almost believe everything was fine. That her life wasn't a mess after all; or at least not any kind of mess that couldn't be fixed with a bit of tidying or a fine-tooth comb.

'So how's your study going?' she asked Claire.

'Good, only two more years to go. It's a long haul, but worth it in the end. I'm wondering whether to specialise. No one wants to be a GP anymore. There's more money and less pain in a speciality.'

Fern wondered if Claire really loved medicine, or if it was just the money that drew her to it. Did motivation really matter? For Fern it would. But maybe that was just an excuse, concocted to hide the simple fact that she was lazy. Her father had said so, over and over - clutching his heart and calling her a lazy no-good bum. But medicine didn't interest Fern. Nothing did. That was the problem.

Fern's ankle was throbbing. She placed it gently on the chair next to her, wondering if any of Cassie's remedies would help. Arnica was for bruising, she recalled. If only she had her pack. Her thoughts were interrupted by a harsh ringing sound.

'Hang on, that's the door,' said Claire. 'Horrible ringer, isn't it?'

A moment later, Fern heard voices in the corridor, a murmuring, growing louder and closer. She knew who it was even before the figure stepped into the courtyard. Cassie had warned her of traps and here she was sitting in one. Her reprieve was over.

Claire stepped out into the courtyard first. 'Grace's here,' she said in her bright voice.

'Hello Mum,' said Fern, her voice heavy with resignation.

'Fernanda dear, are you alright? I've been so worried about you. Thank God Claire rang and told me you were safe.'

Fern wasn't angry, only disappointed. Of course Claire was trying to help. She'd felt she was doing the right thing. And if Fern were honest with herself, the predominant feeling she could identify was relief. Perhaps she'd just needed someone else to make the decision for her.

She stood and let herself be hugged, felt her mother's parchment skin rub against her cheek, smelled the talc, the hairspray, even the washing powder her mother always used, all conspiring to make her a child again. The situation was out of her hands now. She didn't have to run anymore and this realisation brought tears welling into her eyes.

While Claire made more coffee, Fern stared at the walls of the courtyard fighting back her tears. She was bricked in with this woman who both was and was not her mother. Funny how each time Fern saw her, she felt the force of her own strangeness battling with the familiar force of love. Perhaps it was simply the knowledge that the blood in Fern's veins was not her mother's.

Now that she had found her daughter, Grace's anxiety turned to anger. 'Your father's sick with worry,' she said accusingly. 'How could you do this to him?'

At this Fern felt the old weight of guilt and responsibility settle on her shoulders. Alive her father haunted her. Dead he would haunt her too. She'd still be weighed down with guilt but added to that would be the remorse from never having resolved the issues between them. Her father had been sick for so long. She'd been five, or maybe six, that first time when he'd come in from the garden and leaned on the piano right in front of her, his skin pale and a weak trembly look about him. She didn't know he was having a heart attack and neither did he. Even if she had known she couldn't have done anything. The next day he went to the doctor and when Fern came home from school he was in the hospital.

Since then her father had been living a half life, too afraid to live and too afraid to die. He had them wrapped around his little finger, controlling them with his illness.

'Don't you get it?' Fern said. 'Dad's been sick forever.'

'All the more reason not to worry him.'

'He sent you, didn't he? You'd never have come yourself. You'd have been too scared.'

'He loves you, Fern.'

'Some way he's got of showing it.'

'He's not a well man.'

Fern opened her mouth and then shut it again. What was the point? It was the same old argument.

She sat through an awkward twenty minutes or so while her mother and Claire drank their fresh coffees and made small talk, every word, every question, every loaded look of her mother's emphasising the already well-established fact that Claire was something to be proud of and Fern was not. When her mother suggested they go back to her motel and 'freshen up' before looking for her bag and collecting her things from the old place, Fern smiled and nodded. She changed into her own clothes and then waited compliantly for the taxi. It felt strange leaving with nothing. No bag, no purse, not even a jumper.

In the taxi, Fern sat staring through the window. The pavements were teeming with people, the roads clogged with traffic pouring out stinking fumes. Everyone going somewhere. But she was going full circle, back to her old life again and the box her parents had made for her.

'We'll stop off at the hospital and get your ankle looked at,' said Grace.

'That'll take hours. Can't we just leave it?'

'No, it might be fractured,' said Grace firmly. 'It's best if we get it checked.'

Fern sighed. There was no point arguing; her mother would do as she pleased. The taxi dropped them off at casualty and they made their way in slowly, Fern leaning on her mother for a crutch.

'You sit down, I'll go and talk to the nurses.'

Obediently, Fern sat on one of the plastic chairs and waited, her mind focussed on the regular throbbing pain in her ankle. When that had gradually settled to a dull ache, Grace still hadn't returned.

Fern looked at the clock. Quarter past ten on a Saturday morning and the waiting room was almost full. She wondered if people had more accidents on Saturdays or if every day was like this. Bored, she studied the drinks machine, then looked longingly at the chocolate bar and chips machine, suddenly hungry as she remembered she hadn't eaten since the previous day.

Glancing up at reception, Fern spotted a blond-haired man standing with his back to her. Her heart beat faster and she felt a blush rising in her cheeks as the confusion she'd felt last night returned. It was Adam, she was sure of it. Once again Fern felt the tugging inside of her, wanting to go to him yet knowing she needed to keep a distance between them. But she also needed to talk to him. Adam knew the Underworld really existed, and that Shamesh was real too. He would know she hadn't been dreaming. He could vouch for her. She needed that reassurance for herself, and the proof too, so that Claire and her mother wouldn't think she was mad. Fern half rose, then abruptly sat back down again when the man turned and she saw that he wasn't Adam after all. Disappointed, she picked up a tattered magazine and tried to lose herself in old news about celebrities she'd never heard of. It didn't work. Somehow Adam's face had imprinted itself on her mind and she couldn't shake the memory of it. She had never met him before, yet she'd recognised him. It didn't make sense.

Her mother returned a few minutes later They sat side by side, Grace fussing and scolding and making plans, Fern distracted by the gurgles of her empty stomach.

Eventually her mother went and fetched sandwiches from the hospital canteen. Tuna, mayonnaise and limp lettuce on soft white bread. Fern swallowed hers in a matter of moments, followed it quickly with a lamington, then looked enviously at her mother's.

Finally a harassed-looking nurse called Fern's name. Obediently they followed her through the doors and into a small cubicle. 'Just wait here,' she said. 'The doctor won't be long.'

Fern sat on the edge of the bed, her mother on a plastic chair next to the heart monitor. So many times Fern had visited her father in hospital and stared in fascination at the regular pattern of the heart monitor wired up to his body, searching for anomalies, wondering when it would just stop and he would be gone. The ratio between dread and hope changing as the years passed and the distaste she felt for her father deepened.

Soon the doctor arrived. He was young, probably under thirty, with trendy red-rimmed glasses and pockmarks on his cheeks from a bad case of acne.

'Hello there, how are we today?'

Fern was torn between relief and irritation. She hated being addressed as 'we'. And what a stupid question, under the circumstances.

'We're fine,' she muttered with all the disdain she could muster, but the doctor was determined to be cheerful.

'So you've hurt your foot. Let's have a look.'

Fern held out her foot and watched him gently unwind Claire's wrapping. He whistled. 'That's some swelling and a whopper of a bruise coming up.' Fern winced as he pressed his fingers into her ankle, feeling for damage. 'Sorry,' he said. 'You'll have to have an x-ray, I can't tell what's going on in there. I'll send someone with a wheelchair. Won't be long.'

Resigned to another long wait, Fern leaned back and shut her eyes, letting the hospital recede as she slipped into sleep. In her dream she was still in the cubicle but it was dark and a hooded man in the robes of a priest was standing next to her. Terrified, Fern forced her way out of the dream, opening her eyes to a fluorescent room, empty except for the heart monitor and her mother nodding off on a chair next to her. Only a dream, she thought, feeling her heart settle again into a steadier rhythm, but keeping her eyes open nevertheless.

Finally a wheelchair appeared and she was taken for an x-ray. Some time later the doctor reappeared carrying the results. Fern stared at him glumly, dazed by the long hours under fluorescent lights.

'It's looking good. No apparent fractures. Even so, it's a bad sprain. It will have to be bound, and you'll need to get around on crutches for a week or two. I'll organise hiring some from here if you like. Panadol will help with the pain.'

Fern nodded. 'Thanks.'

'Here, put your foot up, I'll bind it for you now.'

Fern did as she was told, staring out past his shoulder at the scurrying nurses.

'Your mother tells me you've had a time of it.'

Fern threw an accusing glance at Grace. But the doctor was looking at Fern questioningly, waiting for her to answer.

'A bit,' she said sullenly.

'Do you want to tell me about it?'

The sympathy in his voice made her want to crumble. 'No.'

'Okay, then what about telling me how you hurt your ankle?'

'I tripped.'

'When?'

'Last night.'

'Were you running?

Fern nodded, still holding out.

'Were you scared?'

She recalled the moment when she'd felt the Bloodhound right behind her, felt his breath on her neck, his hand reaching out through the rain and the darkness. She remembered the terror. Tears filled her eyes as she nodded once again.

'What happened, Fern? Was someone after you?'

'Yes,' she whispered. The floodgates opened then and she couldn't stop herself, the words coming out in a monotone, flat and empty as if there was nothing left inside her. 'He followed me all night. I don't know who he was. But I fell. Twice. Once down some stairs I think. Then later I tripped in the gutter.'

'What happened when you fell down the stairs?'

'There was another man,' she said. 'A bar tender.'

'Did he hurt you?'

Fern shook her head.

'What about your room, Fern? Your mum says you didn't want to leave.'

'No.'

'Why not?'

'I don't know.'

'How long were you there?'

Fern shrugged. A lump had risen up into her throat and she couldn't speak.

'A month?'

She shook her head.

'Two months?'

Another shake

'Three? Four?'

Fern nodded.

'That's a long time to stay in your room.'

The tears were running down her cheeks now and wetting her t-shirt. She didn't even try to wipe them away.

'Why did you run away when your mum came?'

She shrugged again and looked away, trying to pull herself together, but the tears kept coming and she had the strange sensation that there was a bottomless well inside her, dark and still, heavy with grief.

'It's alright, darling,' said her mother, dabbing at Fern's face with a tissue. 'The doctor just wants to help.'

Grace's face was drawn tight with worry and Fern felt a fleeting guilt that she was adding to her mother's burden. They were sitting so close and yet neither reached out to hug the other. Fern couldn't remember when this physical distance had grown between them or how they'd let it happen.

The doctor finished binding her ankle and stood up. 'There you go … Now don't you worry.' He patted her on the shoulder. 'You stay here. I'm going to have a quick word outside with your mother.'

Fern waited obediently for her mother and the doctor to return. She felt like a child again, passive and powerless, letting them mutter and mumble over her. She'd never been good at defying her parents and yet had felt compelled to do it over and over in so many small ways. It was a need and a relief, like opening a window in an airless room. Then there was the punishment. She'd hated the physicality of it, hated the wooden spoon, the broom, the slap of fingers … But it was the words that somehow hurt more than the smarting on the backs of her legs. 'Bad blood,' her father always said as if that explained everything.

Fern remembered her misdeeds well. Looking back they seemed so trivial, yet at the time they were monstrous things: an apple picked across a neighbour's fence, a slice of cake sneaked in the night, an hour at school spent hiding in the toilets, and forbidden but glorious visits to the local park. Then there was the tunnel, one end in the park and the other end unknown, and this the source of much speculation. It was long, though no one knew how long, and it came with all the adult warnings of flash floods and strange men, designed to keep the kids away, but instead making it all the more alluring.

One day when Fern was about ten, a few of them had set out to find the other end. They'd walked out of the sun into the cool shadowy darkness, the tunnel walls covered with graffiti, the ground with cigarette ends. Behind them the patch of light shrank until they turned a corner and it disappeared altogether. Their voices bounced back at them from the walls, which made them whisper at first, then fall silent. No one wanted to be the first to suggest turning back, so they walked on, shuffling in the dark, ears alert, their fingers touching the walls for comfort.

It had seemed an eternity before they turned another corner and saw a tiny patch of light. Fern had been in front, she'd seen it first and called out. They walked faster and faster until, laughing with relief, they ran the final hundred metres and plunged back out into the light. They all gasped then, because it was a paradise they'd entered: a creek, lined with willows and eucalypts, the sun filtering through the lush greens of a silent garden. Eden, Fern had thought, but known it couldn't be. She'd also known they were trespassing, so they could only sit quietly for a few moments, soaking up the mysterious tranquillity, before retracing their steps through the tunnel. Back to where they belonged. Only Fern didn't belong, she never had, not at either end. She'd felt the injustice of it then and swallowed it down, holding it in a place deep inside with all the other injustices.

Now, sitting in this tiny cubicle while her mother and the doctor conspired outside, Fern felt as if she were trapped in that tunnel, right in the middle, with no light at either end. The only thing keeping her there was the tiny and fragile hope that one day she would find an end, and with it something vital and beautiful.

Fern's mother came in first, looking furtive. 'Fernanda, dear, the doctor wants you to stay here for a little while. He thinks it's a good idea to get another doctor to have a look at you.'

'Why? It's not even broken. The doctor said so.'

'Not your ankle, sweetheart. The doctor's worried about you.'

'What do you mean?' Fern could feel all her instincts rising up in warning.

'He thinks you might be depressed.'

'Depressed! Who wouldn't be depressed, spending an entire day sitting in a waiting room for nothing?'

'He's worried, sweetheart. He thinks you might hurt yourself. He just wants another doctor to take a look at you.'

'A psychiatrist? You're kidding.' Fern pushed herself off the bed and onto one foot, tugging at the curtain to keep her balance. 'I'm getting out of here.'

Her mother reached towards Fern as if to restrain her. 'Please, Fern, just for a few hours.'

'No!' She pushed her mother away, sending her staggering backwards into the doctor's arms as he entered the cubicle, still smiling determinedly.

'What have we here? I didn't know I had such an effect on women.'

Three things happened in quick succession: her mother burst into tears, Fern tried to duck around the two of them, and the doctor reached out, his strong fingers circling her upper arm and stopping her in mid-flight.

Normally when encountering authority, Fern would have succumbed and allowed herself to be led away, but this time something unexpected happened. It started as a great pressure building in her chest. Then through the dull dread and the numbness of her world, came a fury so strong it felt too big for her, forcing its way out of the narrow confines of her body.

'NO!' she screamed, the force of it reverberating through the emergency ward and peeling the doctor's fingers from her arm.

Behind her the heart monitor, untouched, crashed to the ground. The doctor looked around in shocked surprise then pressed a red button as Fern started hopping out of there; away from them all, before they locked her up.

She had almost made it to the exit when two security men intercepted her, taking Fern by the arm and turning her around to face the doctor and her mother, who had followed her. Fern struggled and kicked and bit, the surge of adrenalin obliterating the pain in her ankle. 'Take your fucking hands off me. Let me go … Mum, don't let them do this to me. Mum… what's happening?' And then came the realisation. 'You planned this, didn't you.'

A nurse hurried towards them carrying a syringe and gave it to the doctor, who jabbed her in the arm. Fern tried to fight, tried to keep struggling, but knew she was defeated. Soon her muscles began to relax and all she could do was send a look of absolute hatred to her mother, before slipping into unconsciousness.

Chapter Six

Fern had no idea where she was. The room was dark and quiet, aside from the snuffling sound of other people's breathing and the restless rustle of sheets. She tried to concentrate, to focus her memory, but her body and mind were heavy with a deep lethargy that forced her eyes shut again, allowing sleep to reclaim her. From its depths came a terrifying shuffle of footsteps and once again the figure of a man appeared, wearing a long gown, no face visible under the cowl of his hood. Fern watched him, horrified. His hands were folded into the sleeves of his gown as he walked towards her. Like a monk, she thought, but reeking of evil. Trapped in her dream, Fern fought to open her eyes and succeeded briefly, only to helplessly close them again and sink back into sleep. All night the battle continued and the faceless man came closer and closer. Soon he would reach out and touch her and she would be lost.

Waking at last in the light of morning, Fern thought for a moment she was back in her attic. The wall behind her was white, the sheets were white, but the smells and sounds were wrong: sharp edged and unforgiving, with a bustling air of urgency. A white curtain surrounded her bed, not soft and transparent like her mosquito net but thick and heavy. It felt as if she were in a cocoon but there was no doubt she was in hospital.

When Fern tried to sit up, a wave of exhaustion forced her back onto the pillow. There was still a residue of the terror she'd felt in her dreams but she was groggy too, as if awaking from a deep sleep, her brain not sending its signals to the right places. She tried again, more slowly this time, and managed to stay upright, though everything spun around her. Her mouth was dry, her lips cracked and she felt sick, deep in her belly. When the spinning stopped, Fern slid her legs off the bed and tried to stand, but pain surged through her ankle, forcing her back onto the bed. She could feel the dread growing within her as she began piecing together the events of the previous day.

Her own clothes had been spirited away in the night and she was wearing someone else's nightgown, an awful old-lady one with a pink floral pattern. On the side table was a plastic jug of water, a plastic cup and a glossy magazine. Next to the jug of water was the necklace Cassie had given her. She picked up the deep blue stone speckled with gold, comforted by its familiarity, letting it soothe her and clear some of the fuzziness from her mind. It was a small thing but enough to anchor her.

Fern stared at the ceiling with its patchwork of white tiles and listened to the sounds of people waking around her. Strangers separated only by a curtain. She wondered briefly at what point a person could lose themselves entirely. Already, in the last forty-eight hours she had lost her attic room, along with all her belongings, her backpack and even the clothes she'd been wearing. She couldn't keep hold of the thoughts for long though; her brain felt heavy and sluggish. Had she lost her mind as well, she wondered.

With a violent whoosh, the curtain around her was pulled open and a round-faced nurse beamed at her. 'Good morning. How are you today?'

'Where am I?' asked Fern.

'In hospital.'

'Why?'

'You just needed a little rest, darling. Sit up while I plump the pillows … There, that's better. Now, a pill before breakfast and we're done.'

'What's that for?' asked Fern as the nurse poured a glass of water and offered it to her with a small white pill.

'Just to help you rest. There you go, pop it in … Good girl,' said the nurse when Fern swallowed. 'Now, how about breakfast? That ankle will keep you in bed for a day or two so I'll send someone in with a tray.'

Then she was gone, leaving the curtains open and Fern exposed to the gazes of the other patients, all women. Most of them were already up, some dressed, others still wearing nightclothes. They all stared at her, either directly or secretively, except for the young one at the end with a sullen dead face, who just stared at the wall. Fern felt her face going red under their scrutiny.

A square shaped nurse came in, pushing a food trolley towards Fern. 'Here we go,' she said, plopping a tray down on Fern's lap.

The ward quietened as the other women left for breakfast, leaving only Fern, the young girl in the corner and a nurse who was trying to encourage the girl to eat. Fern ate hungrily. As she finished her toast, a man and a woman, both in white coats and holding clipboards, entered the ward, carrying a palpable air of authority with them. They stopped at the end of Fern's bed and consulted their clipboards.

'Hello, Fernanda,' said the woman. 'My name's Dr Whittaker and this is Dr Greenacres.'

'Are you psychiatrists?'

'Yes, that's right.'

'Am I in a mental institution?'

'No, Fernanda, you're in the psychiatric ward of a general hospital.'

'Isn't that the same thing?'

'No, not really.'

'Can I leave then?'

'Well, that's what we're here to discuss.'

'How are you feeling?' asked the man, speaking for the first time.

'Fine,' said Fern.

'We'd like you to tell us what's been happening in your life.'

Fern sighed. So far, every time she had tried to explain something of what had happened, things had become very much worse for her. And neither of these doctors looked as if they would believe a word she said. Dr Greenacres had eyes that were too big behind the thick lenses of his glasses, and scaly skin on his hands and neck that made him look like a fish out of water. Dr Whittaker was suspiciously normal, exuding common sense, right from her flat comfortable shoes to the neat sweep of her hair and the nicely sharpened pencil held poised and waiting. Fern was just one of Dr Whittaker's chores, to be dealt with as efficiently as possible. She was probably thinking about the lasagne she planned to make for dinner, wondering whether it should be meat or vegetarian.

'Well?'

'I always prefer vegetarian,' said Fern, the words slipping out before she could stop them.

Dr Whittaker stared hard at her. 'I beg your pardon?'

'Nothing,' said Fern quickly.

'Okay, let's be more specific,' said Dr Whittaker, consulting her notes again. 'Could you tell us what happened after you fell down those stairs at the club?'

'No,' said Fern, and just then her mother arrived, rushing in as though she knew she was late, as though this was a meeting to which she had been invited. For a moment Fern stared at her mother. The strain of having a daughter locked up in a psychiatric ward was obviously taking its toll. Fern wondered if she was being too tough on Grace who was after all only doing what she thought best. But her resentment grew as she watched Grace listening deferentially to the doctors, nodding and smiling nervously, in league against her own daughter. She hadn't even greeted Fern, hadn't asked how she was.

After conferring briefly with Grace, Dr Greenacres turned back to Fern and repeated Dr Whittaker's question about the club.

'It will help us to know a bit more about you, Fernanda,' said Dr Greenacres. 'It will help us make some decisions.'

Fern pointed disdainfully at her mother. 'Ask her, she seems to know everything.'

The doctor sighed. 'Okay, Fernanda, if that's your decision, we'll have to reach our own conclusions.'

Fern watched them muttering to each other, consulting their clipboards, nodding. In collusion, she thought, their self-importance the vital ingredient in this farce. Yet she couldn't raise enough energy to protest.

Dr Greenacres turned to Fern and smiled as if he'd only just noticed her. 'How about staying here for a few days? It will give you a chance to recuperate before we reassess your case … What do you think?'

Fern stared at them. As if she had any choice in the matter. She felt a mixture of relief and fear at the prospect. A few days didn't sound like much and it might give her time to work out what to do next but she didn't have the resources to convince them she was telling the truth so she was caught in a catch-22. Speak out or stay silent: either way she lost. And that might mean a longer stay.

When the doctors left, Grace sat down wearily beside the bed and Fern wondered if their love and shared history would be enough to sustain her mother through this fresh crisis and the criticism she would face from the rest of the family. She felt a surge of pity for her mother. For years the family had made Grace pay over and over for her decision to bring a stranger into their midst. And although Grace had tried to shelter Fern from the worst of it but they'd trampled Fern too, seizing on every misdemeanour as proof of her bad blood: an impatient word to a cousin becoming a great sin, a broken plate a tragedy not to be brushed aside.

Staring up at the white-squared ceiling, Fern remembered another hospital, a baby lying stranded in her crib. She could see it all so clearly, and smell it, hear the clink and clatter of trays and the squeak of nurses' shoes. How efficient the hospital system was, then and now. Like clockwork. The nurses feeding and changing her every few hours, then leaving her; neither her cries nor her first tentative smiles having any effect on the bewildering world she'd entered. The nurses' hands were gentle, but efficient, never lingering. And they smelled wrong. The bottles they pushed into her mouth smelled wrong too, but she sucked anyway, then screamed with the wind caught in her gut, sucked and screamed and vomited, sucked and screamed and vomited, in an endless round of pain and frustration, until the day she opened her eyes and saw a woman's anxious face peering at her, her hair pulled tightly into a bun and beads of perspiration sitting along her hairline. Behind the woman stood a small thin-lipped man wearing a neat pressed suit, his hands clasped officiously behind his back. Grace and Richard Parsons had come to take her home.

Now Fern drew her eyes away from the ceiling and looked at her mother. 'Did you get me this?' she asked, pointing at the nightdress.

Grace nodded, clearly happy to discuss practical matters. 'I thought you'd need something in here. And it was so pretty. Don't you think? You'll need some day wear too. Most people seem to be wearing their own clothes. And some slippers. What size are you? Thirty-six? Your feet have always been so tiny. Not like my monstrosities.' Grace laughed awkwardly and looked down at her own feet.

Fern turned her eyes back to the ceiling as her mother tried to draw her into a conversation, her voice occasionally wafting into Fern's consciousness as if from a great distance. 'Father sends … the newsagent … something to read … Mrs Lindsay next door … what nice people …' But Fern wasn't listening; long forgotten memories were bubbling to the surface, her mother's or her own, she couldn't distinguish. Flashes and glimpses that blended memory and desire, past and present. Had she really heard the echoes of her birth mother's scream the day Grace and Richard had carried her out of the hospital? A scream that had brought a tearing in her own chest. She must have known her mother well, must have recognised the rhythm of her heart, her moods, her voice, the gurgling of her stomach, her sleep patterns … Perhaps, as Fern's new parents carried her out of the hospital, her birth mother was only just realising that out of sight would never be out of mind. That despite everything, Fern would always be her daughter.

Eventually Grace gave up trying to make conversation and left, promising to come back later. Fern dozed on and off, filled with an intense weariness. Each time she fell asleep she was woken soon after by a brightly fussing nurse who fed her more pills, or by the desolate, slurred voices of the patients, or the gasping fear of a nightmare that quickly passed out of reach. Then she would look at her window where the sky was always the same sullen grey and she would know that hardly any time had passed.

The doctors came again, asking questions which Fern didn't bother to answer, and telling her things she didn't want to know. They said she was depressed. That this was the cause of everything that had happened. They used other words too, ones she didn't want to understand. Fern slipped away from them and into sleep once more, her dream sending her into a lush dense forest which should have been beautiful. Instead, the atmosphere was thick and heavy, forcing her to fight for each step, wanting desperately to be away from the darkness growing around her. Then without warning a strong hand reached into her dream, grabbed her ankle and tried to drag her out of this world and into another.

Fern woke, gasping for air, her heart thumping, her throat tight as she struggled against a heavy weight on her chest. She was becoming afraid to sleep and yet she couldn't resist sleep's call. It was like a beautiful but deadly Siren, luring her onto the rocks. There was a malevolence increasingly inhabiting her dreams, turning them into nightmares. In her sleep Fern was helpless, and it felt as if something was taking advantage of that vulnerability.

Her mother returned that afternoon with a bag of shopping and a happy smile that threatened any moment to dissolve into tears. She waved oversized undies in Fern's face, a beige bra, stretchy trousers she called slacks, and a t-shirt. There were fluffy slippers too and a pink dressing-gown, plus a couple of magazines.

Feeling distant and dull minded, Fern watched her mother proudly pulling out her shopping, remembering the day Grace and Richard had first taken her home. The scream that had forced its way out as Richard had strapped her into the car seat. Then night after night, day after day she'd screamed, her stomach clenched in pain as she brought up the sugared milk they'd fed her. She'd been hurt and afraid and sick, a sickness of the spirit as well as the body. Now it was happening all over again, only she wasn't screaming anymore. Instead she was locked up and dosed up with pills.

Fern remembered the tiny infant she'd been, whose screams had finally stopped after three months, to be replaced by a gaping silence. Exhausted, her head resting on the soft lace pillow that her new mother had made, Fern had slept as though she'd been pricked by a spindle, oblivious to the passing of time. For twenty years, bed had been her safe haven, the place where she could shut down, one bed replacing another until eventually she'd found her white bed in her white attic and locked the door against the world.

Now, in her new cocoon and too afraid to sleep, Fern lay in bed for hours after Grace left, listening to the restless sleep of others. Somehow she had to find a way to engage with the world again. But which world? She could no longer tell what was real and what was not. Perhaps I imagined everything, thought Fern, perhaps none of them are real: not Shamesh, not Cassie, not even Adam with his golden hair and dark eyes.

Despite her resistance, sleep finally overtook Fern, dragging her down into a place so dark she felt she must be blind. She reached out her hands, looking for something solid to help guide her, but there was nothing, and she was afraid that if she waited, the terrible hand would reach out again through the thin membrane that divided worlds, or time, she didn't know which. She took one step, and then another, her hands in front of her. Then she felt a familiar softness and gratefully sank her hands into the bear's fur, feeling its strength seeping into her bones and replenishing her.

When the bear tugged, she followed, knowing without words that the bear wanted Fern to come. After a while there was a glimmer of light and Fern could see they were walking through a narrow tunnel with a rocky floor. The rock became sand and they emerged into a starry night, the silvery moon reflected in a calm sea, lapping gently against the shore. Fern knew without knowing that the bear wanted her to enter the sea, so she did. The water was warm and dark but she wasn't afraid. She took her feet from the bottom as the bear wanted her to, and floated, surrendering to the power of the sea, letting it rock her gently back and forth until, for a moment, Fern became the ocean. As she woke, a single word found its way through the fog of her mind. *Trust.*

Fern lay cocooned in the crisp white hospital sheets, trying to hold onto the last vestiges of her dream. The tension in her chest had eased, she wasn't gasping for breath, and her heart wasn't pounding. Somehow the bear had given her strength and a little clarity, enough to remember she needed to get out of here. But they wouldn't let her out until she cooperated. So be it, she thought, I'll play their game.

As night settled, Adam sat in his darkened room, staring up at the streetlight outside, remembering the gold slippers he'd watched slip past only a few nights before and the purposeful feet that had followed. She was in danger, he knew it. He'd known it then too, only he'd chosen to ignore the warning. Since then, Shamesh had charged him with the care of Fern and he'd let her slip away all over again. Over the past few months, Shamesh had done so much for Adam, giving him the work he needed so badly. More importantly though, Shamesh had expected Adam to do the work well. He'd shown Adam a respect that Adam didn't even feel for himself. For that he was immensely grateful. This was the only time Shamesh had ever asked anything more from Adam and he'd failed him. He scowled at the memory feeling ashamed all over again. But it wasn't his fault. It was that stupid girl. Never mind that he'd frightened her. She didn't have to run away like that. Adam swilled the remainder of his drink in the glass, watching the amber liquid glow in the light. Then he drained it. The bottle was empty; it was time to go.

Clumsily, Adam locked the door behind him and walked the few blocks to the Underworld where Shamesh was waiting in the empty bar. He couldn't have known Adam was coming and yet there was no doubt he was waiting for him. This was one of many things about Shamesh that perturbed Adam.

'I'm sorry, Shamesh, I …' Adam shook his head, not knowing how to explain about Fern, about his own wariness and his need.

Shamesh smiled. 'There is a good deal between you and Fern already. This will confuse your responses but if you are careful it won't blind you.' He put his hand on Adam's shoulder. 'Next time try to be more gentle.'

Adam blushed and stammered out another apology. Then Shamesh's words sunk in. 'Next time? But she's gone. I don't know where she is.'

'Only for now. She will find her way back to you.'

'How?' asked Adam, unable to mask the desperation in his voice.

Shamesh shrugged. 'It is written,' he said, handing Adam a coffee. 'Here, drink this. You need to prepare, and coffee will do you more good than whisky.'

Chapter Seven

In the morning another nurse with a bright smile whisked open the curtains. 'Good morning, Fernanda. Did you sleep well?' she asked, not pausing for an answer. 'I think it's time you had a shower, don't you?'

Fern let the nurse help her out of bed. She felt weak, both inside and out, and so dizzy she had to lean on the bed for balance. Her foot was stronger though and she could put a little weight on it. Nevertheless the nurse gave her crutches and Fern lurched awkwardly after her to the shower room.

'You can have a nice hot shower and then breakfast in the dining room. How does that sound? Here, let me help,' she added as Fern fumbled with the buttons on her nightdress.

Fern obediently lifted her arms and let the nurse pull off her nightdress. Puzzled, she watched the nurse's smile turned into a frown.

'My, you're thin!' said the nurse. 'And look at those bruises. Did you get them when you hurt your ankle?'

Bruises? Fern looked at herself in the mirror, and saw what the nurse was referring to; a pattern of livid bruises on her chest. She shrugged, trying to look unconcerned, but really she was puzzled; she didn't remember hurting her chest.

'Never mind,' said the nurse. 'I'll come back in ten minutes and take you to the dining room for breakfast.'

Fern stood in the shower and let the steaming water pummel her back. Looking down, she noticed another pattern of bruises, this time in a ring above her good ankle. She remembered her dream yesterday afternoon; that hand reaching out and dragging her with it into another world. Fern shuddered. No, it couldn't be. A hand in a dream can't bruise you.

She stepped out of the shower and stood staring at herself in the mirror, shocked by how frail she was, her legs trembling with the effort of standing upright, her face drawn, with dark shadows under her eyes. She could feel the edges of her bones protruding through her skin, and her ribs were sticking out the way they had when she was a child. Fern hardly recognised herself. Frightened, she abruptly looked away: it was too easy to imagine the next step.

Fern dressed herself in the clothes her mother had brought. They made her feel like someone else, the bra gaping and loose, and the trousers too big, threatening to slip down over her narrow hips.

'That's better,' said the nurse when she returned. 'You look like a different person.'

Inside the dining room, the noise hit Fern with a jolt. It felt nightmarish in here; there were too many faces, greedy eyes and open chewing mouths. Obediently, Fern sat where the nurse pointed, at one end of a table of six. She ate her cereal slowly, trying not to notice the person slurping next to her with Rice Bubbles on his chin. Her hands were steady as she buttered a slice of toast and spread it thinly with honey, but inside she was fighting the overpowering urge to bolt.

Fern had just taken the first bite of her toast when a gaunt man with concave cheeks and a scar across his neck came and stood too close, his eyes staring intently into hers. Fern couldn't take her eyes off that scar, so livid it looked painted on, and right across the artery, stitch marks neatly crisscrossing its line. She shuddered, feeling the intent behind that wound, and the despair.

He leaned down even closer and whispered into her ear. 'Beware. You are in danger. Watch out for the aliens.'

Feeling a cold chill running along her spine, Fern shrank away from him.

'Come on, Trevor,' said a nurse, taking his arm and leading him away. 'Sit down at your own table and leave this poor girl alone.'

'Don't worry about him, he's mad,' said the slurping patient, reaching over and taking Fern's toast. 'Hey, I'll tell you a secret: when the end of the world comes, I'm going to be king.'

Fern stood up and reached for her crutches. The gaunt man's warning had disconcerted her. She needed to get away from here, back to the safety of her bed and the relative quiet of the ward, where she could at least try to gather her thoughts. But there was no peace in the ward either. Grace was waiting by Fern's bed and wanting to chat.

'Hello, darling. How are you today? Better? Yes, you look much brighter. And you're dressed too. That's wonderful.'

Obediently, Fern lifted her cheek for her mother to kiss.

'Look, I've brought you another magazine. *Vogue* – I thought you'd be interested in the fashion. Do you remember how you used to pore over those magazines, making your own sketches?'

While her mother talked, Fern listlessly opened the magazine and flicked through the glossy pages, glancing at the fashion and the models. She couldn't think why she had been interested in this. It all seemed so far away from her present world with its pocket-sized patches of sky, oversized beige bras and mad people whispering warnings in her ear; and aeons away from her beautiful white attic room with its floating muslin curtains and mosquito net.

She felt the weariness growing again, an overwhelming tiredness that forced her eyes shut and slipped her into the dangerous world of her dreams, where with just a flick of a malevolent finger her skeleton collapsed in hundreds of pieces onto the ground. Horrified, she picked up one piece and then another, trying to work out how they fitted together, this joint with that, but getting nowhere. She woke briefly, only to slip back into the dream, still clutching her finger bone. It was the missing piece, but when she looked around, the other pieces had disappeared. This finger bone was all she had left of herself. In the distance she could hear the horrible triumphant echo of laughter.

When Fern woke, her mother had gone. Her chest throbbed, the pressure on it taking her breath away. She tried to recall her dream, but it slipped away through the muddled pathways of her mind, lingering only on the edges of her vision and in the fear in her heart. The small reserve of clarity and strength the bear had given her was almost gone.

Wearily she closed her eyes and the Bear Handler was there, smiling. He held what looked like a roughly carved staff. 'This is for you,' he said, placing it in her hand. 'Use it well.'

Fern woke with a start, her hand grasping an empty space where the staff had been. Trevor, the gaunt, scarred man from the dining room was standing next to her bed.

'Shhh,' he said putting his finger to his lips when he saw her mouth open in alarm. He looked around nervously, then leaned in close so that Fern could feel his warm breath on her ear. 'Read this.' He pressed a magazine into her hand and then tiptoed away.

It was a journal of anthropology, dating back a couple of years. On the page Trevor had marked was an article called *Shamanism: The Old and the New* by Trevor Whiteheart, PhD. Fern could hardly believe that this man who talked so casually about aliens was an anthropologist. She began reading at random under the heading 'Initiation' ... *The process of initiation is complex, but its patterns are repeated across many cultures. In fact, shamanism is a world-wide tradition. Usually the person becomes withdrawn and contemplative, sleeps for long hours and has powerful dreams ...*

Too tired to make sense of the words, Fern closed her eyes again, the malevolent force in her dreams drawing her towards it once more.

This time she was woken by a voice she recognised shouting outside in the corridor. 'We are coming to the transition between worlds. The time has come. The earth is shifting to a higher vibration. If we don't shift with it we'll be lost. It's time. We must let go of all our negative energies. Release them so we can live in light …'

Fern pulled back the covers and grabbed her crutches, arriving in the corridor just in time to see two men holding Cassie while a nurse stuck a needle in her arm.

'Get your hands off me, you filthy man. How dare you! I know my rights. Can't you see? We don't have much time. It's in the sky. The warnings are everywhere.'

'Come on, love, settle down,' said one of the guards, struggling to keep hold of her.'

'No, no, no - stop it. I don't want to go to sleep. I have to speak. I have to tell.'

'Jeez, she's as strong as a bloody mule this one. She should have gone under by now.'

'We're on the verge of cataclysmic change. Gaia is breathing out. We have to act now. Can't you - ' Cassie stopped suddenly midsentence as her legs crumpled beneath her.

'There,' said the nurse. 'I'll get a wheelchair. Take her along to Ward C. I think there's still a spare bed in there. If we're lucky.' She rolled her eyes. 'God, if it doesn't rain it pours. There must be a full moon or something.'

Fern waited ten minutes, then made her way to Ward C where she found Cassie asleep behind drawn curtains, her face drained of colour. Aside from the almost imperceptible rise and fall of her chest there was no sign of life. Fern sat on the edge of the bed and watched her friend sleeping. It was strange, she thought, how Cassie said her prophecies were all bad, yet compared to the news on television, they were full of hope. If Cassie was right, this was a new beginning, not an end. Though it all depended on the choices we make.

Cassie frowned and began mumbling incoherently, the prophesying force that appeared to have taken her over battling against the drugs. Realising the battle could take hours, Fern turned to go, but as she reached for her crutches, Cassie grabbed her hand, making her almost lose her balance. 'Don't take the pills,' she whispered.

Fern waited to see if Cassie would speak again, but she was tossing and turning now, the words spilling out, jumbled and meaningless. 'Okay Cassie, I won't,' said Fern reaching out and brushing a strand of hair from Cassie's face.

Later, when the nurse came round with her pill, Fern put it in her mouth and pretended to swallow. She was worried that the nurse would check, as she did with some of the other patients, the ones who insisted they didn't want drugs, but Fern's docile behaviour had disarmed the nurse and she didn't even look up to see if Fern swallowed. When no one was watching, Fern spat the pill into a tissue and dropped it in the bin. That evening she did the same and by the next morning her thoughts were becoming lighter, the pathways clearer and her mood soured as the anger set in once more.

Her mother arrived after breakfast, carrying another shopping bag. 'Hello, dear,' she said, kissing Fern on the cheek. 'I've brought you a nice cardigan to wear.' She pulled out a navy-blue knitted cardigan with silver buttons and held it up for Fern to see.

'Where are my own clothes?' asked Fern, ignoring the cardigan. 'Why can't you bring me my things?'

'They're all in storage, Fernanda darling,' said Grace, looking uncomfortable. 'I didn't know what you wanted so I thought it best to pack up everything.'

'I hate these things. They're not me. None of this is me. And for God's sake will you stop calling me Fernanda?'

'It's your name, darling.'

'No it's not. It's *your* name. You chose it. Just like you chose these bloody clothes. I don't want it and I don't want these.'

'Calm down, you've been doing so well, darling. Don't spoil it now.'

'Doing well! I've been drugged up to my eyeballs, my brain not working. Doing what I'm told. You call that doing well?'

Her mother was crying but Fern steeled herself against sympathy. Right now she didn't care if she never saw Grace again. Her fury was so big she couldn't contain it. Suddenly a magazine lifted off the bed, propelled itself towards her mother and hit her in the face before falling to the floor. Shocked, they both froze. Fern felt the anger draining from her. She knew this was her doing yet had no idea how she had done it. With a growing sense of fear, she wondered at the power in her anger; the thought that it might be stronger than herself was frightening, and the prospect that it might act of its own accord, terrifying.

Clearly deciding it would be best to pretend nothing had happened, her mother wiped her eyes and stood up. 'I'll go now, darling. You seem a little upset.' She hesitated, then leaned over to kiss her daughter. When Fern did not return her kiss, Grace sighed. 'I do love you - please remember that.'

When Grace had gone, Fern felt sorry, as if she had broken something that couldn't be glued back together again. Grace had been doing her best. Even if she was wrong, she'd tried to be kind. And despite her anger, Fern loved her mother.

Ignoring her crutches, Fern got out of bed and limped barefoot around to Ward C, where Cassie was awake, the colour firmly back in her face.

On seeing Fern, Cassie looked dumbfounded. 'Fern! What are you doing here?'

Fern smiled. 'I was going to ask you the same thing.'

'Oh, me - it happens occasionally. I get a bit carried away and the police bring me in. Hector hates it. Says it's destroying his nerves, never knowing when he'll get a phone call. So tell me, are you a patient or a visitor?'

'A patient, I guess,' said Fern, puzzled. 'But you spoke to me yesterday, you told me not to take the pills.'

'Did I?' said Cassie, surprised. 'Can't remember a thing.' She reached out and took Fern's hand. 'What happened, love?'

Fern paused. She was daunted by the prospect of trying to explain it all again, but here at least was someone who would not think she was mad, and the irony of that almost made her laugh.

'Dear me,' said Cassie when Fern had finished her story. 'Poor thing, you have had a time of it. Exciting though.'

'Exciting! I don't call being locked up in a mental institution exciting.'

'It's not that bad, dear. In fact I think I might stay on for a time, try to help out some of the others. You know, a good number of these wackos are sensitive, poor things are trapped in a dark night of the soul. That's all. If they had someone to lead them through they'd be fine.'

'Like Trevor,' said Fern scornfully. 'With all his talk about aliens.'

'Don't be hard on Trevor. His heart's in the right place, and he's got the gift of knowing, though he hasn't got his head around it all yet. He'll come through though. He just needs a push in the right direction … Oh dear, here come the doctors. You'd better go now.' She winked at Fern, 'I'll see you later.'

Fern couldn't help smiling as she made her way back to her ward. It was good to have Cassie around. She made everything seem possible.

Chapter Eight

Fern was bored, which was probably a good sign. Ignoring her mother's magazines, she half-heartedly picked up Trevor's journal and read some more. *Prospective shamans have described the next stage as a light or a strong force that comes inside their head, enabling them to see differently. They can then see through the dark, accessing the past and the future* ... She paused, amazed, before reading on with new interest. *In shamanic lore there is an underworld, a middle world and an upper world. The shaman moves between these worlds, though not without danger. One of the roles of the shaman is to journey into these worlds and recover fragments of lost or stolen souls.*

Fern read the last line again, remembering Shamesh telling her she needed to recover the lost parts of herself. Then eagerly she continued reading. *As part of their initiation, shamans are symbolically torn apart and put back together again. This represents a complete renewal or rebirth into a new way of being.* Scanning the page, she spotted a single sentence that made her gasp: *When the shaman descends to the underworld he is often accompanied by a bear spirit.*

Fern read on, hungrily devouring the long article. *The patterns are always the same. The symbolism of death and mystical resurrection. Descent to the underworld, followed by magical flight ...*

'Fernanda, dear …' Grace's panic-stricken voice jolted Fern out of her absorption. She looked up and saw her mother approaching, a worried expression on her face. 'Your father's had another heart attack, just a few hours ago. He's in the hospital. I have to book a flight. I'll come back as soon as I can. Or should I speak to one of the doctors - wouldn't it be nice if you could come home for Christmas?'

Fern looked at her mother and felt remorse. Grace was torn between the needs of the people she loved, her face creased with worry lines and panic in her eyes. She took her mother's hand. 'I'll be fine here, Mum. Dad needs you more than I do.'

Her mother's relief was evident as she leaned over to kiss Fern on the cheek. 'You mustn't blame yourself for his heart attack, darling,' said Grace. But they both knew who her father would blame: the aberrant daughter, her bad blood. What else had Fern done wrong? Got low marks in maths; not gone to church; stayed out late; come home smelling of cigarettes; and answered back, just once.

When her mother had gone, Fern tried to sift through the confusion of feelings inside her, worrying that this new anger she felt was turning her into a monster, because while she felt compassion for her mother, she couldn't find a trace of sympathy for her sick father. Seeking distraction she picked up the journal again and immersed herself in its pages. *The shamans often receive their instruction in dreams,* she read. Fern considered this. Her dreams with the bear and the Bear Handler did feel like lessons but the other dreams were different. Their malevolence wasn't teaching her anything; they were just nightmares.

Then she found a section of text that someone - presumably Trevor - had underlined. *Some shamans use magical darts that cause and cure illnesses. Bad shamans send these spirit helpers into victims' bodies to make them ill or kill them, while good shamans use their own helpers to suck out spirits.* She reread this, wondering if Trevor had underlined this section to warn her. But no, this was too far outside the realms of reason. It couldn't be possible. She continued reading: *Most people are reluctant to become shamans. Often their acceptance only comes when they realise they will die if they refuse to follow this path.*

Afraid now, Fern heard Shamesh's words ringing in her ears. 'It's simple. If you refuse this call, then you will die.' Fern threw the journal down, rejecting it and its implications. She would not admit any connection between what she was experiencing and an academic article written by a madman.

'Knock, knock.' Cassie's smiling face appeared around the curtain. 'Are you open for visitors?'

'Sure,' said Fern, but her face was sombre.

Cassie picked up the journal. 'Trevor lent you his article,' she said, raising her eyebrows. 'He must like you.'

Fern scowled. 'None of it has any bearing on my life. I am not a shaman. I don't want to be a shaman. I don't even believe any of this.'

Cassie looked sternly at Fern. 'Are you denying your own experience?'

'Everyone thinks I'm mad. My dad's had another heart attack because of it. My mum's being torn in two. I've lost my friends, my boyfriend, my home, my fashion degree, even my job in the pub. I've lost everything I own. I'm not even Fern anymore - everyone calls me Fernanda. I'm wearing crap clothes that don't even fit. I don't have anywhere to go or anyone to turn to and you ask me to believe in wizards.' She sniffed and wiped her eyes. 'And I'm not crying, okay? My eyes are watering.'

Cassie handed Fern a tissue. 'It's hard losing everything, Fern dear. I know it. But sometimes it's what has to happen. All the doors need to close behind you before you find a way forward.'

'You told me I was going on a journey. But practically the very next day Mum brings me here and they lock me up.'

'This is the journey, or at least part of it,' said Cassie, seating herself on the edge of the bed. 'Sometimes journeys aren't about going somewhere, not in the physical world anyway. You're taking a look inside yourself. Finding your power and building up your strength for the real work. And that will take wit and strength and courage. More than you've got at the moment.'

'I don't want to go anywhere. I don't want to be a shaman.'

Cassie laughed. 'Don't worry, no one's going to make you beat drums or eat toadstools. You're not a shaman but what is happening to you is a shamanic process. You do want to get better, don't you? You want to live your life well?'

Fern nodded cautiously.

'The problem with most people is that they take all this stuff literally. The costumes are always metaphorical. It doesn't matter what path you choose; shamanism is just one of many. And if you don't get lost in all the rigmarole people attach to these things, then ultimately all the paths take you to the same place - back to yourself. To the real you not the one that's been constructed by everyone else. A shaman's just someone who has found that real self and because of this, they can help others.'

'I know who I am,' said Fern dismissively. 'I don't want to "find" myself.'

Cassie sighed. 'Sometimes you don't have a choice'

'What's going on, Cassie?' asked Fern, chewing on the remnants of a fingernail. 'Why are there freaky things in my dreams and bruises on my chest and men following me?'

'Bruises?' asked Cassie, clearly shocked.

Fern lowered her voice. 'There's something in my dreams. It's getting closer and trying to draw me in further. When I was taking those pills I slept a lot and every time I woke it was like someone was sitting on me, squashing my chest. There are bruises around my ankle too. Look … ' She lifted up her foot for Cassie to see. 'They appeared after a hand tried to pull me out of my dream into somewhere else. I'm scared, Cassie, I don't know what's happening.'

Cassie sat quietly for a moment. 'I don't know,' she said eventually. 'Someone wants to harm you. But the messages aren't clear to me. There's a mess of things from this life and from other lives too. Somehow they're woven together, though I can't see the pattern. But I do know you're waking up and that scares them. When you find your power they won't be able to stop you.'

'But who are *they*?' asked Fern, bewildered.

'I don't know. It should be one person, but it looks like there may be more … Oh Fern, I'm sorry. I can't help you with this, but you must resist at all costs.'

'I don't know how,' said Fern, groaning.

'Now listen to me,' said Cassie. 'You've got to stop running and you've got to stop hiding. Follow your intuition and you'll find a way.'

'But how can I? I don't even know what I'm running from! And I don't even *believe* in this stuff.'

'Well, you'd better start believing, girl. Listen carefully. There are two ways of knowing. One's up here in your head. That's useful, but with this sort of thing it isn't enough. The other's in your heart. That's where your knowing needs to come from. You have to open your heart again and see what happens. It's about taking risks, Fern. Start trusting.'

Fern sighed. There was that word again. 'It's not that easy.'

'No, it isn't. And you've got a big journey ahead of you. Have you found the boy yet? The one you're travelling with?'

'Adam?' Fern felt a blush flooding her cheeks. 'I'm not going anywhere with him.'

'Why not?'

'He's a drunk. He's violent. He's … ' Fern stopped, not knowing how to explain her contradictory feelings about Adam.

'He is what he is,' said Cassie. 'In the end it's up to you.' She glanced uneasily at Fern's bruised ankle again. 'Listen, have you still got the stone I gave you? The lapis lazuli?'

Fern nodded; it was the only thing she had left.

'Good. Put it on. It helps to block psychic attacks.'

'What do you mean?' asked Fern, really alarmed now. 'What are psychic attacks?'

'Not every attack is physical,' said Cassie. 'Though as often as not the result is. A psychic attack is an amplified form of wishing someone ill. Sometimes we attack ourselves, sometimes the attack comes from elsewhere.'

Fern remembered reading about the poison darts in Trevor's article but couldn't imagine why anyone would want to hurt her.

'Ooh, heavens,' said Cassie, jumping up. 'I've forgotten the time. Hector will be looking for me.'

When Cassie had gone, Fern retrieved the necklace from the drawer and put it on again, feeling comforted by the weight of the stone against her skin. Then she headed to the dining room for lunch.

Leaving the dining room half an hour later Fern stepped into the corridor and looked up to see a familiar figure talking to a nurse at the reception desk. It was the Bloodhound! Heart thudding, she quickly stepped back into the dining room. Cautiously she peered out again just in time to see the nurse pointing up the corridor towards her ward. Fern waited a moment as the Bloodhound walked away in that direction, then she slipped out of the dining room, camouflaged by a group of patients, and quickly made her way to Ward C where Cassie was sitting up in bed looking radiantly happy and healthy. She had a visitor; a short round man, wearing a cheap suit and an embarrassed expression on his face. It was obvious he wanted to be somewhere else.

'Hello, Fern, this is my brother, Hector. I've told him all about you.'

'Hi,' said Hector, holding out his hand.

'Cassie, he's here,' said Fern, ignoring Hector. 'The Bloodhound.'

'Who?'

'The man who followed me after I left your place. He's here. I saw the nurse direct him to my ward.'

Cassie took a deep breath and waited for a moment, thinking, or maybe reaching out into the realms Fern didn't want to believe in. Then she looked at Fern, her face filled with concern. 'I don't know who he is, but I do know his intentions. I'm sorry, Fern, I know I told you to stop running but now I'm telling you to run. This isn't the time for a showdown. You're not strong enough to face him yet - or at least whatever it is that stands behind him, though honestly I don't know what I mean by that … Oh Fern, you have to get out of here.' Cassie looked at her brother sitting by the bed, a confused expression on his face. 'Hector, I want you to slip out with her.'

Hector looked horrified.

'Don't worry, no one will notice. I'll make a scene and distract them.'

'I can't do this, Cassie. If they catch me …'

'Oh shut up, Hector. Live dangerously for once. You'll love it.'

'But what will I do with her? I can't take her home.'

'Just get her out, she'll know where to go from there.'

'Cassie, this is ridiculous,' said Hector. 'Why don't I call the police? Or at least tell the nurses that the man's dangerous?'

'Don't be a fool, Hector. This is a psychiatric ward. No one believes anything we say. Now take that girl's hand and help her get out of here.'

'Okay, okay, but if I get caught they'll never let me keep my job,' Hector said miserably. 'It's bad enough having a mad sister, but colluding and assisting an inmate's escape, and one I don't even know …'

'Oh, for heaven's sake, Hector! Don't worry about him, Fern, he's got nerves of steel underneath that cowardly exterior.' Cassie got out of bed, took a deep breath and straightened her nightie. 'I'll go out and do my thing in front of the nurses' station. Fern, you get as close to the door as you can and then slip out with Hector just as soon as he asks the nurse to press that buzzer. It's not foolproof but it will have to do. Let's hope that man's already left for the day.'

But he hadn't. As Fern limped along beside Hector she saw the Bloodhound in the television room, his back to the door. Any second now and he would turn around and see her. Hector gave Fern a nudge and she forced herself to keep moving, concentrating on putting one foot in front of the other. She peered through the windows of the television room as they passed. Trevor was in there, and. Fern saw him look up and frown at the Bloodhound, recognising an alien when he saw one.

'Looking for someone, are you, mate?' said Trevor calmly.

'Yeah, a chick called Fernanda, though she goes by the name Fern. Know her?'

Trevor looked past the Bloodhound at Fern, his eyes blank. Please don't give me away, she prayed as Trevor rubbed his chin.

'Fernanda, Fernanda … ah yes, I think I've met her. Pretty young thing. The aliens are after her, though. I had to warn her. You know how it is. Hate to think what'll happen if they get her.'

'Know where she is?'

'Mmm, I think she might be in the exercise room. Here, why don't I take you down there,' said Trevor, leading the Bloodhound along the corridor in the opposite direction.

Thank you, Trevor, thought Fern, thank you. Her knees were trembling as Hector grabbed her hand and half pulled her along. Already she could hear Cassie's voice ringing out.

'I need to go now,' she announced to the nurse on duty. 'I have a message for the people … No, I won't go back to my ward. I want you to listen. Where's the doctor? I need the doctor. I want him to sign the papers. It's vital that I pass on my messages. The time is coming when human history will change more quickly than ever before. It's a time of great beauty, can't you see? The vibrations are getting higher and higher and lifting the people up with them … No, I won't be quiet. This is a message for the people!'

Hector winced. 'God, I hate that voice of hers,' he muttered under his breath. 'The trouble it gets her into. And me too, for that matter.'

Some of the patients were beginning to gather around Cassie who had taken up her position near the nurses' station. While Hector asked the nurse at the desk to let him out, Fern stood among the patients, trying to blend in and desperately afraid the Bloodhound would extricate himself from Trevor and find her. Cassie's ranting grew louder and more desperate by the moment, drawing more patients to her, along with the security guards and a nurse with a syringe.

'No, no,' she was shouting, 'don't touch me.'

Hector grabbed Fern's hand again and pulled her towards the door. 'Stand close,' he said quietly.

Fern was almost blind with fear. In the distance she heard the buzzer. Heard Hector open the door. Heard his whisper. 'Come on, Fern.'

It took all her strength to respond, because the Bloodhound was walking back along the corridor, his eyes mercifully on Cassie and the security men. She couldn't tell if he looked up just as she slipped through the door, or if anyone else had noticed as the door shut behind them.

Chapter Nine

Following the exit signs, Hector and Fern walked as fast as they could without running, down one corridor after the next. Every few steps Fern couldn't resist glancing behind, expecting to see the Bloodhound.

'Stop looking around,' said Hector. 'You've got to pretend to be normal.'

'What?'

'I said, pretend to be normal.'

Normal! There was no way she looked normal, escaping from a psychiatric ward, barefoot and in dreary clothes at least three sizes too big. But suddenly she was excited. Life seemed worth living again. Fern felt the laugh rising all the way from her stomach, through her chest, into her throat and then bursting out her mouth.

'Shut up,' Hector hissed. 'We're not out yet.'

Fern laughed again. She couldn't help it.

Hector rolled his eyes. 'Jesus, you're as bad as Cassie.'

'You know, I think Cassie was right. You're loving this,' said Fern.

'Rubbish,' said Hector, smiling in spite of himself.

Outside, in stark contrast to the chilled air-conditioned ward, the heat was a solid force blocking Fern's way. And it was so busy: traffic and people everywhere. Fern stopped for a moment, trying to orient herself. But Hector was impatient, still looking behind for imagined security guards and nurses, and the Bloodhound.

'Come on,' he said, taking her arm. 'The car's this way.'

The footpath was hot under Fern's feet, burning her soft soles, which were unused to the concrete.

Hector had the messiest car Fern had ever seen. It stank too, of greasy food wrappers and spilled drinks. She screwed up her nose. Horrible.

'Sorry,' he said. 'I don't usually have passengers.'

'Do you ever eat anything other than takeaway?' asked Fern.

'Not really. I can't cook and Cassie's food is too wholesome for me - buckwheat everything, and bloody pulses. It's enough to drive you nuts.'

Fern smiled. She could imagine Cassie might get on your nerves if you had to live with her. 'What do you do?'

Hector looked surprised, as if no one had ever asked that question before. 'Me? I'm a meteorologist. I predict the weather.' He laughed. 'It's ironic really. As Cassie says, we're both prophets, but she and her bloody muse are more accurate than I'll ever be with my computers and data and all the information I feed in about cloud patterns and humidity levels.' Hector started the car and switched on the indicator, waiting for a break in the traffic leaving the car park. 'Thing is,' he said, 'they all believe me and no one believes Cassie. Mine's a respectable science and she gets put in a mental institution.' He glanced at Fern. 'Not fair, hey. Whoever said the world was sane?'

'Yeah, it's nuts … and getting nuttier every day,' said Fern. Yet somehow that knowledge didn't bother her as much as it usually did. She leaned back in the seat and felt herself relax. She was out of that place. Hallelujah!

'So, where am I taking you?'

'Oxford Street, the Surry Hills end if that's okay.'

Hector pulled out and drove towards Oxford Street, but they were soon stopped by an amber light. Hector drummed his fingers on the wheel and checked his watch, muttering about being late back from lunch.

A few moments later, Fern looked straight into the Bloodhound's eyes as he crossed the road in front of them. Frightened, she watched as a flicker of recognition appeared on his face, followed by a thin smile that made her shudder. 'That's him,' she whispered.

'Hell, that's blown it,' said Hector, locking the car doors. 'And I thought you were making it all up.'

The lights turned green but the traffic was bumper to bumper and they had no choice but to inch their way along with everyone else, and head-to-head with the Bloodhound as he walked along the footpath beside them.

This was too much for Hector. 'My God, what if he comes looking for me? He knows the car now: if he gets the rego it'll be a cinch to look me up. Oh dear, I won't be able to sleep at nights.'

Fern looked at Hector. At his neat grey suit, shiny at the elbows, stretched tight around the shoulders and too short at the wrists. Too tight round his beer belly as well. And the trousers, lifting high up his calves as he drove, revealing short brown socks and pudgy white calves dotted with hairs. He wore a neatly pressed shirt with a nondescript tie, and his thinning hair was slicked down across his head in an obvious effort to hide the bald patch. Hector was nothing like Cassie in looks or character. He was evidently a timid man yet he'd been brave, stepping out of his comfort zone and helping her like this. And she was grateful for it.

'Hector, he's not after you. And even if he does look you up, just tell him you dropped me in Oxford Street, which is exactly what you're going to do.'

'This is the last time I do anything for Cassie,' said Hector, not listening. 'I mean it. The very last time.'

Fern sighed. 'I'm sorry, Hector, I'll get out as soon as I can. Okay?'

'No! You can't do that, said Hector, looking horrified. 'You don't know what he'll do to you. I wouldn't be able to sleep with the guilt of it.'

Fern smiled. 'Okay, I'll stay until Oxford Street, but stop worrying. Honestly, there's nothing he can do.'

The car inched along for several minutes that felt like hours. When the traffic finally cleared and Hector put his foot down on the accelerator, Fern had to resist a crazy impulse to blow a raspberry at the Bloodhound as they shot off.

'Thank God for that,' said Hector. 'My nerves are completely shot. Look, my hands are shaking.'

Everything looked different in the daylight, but near the bottom of Oxford Street, Fern thought she recognised the street where the bar was. 'You can drop me here.'

'Here? But where are you going? … No, don't tell me, I don't want to know. If he questions me it's best to know nothing.'

Fern leaned over and gave him a kiss on the cheek. 'Thanks, Hector. I really do appreciate what you've done for me.'

As Hector drove off, Fern was almost overwhelmed by loneliness. The relief she'd felt at getting out of that place was quickly replaced by uncertainty about what to do next. And she couldn't work out how the Bloodhound had found her. Only two people had known where she was - no, three: her mother, Claire and Cassie. Fern couldn't believe any of them would have told him. She headed towards the bar, retracing the steps she'd taken that night. She wasn't sure how long ago that was, only a few days probably, but so much had changed since then.

There it was. A nondescript building, the walls covered in graffiti and a tiny sign saying *The Underworld*, next to a red metal door which was locked. The place existed after all; it wasn't just a figment of her imagination. It was mid-afternoon, so the club wouldn't be open. Still, there might be someone about. She pressed the doorbell and waited.

After a minute the door opened and a guy peered out, wearing a t-shirt that was too small and muscles that were too big. He looked her slowly up and down, then raised an eyebrow. 'Two problems,' he said. 'One, you gotta be over eighteen. And two, there's a dress code. You ever heard of style? Nah, reckon not. Oh, and shoes are an essential item. Hang on, there's a third problem - or is that a fourth? - we're shut.' He closed the door in Fern's face.

'Wait,' she shouted, pressing the doorbell again.

The door opened just briefly. 'Piss off.'

Determined, Fern pressed it again.

'What the fuck?' he said, opening the door.

'I need to see Shamesh. Tell him it's Fern. He'll want to see me.'

'Yeah right,' said the tough guy, emphatically swinging the door emphatically shut.

Fern waited. After a few minutes the door opened yet again. This time it was Shamesh.

'Ah, Fern, you're back. I knew you'd make it.'

'Make it! Do you know where I've been?' said Fern, her anger momentarily outweighing the relief she felt at finding him.

'In a cave, I imagine, learning some lessons and awakening your power, or you would have come back sooner.' He bowed and swept his arm in a gesture of welcome. 'Do come in.'

Fern stepped through the door and carefully followed Shamesh down the steep flight of stairs. Last time she'd tumbled down these stairs and landed in a heap at the bottom. It was a wonder she'd survived.

The empty bar looked sad, with just a drizzle of daylight slipping in through barred windows high up near the ceiling. No music, no people, no soft warm lighting; how bland it seemed in the daytime, its mystery dissolved.

Shamesh turned towards Fern. 'Would you like a drink?'

'I'm not staying. I just came to get my bag.'

'Ah, but first I have something to give you, and before I do that I would like a coffee. Can I make you one too?'

Fern took a deep breath, trying to quell her impatience. 'A coffee would be very nice, thank you.'

She watched Shamesh preparing the coffees, heard the hiss of steam as he warmed the milk. His movements were methodical and self-contained, yet graceful, like a slow dance, no sense of haste or impatience. His chiselled features and lean body were flawless. He was beautiful. For a moment Fern let herself imagine making love to him. Shamesh looked at her quizzically and too late she remembered his skill at mind reading. She felt the blush flooding her cheeks.

He laughed. 'Don't worry, young women are not my area of interest.'

An image of the muscle-bound thug at the door flashed into Fern's mind. 'Are you telling me you're gay?'

He smiled. 'I'm telling you that I'm not interested in young women.' He handed her a latte, a serviette tied carefully around the hot glass, the spiralling pattern on the creamy top formed perfectly.

'Why do you wear dark glasses all the time?' she asked.

'Because some people find my eyes disconcerting.'

'Do they always have that strange light in them?

Shamesh took off his glasses and looked at Fern. No light shone from them this time and nothing pushed down into the crown of her head. They were just blue eyes, though still piercing, and she felt they were looking into places she didn't want anyone to go. Troubled, she turned away.

'See,' said Shamesh, putting the glasses back on. 'I take them off and quickly become a social outcast.' He reached into his pocket and drew out a stone. 'This is for you,' he said, handing it to her. 'The tempest stone. Pietersite is its scientific name, though its nature is the storm. This will help you on your journey, showing you how to break free of the contracts you have made in the past - in all of your pasts. It will reveal the power of the spirit world - and your own power. That's the hardest one for most people, coming to terms with just how powerful they are.'

Fern held the stone in her hand and gazed into the amazing richness it contained, whirlpools of colour, oceans, rivers and land masses snaking through it – a world in itself. She could feel in it a power that was beyond sentiment, beyond good or evil; it just was. As Fern held the stone, two parts of her were battling. The part who felt and knew in a way that was beyond words, was telling her she must break free of the past, within this life and spanning all her lives through many thousands of years. This part saw the vastness of life, how it spiralled in endless cycles like the seasons: birth, death and renewal, on and on. Until when? she asked herself. Was it simply repetition or was life evolving, both drawn and driven towards something. But what? she wondered, staring deep into the stone. And why?

But these questions were impossible and Fern found herself leaning back towards the other part of herself, the rational Fern who would not accept what she couldn't see or measure. For this side of Fern, life began at birth and ended at death, ashes to ashes, dust to dust, the past contained only in the experiences of a single life. It was much more straightforward and certainly more socially acceptable, though she couldn't deny that it was a little disappointing. But either way there was something there in the stone, something that was drawing her in, making her dizzy. Fern quickly put the stone down. It was too much for her, she could feel its energy swirling around inside her head, and there was terror in it too – the same terror that sought her in her dreams.

Shamesh picked up the stone. 'This is a stone of vision,' he said. 'You must be careful how you use it.'

'What does that mean?' asked Fern

'It will show you only what you *need* to see not what you *want* to see.'

Pondering his words, Fern looked cautiously at the stone sitting in Shamesh's hand. It looked just like a stone now. Nothing special. And already the dizziness and the fear seemed far away. But even so, something of its power remained and as she sipped the froth from her latte, swallowing its spiral pattern, she felt as if she was following the spiral inwards on an adventure she hadn't asked for, into her very depths.

'What's happening to me, Shamesh?'

'It's an initiation, if you like. A time when you let go of the past and learn new rules for living. It isn't supposed to be easy, though for some it is easier than others.'

Fern sighed. 'Mine's not one of the easy ones, is it?'

'No, it isn't.' He paused, as if uncertain how to go on. 'You people come to earth heavy with the imprint of your past lives and carrying the genetic inheritance of the family you choose to incarnate with. Then there's the environment you grow up in and the events that impress themselves within you. All in all, there's a lot to clear. Most of you never do it, though that's changing now. Some do it instantaneously, but most are destined to peel it away layer by layer. And you are one of them.'

'Why?' asked Fern.

'Firstly, you're carrying too much grief and fear, and that's left you too weak to withstand a sudden transition. And secondly, for you to become a healer of others you have to understand and experience the processes they are undergoing.'

A healer? Fern took a sip of her coffee. She'd never considered becoming a healer. That was Claire's realm and she'd never been drawn to it or the way it dealt with symptoms not causes.

'What if I don't want to be a healer?'

'Then you won't be. Any more questions?'

Lots, thought Fern, so many she barely knew where to begin. 'You refer to us as *you people*,' she said. 'What does that make you?'

He smiled. 'I am Shamesh,' he said, draining his coffee. 'Now listen carefully. There are things you need to know before you venture out again. Your enemy is an ancient spirit, working against human evolution. You've had your head down, Fern - you were betrayed and you shut yourself off. For three lifetimes you've been closed. It kept you safe but neither could you live well. Now you need to face the thing that shut you down and you need to open up again. You need to remember who you are.'

Shamesh stood up and paced back and forth along the length of the bar. 'This is not without its dangers. You open up and he'll notice you. He'll come for you.' He stopped for a moment and a look of concern passed over his features. 'Though that may have already happened. It seems he is already on your trail.' Shamesh took off his glasses and stared at Fern, reading her around the edges and all the way through until she squirmed.

'Can you stop that? It's making me uncomfortable.'

'You've already opened somewhat. Perhaps he's understood who you really are.'

'Who am I? Everyone else seems to know except me. Couldn't you fill me in,' she asked sarcastically.

Shamesh took her hand. 'You are an ancient soul. Once you were very powerful.'

'What do you mean? How was I powerful?'

'Power lies in the ability to live well, in action, not in reaction to events. And its source is the invisible world, if you like - the one most people dismiss. There is power in reason, and power in intuition. And when the two merge there is great power.' Feeling Fern's attention wander, Shamesh paused. 'This is confusing, I know, but please try to concentrate. It is very important. Intent is the wielder of power. It can be used for good or for ill. Your enemy chose to use his power for ill, but he is not as strong as he might be, for the greatest power of all flows through the heart.' Shamesh leaned forward. 'This was your power, Fern. Your enemy knew that and over lifetimes he worked on you and those closest to you, building grief and pain to such levels that your heart was forced to shut.'

As he spoke, Fern felt the dizziness again, then a stabbing pain in her chest and an ache that was heavy with sadness. With it came a sense of despair so encompassing, she had to fight to stop herself buckling under its weight.

'Yes, you are carrying it still,' said Shamesh. 'You will find your power again but it will not be easy. In the meantime there are things you must learn and they are going to hurt. I can only tell you a portion of them. But in this lifetime your enemy has incarnated as your father.'

'My father?' Fern stared incredulously at Shamesh, trying to read his face, to see that this was all a joke. But he was serious. 'Which one?' she asked.

'Your natural father.'

Fern was confused. She had never met her father. She didn't even know his name, and seldom thought about him. Surely he couldn't hate her; he didn't even know her.

'It is difficult to believe, I know. But for your own safety you must believe me. Before your birth there was a prophecy. Your father is trying to break that prophecy and he believes the only way he can do that is to kill you. Until recently he only knew you as his daughter but he may now have recognised that you are also his ancient enemy. This means he will double his efforts. By running you give him power: now you must turn around and face him.'

Fern could feel the fear creeping in once again and taking her over, only this time it was manifesting as anger. 'How do I do that? I don't even know who he is. He's just a blank space on my birth certificate, a faceless bastard who made me and then left.'

'You will find a way. Tell me, has he entered your dreams?'

'No,' said Fern. 'Well maybe.' She explained what had happened in the hospital but Shamesh didn't dismiss it as she'd hoped he would.

'He's breaking through. This is dangerous … Fern, if you see something in your dreams, something frightening, you must not run away. That will give it power. If it is too much for you, then turn around and calmly reject it. Otherwise you must go towards it and touch it. Have you got a staff yet?'

'Only in a dream. The Bear Handler gave me one.'

'Ah, good. Take it with you wherever you go. You will need it.'

'It was only a dream, Shamesh. I don't have a staff. It's not going to rescue me from anything.'

'Trust me.'

There was that word again. Fern was sick of it. Everyone wanted her to trust them, but they weren't the ones being chased by Bloodhounds and they didn't have ancient spirits attacking them in their sleep. She didn't want to trust anyone and it was beginning to dawn on her that she wasn't safe anywhere.

'No,' she said and drained her glass, her head spinning from the coffee, her third for the day which meant she probably wouldn't be able to sleep. The thought crossed her mind that she didn't have anywhere to sleep anyway, but she pushed it aside. All she needed was her bag. There was money in it and clothes and a pair of shoes. Everything that said: *This is Fern.* She would get changed in the toilets here and then at last she would be herself again.

'I don't have your bag,' said Shamesh, reading her mind.

'You're kidding! What have you done with it?'

'I asked Adam to look after it. Things tend to go astray here.'

Despite herself, Fern felt her heart beating harder. She ignored it, letting her anger rise instead and overwhelm her confusion. 'Adam? That drunken slob you introduced me to?'

Shamesh smiled. 'That's the one.'

'You trusted him with my bag?'

'I did.'

'Oh, that's just great … Where do I find him?' she asked grumpily.

Shamesh pulled out a fountain pen and miniature notebook and wrote down an address in a beautiful flowing cursive. 'There, I imagine he will be at home. He'll be your companion on this journey.'

'No he won't.'

'Your enemies are strong, Fern; you should accept all the help you can get. And it won't be as one-sided as you might expect. Adam is on his own journey - perhaps you can help him.'

'Sure, I can add him to all the other helpers: a madwoman who can't stop prophesying, a weird bartender, an imaginary bear and her handler, and now an alcoholic trying to redeem himself. What do you reckon my chances of succeeding are?'

Shamesh burst out laughing and slapped his thighs. 'I imagine your chances just improved.'

Fern stuffed the piece of paper into her pocket and stood up. Shamesh held out his hand and in spite of her ill temper Fern took it. It was warm and firm and she could feel his strength. If she listened to her heart she would trust this man.

'Good luck, Fern,' he said. 'Here,' he added, holding out the tempest stone. 'Don't forget this. It will provide the visions you need in order to remember.'

'Thanks,' said Fern, not sure whether to be grateful or not.

'Adam will be a good companion. You each have something the other doesn't - and you are both in great need of a friend. But you must avoid slipping into Adam's own nightmares or letting him drag you along with his idealism, something not even Adam knows he has. Not yet, anyway.'

'I told you, I'm not going anywhere with Adam,' said Fern, turning away.

'Have it your way,' said Shamesh smiling to himself. He watched as Fern limped up the stairs, then remembering something, he called out, 'One more thing.'

Fern paused and looked down at Shamesh.

'Remember, your journey is to heal yourself, not the world. The world will follow.'

Fern scowled. Here were more cryptic words for her to untangle. She was tired of being treated like a child. He was just a man who was too old for tight jeans; a manager of a seedy bar; a little man who had no hold over her. She turned away again, not willing to give him anything, not even a smile.

Chapter Ten

When Fern left Shamesh it was late afternoon and the sky was even heavier with smoke than before. Signs of Christmas were everywhere: tinsel in shop windows, tinny carols crackling over the traffic noise, and Christmas trees heavy with decorations, framed in windows. People rushed from one place to another, ticking off mental lists as they went. It was an energy that was hard to resist, a whirlpool that caught you and sucked you in. Stopping outside a newsagent's she checked the date on the paper: Friday, December eighteenth. Only a week until Christmas. The thought sent her into a panic. She had nowhere to go. She couldn't go to Claire's, or home to Adelaide. They'd probably just send her back to the hospital.

Then it struck Fern that people might be looking for her. After all, she was an escapee from the psychiatric ward. Nervously, she scanned the crowds for the Bloodhound or whoever else might be out looking for her. But there was no sign of him and no one else showed any interest. Even barefoot and in these stupid clothes she was just one person among many. Usually people noticed her, especially men, but today, wearing these dreadful stretchy slacks and shirt, she might as well have been invisible.

Adam's address led her to a huge old terrace house divided into three flats: upstairs, ground level and basement. Fern pressed the buzzer to the basement and waited. There was no response. Impatiently she pressed it again. Shamesh had said Adam would be home and Fern hadn't even questioned how he knew this, or what she would do if he were wrong. She pressed the buzzer three more times in rapid succession – long presses that brought no response. She would have to wait.

Fern had been walking on her ankle for the first time without crutches and now it throbbed angrily. She sat down on the steps, caressed by a mottled, shifting pattern of shade from the giant plane trees that lined the street. The stone beneath her was warm from the sun. Leaning against the wall, Fern listened to the hum and roar of the traffic, the wail of sirens, and among all this the shrill calls of the birds in the trees. She had always found it amazing that even right here in the city there existed stubborn pockets of nature. Maybe there were more birds coming in from the desert - refugees, like the rabbits and the country people. Towns shut down one after the other, with no water for years and then massive storms that flooded everything and washed away what crops were left; then the dry again, months or years of it, dust and wind and raging bushfires.

Fern felt like a refugee too, with nowhere to go and nothing to call her own, at least until she retrieved her bag but to do that she had to deal with Adam again. Exhausted, she closed her eyes and let her mind wander, roaming freely until she slipped into a dream, glimpsing a flash of coloured robes, dark skin and fear.

'What you want, girl?'

Fern jumped awake, trembling, confused. A gigantic Maori man was peering down at her. His arms were at least twice as thick as her thighs, the muscles, worked on and taut, could crush her in a second, and yet his face didn't look dangerous. His expression was suspicious but not unkind. He ran his eyes up and down her arms, no doubt looking for marks, something to explain why she was sitting on these stairs.

'You alright?' he said at last. 'You were twitching all over the place.'

Fern nodded. 'I'm waiting for someone. Adam. Do you know him? The guy in the basement flat.'

The man looked puzzled. 'Adam? But he's home. He's always in daytimes.'

'I rang the bell,' said Fern, 'over and over.'

The man smiled. 'He'll be asleep. Here,' he said, putting a key in the lock. 'I'll let you in.'

Fern followed the man through the door into a dim hallway lit by a dusty chandelier, with only one of the bulbs working. It looked out of place surrounded by grimy walls and a torn lino floor.

The man followed her gaze and spat. 'Bastard landlord, never does anything here. Adam's downstairs. Just bang on the door. '

'Thanks.' Fern made her way down the stairs and into the darkness of the basement, running her hands over the walls searching for a light switch but without success. The stairwell stank of garbage and the sweet stuffy smell of mice or rats. She knocked on the door and waited, then knocked again, louder this time. Eventually she heard movement behind the door. Someone fiddled with the lock and the door opened a little. Adam peered into the darkness, puffy-faced and bleary-eyed.

'Hi,' said Fern. 'I think we've already met.'

Adam blinked, confused, and ran his hand through his hair, which was standing up in a riotous mess. 'Yeah, right … So what are you doing here?'

'I came for my bag.'

'Your what?'

Fern felt the panic rising inside her. 'Shamesh said you were looking after my bag.'

The understanding reached Adam's eyes. 'Oh yeah.' He opened the door further, and Fern tried not to notice that he had on nothing but a pair of faded boxer shorts. 'Come in.'

The room was almost as dark as the stairwell, and stank of dirty socks, old alcohol and sweat. Adam pulled up the blind, letting a slither of light through from the footpath above. He pushed open the window, swearing as two crushed beer cans and a syringe rolled in through the bars, landing on the table.

'Bloody arseholes throw their rubbish down here.' He groaned. 'Shit, I've got a killer hangover.'

Fern watched as Adam opened the fridge, pulled out a two-litre bottle of tomato juice, poured it into a dirty glass, added Tabasco, then Worcestershire sauce, and drank it down in one gulp.

'Ahh … Good stuff this, makes your eyeballs sweat.' Then, remembering he had a guest: 'Want one?'

'No, thanks.' Fern hesitated, realising how thirsty she was. 'A glass of water would be good though.'

Adam rinsed a dirty glass, filled it with tap water and handed it over before pouring himself another tomato juice.

'Thanks.' Fern took a sip from the smudgy glass. She could smell the traces of last night's whisky blending with the tepid water.

Suddenly curious, Fern looked around the dingy room, searching for something that would tell her more about Adam. There was a double bed with a quilted cover, the stitching gone in most places; clashing floral curtains in a faded print hung crookedly over the window. The floor was worn lino, lifting up around the cracks. There was a second door, which Fern assumed led into the bathroom. And in one corner was the kitchen: a bar fridge with a television perched on top, a microwave, a kettle, and a small bench cupboard painted lurid orange. The table was pushed up against the window. On it were a bottle, glasses, an empty takeaway container, a mess of papers and a laptop. Beside the table was an overflowing bin.

Adam followed Fern's gaze and shrugged defensively. 'It's a shit hole, but it suits me.'

Fern nodded. It was a nothing room. There was nothing of Adam here, except maybe the guitar propped up in one corner. She felt her curiosity aroused even more. He was young but his eyes were old, like someone who'd seen too much too soon. The whites of his eyes were bloodshot, but the pupils were a deep brown, unlike his hair which was blond. His eyes made her nervous. She couldn't read them.

Adam was curious too. Fern was so tiny he could have crushed her with his hands but instead he felt an irrational urge to protect her. She was pretty, with huge round wary eyes, but she looked so young, like a helpless half-starved child. Close up, though, he could see Fern was older than she first appeared, maybe twenty. And not helpless either. There was a strength about her that made him nervous. She was holding herself upright, her shoulders tense, the muscles in her neck taut, all her fight-or-flight reflexes on red alert.

'So,' he said, realising he'd been staring too long. 'Where have you been?'

'Just around,' said Fern.

'Shamesh said you'd come.' He paused and looked uncertain, before continuing awkwardly. 'He also said I had to stick with you.'

'Well he was wrong,' said Fern crossly.

'That's what I thought,' said Adam quickly. 'But he also said I needed company. That we needed to stick together.' He stopped. He was nervous and saying too much and Fern still looked ferocious, making him want to laugh but he resisted the impulse, knowing that would be a disaster. He needed to placate her but placating wasn't his style. It would be so much easier if she just took her bag and left.

He went on. 'Look, I told him I thought it was bullshit, but there's something about Shamesh, you know. He's a weirdo but he gets things right.' He pulled Fern's pack out from under the table. 'Here's your bag. Take it. Shit, I don't care one way or the other where you go. I don't know why I promised to stick with you.'

Fern picked up her pack and slung it over her shoulder. Adam was blushing and that made him seem safer somehow, softer, less certain. She wanted to trust Shamesh; she wanted to trust them both. But Fern was too tired and frightened to trust her instincts. No one knew she was here. Adam could murder her and chop her up into little pieces and no one would ever know, except maybe Shamesh, and the man who had let her into the building. She knew that whatever choice she made now would shift the scales one way or the other. There would be consequences and not just for her - for Adam too.

Adam watched Fern chewing her nails, clearly undecided. Suddenly he really wanted her to stay. 'You know, when you're on the run from someone …'

'What?' Fern gave Adam a sharp look. How much did he know?

Seeing the suspicion on her face, Adam explained. 'Shamesh filled me in on some of what's been going on, and anyway, it's not so hard to pick someone who's being hunted. There's an air about them. You can smell the fear.' Adam hesitated, afraid he'd said the wrong thing again. 'Anyway, it's good to stop and think things through. Kind of gather up your defences and work out what's going on. Otherwise you make mistakes and eventually you get caught.' He paused, wondering who he was trying to convince. 'What I'm trying to say is you're safe here. Okay?'

Fern tried to smile but it came out like a grimace; she could feel it distorting her face. Adam was trying, harder than he wanted to, and she needed to give him something back. It was getting late and Fern had no idea what she would do when she walked out of here. He was right, too: she needed to think things through, to gather her strength and make plans. And if she took Shamesh's advice, she needed to turn around and hunt the hunter. Not a thought she relished.

She was intrigued by Adam, standing there all vulnerable in just his boxer shorts. He had a great body: a clearly defined six-pack and muscly legs, the calves covered with curly blond hair. He didn't look well though. The alcohol hadn't reached his middle yet, but there was already a softening at the edges. And his skin was pale and sickly looking, as if he hadn't seen the sun for a long time.

'Okay,' said Fern, putting her bag down again. 'I'll stay for a bit.'

Adam nodded, both relieved and irritated. 'Suppose I'd better get some clothes on,' he said, suddenly embarrassed. 'Make yourself a coffee while I have a shower.'

Fern didn't want another coffee but she was impatient to get changed back into her own things. She dug about in her pack and found fresh clothes: undies, a bra that fitted, a t-shirt, and her favourite skirt, the one with the dragonfly embroidered across the front. When she'd changed, Fern rolled the dowdy clothes her mother had bought into a ball and crammed them into the bin.

Adam emerged from the bathroom and stopped in his tracks, amazed at how different Fern looked. Hers was a kind of fragile beauty that made Adam want to tiptoe around it. So fine. Realising he was staring, Adam blushed again and then felt a surge of anger at how quickly Fern had got through his defences. 'You hungry?' he asked, tersely.

Fern nodded, unsure what to do next; she sensed Adam was angry, but didn't know what she'd done wrong.

'I'll get some supplies,' said Adam, grabbing his keys and wallet.

'I'll come,' said Fern.

'No, you stay here. It's best not to show your face for a bit.'

Fern nodded again, relieved. When Adam had gone, she looked through her bag more carefully. Everything was exactly where she'd left it. She pulled out the supplies Cassie had given her and took a drop of Rescue Remedy. Almost immediately the tension left her neck and shoulders, a release that made her feel at once more lucid and sleepy. The feather was still there, so she hadn't imagined that great bird after all. Even now if she concentrated, Fern could feel the places on her upper body where the wings had moved. How strange the world had become. Almost overnight it had transformed from a black and white place of logic and reason into a magical place filled with possibilities and a different way of knowing. Despite everything she felt more alive than she had for many years.

Suddenly remembering the tempest stone, Fern pulled the trousers from Adam's bin and retrieved it from the pocket. She looked at it warily, aware that it was dazzling her somehow, drawing her into its rich veins of colour, rivers and islands, swirling strands of gold and red. It was like the earth, yet it didn't look solid, at least not on the inside.

As Fern was about to put the stone in her bag, something happened that stopped her in her tracks. The dizziness descended again, and then her vision filled with soldiers in a uniform she didn't recognise, knowing only that it belonged in the distant past. Their helmets where white with a blue pattern, a nose plate reaching down the middle, their tunics blue and white. She felt the soldiers holding her arms while she struggled, and the tight painful grip of their fingers. But there was something else there, far more frightening yet blocked from her view. She needed to see it but couldn't at first. Then, as she lifted her head, she caught a glimpse of a man, and the intent in his eyes filled her with terror. Fern dropped the stone as if it were on fire, feeling its heat burning through her palm.

It was hot in Adam's bedsit, but Fern was shaking, her heart racing. She couldn't explain what had just happened or comprehend the power that had drawn her into the stone and opened up pictures in her head that seemed as real as this room.

Fern had always used music to calm herself. Now she pulled out her pipe and for the first time in months held it to her mouth and played; quietly at first, afraid of the notes that broke the silence around her, then louder, more firmly as her fingers loosened. She played and played, weaving the notes together, slipping in and out of the music, the haunting tunes settling her until she lost herself in the playing and forgot to be afraid.

Something, a noise or a movement, made Fern look up. Adam was standing in the doorway, staring hard at her again. Confused, she stopped mid-tune with a jolting off-key note that broke the spell the music had woven. Feeling her face redden under his gaze, she looked away.

'What instrument is that?'

'A pipe … well, actually it's called a tin whistle. It's a Celtic instrument. I heard a woman playing it when I was a kid and loved the way it sounded, so I bought one with my pocket money and taught myself.'

Adam had never heard of this instrument that made notes so fragile they rose up and hovered gently in the air, before being dispersed by the tiniest breeze. 'You play well,' he told her, because something needed to be said, and she did. But the music destroyed him. Those notes played havoc with his heart, tugging at the armour he'd surrounded it with.

'Thanks,' said Fern, embarrassed again.

Adam carried the shopping bags in and began unpacking them; a six-pack of beer, a bottle of wine, milk, ice-cream, a tin of peaches and a family-size pizza.

'Here,' he said dumping the pizza on the table. 'Dinner. Get started, it's probably cold by now.'

'How much do I owe you?' asked Fern.

'This one's on me,' said Adam, trying to stuff the ice-cream into the tiny freezer in the bar fridge.

'I'd rather pay my share.'

'Look, I'll pay for this meal, you do the next. It's easier this way. Okay?'

Fern hesitated, before putting the money back in her wallet. She didn't know how she felt about Adam's assumption that there would be a next time. 'Okay… Thanks,' she added, hoping she didn't sound surly.

Adam opened a beer with his teeth and drank it straight out of the bottle. 'Ah, that's good. You want one?'

'Yes please.'

They sat at the table eating soggy ham and pineapple pizza, Fern matching Adam for every slice. She loved the sensation of filling her belly, loved washing it down with cold beer. Perhaps it was hope that was giving her an appetite again, or simply the need to replace the weight she had lost.

'Shit, you can eat,' said Adam after a while. 'I'd better go out and get another one.'

'No, no, I've had enough,' said Fern, restraining herself from reaching out for the last slice. 'You have that.'

'You sure?'

'Yeah.'

'Here, have another beer.'

Fern sipped on her second beer, already feeling the effects working their way up her legs, turning her feet, her calves, her thighs into a weary weak jelly. But she felt better, stronger; it was wonderful to be out of that madhouse, with real food in her stomach and no one chasing her – for now at least. Even if she was sitting in a basement flat with a stranger, even if no one in the world knew where she was, just for the moment life seemed almost normal.

'You want to talk about this bloke who's chasing you?' asked Adam.

At the mention of the Bloodhound, Fern instantly felt the tension return to her shoulders. She took a swig of beer and pondered what she should tell Adam. He'd taken her in and the laws of hospitality meant he deserved some sort of explanation. 'Okay, I'll tell you some of it. But I'm warning you, it doesn't make sense.'

Adam opened his fourth beer and poured Fern a glass of lukewarm Riesling. Choosing her words carefully, she told him about getting stuck in her attic for months on end. 'I don't know why,' she said, her eyes filling with tears. 'Something happened inside me and I couldn't manage anything anymore. I don't know … Maybe it was depression or a breakdown.'

'Yeah,' said Adam, 'it happens.'

Fern paused, cautious about opening herself up to this stranger but his casual acceptance of her story and the alcohol, were loosening her tongue. She took another sip of wine and then told him about the landlord breaking down the door, her encounter with Cassie, the Bloodhound chasing her and how she met Shamesh, although she left out most of what happened at The Underworld – she wasn't sure what Adam would think of power animals and bear handlers. Fern gulped down the rest of her wine, her mouth dry with the effort of talking.

Then she told Adam about her time in the psychiatric ward - only a few days but it had felt like an eternity. Fern shuddered at the memory of that dead space she'd inhabited and the nightmares that had forced their way into it. She avoided mentioning the dreams, instead telling him about the Bloodhound finding her this afternoon, and how Cassie and Hector had helped her escape.

As she talked, Adam kept his eyes fixed on her. Not questioning, not judging. She was grateful for that.

'And here I am,' she said, flashing Adam an uncertain smile. 'Picking up my bag.'

So far Adam had followed the gist of it. As far as he was concerned, it was straightforward: Fern was being stalked by a pervert. However, it was pretty obvious that she wasn't telling him everything, and neither had Shamesh. He would find out the rest eventually, but for now he'd work with what he knew.

'You think you've shaken this bloodhound guy?'

'There's no way he can know where I am.'

Adam nodded and leaned back in his chair. 'So what next?'

'I have to visit my mother.'

Adam raised his eyebrows questioningly and Fern realised there was another whole story there. She felt weighed down by back stories and wished for a moment she could take a sharp knife and slice through all her ties and connections: to people and places; to memories, hidden and conscious; to fears, guilt and duty. Just sever the lot, and then she would fly, weightless as a balloon, letting the wind take her where it would.

Fern sighed. 'Not the one who committed me to hospital. I'm adopted. This one's my birth mother. She'll know things about my father that I need to find out.'

'Such as?'

'His name. And where he is - I have to find him,' she added, though she couldn't think of anything she'd less like to do.

'But what's your father got to do with this?' asked Adam, confused.

This was another story, one Fern didn't know yet. 'According to Shamesh, he wants me dead.'

Adam's beer stopped midway to his mouth. 'Shit … Why?'

'I don't know, something about a prophecy. Shamesh wasn't clear about that.'

Adam let that pass; prophecies belonged to a realm he didn't want to consider. There was nothing practical you could do about a prophecy. 'So what's the connection between your father and the Bloodhound?'

'I don't know.'

'This is crazy stuff, you know that?'

Fern shrugged and looked away, wondering why she felt so disappointed at his reaction. After all, it wasn't surprising. She'd known he wouldn't believe her. Now she was relieved that she hadn't told him the rest of it.

'Sorry,' said Adam, seeing Fern retreat and realising he'd said the wrong thing. 'I didn't mean you're crazy or anything. I believe you, really I do.'

Fern poured herself another wine.

'Look, there's one thing I don't understand,' said Adam. 'Why are you looking for your dad? If he wants you dead, wouldn't you be better off going into hiding or something?'

'Yeah, you'd think so, but Shamesh told me to turn around. He said that running makes you lose your power.'

Adam nodded; Shamesh was right, though sometimes there wasn't any choice, sometimes you had to run. 'Where does your mum live?'

'Katoomba.'

'Okay, not so far then. Katoomba it is. We'll head there to-morrow, and after that we'll go hunt down your father.'

'We?'

'Shit yeah, you need a bodyguard … Hey, how about some ice-cream?'

Fern was touched that Adam had offered to come. He didn't owe her anything – if anything, she owed him. She watched him hunting around for a tin opener, swearing when he couldn't find one and picking up what looked like a hunting knife instead. He jabbed it into the top of the peaches, then cut around the lid in jagged cuts.

'So how about you?' she said.

Adam stopped spooning out the peaches and looked at her quizzically. 'Me?'

'Yeah. What's your story?' asked Fern, watching him shut down as the question sank in.

'Me? I'm nothing. A nobody. You don't want to know about me.'

Fern smiled. 'Okay then, mystery man,' she said, draining her glass. 'Can I have three scoops?'

Chapter Eleven

Early the next morning, Fern paused at the door and looked back at Adam as he lay snoring on the floor. She felt bad running away like this when Adam had been so kind, feeding her and letting her sleep in his bed while he slept on the floor. It wasn't as if she wanted to go back out there alone and risk being spotted by the Bloodhound or murdered by her father. And she was afraid of meeting her mother. Terrified of what she might find if her mother opened the door, and just as terrified of having the same door slammed in her face. Still, Fern needed to do this alone. It wasn't the sort of thing you shared with a stranger. And anyway, it wasn't fair to involve Adam in her story when he obviously had some serious issues of his own to deal with.

As she opened the door, Adam rolled over and started muttering, his arms waving around as if warding something off. 'No, no, no, get away,' he shouted as Fern quickly shut the door behind her and ran up to the ground floor.

Outside, the air was cool and relatively fresh, though smoke was already building in the sky, taking the glare from the sun but not its heat. By midday she would be choking on the smoke and the sun would be a gentle orange orb, like a fading torch. The morning was quiet, apart from the dawn chorus of birds ringing out invisibly from the trees that lined the street and the occasional sound of a siren. Everywhere there was evidence of the night before: empty cans rolling down the pavement; greasy pizza boxes; kebab wrappings blowing this way and that; puddles of vomit in splattery circles; and pigeons picking at crumbs, pizza crusts, bits of plastic, anything.

As she approached Taylor Square, Fern could see a group of party goers still chatting and laughing in the early morning sun while the city slowly came to life. There were police too, at least ten of them, watching as glazed-eyed clubbers tottered out of nightclubs and onto the streets, shielding their eyes from the sun. For a moment Fern imagined they were pale-skinned vampires that the light of day would reduce to dust, but they stayed intact as they staggered down pavements and reached out hopefully for taxis. Some called out to her. A lurching man wearing a Santa hat smiled a wide insincere smile, flashing white teeth and hungry eyes.

Fern had intended to get some breakfast on Oxford Street but in an effort to get away from last night's revellers she turned down a side street instead, deciding to take a short cut to the station and avoid Taylor Square. But even here there were people. A man walked past, his clothes thick and blackened with age and wear, his bones sticking out through skin which had become too tight for his body. Two men in business suits, collars open, ties askew, studied the morning with bleary eyes, talking uncertainly on mobile phones.

It felt safer in Belmore Park, where a group were doing tai chi, their movements synchronised in a graceful dance, a contrast to the rigid shapes of high-rise buildings looming behind them. An old woman was feeding the pigeons, hundreds of them cluttering the path and hardly bothering to get out of Fern's way as she walked. On the grass a man was asleep, surrounded by his belongings, curled into himself, oblivious to Fern and the other passers-by, who all seemed to be going somewhere, who all had some purpose, no matter how futile.

On Eddy Avenue, a Chinese man sat on a milk crate, plucking haunted notes from an instrument she didn't recognise. Behind him was a sunlit wall, covered in graffiti and blackened by the grime of bus exhausts; at his feet the pavement was almost white with pigeon shit. But the notes he played made everything exquisitely beautiful. Fern found a coin in her pocket and put it in the plastic container that sat near his feet. He looked up at her briefly, stared solemnly into her eyes and then smiled, his face crinkling into a thousand wrinkles. Fern smiled back, then as he became immersed again in his instrument, she turned, the notes following her into the station.

The cafes were open, luring Fern in with the smell of coffee and bacon, fried eggs and toasted fruit bread. She bought coffee and a bacon and egg sandwich, hoping the grease would help with her hangover. Instead, the white bread turned into doughy balls that seemed to get stuck in her throat. In the end she gave up, leaving half the sandwich uneaten. She bought a bottle of water and drank most of it down in one go, then bought a return ticket to Katoomba and sat on the dreary platform to wait, already regretting that she'd left Adam asleep on the floor.

The previous evening kept slipping back into her mind. When the beer and the wine had run out, Adam had poured himself a whisky, then picked up his guitar and started strumming. He'd held it tenderly, with reverence, and watching him Fern had realised that no one had ever held her like that. For the briefest of moments she'd envied that guitar. Then Adam had started playing 'Scarborough Fair' and unable to resist the call of the music she'd picked up her tin whistle and joined in, sending the notes out and across to the guitar, communicating with Adam in a way she hadn't been able to do with words. In the space of that music she'd felt completely at ease with him.

'G'day. Mind if I sit here?'

Fern's heart lurched at the sound of Adam's voice. She looked up at him standing there in front of her. Despite his smile, he looked pretty rough, with dark circles under his eyes, and hair sticking up, wearing a grubby t-shirt, baggy shorts and runners without any socks. He was holding two coffees in a cardboard tray.

'Well, do I have your permission?'

'Sure.' Fern smothered her own smile. She couldn't decide how she felt about this, whether she was pleased he was here or irritated that he'd found her.

'You left a couple of things behind,' said Adam. 'This.' He held up the pipe. 'And this,' he added, pointing at himself.

Fern bit back a laugh and reached for her pipe, but Adam dangled it just out of her reach.

'Uh-uh,' he said, shaking his head. 'Not until you admit you did it on purpose. You couldn't bear the prospect of never seeing me again, so you left it there, knowing I'd be forced to chase you through the streets at some God-forsaken hour on a Saturday morning.'

Now she was really laughing. 'Never,' she said, jumping up and grabbing one end of the pipe. But she couldn't wrest it from Adam, he was too strong.

'Come on, admit it.'

'Okay, okay, I confess … Happy now?'

'Repeat after me: I couldn't bear the prospect of never seeing you again.'

'Icouldn'tbeartheprospectofneverseeingyouagain,' said Fern screwing up her face and speaking quickly, so that the words ran together.

Adam grinned and handed over the pipe. 'I guess that will have to do … Here, I got you a coffee.'

Fern sipped her second coffee for the day and wondered again about Adam. This was a different person from the withdrawn angry drunk she'd first met or even the gentle musician of last night. Perhaps they'd slipped past each other's defences. The thought of that made her afraid all over again. She felt too fragile to risk letting Adam in.

'Are you sure you want to come with me?'

'Yep.'

'But you don't know what you're getting yourself into. I'm depressed, I'm probably mad, I've got the Bloodhound chasing me and a father who wants to kill me.'

'Yeah, yeah, it's not a problem,' he said, then paused. 'Though when you put it like that … I'm joking,' he added quickly when Fern looked at him. 'You know, my dad told me once that everyone's wacky. They seem normal at first and then as you get to know them they get weirder and weirder. The only difference with you is that you started off weird … Only kidding.'

As soon as the train pulled out of the station Adam leaned back in the seat. 'If I have a little doze will you promise not to do another runner?'

Fern smiled. 'I promise.'

'Okay, night.'

While Adam slept, Fern stared out the window as the train streaked past the backs of houses and offices, showing the dreary scribbled-on face of Sydney. The suburbs went on and on, kilometre after kilometre, until Fern thought the city would never end. Eventually, though, they reached Penrith and the train began its slow climb into the mountains, passing thickets of burnt-out trees, with houses perched precariously nearby and plumes of smoke dispersing into the sky. It didn't look anything like the last time she'd come up, a year and a half ago. A dirty weekend with Jeff, as he'd described it, though it hadn't felt dirty. If anything it was clean and bright, a memory that shone. It had been winter and they'd walked in the mist and rain, then dried out in front of an open fire in the hotel. Back in their room they'd made love, before going to a restaurant where they'd ordered too much and eaten it all. Then they'd gone back to their hotel and made love, and in the morning they'd made love all over again. The memory made Fern wince. It wasn't an unhappy memory but that weekend was the closest they'd been as a couple, and things had gone downhill after that. Fern wasn't sure why, but she suspected that the door she'd opened inside herself that weekend had simply clanged shut in panic. Perhaps this was her only response to intimacy.

Adam was snoring gently next to her. Occasionally the snores would rise into a crescendo and Fern would dig him in the ribs, making him splutter and the snores recede. Fern shut her eyes too but she couldn't quieten her mind. Her thoughts kept racing along with her heart at the prospect of confronting her mother. She wasn't sure if she could go through with it.

At Katoomba station, she woke Adam and they stepped out of the train into an atmosphere so dense with smoke it was hard to breathe. And it was hot, hotter than Sydney had been. Fern had always thought of the mountains as cold, but then she had only visited in winter, feeling the chill grow as the train ascended and then stepping out into the fresh icy mountain air. This was completely different, a dry heat, less oppressive than Sydney's polluted humidity, but harsh with smoke.

'Shit, it's bad,' said Adam, between coughs. 'They say the fires never go out these days, only die down when it rains and spark up again at the first sign of a dry spell.'

Fern tried to imagine the flames roaring through valleys, leaping from one cliff to another, crossing roads, burning houses. In such a short time the area had turned into a nightmarish place to live, the air heavy with smoke, ash settling on gardens and washing lines, everyone on alert, ready to evacuate.

'It reminds me of Tassie,' said Adam.

'Tassie?'

'Yeah, where I grew up. In a hot northerly the bushfires are killers, sweeping through everything. Then in the autumn, Forestry light the fires. Burn-offs, they call them but really they're bloody infernos that kill everything …' Adam stopped, surprised by his bitterness. He hadn't even noticed a tree for the past two years. Still, he used to love the bush. A few years back when he was still in Tasmania, he practically lived out there, spending weeks at a time down the south coast, surfing and living off abalone and oysters. His mum used to say the forest fed his soul.

They walked down the main street, passing cafe after cafe, the chairs outside empty, the people crowding inside, away from the smoke. With each step they took, Fern felt her feet dragging as she grew more and more reluctant to go through with it.

'Are you right from here?' asked Adam, stopping at an intersection. 'You know the way?'

Fern nodded.

'Okay then, I'm off for a walk. See you in a couple of hours.' He glanced at his watch. 'Say twelve thirty in that first cafe near the station.'

'Okay.' Fern took a deep breath and turned away. Well, she thought, Cassie said I needed to find out who I am. Here we go.

Her birth mother's house was in a deep valley. As Fern descended the hill she felt the heat go out of the air. There was no wind, and the atmosphere felt unnaturally still. The sun hadn't reached into the valley yet and when it did it wouldn't stay for long. The sudden chill shuddered its way through Fern's spine. If there were good places and bad places on earth, this was a bad place. There was something toxic about this valley, as if the very earth oozed poison. Or perhaps it was a human legacy, the site of a murder or massacre, a place haunted by violence.

This was the down side of the changes Fern felt were happening within her. She didn't know what had sparked these changes but the results were evident as she began to sense atmospheres and read people's moods as well as their intentions. The world was becoming more vivid, its colours richer. Even sounds were affecting her physically, her body responding dramatically to both discord and harmony. Now here, so close to her birth mother's home she felt poisoned by the atmosphere.

The houses on her birth mother's street were all fake brick or weatherboard, and small, definitely not the homes of the rich or even the comfortably well-off. But they were respectable: neat front gardens, a rope swing hanging from a tree, and Christmas lights strung across front porches. All of the houses had For Sale signs out the front. She assumed they weren't foreclosures, simply people trying to get away from the fires. Number seventeen, her mother's house, had a lattice framed front porch and a garish garden gnome on the step.

Before she could change her mind, Fern pressed the doorbell, hearing it echoing down the hallway inside. A dog barked, just once, then fell silent. Fern waited, her heart thudding in her throat, her palms wet; she wanted to run but forced herself to stay and face whatever was behind that door. She heard footsteps approach and then silence. The door had a spy hole in it and Fern sensed an eye behind it peering out. Then a key turned in the lock and slowly the door opened.

A woman stared at her, curiously, but with no recognition in her eyes. For a moment Fern thought she must have the wrong address. This woman seemed too young. She was short, like Fern, and wearing a faded blue dressing-gown, toast crumbs clinging to the front. Her features were fine, but her face was puffy. Her hair was short, cut into a bob that was longer at the front than the back. A stylish cut, but slept on and scruffy.

'Hi,' said Fern. 'I'm looking for Joan Childe.'

'Yes, that's me. Or it was, I'm McFarlane now,' the woman said guardedly.

Fern felt her heart lurch and her knees threaten to buckle. Of course, she reminded herself, her mother was only thirty-eight. She had known this, had done the arithmetic over and over, wondering what it would have been like to have a young mother. Her adopted mother was sixty-one, old enough to be this woman's mother. But then Grace and Richard had always seemed old, the way some people do, as if they'd skipped their youth and moved straight into comb overs and grey hair, creaky joints and wrinkles.

'My name's Fern,' she said, forcing the words out. 'Fernanda Parsons.' She paused, finding it hard to shape her mouth around the next words. 'I'm your daughter.'

Joan recoiled, stepping back into the hallway, the look of terror on her face sending a knife plunging into Fern. 'No,' she gasped. 'You must have the wrong person.'

Fern shook her head, determined to finish what she'd started. 'I don't think so. I was born in Adelaide on the second of January 1989.'

'No, it can't be.' Joan breathed in raggedly and covered her mouth with one hand, the other blindly reaching out and grabbing the door frame.

'Your name is on my birth certificate, Joan Childe. You called me Erica.'

'Erica! I can't believe it.' Joan looked around nervously. 'Come in, the kids are with their dad until lunchtime, so we're safe for a while.'

Fern stepped inside, wondering what the woman meant by safe. Then it struck her that Joan's husband and children probably didn't know about her. Until now she'd been nothing but an ugly secret fermenting inside her mother. Now Joan's secret had manifested in the outside world, threatening to throw her life into disarray.

As she made her way down a dark hallway, Fern felt a chill enter her, penetrating so deeply that her bones trembled. The back of the house opened into a kitchen-cum-dining room. It was lighter here, but that only highlighted its drabness. The odour of dog's piss was almost masked by the sharp smell of burnt toast. Toys were scattered here and there, the carpet was stained, and dirty dishes were piled up on the kitchen sink. It was so unlike the ordered house in which Fern had spent her childhood; Grace fiercely conscious of the need to keep up appearances was always cleaning, ensuring that everything was in its proper place.

'Excuse the mess,' Joan said. 'My husband left twelve months ago. Just before last Christmas it was. The bastard, doing that to the kids.' She looked at Fern and sighed. 'Your dad was no better. I've never had any luck with men.'

In one corner of the room was a Christmas tree, a cut pine, decorated roughly with swathes of tired tinsel and an odd assortment of decorations. So unlike Grace's tree, the plastic one she folded open each year, with its tinsel and matching baubles hung so neatly.

In the opposite corner was a cane dog basket. A large old Labrador lifted its head briefly and wagged its tail before falling back into a comfortable slumber. Fern had never had a dog, although she'd always wanted one. Grace and Richard had once given her a bird in a cage - a budgie that didn't sing - but it wasn't the same as a dog.

'Benji's old now,' said Joan, reaching down to give him a pat. 'He doesn't do much these days. He's over fifteen, you know, and incontinent, but I couldn't bear to have him put down.'

Fern looked out into the back garden, a wasteland of junk and long grass, so different from the clipped lawns and pruned rose bushes in Grace and Richard's garden.

Joan followed Fern's gaze and sighed again. 'I ought to clear it out, it's a fire hazard, but it's gotten out of control. I can't even let the kids out there now, there are too many snakes. They come looking for water.' She filled up the kettle. 'Would you like a cup of tea?'

'Yes, please.'

While Joan put on the kettle and gathered cups and sugar and milk, Fern studied the photographs on the wall, a montage of smiling faces, bright colours, sandy beach shots, wet dog shots … the stuff of families. Fern's family. On the large old-fashioned television sat a couple of school photos: a pretty young girl with fine features like Joan's, and a boy, neat in his uniform but with eyes that were too responsible. Those are my brother and sister, thought Fern; the knowledge settled inside her, making her feel lighter and heavier at once. She had a family, actual blood ties. It made her feel a connection to life that had been missing yet looking at Joan and the heavy melancholy she carried, Fern realised that growing up with her as a mother would not have been ideal either.

'My children,' said Joan. 'Jack's eight now and Fi's just gone six. Aren't they beautiful?' She talked on, her mood lightening momentarily. 'Fi's doing dance, she's like a little angel, and Jack plays soccer. He's so good at it, a real sportsman. And so bright. He's reading way beyond his age …'

As Joan spoke, the pride in her voice was unmistakeable and Fern felt the knife again, plunging deeper into her. Her mother hadn't connected with the fact that Fern was her daughter too; she didn't seem remotely curious about her life.

Was it blood or environment that made a mother? If it was a combination of both, then what were the proportions? Fern had asked herself these questions many times. As a child she'd been cast aside from blood ties yet accused of having tainted blood and held responsible for her birth parents' failings. It had left her confused and lonely. But in a way this isolation had also been a blessing, giving her a potential freedom to construct herself in the way she chose, not in the mould of her family. A freedom she hadn't yet used well. If at all.

'Here, sit down,' said Joan, pushing a pile of papers to one end of the table and making a space for the cups. 'Milk?'

'Yes please.'

Fern watched Joan's hands shaking as she poured in the milk. They were slender, the nails chewed right down just like her own. She scrutinised her mother, searching for likenesses. The eyes perhaps? The hair too, thin and mousy like hers. But not much else she could pick. Joan must once have been petite like Fern. Now she was all bosom and belly, with an extra chin.

'Sugar? … No, I didn't think so. That's how I have it, you know. Milk and not too strong.'

They sat opposite each other, their mugs between them, while Joan talked and talked, filling in all the spaces. Telling Fern about her life: how much work the kids were; her job in telesales down in Penrith, only part-time but the hours were awful so she had to juggle the children; the dreadful house she lived in because no one would buy it and why would they when there was so much else on the market and these bloody fires were draining the life out of the mountains. Where would she go anyway? They couldn't afford to move to Sydney, with only one income now her husband had left her, just like that, for another woman. How dare he!

While Joan talked, Fern sat and sipped her insipid tea with its skinny milk that was *not* how she liked it. She was only half listening, knowing that this was just a prelude, an intricate dance as they circled each other, knowing there were more important things to discuss. But by the time her tea was finished, Fern had begun to wonder if they would ever move on from the mundane. Perhaps Joan was so caught up in being a victim that she had no room to consider Fern's needs. Perhaps it was her way of explaining, of evading her guilt. Perhaps she was saying: look, my life's been crap; it's not my fault; you were lucky to grow up somewhere else. Fern was torn. She felt for Joan, sensing how afraid she was. But Joan's lack of interest in Fern, her gabbling monologue and every question she didn't ask, twisted the knife that was already embedded in Fern's chest. Fern had a question on her own lips, but Joan wouldn't stop talking. On and on she went, throwing words out as if she was under attack, leaving no spaces for Fern to step through.

In the end Fern just said it, tossing the word into the air right in the midst of Joan's words. 'Why?'

Joan stopped in mid-sentence and looked at her, blinking, as if she'd only just realised Fern was there. 'Pardon?'

'Why? What happened? Why didn't you keep me?'

Joan took a deep breath. 'I wanted you. I always did. Can you believe that?' She paused and stared at Fern with tears in her eyes, as if that was enough to make it true. Embarrassed, Fern shifted uneasily under her gaze. There was something inauthentic here. Something hidden. Her mother was not speaking the complete truth. 'Not a day passes when I don't think about you. When I don't wonder what happened.'

As Fern tried to untangle the double negatives, Joan started to sob.

'I took so long to get over it. You haunted me. I saw you everywhere, in every baby, every child. Even now … Oh God, you don't know what it was like.'

Fern wasn't a mother. She didn't know what it would be like to abandon a baby. She didn't know how heavy the guilt of that would be, though she had her own guilt to carry. But she knew what it was like to be abandoned. She knew what it was like to live a life where you don't belong, not to family or place or even to history. She had an intimate and uncomfortable relationship with the word illegitimate. She understood the not knowing, the wondering, the waiting. And she also knew that Joan had never searched for her. But she couldn't say any of this, because if she started it would come out in such a rush that Joan would be struck dumb with it. Fern knew the power of words; she feared the consequences of speech. She would stay silent.

Joan's expression changed. 'It was him … ' she hissed angrily. 'I did it to keep you safe.'

The words echoed in Fern's ears. *To keep me safe*. She felt a strange satisfaction, as if a missing piece of a puzzle had found its place. But along with that she felt a familiar fear rising. 'From what?' she asked, needing to be sure.

'Your father.'

'Why?'

'There was a prophecy; I can't remember the exact words. It happened just before you were born. A load of rubbish, I know, but your father took it seriously. I never could understand him, the way he dismissed important things and made mountains out of other things.'

Fern felt a chill down her spine. Shamesh had been right. 'What was the prophecy?'

Joan frowned, trying to remember. 'How did it go? That you would be the death of your father, something like that. Simple Simon said it. He was an old gardener at the Botanic Gardens, blind in one eye.'

'What did it mean?'

'It didn't mean anything. It was a stupid thing to say. But it caused a lot of harm because your father thought differently. He was furious. He… ' She stopped and looked at Fern, with haunted, fearful eyes.

'Yes?' said Fern, sensing Joan was shutting down again. 'He what?'

'Then you were born,' Joan said quickly. 'That very day. A few weeks early, it was. I didn't even make it to hospital. You were born on the footpath while I waited for the lights to change.' She smiled nervously, a smile that didn't reach her eyes. 'How's that? Not many people can say they were born on the footpath.'

Fern was certain her mother was holding something back. She could almost see it, almost reach back to the memory … There it was, a fist and a pregnant belly, stretched tight. It was too much and Fern tried to look away but felt hands on her face, holding her head still. *You must see*. The words came as the fist hit the pregnant belly. Fern shuddered, tears forming in her eyes. My father, she thought. He tried to kill me. Even then he had wanted her dead.

With an effort Fern pulled herself together and addressed Joan once again. 'What's my father's name?'

Joan looked startled for a moment. 'Of course, you wouldn't know. I didn't tell them.' She paused. 'Eric Hannson was his name, Hannson with two n's. I never saw him again after I signed the papers,' she added, a bitterness creeping into her voice. 'He only stayed around long enough to make sure I wouldn't change my mind.'

Eric Hannson. Fern tossed the name around in her mind, testing it out. 'So that's why you called me Erica.'

'Yes. It was stupid really. I wanted to give you something of him, some link or clue to who he was.' Her eyes filled with tears. 'I did love him you know, despite everything.'

Fern didn't know how to respond, so she waited, watching Joan chew her nails and glance around as if she was afraid of being overheard.

'Strangely enough, he rang just over a year ago. Just like that, after twenty years of nothing.'

'What did he want?'

'He wanted to know if I was in contact with you. When I said no, he tried to talk me into starting a search. He said he'd never had another child and felt bad about letting you go. I said he should look for you himself, but of course he couldn't because his name wasn't on the birth certificate. Though I imagine he'd have his ways - that man could get around anything. Still, I didn't trust him, so I said I wouldn't find you for him, and if I ever heard from you, I wouldn't tell him.' She bit her lip anxiously. 'You can imagine that didn't go down too well. He's a man who likes to get his own way.'

For a moment hope flickered inside Fern. Perhaps her father did want a daughter; perhaps he would find it in him to love her. Quickly she extinguished it. After all, he'd tried to kill her at birth and Shamesh said he still wanted her dead.

'Someone came here, you know. Just the other day. He asked about you. He wanted to know if you'd been in touch. And he said your father wanted to find you.'

'What did he look like?' asked Fern, already knowing the answer.

'Skinny and oldish, probably in his late fifties, with a pot belly and drooping cheeks. There was something about him. He frightened the kids.

Now Fern knew for certain what she had already suspected. The Bloodhound had been sent by her father. 'Do you have any photographs?'

'Of that man?' asked Joan, looking surprised.

'No, my father.'

'No, I tore them all up when he left. I didn't want anything more to do with him. But you won't have trouble finding information about him. He's a powerful man and a rich one. He always was ambitious. Only I wasn't part of those ambitions.' She studied Fern carefully. 'You're like him, you know. You've got his features, and a strong will. I can tell. And there's a way about you as if you're seeing more than what's there, kind of otherworldly … That way of his always used to frighten me.' Joan shuddered. 'If I were you I wouldn't try to find him. But if you must, then be careful. Don't trust him - he's a control freak. He forces people to do what he wants and then he drops them and never looks back.'

Fern pondered the surprising possibility that she was like her father. Strange how other people see you. A strong will was not something she associated with herself.

'Do you know where he lives?' she asked.

'I think he said he was based in Tasmania, running a guest house or something. It seemed strange. I expected him to be living in Sydney or New York, not Tasmania. Joan glanced at the clock. 'Heavens, it's nearly midday,' she said, standing up and collecting the mugs. 'The kids'll be back soon. I'd better get moving.'

Fern stood too, understanding that it was over. That this was all she would get, a name and yet another warning. On the front porch they were awkward with each other, not knowing how to say goodbye. Joan's stream of words had dried up now, leaving a silence that neither knew how to fill. In the end Joan spoke first.

'Come back again sometime,' she said, a pleading note in her voice. 'I want you to meet the kids. They're your brother and sister, you know. I'll tell them. They'll be excited.'

Fern smiled, recognising the intent behind her mother's words and accepting her gift. 'I'll come when I can.'

As she turned away, her mother finally asked a question. 'You were happy, weren't you?'

Fern stopped on the step next to the grinning garden gnome, and turned around to face her mother. Answers rushed through her head in a confused tangle. Happy? No, she hadn't been happy. She'd been alone, isolated, sobbing quietly in the backyard on her birthdays. She hadn't been happy but she'd been cared for, more than many other people. So what that Richard had kept accounts. So what that they never let her forget her origins. They'd fed her and Grace loved her, she knew that. An honest answer would be full of contradictions. She looked at her mother, waiting there framed in the doorway, a hungry look on her face. No, she hadn't been happy. But would she have been any happier elsewhere? Joan was so eager to hear that she'd done the right thing. Could she absolve her mother's guilt with a single word? No, she couldn't do that either.

In the end, Fern shrugged. 'I don't know.'

Chapter Twelve

Fern stepped into the cafe and scanned the tables for Adam. He wasn't there. The clock on the wall opposite said 12.35. Fern sat down at a table near the window and ordered a coffee and a piece of chocolate mud cake. All in all, she felt she'd handled the meeting with her mother quite well, stayed calm when Joan cried, asked the right questions and even drunk that awful tea. Yet now she was fighting back tears and trying desperately to swallow the lump in her throat. She had finally met her mother and yet in a way she hadn't met her at all. This mother was not the same as the one who had carried Fern in her womb and given her a name. She was not the same woman who had signed the piece of paper that had placed Fern in the arms of strangers. She'd lost that mother forever. Twenty years had passed since then and they had not shared the same path.

Behind her was a long table with a couple of computers. To distract herself while she waited for Adam, Fern moved over to one of the computers and googled Eric Hannson. There was a long list of hits. She opened the Wikipedia entry and started reading. He was born in Adelaide in 1960, to a Swiss German family. His father and mother ran a cafe in Hahndorf; Eric had helped out there as a child but at the age of sixteen he left school and took a job selling computers. While his peers were improving their minds at university, he was improving his bank balance. He started a small IT company in Adelaide, then expanded, buying up other companies until he'd formed a mega corporation. He'd made most of his money in the internet boom, then sold out before it all crashed. Intrigued, Fern read on. These days it seemed as if he was into everything: a CEO of a major corporation with a good many subsidiary companies, he was on the board of several others, including a mineral company. He was also a property speculator. She wondered if he'd lost some of his wealth in the recent recession or if he had managed to insure himself against that too.

Fern studied his photograph carefully. Joan had said she looked like her father but Fern couldn't see it. He had a strong jaw, dark hair, a slightly receding hairline and eyes that looked right into her. She tried to read their expression - perhaps a mixture of amused and haughty? It was just a head and shoulders shot, one of those corporate black and white ones, taken at an angle, with careful lighting; the sort that make everyone look the same. Still, this was her father. Eric Hannson. How strange that an hour ago she didn't know who her father was and now she was sitting here looking at a picture of him. And even stranger that an hour ago he could have been anything - a fisherman, an athlete, a carpenter, even dead - but now he was only one thing: a successful man, probably quite famous in the rarefied world of *Financial Times* readers. All this time he had been living his life and she had never known.

'An espresso thanks, mate,' said Adam. He plunked himself down onto the seat next to Fern, wincing as he bumped his knee on the table top, his legs too long to fit properly underneath. 'Phew, that was hard work. Can't think what made me go bushwalking on a day like this. It's hellish out there.' He poured himself a glass of the complimentary water and drank it down, then another, until he'd drained the bottle. 'That's better. I didn't take a water bottle or a hat. Pretty stupid, hey … How did it go with your mum?'

'She's not my mum, she's my mother, okay … She'll never be my mum.'

'As bad as that?'

Fern felt the lump rising in her throat all over again. She swallowed, forcing it back down. 'No, it was okay,' she said. 'Just a bit overwhelming.'

'Thanks,' said Adam as the waiter delivered his coffee. He spooned in three sugars, gave it a cursory stir and then downed his espresso in one gulp, before holding the cup upside down and letting the undissolved sugar drip into his mouth. 'I needed that,' he said, taking his teaspoon and helping himself to Fern's cake. 'So, did you find out anything?'

Fern pointed at the computer screen. 'That's my father. Eric Hannson.'

'Where does he live?'

'Tasmania. He's got a guest house down there. But why would a financial speculator and CEO of a major corporation want to run a guest house, even an upmarket one?'

'Probably a tax dodge,' said Adam.

Fern clicked on another site and waited as a picture downloaded. It showed Eric's guest house: a historic mansion called Pine House, which, according to its caption, offered exclusive holidays, golf, fishing, bushwalking, a restaurant and a bar stocked with 132 different whiskies. The grounds were spectacular too, landscaped, with a lake, a golf course, European trees and a perfect lawn. An aerial shot showed all this surrounded by bush.

'Where is it?' asked Adam, scanning the screen for something to identify its location. 'Somewhere in the west, I reckon, near Strahan. There used to be a load of mining going on over there. The house was probably built by some mining tycoon.'

'The website says the only access is by boat or helicopter.'

'Nah, I don't believe it, that's just to keep the plebs out. There'd have to be a service road somewhere.'

Fern took a bite of her cake before Adam could finish it, hoping the chocolate would give her some energy. The hangover, the early morning, the emotional roller coaster she'd been on all day were all taking their toll. Outside the wind had started, blowing in short sharp gusts, swirling dust and ash around the street. The scene looked wild and hostile. There was hardly anyone out there, and the few that were had screened their eyes and closed their mouths against the grit, smoke and wind. A mother pushed her baby, the pram draped in muslin that was pegged on but still lifting at the corners; a couple of young girls tried uselessly to keep their hair in place; and a man strolled slowly past, his dark glasses a protection against the dust. As if aware that someone was watching him, the man turned his face towards the window. Recognising him, Fern looked away quickly, the colour draining from her face, the cake lodging in her throat and making her cough.

'You all right?' asked Adam, thumping her on the back.

'The Bloodhound's outside. He's seen me.' Fern's mind was whirling. How did he know she was in Katoomba? Someone must be telling him her movements. Was it Adam? No, she reminded herself - the Bloodhound had found her yesterday, too, in the hospital and it couldn't have been Adam then. Nor would Joan have known she was there. Besides, she couldn't think of any reason why either of them would have given information to this man. Despite that there was no way his presence here was a coincidence. The Bloodhound must have followed her to the cafe from Joan's house, or spotted her on the main street; maybe he'd even been following them from Sydney. She shuddered.

'Act as if you haven't noticed him,' said Adam, glancing casually out the window.

Obediently, Fern took a sip of her latte and tried to look unconcerned.

'Yep, I see him,' said Adam. 'He's crossed the road and now he's looking in a shop window. This is good. Obviously he doesn't think you've seen him. Let's keep it that way.'

'Why?'

Adam looked at Fern as if she'd just failed a basic maths test. 'Because it gives us the upper hand, of course. Okay this is what we're going to do. You go out there and make sure the guy sees you. I want you to lure him somewhere quiet. There's a park just around the corner, up near the station on the right. Go there. And make him think you don't know he's following you.'

'What about you?'

Adam smiled. 'I'm going to finish your cake and pay the bill. Then I'll wait up in the park for you and we'll have a chat with the Bloodhound.'

'What if he has a gun?'

'He won't.'

'He might.'

'Well, he won't use it.'

'How do you know?'

'Believe me, I know about these things.'

Seeing the look on his face, Fern believed him. 'What if I get to the park before you?'

'You won't. Just saunter along. Stop and peer in windows, buy some chips or something, then head for the park to eat them. But above all, don't look nervous.'

'I *am* nervous.'

'Well, try not to look it.'

'What if you don't come?' she asked, distrust creeping in again. Where had Adam *really* gone while she'd been talking to her mother? Had he been meeting with the Bloodhound? And had he contacted him the night before while she slept?

'Of course I'll come,' said Adam impatiently.

Fern sighed. She had to ask. 'I don't know whether to trust you, Adam. How did that man find me? You and Joan are the only ones who knew I was here.'

'You think *I* told him?' Adam looked so astonished that Fern backed off a little.

'I don't know.'

She expected him to be angry with her, storm out maybe, but instead he softened.

'It's okay, you're right to question me. None of this makes sense and you have to check every possibility. Look, Fern, I might be an arsehole in lots of ways but I wouldn't lie, not to you. I don't know how he found us but one thing I do know is that there's no such thing as a coincidence. Someone must have told him and we'll find out who. But I promise it wasn't me.' He put his hand on his chest. 'Cross my heart and hope to die.' He looked at her imploringly. 'Will you trust me?'

Fern looked at Adam, sensing the sincerity in his words and seeing it in his eyes. She nodded.

'Good,' said Adam, switching back into practical mode. 'Come on, he's watching. Give me a kiss, then stand up and leave.'

'*What?*'

'A kiss. We want him to see us saying goodbye.'

Fern hesitated, a blush rising up into her cheeks. Then she leaned over and kissed Adam on the mouth. It was supposed to be a quick peck but it turned into something else; a slow lingering kiss that tasted of coffee, last night's whisky and smoke. When Fern pulled away, their eyes met, caught in the enchantment of that kiss.

'Mmm,' said Adam, 'that was nice. Now, see you later.'

As Fern stepped outside, the gusting wind blasted ash and smoke in her face and for a moment she was blinded. Heart pounding, she rubbed her stinging eyes, wondering where she would find the courage to go through with this. She could feel Adam watching, urging her on, but she could also feel the Bloodhound's eyes, and in her newly sensitised state they felt greedy, fuelling her desire to run. Forcing her feet to move slowly, Fern walked up the hill towards the station. From the edge of her vision she saw the Bloodhound begin to follow. She paused, peering into a shop window, pretending to look at the crystal jewellery display but instead studying the reflections, trying to make him out. Then she moved on again, stopped in a bakery and ordered a pie, quickly turning her head to see the Bloodhound crossing the road.

'Just meat,' she squeaked when the girl asked what type of pie she wanted. Fern handed over a note and forced herself to wait for the change, her fingers trembling so much she almost dropped it. The girl looked at her strangely.

Back outside, Fern crossed the road once more and the Bloodhound crossed with her. At the top of the road she turned right and walked into the park, aware that the Bloodhound wasn't far behind. If it hadn't been so hot she would have thought it was winter: the grass had a grey frosting from the ash, and the smoke hovered like mist. Nervously she headed towards a cluster of bushes. To her left a wallaby calmly nibbled at the grass as if this manicured urban park was his home. Fern kept walking, hoping Adam was already in place, watching out for her. It was all she could do to stop herself from running. She could hear the Bloodhound, feel the triumph in him. He believed he had her.

Finally she couldn't stand it anymore – she turned and saw his ugly face leering into hers. Just then Adam lunged out of the bushes and grabbed the Bloodhound by the neck. As Adam dragged him into the bushes, fear swept over the Bloodhound's face and Fern remembered from her school days how cowardly the bullies usually were, throwing stones and abuse and then denying it. They were easily defeated if you knew how - only back then she never had. Still shaking, she followed the two men.

'Right, mate, you've got some explaining to do,' said Adam, slightly loosening his stranglehold on the Bloodhound's neck.

'Let me go, I've done nothing. You got nothing on me.'

Adam tightened his hold again and Fern watched the Bloodhound's face go red before a blackness entered the edges of her vision, spreading inwards and wiping out her sight. Her legs gave way and she slumped to the ground. She could hear Adam's voice, worried and then irritated. 'Fern. *Fern!* This isn't a good time to faint on me … Shit. Well you have a nice rest while I get on with it.'

Adam squeezed the Bloodhound's neck tighter still, until the veins were swollen in the man's temple. 'I'm going to ask questions and you're going to answer them. If you don't cooperate, I'm going to squeeze harder until you can't breathe at all and then you'll die. You get that? Just nod … Good.'

Fern lay on the grass; her vision was gone and she couldn't move but she could hear everything. She felt as if she'd slipped into a movie, the sort with spies and underground mobsters. The sort she could never imagine herself in.

Adam loosened his grip again and the Bloodhound gasped for air.

'Name?'

'Reg … Reg Blackett.'

'Okay, Reg, why have you been following Fern?'

'It's my job,' said Reg, still gasping.

'Who's paying you.'

Reg hesitated. 'Dunno.'

'That's not good enough, Reg,' said Adam, with a squeeze of the man's neck.

'I dunno. Really! He just calls me and, you know, gives me orders.'

'Reg, I'm disappointed in you,' said Adam. 'Now, if I loosen my hold, will you promise to tell me the truth?'

Reg nodded. 'I shouldn't be telling you this,' he said. 'He told me to keep it quiet. Mr Hannson his name is. Eric Hannson. He contacted me out of the blue, said he wanted someone followed. He told me where to find her, said he didn't want her hurt or anything. "Just scare her," he said.'

Fern's vision was coming back, spreading in reverse from the inside to the outside. She was lying down, her face scrunched up on the grass, her senses vivid, hearing the roar of cars on the road above, the distant laughter of children, leaves rustling in the wind, the meaty smell of the pie she'd bought, which lay uneaten on the grass next to her, and the sharp burnt tang of the ash smeared on her face and hands. With a great effort she sat up and looked around, blinking, confused. The Bloodhound's last words were ringing in her ears but she couldn't imagine why her father would want her scared instead of dead.

'Ah, Fern, I don't believe you've been formally introduced. Fern, this is Reg. Reg, Fern. Where are your manners, Reg? Say hello to the lady.'

'Hello.' The Bloodhound's voice was sullen.

Fern studied him. Up close he wasn't so frightening. She'd been afraid of the Bloodhound, but it was harder to be afraid of someone called Reg.

'Okay,' said Adam. 'Let's get back to business. Any ideas why Mr Hannson wanted Fern scared?'

'I asked him. Told him I wouldn't do it unless I knew. I've got standards, you know. He said he was her dad, and she'd run away from home. He thought if he gave her a scare she'd come running back. I understood. I got kids of my own, you know. It's not easy being a dad.'

'And you believed what he told you?'

'Course I did. He wanted her back. He just said to keep on her tracks. Make sure she was nervous, like.'

'Eric Hannson has never had the honour of actually meeting his daughter,' said Adam.

'You're kidding me,' said Reg, looking genuinely surprised.

Fern was still pondering why her father would hire someone to frighten her. It seemed pointless, but the little she knew of Eric suggested he did things for a reason. Fern felt the answer was already there, somewhere inside her, like a word on the tip of her tongue but as hard as she tried, she couldn't locate it.

'How did you find me today?' she asked, thinking a clue might lie in the answer to a different question. And at the hospital – how did you know I was there?'

'I lost your scent a couple of times,' said Reg, looking embarrassed. 'Mr Hannson wasn't too happy about that. It was weird, though - both times he rang back and told me where to look.'

'How did he know?'

'I dunno - really I don't. He must know a lot of people. Maybe he's got someone else looking out for you.'

Fern tried to think it through. She couldn't fathom what reason her father would have to employ someone else to follow her. No, he had to be getting his information from someone she knew. She was going round in circles and getting paranoid all over again - Adam? Shamesh? Grace? Joan? Claire? But none of them had known where she was all the time over the past week.

'Where does Hannson live?' asked Adam.

'I dunno, he only rings me. He puts money in my bank account. There's no other contact. Honest.'

'Here, Fern, check his pockets, see if you can find anything.'

'I'm not putting my hands in there,' protested Fern, looking at Reg's tight jeans.

'Well, that's difficult, I don't have a spare hand. So you either check his pockets or take over from me. Your choice.'

Reluctantly Fern slipped her hand into Reg's back pockets, one at a time. She pulled out a wallet and checked its contents: a few dollars, some credit cards, a photo of two children, and a driver's licence, confirming his name. He lived in Strathfield. An ordinary wallet, an ordinary man.

'And the rest.'

Fern scowled at Adam and slid her hand into Reg's front pocket, quickly retrieving a mobile phone.

'Okay, check the directory, Fern - voicemail, texts, anything that might tell us where he is.'

Fern fiddled with the buttons, trying to figure out Reg's phone. There was nothing in the directory and no voice messages. But among the text messages she found one dated today, 7.35 am. It was short and to the point: *Visiting mother in Katoomba.*

'It's a mobile number,' she said, hunting around in her pack for a pen and writing the number on the back of her hand. 'It's useless. It doesn't tell us where he is.'

Adam seemed unconcerned. 'Give Reg back his wallet,' he said, 'but keep the phone. We're going to make a phone call.'

'No,' said Fern, as she realised what he was planning to do. 'You can't.'

'Watch me,' said Adam.

Fern felt profound terror surging through her. She didn't want to come any closer to Eric Hannson, not even over a mobile phone. 'No!' she almost shouted.

Adam spoke patiently. 'Fern, remember what Shamesh said? What we talked about? You've got to turn around and hunt the hunter. He'll find other ways to get you. Hunters always do.'

Fern sighed. 'Okay, but you do the talking,' she said, uneasily pressing the return call option and handing the phone to Adam, who switched it on to speaker and waited.

The ringing stopped and a man's voice came on, cultured and supremely certain of itself. 'Reg?'

'Ah, Mr Hannson, how are you today?' Adam said smoothly.

'Who is this?'

'I'm just letting you know that Reg won't be working for you anymore. We know who he is and we know who you are, Mr Hannson.'

'What do you mean? Who are you?'

Fern thought she could detect a note of fear in her father's voice but even so she writhed in terror, feeling the tentacles of his intent reaching out across space, blindly feeling for her.

'I suggest you stop playing games with your daughter and leave her alone. Because, if you don't, believe me, we'll come and find you.'

There was a short barking laugh from Fern's father, just as Adam cut him off. 'Always best to have the last word in these situations,' he said, smiling at Fern.

'Hey, that's my phone,' said Reg as Adam shoved it into his own pocket. 'It's got all my contacts on it.'

'That's what comes from working for the wrong people,' said Adam, letting go of Reg and shaking his head sympathetically.

Reg sighed and turned away, defeated.

'Uh-uh, not yet, you've got an apology to make.'

'Bullshit,' said Reg.

Adam stretched out a leg, hooked Reg's feet and pulled them from under him, sending him thudding to the ground face first. 'I want you to apologise to Fern.'

Reg groaned and rubbed his nose. 'Sorry,' he muttered.

'Not good enough. Repeat after me: I'm sorry for scaring you, Fern, and I promise I won't do it again.'

Reg repeated the words, his voice disgruntled.

'That's better,' said Adam. 'Don't you ever come near Fern again or I'll kill you. Got that?'

'Got it,' said Reg.

Chapter Thirteen

As they walked towards the station, Adam's mood darkened. He walked briskly, Fern half running to keep up with him. She could sense his anger but couldn't understand where it had come from.

'You were really amazing back there,' she said.

Adam scowled. 'Yeah, I'm well trained in that kind of shit. It's the only thing I know how to do,' he said, his voice laced with bitterness.

A man wearing a white robe and carrying a wooden cross thrust a leaflet into Fern's hand. 'Repent,' he said, 'the end of the world is nigh.'

'About bloody time,' said Adam and the man sent him a shocked glance before moving on.

On the train, Adam sat down and closed his eyes, shutting out the world. Fern sat down next to Adam and glanced nervously at him. 'I just wanted to say thank you,' she said, hesitantly. 'I really appreciate the way you've helped me.'

Adam opened his eyes and looked at Fern but she felt he didn't really see her. He was somewhere else, far away. 'Yeah, no worries,' he said and closed his eyes again.

Fern tried to relax but it wasn't easy. Her whole body was trembling from the combination of coffee and nervous tension. She forced one shoulder down and then the other, rubbed her neck and rotated her head in circles, trying to loosen all her muscles. Gradually she relaxed enough to feel the fatigue that was creeping up from her feet and into her legs, then her arms, before sinking into her chest. Her exhaustion was mixed with relief. She'd gone through with this, had met her birth mother and faced the Bloodhound.

She looked at Adam, sitting next to her with his eyes resolutely closed, blocking her out. Yet in the cafe he'd asked her to kiss him and the memory still lingered on her lips. Maybe he was angry with her for drawing him into all this. Or perhaps he hadn't forgiven her for doubting him. He hadn't said it but she could sense the unspoken question: 'do you believe me now?'

Fern wished she could understand Adam, make sense of his moods. He was like a multi-faceted crystal, one minute showing one face to the world, the next another face. A dark crystal not letting anyone in, yet turbulent inside, all caught up in its shadow self.

Outside, the wind was whipping the dust, leaves and rubbish into furious eddies that buffeted the carriage. Sighing, Fern closed her eyes and tried to escape into sleep but her mind was racing, throwing up images of the Bloodhound, Shamesh, Cassie, her birth mother, that photograph of her father staring into her, and all their voices echoing in her mind keeping her senses alert and buzzing: 'Just scare her' … 'Adam is on his own journey' … 'You're waking up and that scares them' … 'This lifetime he has incarnated as your father' … She opened her eyes again and stared through the window; it seemed the whipping wind outside was calmer than her mind.

Remembering her knitting, Fern reached into her bag to retrieve it. She'd always used knitting to keep herself focused. It felt like a mini meditation; the rhythm of it, the way it settled her mind. This was a straightforward piece, a tank top, pretty much up and down. The wool was six-ply, its colours a blend of royal blue and turquoise. Even the feel of it in her hands calmed her. But as she unrolled the section she had been working on, the tempest stone slipped out, landing in her lap. Fern looked at it warily. There was something about this stone that was both repellent and alluring.

Her hand reached out and her fingers clasped the stones smooth surface. Almost immediately she felt the dizziness again and then without warning the soldiers were back, as if a page were turning on a continuing narrative. This time she could feel the bruises forming where their fingers were clutching her upper arms. She could see the blue and white of their intricately painted shields. Next to her was a young girl of about nine or ten, wearing a dirty shift, her dark long hair tangled. The girl was struggling and crying. Noticing this, Fern struggled harder to free herself from the soldiers, feeling overwhelmed by a great need to hold this girl in her arms, to protect her from the looming threat around them. They were linked in some way, mother and daughter perhaps, because the fear she felt was not for herself but for the girl.

An air of expectation arose among the soldiers and they fell back silently to make way for a man who walked towards Fern, his movements studied and understated but exuding power. He was wearing a long gown, a cape of some sort with a hood that covered his face, the material ornately embroidered in gold thread. Recognising the gown from her dreams, the fear Fern had felt for the girl turned into terror. She struggled to free herself but the soldiers' hands were unyielding. When the man in the robe stopped a few paces from Fern and pushed back his hood to reveal his face, the terror rose to an unbearable pitch inside her. She did not want to see that face, did not want to make the connections. She tried to turn her own face away but some power beyond hers pushed it back, forcing her eyelids open, forcing her to look.

It was the smile she noticed first. A self-satisfied smile; that of a spider who has caught its fly. Fern was mute, transfixed with horror; her gaze was released only as the girl struggled again, crying out in fear. At this the robed man casually lifted a finger, sending a soldier's sword swinging. Where the girl's head had been only a second before was a severed neck, the bone gleaming white, blood fountaining, the body still moving. It had been too quick to comprehend yet an irreversible action. Fern cried out in bewilderment and horror. It was too late. She had failed the girl. Yet before the grief could surge into her heart and merge with the heavy weight of her guilt, a spear entered her chest, propelling her backwards, jerking and twisting. The last thing she saw was the Against her will, her eyes were drawn away from the girl and back to the robed man. In his face she could read an immense gloating satisfaction.

Adam watched Fern twitching and moaning next to him. At first he'd thought it was a dream but her eyes were open. Now he was worried it was a fit of some sort.

'You okay?'

Fern jumped and let go of the stone, the vision disappearing as the stone hit the floor.

'What's going on? You were thrashing about all over the place - and you look like shit.'

'Thanks,' said Fern, trying to smile through trembling lips. 'I must have had a dream.' But it was too real to be just a dream. Somehow this stone was taking her into the past. Shamesh had said it would help her remember. Was she seeing herself in a past life? No, she thought, more likely it was genetic; a memory she'd inherited somehow, that had been passed down through generations.

Adam reached down and picked up the stone. 'What's this?' he asked, turning it over in his hand. 'Hey, it's amazing, those veins look like gold.'

'Shamesh gave it to me,' she said. 'It's called a tempest stone.' She hesitated, then asked, 'Does it make you feel strange?'

Adam looked at her quizzically, then studied the stone again. 'It's beautiful,' he said after a pause. 'But it's only a stone.'

'It makes me see things,' said Fern without thinking.

'Like what?' asked Adam, sounding sceptical.

'I don't know,' she said, backtracking. 'Nothing really. I must have been dreaming.'

'Yeah, I reckon,' Adam said, wishing he'd kept the cynical tone out of his voice. He understood that Fern had offered him something but instead of accepting her gift, he'd thrown it back at her.

Adam handed the stone to Fern and watched as she stowed it away carefully in her bag then pick up the knitting on her lap. She seemed too young for that. Knit one, purl one: it reminded him of his mother, knitting away every night in front of the television. The comforting click of the needles, making something from nothing. With the memory came regret for a childhood that could never be reclaimed. And the guilt. There was always the guilt. It had been too long since he had seen his mother.

They stepped off the train into a muggy airless afternoon. A red-faced Father Christmas sat miserably on his temporary throne in the main part of the station, half-heartedly ringing a bell and muttering the occasional 'Ho, ho, ho'. In spite of his lack of enthusiasm, the smaller children were convinced, some standing back awestruck and clinging to their mother's hands for safety, others crowding around him, pulling his beard and shouting wish lists.

Every time Fern remembered that it was nearly Christmas, she felt loneliness threaten to engulf her again. It reminded her that she needed to move on. She couldn't let Adam get caught up any further in her mess. It wasn't fair on him. She would have to act immediately.

Fern stopped walking and watched Adam carry on for a few paces until he realised she wasn't next to him. He stopped too and looked back, then rolled his eyes.

'Don't even think about it,' he said.

'I can't lay my stuff on you anymore. It isn't fair.'

'Fair! Shit, don't be an idiot. Life isn't fair. And what are you going to do without me? Where do you plan to go? Back to the nuthouse?'

Fern steeled herself against Adam's words. 'I haven't got a clue where I'm going,' she said, 'but I can't involve you in this any longer. I hardly know you. Look, you've seen off the Bloodhound and you were fantastic. I've met my mother. I've found out about my father. You've helped me a lot and I'm grateful but I can manage by myself now.'

Adam was really angry now. 'So, I'm just some jerk you can use when you feel like it and then dump?'

'That's not what I meant.'

'You still don't trust me, do you?'

'I do,' Fern protested. 'It's just that … '

'I'm only here because I promised Shamesh, otherwise I wouldn't bother chasing you all over the place.'

Now Fern could feel her own anger rising. 'Then leave me alone. I can look after myself.'

Adam stepped closer to Fern, his voice quieter now. 'Do you really believe it's over? Do you really think that man is going to stop just because we caught his hired hand?'

Fern shook her head despairingly, feeling more and more like a trapped animal. 'I don't know. I want him to stop. I want all this to stop.' Despite the heat she was shaking, her teeth chattering and the tears threatening to spill over.

Adam put his arm around Fern, holding her close. 'Hey, it's okay. We're in this together now.'

In Adam's arms, Fern felt her panic slowly subside. 'Why were you so angry with me on the train?'

Adam sighed. 'I wasn't angry with you. I was angry with myself.'

Fern was baffled. 'Why? You were great.'

'Yeah, I was good. And I enjoyed it. You're not supposed to enjoy squeezing someone's neck until their veins pop out. But I did. Come on.'

He grabbed her hand and started walking again, so fast that Fern had to half run to keep up.

The flat stank. Even Adam noticed it. 'Jeez,' he said, embarrassed. 'This place could do with a clean.' He opened the window, letting in the heat but no fresh air. Then he stuffed yesterday's pizza box and a half dozen empty beer bottles into an overflowing garbage bag and dumped it outside the door. 'That's better. Want a beer?'

'No thanks.' Fern was desperately thirsty but the last thing she wanted was beer. She dug around in the shopping bags looking for the juice she'd bought on the way back from the station, then drained two glasses in a row before she felt ready to unpack the rest of the shopping. Adam didn't seem to care one way or the other, but Fern had decided that, under the circumstances, cooking dinner for him was the least she could do. She was keeping it simple, though, spaghetti Bolognese, just mince, a jar of ready-made tomato sauce, parmesan, some salad ingredients and a ready-made dressing.

'Where is everything?' she asked.

'What in particular were you looking for?' asked Adam, grabbing another beer from the fridge.

'You know, just the usual - saucepans, a chopping board, a wooden spoon, bowls, that sort of thing.'

'There might be something in that one above the fridge,' said Adam pointing at a cupboard out of Fern's reach.

Fern rummaged around among a thick tangle of spider webs, finding a small dented saucepan with no lid, a flour sifter, a cake tin, a plastic icy-pole maker and a metal bowl that would do for the salad.

'Don't you ever cook?'

'Not often.'

Fern sighed and looked around the kitchen. 'Where's the stove?'

'There isn't one.'

'How am I supposed to cook then?'

'In the microwave.'

'I can't make bolognese sauce in the microwave.'

'Course you can'. Adam opened another cupboard and pulled out a plastic bowl. 'Just throw it all in here and stick it in the microwave.'

When Fern looked at him, astonished, Adam grabbed the jar and the meat and did it himself.

'Don't you know how bad those things are for you?'

'Yeah. If I'm really lucky it'll turn my brains to jelly.'

'Why don't you look after yourself more?'

Adam ignored her and switched on the television. Fern bit her lip and sat down at the table with the salad things. She pulled the lettuce apart and layered it in the metal bowl, then sliced the cherry tomatoes in half, popping one into her mouth and savouring its sweet tartness. Then she cut the cucumber into thin slices. The snow peas were glorious, their flesh crisp and sweet. It felt good doing something normal for a change. After the past week, the simple routine of preparing food felt like a precious gift. In its simplicity she could almost forget herself for a moment. And in it she could find space for this sudden burst of happiness that had ambushed her so unexpectedly.

Fern finished the salad, put the pasta in a bowl of water in the microwave and then sat down with Adam to watch the news. She was reminded of the last time she'd seen it - in another era it seemed, when she'd been part of life and a future had seemed possible - sitting in the lounge room of their terrace house with her friends, drinking tea and discussing politics and the environment, as if there were some point to their conversations, as if they could make a difference. One day she'd realised how much she hated the news – the feeling it triggered in her stomach, a twisted surging fear. She'd wondered then what point there was to watching it, whether it made her a conscientiously well-informed citizen or just kept her fearful. They'd argued about it, the others saying it was a responsible thing to do, that ignorance was dangerous. 'Don't you care what happens in the world?' they asked, and Fern couldn't find the right words to explain that she cared too much. Now here she was, watching the news again with a near stranger in this smelly flat and nothing had changed. Next to her Adam was becoming angrier and angrier as he watched.

'It's a fucking mess,' he said. 'The world's unravelling.' He drained his beer. 'Fuck it, who cares?'

'You do,' said Fern, seeing clearly the hurt inside of him.

Adam glanced sullenly at her. 'I don't give a fuck about anything.'

But Fern could see that wasn't true. Like her, Adam cared too much, only he dealt with it in a different way.

She got up and drained the pasta, then mixed it with the sauce and put it on the table. She found a couple of plates, opened a bottle of white wine and dug out a couple of mismatching wine glasses. 'Dinner's ready.'

Adam turned off the television and promptly switched moods. 'Great,' he said, helping himself to pasta. 'Mmm, it's good.'

As they ate, Fern savoured the sense of safety in this domesticity. If they could just go on acting normal like this maybe it would be enough to keep out the demons.

'Guess we'd better talk about Tassie then,' said Adam, dispelling Fern's contentment.

'Tassie?'

'Yeah, isn't that where your dad is?'

'I don't want to go to Tasmania.'

'Got any better suggestions?'

Fern thought about it. There was nowhere she could go, except Adelaide. But what then? She had just under a thousand dollars in her bank account, no job, nowhere to live, and no friends - except Adam. But she couldn't stay in his basement flat indefinitely.

'We could tell the police.'

Adam laughed. 'Tell them what? That your father who you've never met, wants you dead? And how do you know that? Because Shamesh told you.' He poured another glass of wine. 'Oh, and you could mention the prophecy, that would go down well.'

'He had me followed.'

'There's no crime in that. He employed a private detective to find his long-lost daughter. It's a heart-warming story.'

Fern sighed and pushed her food away, half eaten. 'You don't have to come with me to Tasmania,' she said.

'Will you stop trying to shake me off? … Anyway, it's a good excuse to visit the family. Christmas, too, they'll be pleased.'

'How long since you've seen them?'

Adam grimaced. He hadn't contacted them once in the past two years. His mum would be beside herself, he thought, and must feel trapped too, just her looking after his brother. 'Too long, probably,' he said, switching on the television again, its panicked blare cutting off their conversation.

Exhausted, Fern washed up the dishes then slipped into Adam's bed and into sleep, while the television flickered and shouted and Adam sat up drinking beer after beer.

She woke into a nightmare. The room was dark and she didn't know where she was but had no space to wonder, because everything else had been pushed out by one simple certainty: she was dying. Fern leaped out of bed, rubbing her arm, trying to get some feeling back, but the whole left side of her body had disappeared into a numb and tingly weakness.

'Help me,' she cried in a hoarse whisper. 'Help me.' She was too far away from herself, a part of her caught in the world of her dreams. Her body was panic-stricken. There was no way she could make it back, She'd gone too far. It felt as if something was stopping her, sucking the energy out of her.

'What's going on?' asked Adam, flicking the light switch and banishing the shadows. It should have helped but it didn't. There was no clarity or safety in the light because Fern was somewhere else, caught in a murky dark world where the air was as thick as quicksand.

'Help me,' whispered Fern, somehow knowing that she mustn't keep still. She had to keep moving. Rubbing. Pacing. Rubbing. It was the only way to bring herself back.

Adam was following her, trying to calm her. She could hear his voice, low and measured, though underneath he was panicking too, she could tell, could see right into him, into the black areas he tried to hide, and around him where the Furies lurked, tormenting him. In that moment she knew him inside out, knew that he was haunted too. That something had to change inside him before he could be free of it. The knowing came from another part of herself that she'd never noticed before, a steady calm aspect that was watching, that knew exactly what was happening and what to do. But she couldn't speak except to keep mouthing the same words. 'Help me.'

'Should I call an ambulance?'

Fern shook her head impatiently, then pointed at her bag until Adam obeyed and brought it to her. She pointed at the front pocket until he opened it, then she gestured for him to pull out the little velvet bag Cassie had given her. He tipped out the bottles onto the bed and, not knowing how she knew, she pointed again, at the aconite and the Rescue Remedy.

Adam held her still for long enough to push an aconite tablet into her mouth then he squirted a couple of drops of Rescue Remedy. For a few minutes Fern didn't think it would work. This was too much for a tiny tablet to fight and she only had Cassie's word for it. Panicking, she pointed again and Adam gave her another aconite. Then she felt it, the calm spreading through her, enough to stop her frantic pacing. Fern slumped on a chair, cold now, her whole body filled with a dreadful flatness.

'You okay?' Adam was rubbing her back. The warmth of his hand was welcome. She tried to nod but could only sit and stare ahead. She'd used every last scrap of her strength to come back. And now her whole body was shaking uncontrollably, her teeth chattering.

'It's shock,' said Adam, wrapping her in a blanket. He poured some whisky into a glass. 'Here, sip this, it'll warm you inside.'

Fern couldn't hold the glass, so Adam held it gently to her mouth and let her sip. His other hand massaged her shoulders until slowly the tremors eased and she was still.

'Are you okay now?'

Fern nodded.

'Do you want me to call a doctor?'

She shook her head.

'You frightened the hell out of me, you know that?'

Fern leaned her head on Adam's shoulder, overcome by the dread that still sat heavily inside her. 'Me too,' she whispered.

'What happened?'

Fern tried to think of a way to answer Adam, but she couldn't begin to explain what had sent her lurching out of bed, feeling her heart strained to breaking point. She ran through the possibilities: stroke, heart attack, or perhaps a nightmare. There was a tension around her heart, as if its edges were raw, but if anything, her pulse was slow.

'I don't know. It was like I was stuck somewhere a long way away. I thought I was dying.'

'So did I,' said Adam. It had given him the creeps, seeing Fern like that. He couldn't tell if she'd looked like someone who was trying to get away from herself or someone who was trying to get back in.

Fern attempted a smile. 'Thank you,' she said. 'Again.'

'No problem. You can wake me up anytime. I don't mind. I can't think of anything more fun than chasing you round in circles while you shout for help.'

Fern could hear the relief in Adam's voice, mingled with anxiety. He didn't understand what had just happened. Neither did she, though she was beginning to form a theory. 'I owe you a lot, don't I?'

'I'm not keeping count.'

'But I am. I feel like Lois, always needing to be rescued by Superman.'

'Shit, Fern, you can't tally things up like that. If you need help, I'll help you. Okay?' Adam met Fern's eyes for a moment and blushed. She had no idea how much she was giving him.

Fern smiled. 'Okay.'

'Good. At least we understand each other. Now get into bed, you're shivering again.'

Still wrapped in the blanket, Fern climbed into bed and pulled the duvet over herself. She curled her body up in the foetal position, trying to warm herself but the shivering only got worse. 'I can't get warm.'

'Your hands are like ice,' said Adam. 'Here, let me feel your feet … Bloody hell. Look I'm not trying anything on, I just need to feel your stomach, or your back, it doesn't matter.'

Fern nodded and let him unwrap the blanket and slip his hand down the back of her t-shirt. It felt burning hot against her skin.

'It's a hot night, you shouldn't be this cold. Here, let me take that blanket. There's no point wrapping you up if you've got no warmth in you.' He stretched the blanket out over the duvet. 'I'm going to have to get in. Is that okay? You need my heat to warm you up.'

Fern nodded, half smiling at the blush that spread up Adam's cheeks as he climbed in, gingerly shifting his body against hers and drawing her close. She felt safer with him there, his warmth seeping into her, gradually bringing her body back to life.

'You warming up?'

'A bit,' she said. Her eyelids were getting heavy, the way they used to when she was a child. She shuddered. 'I'm afraid to go to sleep.'

'It's okay, I'm here.'

'No, you don't understand. There's something out there. It's waiting for me. Next time it will get me.'

'Anything that's hunting you is doing it in the real world,' said Adam, sounding more certain than he felt.

Fern shook her head but she was too tired to explain. Besides, any story she could tell would be so fragmented and outlandish it would make no sense. 'He's reaching into your dreams,' Shamesh had said. And now Fern was certain it was true. This must have been how her father had found her. And this was why he'd wanted her frightened. It weakened her, and when she was weak he could get past her defences.

'Stop worrying, I won't let anything get you.'

'Even in my sleep?'

'Even in your sleep. Just call me.'

As Fern's eyes closed, Adam felt the weight of her trust and wondered if he was making promises he might not be able to keep.

Chapter Fourteen

'Look,' said Adam, peering out the window. 'There's Tassie.'

Fern looked at the curved coastline extending as far as she could see, then back at Adam who was staring, transfixed, with something new in his eyes. A fierce joy, even pride. This was his home. She wondered at the strange twist of fate that had sent them to Tasmania. There was no doubt they both had something to find here. An ending perhaps, a conclusion of some sort. And maybe a new beginning.

'It's green,' she said, stating the obvious as the plane soared above lush farmlands and mountains. She'd almost forgotten what green looked like.

'Isn't it beautiful? The south is pretty special too, though it's much drier there.'

Fern shifted uncomfortably in her seat. It had been two days since the night attack, but she was still weak on her left side and experiencing shooting pains in her head and a rawness in her chest as if her heart was wounded. She'd wanted to get on a plane the next day but Adam said she wasn't well enough, that there wasn't any hurry. In the end she'd agreed to see a doctor, and spent an hour in a waiting room, before an ageing doctor told her she was too young to have heart problems.

'Probably just a panic attack,' he said, dismissing it as a small and embarrassing piece of hysteria. Women's stuff.

So it appeared that whatever was wrong with Fern was not measurable and therefore not serious. But her instincts told her that she'd been lucky to survive; that her heart had experienced a huge jolt, a giant rush of adrenalin; that something had temporarily cut off her life source. She'd fought back instinctively and now wondered if that was what Cassie had meant when she'd told Fern to follow her intuition. It was as if she had an innate knowledge inside of her and all she had to do was remember how to access it.

As a teenager the idea of astral travelling had appealed to Fern and she'd spent hours trying to clear her mind and imagine herself out of her body, each time slipping into sleep instead or getting lost in her thoughts. In the end she'd given up. Now she wondered if she'd been astral travelling the other night. Could it be possible that she'd met her enemy out there in the ether and he'd tried to kill her by severing the life cord that was supposed to connect the astral body with the physical body. No, she thought, that's the stuff of horror films not real life. But despite her doubts she couldn't shake the idea.

'See out there,' said Adam, 'that's the Great Western Tiers, some of the best walking country in Tassie. I'll take you there, you can see for yourself.'

'Great,' said Fern. She wasn't exactly familiar with camping, or particularly keen on the idea of bushwalking in snake-ridden wilderness, but Adam's excitement was infectious. As she leaned over him to peer through the window, her arm accidentally touched his chest and she jumped as if she'd been shocked. This strange electric tension between them had started the morning after the panic attack. She'd woken late, to find the blankets thrown off and Adam lying stretched out on his back, one arm still pinned under her. She'd watched him for a while, studying the almost imperceptible pulse in his neck, his chest rising and falling, the blond hairs sprinkled between his nipples, the mole just under his belly button, the thick muscles of his legs, and his boxer shorts gaping just a little at the front. She had to fight a powerful urge to run her fingers down his chest and slip her hand into those shorts. She wanted him so much it hurt. Wanted to lean over and kiss him again, losing herself in his mouth, imbibing his strong smell of sweat and beer, her skin rubbing raw against the stubble on his chin. But just then Adam had opened his eyes and stared straight at her. He'd given her a sleepy smile and for a moment she thought he was happy to find himself beside her. But a second later, his eyes had clouded over with confusion and then embarrassment, and he pulled his arm out from under her and sat up abruptly.

That night had been a torture for Adam. While Fern slept, he'd spent hours cradling her against him, letting his warmth flow into her, and trying not to feel anything or, more precisely, trying not to let her feel anything. The tension had built inside him as the night wore on. Her skin was soft and silken and he'd desperately wanted to stroke it but hadn't dared move. When he finally shifted one arm a little to try to ease the pins and needles, she sighed and snuggled closer to him, her face right up against his chest. Then it was all he could do to stop himself from bending down, lifting her chin and kissing her. Instead he lay statue still, staring at the ceiling and attempting to distract himself. First he replayed in his head every song he knew, then feeling idiotic, played a game he had used as a kid when he couldn't sleep, trying to think of every fruit or vegetable starting with A - apricot, apple, avocado, aubergine – B - lots of berries there, blackberry, blueberry boysenberry - and so on through the alphabet. Then he started again on animals. It was only when he reached Q and dawn was approaching that he finally succumbed to sleep and then it seemed only a fraction of time before he opened his eyes again to find her looking at him. Her face was open, her eyes soft and filled with a yearning that made him want to reach out and enfold her. Instead he blushed and turned away, muttering something stupid about getting breakfast, and regretting the lost intimacy even as he spoke.

After that they were wary, holding their bodies away from each other. If Fern's hand brushed against his she quickly snatched it away, and when they came face to face in the tiny flat, they hastily sprung apart. Neither was able to step across the abyss they'd created between themselves.

Fern felt the pressure change in her ears as the plane began its descent. She hated this bit, flying through clouds until suddenly they were too close to the ground, the wings tossing one way and then the other. She did up her seatbelt and waited, feeling the nerves set in, exacerbating the rawness around her heart. The plane would land because it always did. And then what? A new place, new people, Christmas with strangers, and eventually a meeting she feared.

Adam was listening to his iPod as if he didn't have a care in the world. But he must be nervous too, thought Fern. Two years was a long time to be away from your family, especially when it was just his mum and his brother. There was something going on there, but he wasn't forthcoming about it.

Despite her arguments, Adam had insisted that Fern spend Christmas with his family. 'They'd want you to,' he'd said. 'They're like that.'

But Fern wasn't so sure. He hadn't even rung to say they were coming. When she'd suggested it would be a good idea to give his mother some warning, he'd shaken his head.

'Nah, it's easier this way. We'll just show up.'

Adam had kept his voice casual, but he was secretly worried. He didn't know how to face them, how to say sorry. He'd left it too long, so now there was nothing he could do to make it easier. If he could have left a message, just said, 'See you tomorrow,' that would have been okay, but his mother would want explanations, there'd be tears, and he'd change his mind. He knew it.

The engine noise dropped suddenly and Fern's knuckles whitened, then it roared again as the plane reached for the runway. She braced herself as they hit the ground, feeling the force of the brakes fighting the heavy machine that was propelling itself forward. For a split second the battle hung suspended. Then as the plane slowed, Fern relaxed, breathing easily again, and excited now. She'd never been to Tasmania before.

Heads down against the wind, they made their way across the tarmac and into the baggage claim area where they waited for Adam's bag. Fern had taken her own small backpack onto the plane with her. Adam had booked the tickets yesterday and paid for them on his card, so no one could trace Fern's movements via her accounts. Then he'd made her take money out at a flexi-teller on Oxford Street this morning. 'Take as much as you think you'll need,' he'd told her. 'You don't want to be making transactions in Tassie.'

Fern had done as Adam suggested, but wondered if it was necessary. Perhaps Grace would be pushing the police to start searching for her, trying to get her placed on the missing persons list, but she didn't think Eric would employ another Bloodhound to find her. There was no reason to attack her in the 'real' world when it appeared he could do it so much more efficiently in her sleep.

Even so, as they waited for Adam's bag, Fern looked around anxiously. A man standing a few paces away caught her eye, then looked away quickly, freezing her to the spot and sending her heart racing. Just then a child ran up to him shouting 'Daddy, Daddy,' and he scooped her up smiling. Relieved, Fern thought about her own fathers: one sick with a broken-down heart; and the other, Eric Hannson, a name that still felt strange to her tongue. In all the years she'd wondered about her birth parents, it had been her mother that she'd focused on, not her father. There'd been only a fleeting sense of disappointment when she saw the blank space on her birth certificate where her father's name should have been. Now Fern was on her father's turf, and she wondered if he could sense somehow that she was there.

'Shit, what's happened to the place?' Adam said as the airport bus drove them into town. They'd already passed a new airport motel and now they were passing a sprawling shopping complex. 'Last time I was here, this was all just dirt.' Adam laughed. 'Tassie's really coming on, hey! It'll be on the map next.'

The bus turned a corner and a massive mountain loomed in the distance, the city of Hobart rising from its base. 'Mount Wellington,' said Adam. 'There are some great walks up there.'

Fern stared at the mountain as they approached. It looked stern and heavy, looming over the houses that sat at its feet and overshadowing the city in the afternoon light. Even the way it was softened and split in two by clouds took away none of its certainty.

'In winter it's often covered in snow. Even snows in summer sometimes. Though most summers it bakes dry - it's a bushfire waiting to happen.'

They crossed a wide river, the bridge curving up and over it.

'The Derwent River,' said Adam as if just the name could describe the play of light on the water as the wind tossed the surface, and the joyful triangles of sails as yachts tacked playfully to and fro. Beyond was the city: a collection of miniature high-rises reaching above period buildings. Docked in the harbour was a cruise ship almost as tall as the high-rises, and around the city centre houses stretched from the water's edge, up the hills and into the mountain. It was beautiful.

'Fucking log trucks,' said Adam, his mood souring again as a truck laden with gigantic tree trunks drove past them. 'I'd almost forgotten about forestry.' He scowled. 'That's how it is with Tassie, when you're not here you hardly think about it, but the minute you get back, the politics take over. You have to take sides about everything. Shit, I hate this place.'

'I thought you loved it.'

'Yeah, it's complicated. I hate it that I love it. You know, if you love something you want to protect it. And every time someone hurts it, they hurt you. Then you get trapped somehow. You're not autonomous anymore. You're not free. That's what Tassie does to me.'

Fern wondered if that conflict extended to all Adam's relationships - if he had any. He hadn't seen his family for a long time and in the few days she'd known him his phone hadn't rung and no one had come by. He hadn't mentioned friends or girlfriends. Maybe it was his way of trying to be free. But it didn't work. Running away was just another trap. She should know.

There was a two-hour wait for the next bus down the Channel Highway to Kettering, where Adam's mother lived with his brother. They passed the time down by the harbour looking in shop windows and browsing in a bookshop. As they walked through Salamanca Square, a guy with dreadlocks and an earring in his nose called out Adam's name.

Adam stopped, looking blank for a moment. 'Matt! I didn't recognise you,' he said, then gave the guy a bear hug.

Fern liked the look of Matt. He was beautiful, with gentle eyes and an earthy feel about him. Perhaps it was the clothes, in shades of brown, or the mud-caked walking boots.

'What you been up to?' Matt asked.

'Oh, this and that,' said Adam vaguely.

'I heard you'd joined the army.'

'Yeah,' said Adam dismissively. 'A short stint, least it got me out of Tassie. How about you?'

'Been camping down at the Florentine for the past few months, trying to stop the loggers … You back for good?' Matt asked, all the while eyeing Fern curiously.

'Nah,' said Adam, looking uncomfortable. 'Just visiting the family'

'Shame … Hey, I'd better get going.' Matt scribbled something on a piece of paper. 'Here's my number. You should come down and have a look while you're here. We could do with more people.'

'Yeah,' said Adam, pocketing the number. 'I'll try.'

So Adam had been a soldier. Fern felt a momentary satisfaction at having one question answered, but it only raised more. He didn't seem like the soldier type, but then again, she'd never met a soldier before. At least it explained the way he'd handled Reg, as if he'd been trained for it. She looked at Adam curiously wondering what had made him join up, but the expression on his face was forbidding.

'Don't ask,' he said. 'Let's get a drink.'

They found a table in the sun, ordering a coffee for Fern and a beer for Adam. Fern untied her hat from the back of her pack and slipped it on, holding it in place with a silk scarf that she'd hand-dyed in college.

Adam sat opposite Fern, drinking his beer and watching her dip her teaspoon into her latte and delicately lick off the froth. A week ago he would have laughed if anyone had told him he would soon be in Tasmania again, sitting in the sun in Salamanca with a girl like this. She was beautiful, in a head-turning way. People looked at her - men and women. Adam felt a mixture of pride and jealousy welling up inside him as he caught another man glancing over at her. However, Fern seemed oblivious to all the attention. A shawl was wrapped loosely around her shoulders and she wore a pair of flat sandals, the fine leather lacing up her ankles, a plain singlet top, a skirt that swished softly around her knees as she walked, and that hat. He couldn't decide if she was a hippy, a sophisticate, or maybe something else entirely. But whatever she was she made him feel like his brother - a clumsy, oversized oaf.

'Do you believe in reincarnation?' Fern asked suddenly, jolting him out of his thoughts. Great, he noted wryly, another weird topic he'd rather not think about.

'No,' he said, abruptly.

'Mmm, I suppose it doesn't make much sense, but then neither does just stopping. How can our life just stop? What would be the point?'

'That's just the way it is,' said Adam, dourly. 'There isn't any point. We live and then we die. Ashes to ashes, dust to dust.'

Fern licked more froth from her spoon. 'In high school I did physics for a term. I was dreadful at it, didn't understand anything, but I'll never forget the teacher telling us that energy never dies, it simply changes form. That's when I started believing in eternal life. It was like an epiphany.' She smiled. 'Hey, maybe we knew each other in a past life. I could have been your mum or something.'

Adam laughed and ordered another beer. 'You! I don't think so.'

No, thought Fern, more likely a lover. There were things about Adam that she knew too easily. Connections already forged. And this strange reluctance they both felt. To accept destiny, maybe, because once they did there would be no going back.

Fern shivered as a cloud crossed in front of the sun. 'What if you made an enemy and that hatred carried on through life after life? she asked. 'A very powerful enemy who wanted to destroy you.'

'No way,' said Adam. 'Not possible.' But he'd felt the shadow cross into Fern and a fraction of her fear transferred itself to him. He couldn't fight Fern's demons - he couldn't even keep his own at bay. But it was different for him, his enemy was himself. Maybe that's how it went with enemies, he thought, that somehow they bring out the part of yourself you're afraid of and for that you can't forgive them.

He looked at his watch. 'Hey, we'd better get a move on or we'll miss the bus.'

As the bus made its way down the Channel Highway, Adam withdrew further and further inside himself. Fern remembered how it was for her the first time she went back to Adelaide after moving to Sydney, everything sparking off memories, the joy of return, the old memories, mixing uneasily with the anticipation of seeing her father.

She left Adam to his musings and stared through the window at the countryside. Some of the paddocks they passed were mown, dotted with round hay bales, but in most the grass was long and yellow, the wind brushing it this way and that like a gentle hand smoothing the finest velvet. A sweet grassy smell made its way into the bus, tickling her nose and making her eyes water. She sneezed three times with not even a 'bless you' from Adam, and dug around in her bag for a tissue. They passed through small towns; first Margate and then Snug, then more countryside, nearly always with views of the water. Houses sat on large blocks, with sheep grazing in the paddocks, and orchards with ripening fruit. Fern felt something softening inside her as the bus made its way south. A vague longing, as if she too were coming home.

Chapter Fifteen

The dog noticed them first, setting up a riotous barking before hurtling down the hill to welcome them. They'd got off the bus at the shop in Ferry Road and were walking up a long steep driveway towards a white weatherboard house shaped in a broad V, as if it were opening its arms to embrace the view of the harbour below.

As they walked, a small group of sheep fled across the long grass, panicking at the intrusion. Fern counted five of them.

'Hey, Mutt,' said Adam, as the dog reached them and went into paroxysms of excitement, the back half of his body wagging so hard he looked as if he would snap in two. He paused a moment to give Fern a half-hearted sniff before returning to Adam, whining and whimpering with delight.

'Thought you would have carked it by now.' His eyes brimming with tears, Adam dropped to his knees and let the old dog lick his face.

Fern watched this reunion, a part of her wishing there was someone, somewhere, who would greet her like that. Dogs loved you no matter what. She'd needed that when she was a kid - something to cuddle and confide in. In the end she'd given that honour to a stuffed elephant Grace had made for her one Christmas.

Adam, stood up, laughing. 'Look at him, panting away. After this he'll probably need to sleep for the rest of the day.'

Fern reached down to stroke the old dog. His hair was grey in places, there were bald patches on his back and he smelled pretty horrible, but the love in his eyes made up for all that as he followed them, wheezing, up the hill to the house.

'Hello?' someone called, a question mark in her voice.

Fern looked up to see a woman standing near the gate at the top of the drive. She was shielding her eyes from the sun, trying to make out the figures walking up the hill. As they got closer, Fern could see she was stocky, with thick solid ankles and sturdy calves below her dress. Her dark hair was pulled back into a ponytail and streaked heavily with grey, and her face was weathered and heavily wrinkled, especially around the eyes. She looked as if she'd spent her life outdoors.

'Hey, Mum,' said Adam, a note of resignation in his voice.

There was a pause. 'Adam? Is that you, Adam?' They were close now and the woman let out a quick gasp and put her hand to her mouth. 'Oh Adam … I didn't … I didn't know what had happened to you.'

Adam and his mother stood facing each other awkwardly, as if unsure how to step across the space between them. Fern watched the flood of emotions cross the woman's face - love, excitement, joy, disbelief and anger - all in the space of a few seconds.

'You're safe,' she said finally. 'That's all that matters.' Then she stepped forward, taking Adam in her arms and holding him tight, the tears pouring down her cheeks and onto his t-shirt. 'Here,' she said eventually, pushing him away, 'let me look at you.' She stared at her son with a look of increasing concern. 'You've changed. Oh, Adam, where have you been?'

Adam's voice was gruff, almost angry, as he spoke. Fern could see he was struggling to hold himself together. 'In Sydney,' he said. 'Hanging out.'

His mother looked puzzled. 'But why?'

Adam shrugged. 'Hey,' he said, glancing at Fern. 'Guess I should introduce you. Mum, this is Fern. Fern, this is my mum - Iris.'

Iris held out both hands and took one of Fern's, shaking it eagerly. 'You're tiny. And so beautiful. Oh Adam, I'm so pleased you've brought your girlfriend home for Christmas.'

Adam and Fern exchanged panicked glances. 'She's not …' said Adam. 'She's just a friend.'

Iris smiled. 'Yes, a special one. I can tell.'

Fern sent Adam a desperate look, but he just smiled fondly at her, a big open smile so his mother could see. 'Yeah,' he said. 'She's pretty special.'

The pause that followed Adam's pronouncement stretched too long for Fern's comfort. They all stood there: the dog panting, a long strand of saliva dribbling from the corner of his mouth; Fern blushing and wondering what the hell Adam thought he was up to; Adam smiling without a hint of embarrassment; and Iris's eyes shining with happiness once more.

'Come in, come in,' said Iris, pushing open the gate. 'Make sure you shut it behind you, those bloody sheep keep getting in and eating the rhubarb. I thought the leaves were supposed to be poisonous, but those stupid creatures don't seem to care.'

They followed her into the back garden, which was dotted with outbuildings: a laundry, a dilapidated shed, and a chicken pen with a rusty galvanised iron roof. Behind the house a rough driveway circled an array of fruit trees. Near the house an old station wagon was parked next to a rusty water tank on a stand, a profusion of mint growing underneath, and next to that was a large, fenced vegetable garden.

As they passed the water tank, Iris rapped her knuckles on the galvanised iron, listening for the change in tone that would tell her the water levels. 'Almost out,' she said sadly. 'It'll have to be short showers till the next rains.' She ushered them into the house. 'Shoes off,' she said apologetically. 'I have to make that rule, otherwise Michael comes galumphing in still wearing his muddy boots and it takes me an hour to clean up after him.'

'Where is Michael?' asked Adam.

'Oh, he's out somewhere, probably helping Stan on his boat … He's good with his hands,' she added, her voice taking on a defensive tone that made Fern wonder if Iris was always having to explain away her younger son. Iris smiled at Adam. 'He'll be so pleased to see you.'

'Yeah, me too,' said Adam, although Fern sensed from the look on his face that Adam's relationship with his brother wasn't straightforward.

They stepped into the lounge room, which was huge and lined with windows stretching from floor to ceiling. Fern felt a wave of vertigo as the vast, beautiful view spread out before them: the curved detail of the hills opposite, the flurry of colour from the hundreds of yachts moored in the bay, and the water, its sparkling silver blue filling the room and sending rippling shadows of light and dark across the far wall.

'It's lovely,' she gasped.

'Yes, isn't it,' said Iris proudly. 'Even after all these years, I still love it.'

Fern looked around the large room with its polished wooden floorboards. At one end an ageing leather lounge suite was arranged around an open fireplace, a television and a colourful rug. At the other end stood a dining table and chairs and a huge dresser. The middle of the room was taken up with an ancient slow-combustion wood fire; and opposite that, double doors led out onto a verandah.

Her eyes were drawn to the mantelpiece, which was cluttered with framed photographs. One was of a young, beaming Iris with her husband on their wedding day; another showed what must have been Adam as a baby, bald except for a blond tuft on his forehead, his face round and dimpled.

'Cute,' said Fern, laughing as Adam winced.

Fern looked at another photo of Adam, in his school uniform this time and wearing a wicked smile, with his hair slicked down neatly as if someone had just wet the comb and shoved it in place for the photograph.

'He was such a mischievous little brat,' said Iris, smiling fondly at the photograph. 'Always getting himself into trouble.'

'Still am,' said Adam, putting his arm around his mother's shoulder.

'And that's Michael and his dad, just before …' Iris's voice changed as she stared wistfully at the photograph Adam had lifted off the mantelpiece. It was easy to spot the similarities between Michael and his father. They had the same large mouths and open smiling faces.

Iris sighed. 'Now, would you like a cup of tea, or a cold drink?'

'Tea please,' said Fern. She left Adam staring at the photograph and followed Iris into the kitchen, where a long row of windows looked out over the back garden. This had to be the sunniest house Fern had ever been in.

'You'll have to excuse the mess,' said Iris. 'I was just making the Christmas pudding. What luck you've arrived now, you can both give it a stir and make a wish.'

'Come on then,' said Iris, 'before I put it on the stove … Adam!'

Fern didn't know what to wish for, or at least couldn't formulate her desires into anything concrete, so she let Adam go first, watching him stirring the pudding mixture, and wondering what was he was thinking. When Adam handed Fern the spoon she was suddenly overwhelmed with wishes. As she stirred, she wished for a safe end to this journey, then for somewhere that she could belong and for a path in her life that she could follow. And, she added silently, hoping she wasn't being too greedy, she wanted to kiss Adam again.

'Now, where did I put the brandy?' Iris opened a door and stepped into a large walk-in pantry. Fern peered in at the shelves lined with jars of jams and chutneys, rice and flour, lentils and chickpeas, oats, icing sugar, all neatly labelled. It felt safe and ordered. With a pantry like that you could never starve.

'There,' said Iris, when she'd put the pudding on to steam. 'Now let's have that cup of tea before I make the dinner. Adam, there's a beer in the fridge if you'd rather.'

They sat at the dining table in the living room, Fern's eyes straying constantly to the view while Iris poured tea from the pot. Her wrists were thick and her hands square, the fingers stubby and capable - the sort of hands that could open jars or turn stuck taps. Fern took a sip of her tea; it was strong, just the way she liked it. She began to relax, feeling almost as if she was on holiday. Christmas was so close, they'd need to stay with Adam's family for a few days so she could put off tracking down her father until later.

'How long have you two known each other?' asked Iris, and immediately Fern tensed warily.

'A couple of months or so,' said Adam, answering for her.

'Not long then,' said Iris, sounding momentarily disappointed. 'Still, love works in funny ways. When I met your father, I knew. We both did. Six months later we were married.'

Blushing, Fern stared out the window, concentrating on the view.

'Are you from Sydney, dear?' asked Iris.

'No, Adelaide. I was studying in Sydney.'

'What were you studying?'

'Fashion design.'

Fern saw the look of surprise on Adam's face and then his attempt to hide it. This was a ridiculous farce: they hardly knew anything about each other.

'That sounds interesting. Very glamorous, I imagine.'

'Not really.' Fern didn't want to talk about herself, and anyway, she could see that Iris was itching to ask Adam questions - the important ones: Where have you been? Why didn't you get in touch? But she was too polite to do so in front of Fern.

'Ah, here comes Michael now,' said Iris.

They watched a giant of a man come striding up the hill and disappear around the side. A few seconds later a voice called eagerly, 'Mum, look at …'

'SHOES!'

Fern heard the thud of boots landing on the floor before Michael came into the living room, cradling something carefully in his hands, on which his eyes were fixed. 'Look, Mum… he said without looking up. He opened the palms of his hands to reveal a bird, carved delicately and with amazing detail, out of a single piece of wood.

'Oh Michael, that's lovely.'

All at once his face reddened and he snatched it away. 'It's a surprise,' he said.

'That's okay, sweetheart, I'll forget all about it, I promise … Look, Michael, we've got visitors.'

For the first time he noticed the other people in the room. 'Hello.' His face opened into a shy smile before he suddenly recognised his brother. 'Adam!' he cried and rushed to embrace him. Adam stood up and was engulfed by his younger brother, who sobbed openly, banging him on the back and squeezing the breath out of him.

'Adam, oh Adam.'

'Hey, Michael, it's good to see you.' Adam could feel something happening inside of him. It had started when the plane landed at Hobart airport and it was getting worse by the minute. Now he felt as if his heart was tearing open. Unable to hold it in any longer, he dissolved into tears, his chest heaving as sobs racked him.

'It's all right, Adam, don't worry, I love you,' said Michael, stroking Adam's head while he cried.

Mastering his emotions, Adam smiled and wiped his eyes. 'How are you, mate?'

'Good.' Michael nodded his head vigorously. 'Good.'

Adam was surprised at the sudden love he felt for this brother of his. He'd always resented Michael, the little brother who'd followed Adam around everywhere, scattered his toys, broken his favourite train set. The brother who never grew up. The one for whom Adam was always responsible. 'Adam, can you look after Michael?'… 'Adam, I thought I told you to watch your brother.' And then that last time when his world had fallen apart forever: 'Adam, where is he?'

When Iris introduced Michael to Fern, he said hello and hung his head shyly. The small group sat at the table finishing their tea, somewhat awkwardly. Michael was silent, staring at his brother and at Fern in turn. Iris talked to fill in the spaces left by all those unasked questions.

'I didn't get any work in the shop this year,' she said. 'Sales are down. They're just hanging in there, poor things. Wouldn't it be a shame to see the shop close?'

'How are you managing?' asked Adam.

'Times are tight, but we're growing a lot of our own food and that saves on costs. And Michael's got green fingers, haven't you, darling?'

Michael smiled and proudly held up his hands to show Fern. They were big and grubby, with dirt under the nails. Fern smiled. He's a clay man, she thought, fashioned from the earth.

'We've just finished planting most of the summer vegetables,' said Iris. 'But the rabbits are out of control. Michael's had to dig the fence deep to stop them burrowing under. The rainfall's down this year too, so I don't know how long we can afford to keep watering the vegies as well as the fruit trees. As it is I'm carrying out the dishwater for the herbs.' She sighed and Fern could see how tired she was, drawn down with worry and responsibility. 'It'll be another month before we get the plums and nectarines and maybe another two before the apples start. They'll see us through the year if I can get all the preserving done.'

'You've still got the sheep, though.'

Iris nodded. 'They keep the grass down, but it's so dry this year I don't know if we'll have enough for them all. If I could catch one of the young ones, I'd send it down to the butcher's and have it brought back in a cardboard box. That'd be meat for a few months … Maybe you could do it, Adam. Michael's useless, he won't hurt a fly.'

'Sure Mum,' said Adam, 'I'll do it.' He felt heavy with guilt. It was obvious how much she needed someone to hold things together and he'd been too busy wallowing in his own concerns.

Iris smiled at Adam, her eyes filled with love. 'Oh well,' she said, gathering up the teacups. 'I'd better stop my whingeing and get on with dinner. Would you mind picking some cherries, Adam? They're just ripe in time for Christmas. I'll do us a cherry pie.' She smiled at Fern. 'That's always been a favourite with the men in our family.'

'Sure,' said Adam.

'I'll help,' said Fern, rushing out after him. She was afraid of being left alone with Iris. Afraid of being asked unanswerable questions. If they were going to get through this visit they would need to work something out, make sure their stories matched.

'What are we going to do?' she asked when they were out of earshot.

'Do?'

'Yes, you know, about the girlfriend-boyfriend stuff.'

Adam smiled, then leaned over and pulled Fern close, kissing her hard on the lips. The suddenness of it surprised Fern into letting down her defences. She could feel herself melting into Adam, could feel the hardness in his groin as her hips rubbed up against him. In those few seconds she knew. They both did.

'Look, Mum, they're kissing,' shouted Michael, bringing them back to their senses. Iris looked up from the kitchen bench where she was working and smiled through the window at them.

'There,' said Adam, releasing her. 'That should do it.'

'Do what?' asked Fern. This was ridiculous. Her heart was pounding in her chest, shivers were running up and down her body, and anger was rising inside her as she realised just how much she wanted him.

He looked at her with a strange smile and shrugged. 'I don't know, make it look real or something.'

'You can't do this to me,' she said, her voice sounding high and strangled.

'Shhh.' Adam put his finger against her lips.

Fern glanced back at the kitchen where Iris was still rolling pastry and smiling to herself.

'It isn't fair,' she hissed.

'What?'

'Don't act all innocent. One minute you kiss me and then …' She stopped, not knowing how to go on without revealing how she felt.

'Then what?'

'Then nothing,' she said savagely, grabbing the bowl from him and ripping cherries off the tree. They kept working until the bowl was full and Fern's anger had drained away. Then they picked more anyway, stuffing the sweet fruit into their mouths until Adam laughed and said she looked like she'd been sucking someone's blood.

'Why can't we have a serious conversation?' asked Fern.

'What do you want to talk about?'

'I don't know … How does it feel, coming home like this?'

'It's complicated.'

'See, you never say anything. You've got a beautiful home and a lovely mother and a brother who loves you to bits and all you can say is *it's complicated.*'

Adam sighed. 'Yeah, it's a great place, but things only ever look perfect from the outside. When you're in them there's always crap to deal with.'

'Like what?' she asked.

'This was never really my home. Physically yes, but that was all.' He leaned against the cherry tree and stared past Fern. 'When I was little we used to live on a sheep station up in the Midlands. It had been in the family for generations. I loved the place. I was supposed to take over from Dad, just like he'd taken over from his dad.' He paused. 'Only he went and died when I was eleven.' There was a bitterness in Adam's voice, as if he blamed his father for dying.

'What happened?'

'It was stupid. Michael went and ran in front of the tractor. Dad turned the wheel quickly, trying not to hit him and it rolled.' His voice broke. 'Right on top of Dad.'

Fern reached out and took Adam's hand. 'I'm sorry.'

'Thing is, I was supposed to be looking after Michael.'

Fern caught a glimpse of the hurt in Adam's eyes before he looked away. 'You were a kid,' she said. 'You have to let that go.'

'Yeah, right,' said Adam, unconvinced.

'So why did your family move here?' asked Fern.

'Mum reckoned she couldn't manage the farm alone. I would have helped out, but she sold it anyway. I dunno, maybe her heart wasn't in it after Dad died. I never asked. We moved down here, nearer to her folks so they could look after us while Mum worked. Though they're dead now.'

Adam sighed again. There were too many deaths, too many disappointments. If only he could focus on what was here, now: a cherry tree, Fern, and the sun sparkling on the water. It would be perfect, if only he could banish the certainty that he didn't deserve such perfect moments. It wasn't just his dad dying like that, it was Michael too, born with a cord wrapped tightly around his neck and his face blue, his brain starved of oxygen for too long. After that, Adam had always felt his own normality as a reproach in the face of his brother's weakness. He knew it was stupid to be alive and not live, but it wasn't just him - that was the way most people existed, day after day, year after year.

'Ouch,' said Fern, jumping as something nipped her calf. Looking down she met the eye of a large white duck, its head cocked to one side as it peered up at her.

'That's Doreena,' said Adam, his mood lifting suddenly. 'She's usually very friendly. Must have thought you were a worm. Here, pat her like this, she loves it.' Adam leaned over and stroked the back of the duck's neck. 'Hey Doreena, that's good isn't it,' he crooned.

It was as if he'd hypnotised the duck; her long neck stretched out and the lids of her eyes folded upwards as she surrendered to an ecstatic trance. Fern smiled wryly, thinking how similar they were, she and the duck, helpless to resist the minute Adam touched them.

'I've been saving this for a special occasion,' said Iris, opening a dusty bottle of red wine. 'And I can't think of anything more special than this.'

Michael, his eyes fixed unnervingly on Fern, held out his glass and Iris poured in a small amount, topping it up with water. 'Just a drop,' she said. 'You know you're a useless drunk.' She held up her glass. 'Cheers. To a real family Christmas.'

'Are we going to Bruny?' asked Adam, when they'd all clinked glasses and drunk.

'Of course,' said Iris, as if she was shocked by the question.

'We have a shack over on Bruny Island,' Adam explained to Fern. 'It's where we always go for Christmas and Easter, kind of a family tradition.'

Iris spooned out lavish helpings of pasta with home-made pesto sauce and thin-sliced parmesan on top. 'We'll go Christmas Eve. I've got too much to do tomorrow – we'll have to get some supplies. Iris rolled her eyes. 'It'll be chaos in town, everyone running around doing their last-minute stuff. But there's nothing for it, seeing as you insist on coming without notice. I can't have you starving now, can I?

'Don't worry, Mum, we'll help with the shopping, hey Fern?'

Fern nodded but she was feeling more and more self-conscious. Michael's eyes were still fixed on her and she didn't know where to look.

'Michael, it's rude to stare,' said Iris, noting her discomfort. 'Michael …'

Suddenly, mid-mouthful, Michael launched himself out of his seat and embraced Fern. 'I like you,' he said.

Iris laughed. 'Well, that's a compliment Fern. The boy doesn't say much, but he means what he says and he's not usually easy with new people.'

Fern smiled. 'I like you too,' she said.

As the meal progressed and Fern downed a second glass of wine, she was able to relax. Adam cleared the table then returned carrying a beer and joking with his brother. This was a whole new side of Adam, and one that Fern liked.

Iris came in, triumphantly carrying the cherry pie. 'Here you go, I haven't made one since you left, Adam. Couldn't bring myself to eat it without you.' Her eyes were brimming with tears as she cut the pie, doling out huge portions and pouring generous amounts of cream over each serving.

Fern only managed to eat half of hers, but Adam was a bottomless pit. 'I'd forgotten how good this pie is,' he said, reaching for a third helping.

Fern tried to stifle a yawn but failed. It had been a long day.

'Heavens, you must be exhausted, poor thing,' said Iris. 'You two can sleep in my bedroom.' She waved away Fern's wide-eyed protest. 'Don't be silly, of course you should. It's the only double bed in the house.'

'Where are you going to sleep, Mum?' asked Adam.

'In the little room. You know, the one that used to be my sewing room. I've got a perfectly good camp bed we can put up in there.'

'You can't sleep on a camp bed.'

'Of course I can.'

'I'll sleep in the sewing room.'

'Adam dear, I don't think Fern would want to share a bed with me.'

'Put Michael in it then.'

'He'd break it. Now I don't want to hear any more arguments, Adam,' said Iris sternly. 'It's not every day I get a surprise visit from my son and his girlfriend.'

'Yeah, I know. I should have rung.'

Iris kissed Adam affectionately on the cheek. 'Never mind, love, I'm just pleased you're here. This is the best Christmas present I've had for years.'

'This is creepy,' said Adam, as he shut the door behind them. 'I can't sleep in Mum's bed.' He looked at Fern. 'Not with you. I mean, shit, it wouldn't feel right.'

'It's your fault. Why did you let her think we're together?'

'What else should I have said? Hey Mum, I met this girl a few days ago, she'd just escaped from the nuthouse, thinks her dad's trying to kill her, thought I'd bring her for Christmas … ' He looked at her sardonically. 'Should I go on?'

Fern laughed uneasily. 'When you put it like that, I guess we don't have much choice. I'll get changed in the bathroom.'

It was a big bed, but even with them both hugging opposite edges, the tension between them was strong. On the dressing-table a clock ticked loudly, Fern's heart beating in time with it until she could no longer tell them apart and she was afraid that if the clock stopped then her heart would too. Fern had always found it difficult to sleep with a clock in the room, but tonight it was impossible. She listened to the silence descend on the house as Iris switched off the lights and settled in her creaky camp bed in the next room. Outside was noisy by comparison: the occasional furious shrieking of the plovers as something approached too close, a growing symphony of frogs around the neighbours' dam; the scuttle of mice, a ghostly hiss of a possum, a sheep briefly left alone and bleating for the others, and sometimes the clear sound of voices rising up from the still valley.

After a while Adam got up quietly and left the room, leaving Fern alone with the clock, its noise filling her head, her tension boiling over into anger. A great ball of energy rose inside her. It grew, swelling without direction, and she grew with it, feeling herself suddenly inside the skin of a bear, catching a glimpse of the soft black fur in the corner of her eyes, as if she'd shape-changed. Feeling huge and unstoppable, Fern directed all her frustrated fury at the clock, her anger surging, tumbling over itself towards it.

The ticking stopped.

At first Fern thought she must be imagining it; that somehow she'd shut out the sound, let it merge with all the other sounds of the night. In the dim light of the moon, she slipped quietly out of bed and looked closely at the clock's hands. There was no doubt about it: they weren't moving anymore. She wondered if this was her doing, and remembered the magazine that had hurled itself at her mother, a small thing but not so easily dismissed.

Wondering where Adam was, Fern lay down wearily and closed her eyes, the remaining night sounds fading around her as she finally slipped into sleep. Almost immediately she found herself climbing up some rusty metal stairs on the side of an old warehouse building, where she was met at the door by the Bear Handler. 'Come,' he said.

Fern followed him through the door and into a vast open room, the walls rough stone, the ceiling laced with giant wooden beams.

'You are in grave danger,' said the Bear Handler. 'It is time for you to learn how to let go of your fear and for that you will need to call on the courage and playfulness of the bear. You must face your enemy and be strong, or you will die.'

'But I don't know who he is. I don't know why he hates me. How can I face him?

'We are all made up of many stories, but they are of no importance. The stories themselves will not release you from your prison. If you get caught in them they will provide new traps. Only the patterns matter. It is in those that you will see the places you are caught, repeating yourself, lifetime after lifetime.' He glanced past Fern as if he was expecting someone, his cloak shimmering softly in the light. 'There is time for one more warning. You are remembering many things that you had forgotten. Be wary of becoming absorbed in childish tricks.'

'Like the clock?' asked Fern.

He nodded gravely. 'You must look beyond these tricks, for they are only the side-effects of something far greater.' He took a step away from Fern. 'Now you must learn to let go of your fear. Remember it is all in your breath … Prepare yourself.'

'Wait,' cried Fern, then gasped as the huge room filled with a sudden urgent sense of danger.

'Breathe out,' said the Bear Handler, and she did so, in a rush, breathing in and out, in and out, as the sense of menace grew. 'Slowly,' said the Bear Handler.

Fern tried to breathe slowly, taking her time, a long slow out-breath, rather than quick gasping in-breaths - the opposite of everything her instincts told her to do. Gradually she felt lighter and lighter until her feet left the ground. It happened slowly at first, just a few centimetres until she felt suddenly afraid and instantly landed with a thud. After a time she was doing it easily, sometimes floating, sometimes sinking, once rising high enough to touch the roof of the warehouse. The floating made her laugh with joy, but always she felt the danger there, lurking too close for comfort.

'Good. Remember, it's the fear that holds you down. Without it you can fly.'

The Bear Handler smiled at Fern. 'Now, it is time. This you will have to do alone.'

'No,' she said, alarmed. 'I'm not ready.'

But he had disappeared, leaving Fern standing at the edge of a deep pit. Below her a circular stone staircase led to the bottom where she knew without being told that the thing she feared was at the bottom. She also knew that if she went down there it would try to kill her. Fern wanted to turn away but knew that would give it power and only defer the moment when she must eventually confront it.

Reluctantly Fern began walking down the stairs. There was no banister to hold onto and she didn't know how deep the drop was. She stepped carefully, feeling her way in the dark, leaning close to the wall for safety. The atmosphere thickened as she descended and her heartbeat grew louder and louder in the silence because even the sound of her feet was muted by the thick dust that lay on each step, undisturbed for many lifetimes. The air became dense, sucking her in like quicksand and sapping her strength. Her breath quickened as she struggled to find oxygen in the impenetrable darkness and felt her dread growing with each step. This was madness, she told herself, there was something down there and she was walking into a trap.

The moment her foot touched the floor of the pit she felt its surging anger, not circling her, not waiting, just an awful intent, so focused it was impossible to deflect. This was a monstrous creature she felt in the dark, its form not recognisable, but its intention clear as it surged at her, bringing a gigantic axe down on her head. Instinctively she crossed her hands above her head in a futile gesture and a second later it forced its way through her hands, splitting her head, the blood gushing …

Gasping, Fern opened her eyes and reached for the place on her head where the axe had landed, fully expecting to feel the warm wetness of blood, but there was nothing there. As her breath eased and her heartbeat slowed, the dread she'd felt was slowly replaced with an immense gratitude that she was still alive. The Bear Handler had given her a lesson, and then a challenge. She had lost this round, forgotten her staff again, but at least she'd faced whatever it was - a man or a monster, she didn't know. Despite her fear, Fern felt a sense of triumph. For the first time she'd chosen to seek it out.

Chapter Sixteen

They left early on Christmas Eve to beat the rush but even so the queue already stretched a long way down Ferry Road.

'The worst time of the year for the ferry,' Iris grumbled. 'You'd think they'd let residents on first wouldn't you, but no, we've got to queue along with all the tourists.'

Michael and Mutt were sitting in the front next to Iris. Fern and Adam were in the back seat, an esky between them, the floor packed with sleeping bags and presents, leaving hardly any room for their feet. The back of the station wagon was full too, laden with more eskies and bags, and a tent, because Iris had discreetly suggested it would be more private outside for Adam and Fern than in the shack. Every spare space was filled with supplies, most of which they'd bought in town the previous day.

Fern had been surprised at how small Hobart was. The centre was tiny compared with Sydney; but even so it was busy in the run-up to Christmas. They'd separated, agreeing to meet two hours later. At first it had felt strange being alone again. Adam had stayed so close to her since the trip to Katoomba, never really letting her out of his sight. An unofficial bodyguard. Fern glanced around once or twice, but couldn't convince herself she would be followed here. The crowds were too intent, rushing past each other with lists running over and over inside their heads. Fern was swamped by the thoughts of the people around her; if she concentrated she could work out what was on each person's list. She tried to switch her mind off, but the impressions kept foisting themselves on her, leaving her tired and confused. The Bear Handler was right, these tricks weren't so great. She had to pull herself together.

Fern decided she wouldn't send anything to her mother; it was too late and anyway she didn't want to let Grace know she was in Tasmania. Even so, it hurt to think of her mother alone at home in Adelaide, her father in hospital, neither of them knowing what had become of her. She pushed these thoughts out of her mind and concentrated on the task at hand. She only had to buy three presents so it should be easy but she knew so little about Adam's family. In the end she found everything she needed in a bookshop: a cookbook for Iris with recipes for garden produce, an illustrated book of birds for Michael, and for Adam she bought a book about the Tasmanian wilderness. The shop had wrapped them for her and now they were safe in her backpack stowed at her feet. Not much, but something at least to repay the kindness of this substitute family.

Once on the ferry they left the car and stood at the front, the cold wind on their faces, water splashing up occasionally as the ship ploughed across D'Entrecasteaux Channel. Feeling inexplicably happy, Fern licked her lips and tasted salt. Michael started dancing, jigging from one leg to the other, waving his arms. A happy dance to the ocean and the sky. Adam was embarrassed and turned away, but Fern loved it. She felt good here on the water, so far from the tensions of Sydney. Then Michael took her hand and pulled her this way and that until she was dancing too, not caring about Adam's red face or the stares from people in the cars lined up behind them.

'An island off an island off an island,' said Adam as they drove onto Bruny Island. 'I always love getting off the ferry at this end. It feels like I'm leaving the world behind. Some people feel isolated here, but I never do.'

Fern nodded, still savouring the relief of leaving behind her problems. As they wound their way along the narrow isthmus from north to south Bruny, she stared intently out the window. On her right was the channel, calm and still, and to her left was the ocean, its waves beating against the coast. One side tranquil, the other wild: two faces of nature. Fern felt she recognised it all, that she was returning home. Her usual disquiet had been replaced by an unfamiliar sense of wellbeing. Perhaps this was what it felt like to belong somewhere.

When they arrived at the shack, Adam showed her around, more enthusiastic than she'd ever seen him and filled with memories of his childhood. 'This was my grandparents' shack,' he explained. 'They built it years ago, when they were first married. I spent heaps of time here.'

It was a ramshackle place with crooked lines and a wobbly stone slab for a front step. The walls looked as if they had been built from driftwood, the planks weathered by the wind and the salt. Years ago someone had painted it the deep blue of a late afternoon sky, though that was flaking and now it was a motley mess of peeling blue paint, a creamy undercoat, and beneath that the variable tones of natural wood. Rooms had been added as needed. First a long kitchen running along the entire length of the front of the house, and two dark rooms behind, one stuffed full of junk, the other a small lounge with a fireplace and couch squeezed in.

'That's where everyone used to sleep when I was really little. Then later I helped Grandad build the upstairs bit. Come and see.'

Fern followed Adam up a wooden staircase that wound in a spiral from the lounge room. Upstairs were two tiny bedrooms, both with sloping ceilings and wide windows looking out over the ocean. It felt organic, fresh and wild, yet safe from the elements, even with the wind creeping its way through the cracks. Fern liked the building's eccentricity too, so many styles and hardly any ninety-degree angles.

Outside one of the windows was a wide old rambling oak tree that dwarfed the house. 'I used to climb out this window onto that branch and sit there for hours, listening to the wind and the sea,' said Adam, smiling at the memory. 'Michael tried to climb out once and fell. He broke his arm, I think. After that he didn't try again.' He sighed. 'It was the only thing that was all mine. Aside from the surfing - Michael couldn't swim.'

Adam thought about the hours he'd spent in the sea, sitting on his board waiting for the right wave. Only it wasn't just about the waves: it was the space he'd wanted. Just him and the ocean and nothing to be responsible for. Standing in this room, immersed in his childhood memories, he felt a surge of pity for the boy he'd been, confined and moody. A boy without a dad. His granddad had tried to fill in the gaps for him, but Adam had resisted, building walls around the hurt and the loneliness.

'Come on,' he said, forcing himself back into the present. 'Let's unpack the car.'

Later that day Fern was standing in the kitchen peeling potatoes for tomorrow's Christmas lunch. Michael had disappeared hours ago, Adam was putting up the tent and Iris was next door chatting with the neighbours. Fern could hear the rise and fall of their voices, the odd burst of laughter, and behind it all the rhythm of waves breaking on sand. The view from the kitchen was even more beautiful than the one from the living room in Kettering. It looked out across Storm Bay to the wide open ocean, a headland at one end, the water changing colour and tone from one minute to the next. You could never be bored with this view. Fern opened the window and breathed deeply of the sea air, seaweed and salt mingling with the scent of thyme and oregano, parsley and basil from the herb garden that ran along the front of the house.

Despite a blunt peeler and too many potatoes, Fern felt content. Her tense jaw had loosened, as had her shoulders, and her feet rested on the ground as if they were supposed to be there. It was only by relaxing that she realised how tense she usually was.

As Fern dropped another peeled potato into the bowl of water there was a creaking sound behind her like a door opening. She looked up, trying to locate the sound, but it hadn't come from any door she could see. If anything it seemed to emanate from the middle of the room. Fern dismissed it and went back to her peeling, but seconds later Mutt turned up at her feet, whining, his tail between his legs.

'What's wrong, Mutt?' She reached down to pat him and he nuzzled into her, trembling. 'It's okay boy, there's nothing to be afraid of.'

With the dog close at her heels, Fern walked to the middle of the room to investigate; peering at the floor she noticed a line of raised wood that suggested there had once been a wall here. The room must have been extended at some stage. She wasn't surprised; the shack had the organic feel of a place that had started as one thing, but had been reshaped many times according to the needs of the residents. With Mutt following, she checked in the tiny living room then climbed up the curving wooden staircase to the bedrooms upstairs. They were empty, but the dog was becoming more nervous and making her uneasy. She led him downstairs and opened the back door. 'Out you go, boy.'

Mutt slunk out, leaving Fern alone in the house, but the atmosphere had changed and the contentment she'd felt earlier had disappeared. Now the sun had slipped behind a cloud, the sea looked ominous and the laughter next door was too loud. Fern dismissed the goose bumps on her arms and went back to peeling potatoes, occasionally looking around to check there was nothing behind her. She was relieved when Iris came in carrying a bowl, just as Fern finished the last of the potatoes.

'Are you coming or going, Mutt?' said Iris impatiently as the dog stood undecided in the doorway, whining. 'What's wrong with that dog? ' She put the bowl on the bench and Fern found herself looking an enormous lobster in the eye. 'Rick gave us a cray. What a beauty! We'll have it tomorrow night with the prawns.'

Adam came in, grabbed a beer from the fridge and sat down at the table. 'Christmas Eve,' he said. 'God it's good to be back.'

Iris smiled at her son and kissed him on the top of his head.

Fern cleaned up the peel and wiped down the bench top, trying to find her way back to the relaxed space she'd been in only minutes before. But she was unable to shake the feeling of uneasiness. Though Iris and Adam seemed oblivious to it, there was a tightness in the atmosphere, as if something was pressing in on her.

Then Michael came in, a broad smile on his face. Two steps inside and his smile disappeared. First he looked puzzled, then he cringed, leaning backwards as if he was under attack. 'Away!' he shouted, dashing towards Fern and standing, arms outstretched, between her and something she couldn't see. Still trembling, Mutt joined him in front of Fern and began barking.

'What's going on?' asked Iris.

'What is it, Michael?' asked Adam.

'Away!' shouted Michael again, pointing at the spot in the middle of the room where Fern had heard the creaking.

'Really, this is ridiculous,' said Iris, taking Michael's arm. 'Calm down, dear. And you,' she turned to Mutt, 'stop that barking.' Mutt ignored her, so Adam took him by the collar and led him outside where he started whining again.

Michael grabbed Fern's hand and peered intently into her face. 'It wants you,' he said.

Fern shuddered.

'Michael, stop it, you're scaring Fern,' said Iris. 'Adam, why don't you take him outside and show him the tent? I'm sorry, Fern, you'll think we're mad. Michael's just sensitive, that's all. One foot in this world and one in another. That's the way he's always been. You ignore him.'

'Come on, Michael,' said Adam. As he left he caught Fern's eye and raised his eyebrows in a question.

Fern shrugged and shook her head, as if it meant nothing but her instincts were screaming at her to beware. A part of her understood what had just happened. Somehow the malevolent force in her dreams had stepped through and both Mutt and Michael could see it, though Fern could only feel it. She clasped her hands together trying to stop them shaking. Even here, on an island off an island off an island, she wasn't safe.

The rest of the day was awkward and strained, with Michael and Mutt staying close to Fern, Adam looking puzzled and Iris trying unsuccessfully to pretend nothing was wrong. Fern was relieved when she could politely excuse herself and go to bed.

The tent was tiny and smelled as if it hadn't been used for some time. Adam had called it a two-person tent but it looked only big enough for one. She unzipped the flap and crawled in, then changed quickly into her pyjamas and slipped into her sleeping bag. Immediately she could feel something hard pressing into her back through the thin mat. The torchlight cast strange shadows on the sides of the tent, which billowed gently in and out with the breeze. Just a thin piece of material between her and nature, but it felt safe. Unlike the regular ticking of the clock in Kettering, the regular crashing of the waves calmed Fern. She wriggled around until she found a comfortable position then lay still, listening to the sounds; at first just a mass of noise, but after a while she began to distinguish between them: the hum of insects, the hoot of an owl, the occasional crack of the galvanised iron roof as it cooled in the night air …

Fern jumped when she heard the sound of the zip, realising she must have dozed off.

'Sorry,' said Adam, as his elbow dug into her leg.

They lay side by side, almost touching but not quite, both cocooned in their sleeping bags and trying to ignore the electricity building between them. Fern knew Adam's kisses had been fronts to deceive the Bloodhound and then his mother, but surely she wasn't the only one who'd felt it was more than that.

The tension was becoming too much for Fern. Tentatively she reached for Adam, putting her fingertips lightly on his chest. She heard his breath catch and he turned his head slowly towards her. It was too dark to read the look in his eyes, to know if they held a question mark, disdain or desire. This time she took the lead, reaching for his mouth, pulling his head closer, and Adam responded hungrily, devouring her lips as if he'd been waiting, poised and ready for this moment. They unzipped their sleeping bags, Fern's hands sliding under Adam's t-shirt, feeling the light hair on his stomach, his soft skin, her lips sliding down to his neck, his chest, as she took in the smell of him, memorising it. Adam groaned and rolled onto his elbow, his hand running roughly across her breasts, his mouth following, sucking her nipples, then moving down to her belly where he licked his way across her hips. Her hands tugged at her shorts and then Adam's tongue searched between her legs, probing deeper and deeper. Fern writhed and arched, trying to ignore the sounds from outside – it was Mutt scratching insistently at the tent door, front paws scraping up and down the material as he whined desperately to get in.

'Go away,' growled Adam, but Mutt only became more insistent. 'Damn it, he'll put a hole in the tent.' Adam sat up and unzipped the door, snapping, 'Piss off, Mutt,' but the dog ignored him and darted into the tent, settling himself down next to Fern.

'It's pretty obvious who's boss around here,' said Fern, laughing and patting the dog. 'Phew, he stinks.'

'Mutt. Out,' said Adam sternly.

Mutt whined but refused to move, so Adam pushed him roughly out of the tent before turning back to Fern. But the mood was dispelled.

'I need the toilet,' said Fern, filled suddenly with misgivings, and aware that she had made a promise to herself not to get close to Adam. A promise she was already breaking.

She made her way towards the outhouse behind the shack. The moon was high, casting a ghostly silver light across the ground which was scored with deep shadows. Mutt was at her side, staying close, tail right down between his legs and whimpering quietly to himself. Fern didn't notice. She could still taste Adam on her lips, feel his hands on her skin, her body still trembling from his touch. She wanted him but she was afraid. Leaving the toilet door open she sat down and peered out at the stars, the Milky Way so vivid and close it made her dizzy.

As Fern reached over to flush the toilet something surged towards her. She felt its impact though she couldn't see it. Mutt barked furiously then howled briefly before cowering in the corner of the toilet and whining. *Turn away:* the voice came from within her, a deep certainty that this was what she must do. But it was too late, the thing already had her in its clasp. Fern was fighting against something she couldn't see, or even feel. There was nothing discernible, no hands, no outline, or perhaps only a hint of a shadow, shifting and changing, giving her fleeting glimpses of its various forms: a hooded cape, strands of black hair, dark eyes staring through her. Fern knew instinctively that she mustn't stare back. She closed her eyes against it, but that was all she could do. Its strength was immense and its attack focussed on her stomach and chest. She doubled over, trying to protect herself, but again she was too late; she could feel it draining away her strength, as if it had a straw to her belly and was sucking the warmth from her body. First her fingers and toes turned icy, then her arms and legs, her head, and finally her torso. And all the time she could sense its triumph, the glee it felt in the knowledge that it had her.

Everything moved in slow motion as, losing consciousness, she slid to the ground, a part of her lifting up and out of her body. Fern's fear was gradually replaced by a detached curiosity. She could see herself from above, her body slumped on the ground, half in and half out of the outhouse. Then Michael was there, and Adam behind him. Something cold and wet hit Fern's face and she felt a huge jolt, drawing her instantly back to herself. She was lying on the ground, her clothes drenched, the water dripping from her hair and down her face. Shocked, she opened her eyes and saw Michael holding an empty bucket. He was staring at her intently, his whole body shaking with terror. Somehow he'd known what she needed, something to bring her back. Cold water was perfect. Michael had saved her.

Fern tried to thank him but couldn't find a way to form the words. She couldn't smile either, to reassure him, but her mind was crystal clear. Incongruously, a memory came of a time when she had been too frightened to go to school because some of the other kids had been teasing her, calling her names. Her teacher had come to visit, sending her mother into a nervous panic, clattering teaspoons and hauling out the best china. 'True courage,' he'd said to Fern when Grace was out of the room, 'isn't to live without fear. It's to recognise how afraid you are and do it anyway.' Then he'd drained his cup of tea and stood up. 'Don't let the bullies win.' The next day Fern had gone back to school;

she'd decided to stop being a victim. She couldn't remember her teacher telling her that last bit, but she knew it for certain: victims make monsters, monsters make victims. Neither is completely innocent.

Now, lying soaking and shivering on the ground, Fern sensed that she had reached a turning point. She was more afraid than she could remember being. This thing had already weakened her, and now it had taken her to the very brink of death. It could come again at any time; it would come, she had no doubt about that, and next time Michael might not be there to help her. Fern had known for some time that she had to stop running, yet that knowledge had only been in her head, it hadn't penetrated into her heart. With Adam's help she'd turned around physically, catching the Bloodhound and tracing her father, but even so there was something inside her that was still running, still afraid. And this *thing* was feeding off that. Like a vampire it had taken nearly all her energy, stripping her of her life force. If it had succeeded, then she would be dead.

Until now a part of Fern had felt as if she was a character in a fictional story, caught in the pages of a book she could close whenever she wanted to. Now she knew in her heart that she had no such choice. She had to see this through. She had to stop running. From now on, every part of her and every moment of time would be imbued with that knowledge. As she lay on the ground looking up at Michael, his head framed by the moon as if he were an angel, she knew without a doubt that she had to fight.

It could only have been a few seconds since Michael had thrown the water, yet it was as if Fern, Michael and Adam were held, frozen in time. Then Mutt crept up and licked Fern's face, somehow releasing the spell that had held them all in place like statues in a children's party game.

'What the hell's going on?' asked Adam, staring from Michael to Fern and back again. He had seen more than he wanted to admit to himself or anyone else. At first he'd thought Fern had gone mad, struggling like that against nothing. But as she'd fallen to the ground, he'd caught a glimpse of something: a flash of a shoulder, the tilt of a head.

Michael dropped the bucket and sat down suddenly, crumpling as if a puppeteer had let go of his strings. The clarity Fern had felt now fled, leaving a space for shock to set in. She began shivering violently, her teeth chattering uncontrollably.

Adam reached down and picked Fern up in his arms as though she weighed nothing. She felt hollow to him, as if the life had been sucked out of her. 'You're shivering, we'd better get you dry … Jesus, Michael, why'd you throw water all over her?'

'Had to bring her back,' mumbled Michael.

'What the hell are you talking about?' Adam's voice was harsher than he wanted it to be, but Michael seemed oblivious. He was rocking backwards and forwards, staring at the moon and humming to himself. Adam hadn't seen him do that since their father died.

Adam carried Fern back to the tent, tugging a beach towel off the line on the way. He stood her up outside the tent and handed her the towel. 'Here, dry yourself while I get Michael back into the house.'

When he returned, Fern was still standing in the same spot, motionless. She hadn't even begun drying herself.

'Jesus, this is crazy stuff,' said Adam. 'Here, hold your arms up,' he added then pulled off her t-shirt for her and tugged down her wet shorts, lifting her legs one at a time so Fern could step free of them. Then he rubbed her down vigorously with the towel, trying to get the blood flowing through her again. When she was dry, Adam reached into the tent and rummaged around for his shirt. He slipped her arms into the sleeves, then fumbled with the buttons, and rolled up the sleeves so her hands could find a way out of them. Then he helped her back into the tent. Mutt pushed in behind them but this time Adam let the dog stay.

He zipped their sleeping bags together then climbed in next to Fern. She snuggled close to him, slipping her feet under his legs and her hands between his arms and his chest. He flinched from the cold but let her stay there, soaking up his heat.

Gradually her shaking subsided as the warmth entered her belly, working its way back in, her torso first, then her head, her arms and legs, though her feet and hands were still icy. Fern wanted to talk. Wanted to explain things to Adam, to use words to push away the menace of what had happened, but she still couldn't make her mouth work. She was afraid she might slip away again, up and out of the tent, dispersing into the sky, losing herself. She needed boundaries, edges, certainties to hold everything together. Fern snuggled closer to Adam, burrowing in like a mouse. She kept her eyes open, looking at Adam, seeking out his eyes to help her stay grounded.

He reached down and kissed her on the head, then closed her eyes with his fingers. 'Go to sleep. We'll talk in the morning.'

Fern didn't want to sleep, but found no solace in being awake. This thing had stepped through her dreams and into her waking life. Now she wasn't safe anywhere. If she didn't act, it would fill her mind and send her over the edge into insanity. As Adam's warmth seeped into her, she felt her resolve strengthening again and with that came the anger. She'd already used this anger to hurl magazines and stop clocks; now she would find a way to use it as a positive force. She might win or lose but either way she had to see it through. That was all that mattered to her now. She would not let the bullies win.

Chapter Seventeen

'Leggings?' Fern disentangled a pair of yellow and black striped footless tights from the wrapping paper. Puzzled, she looked at Adam for an explanation.

'Thermals,' he said.

'Only you would buy that sort of underwear for your girlfriend,' said Iris, rolling her eyes. 'Really, the boy has no idea.'

'She'll need them when we go bushwalking,' said Adam defensively.

They were sitting in the tiny living room, surrounded by a growing mound of discarded wrapping paper. Proudly wearing a Father Christmas hat, Michael was handing out the presents. Aside from Fern's weariness and lingering sense of foreboding, it was as if the attack last night had never happened.

When she'd woken that morning, Adam hadn't been there. Fern had found him on the beach, sitting on a log and watching the sun rise. Even from a distance she could read the confusion inside Adam and she felt it collide with the resolve she'd found the previous night.

'It's lovely,' she said, sitting down next to him on the log and gazing at the first rays of light on the horizon.

'Yeah, it's my favourite time of day. I'd almost forgotten - in Sydney I sleep through it.'

They sat quietly for a while, watching the smooth surface of the water shift through a multitude of luminescent colours. The ocean was peaceful now, the waves lapping gently against the sand, their sound a lullaby, though not soothing enough to calm Adam's mind.

'What happened last night?' he asked, breaking the silence.

'Something attacked me,' said Fern, then paused, wondering how best to explain it. 'I think it's the same thing that happened in my dream in Sydney, when I woke up in a panic. Only this time it stepped through somehow.'

Instinctively, Adam wanted to scoff, but he couldn't deny that he'd seen something. 'What was it?' he asked, trying to keep his voice neutral.

'I don't know … The thing Michael saw yesterday, whatever it is. The thing that's chasing me.'

'I thought that was your father.'

'So did I. And I think it's connected somehow. Maybe he sent it. Or …' Fern stopped, wondering for the first time if the creature was linked in some way to *her*, that somehow *she* was giving it shape. But how could she be responsible for something like that?

'I don't get it. How did that thing find you?' asked Adam.

Fern shook her head. 'It's as if there's some kind of tracking device inside me, giving off a signal. That must be how my father found me when the Bloodhound couldn't.'

'That's crazy,' said Adam. 'It isn't possible.'

'That's what I thought at first.' She paused. 'But then things happened …'

'Such as?'

Fern sighed. She'd told him very little when she'd first met him. Now it was obvious that Adam needed to know more, but she was afraid that describing all of her recent experiences would drive him away. 'Okay,' she began reluctantly. 'I guess it started when I saw Shamesh one night, standing on the pavement outside my window. He took off his sunglasses and something happened; a kind of waterfall forcing its way through my head. From here,' she said, tapping the top of her head. 'It was so strange. It should have been terrifying, but it wasn't. I wanted it to go on and on forever.'

Adam nodded; he was all too familiar with Shamesh's strange eyes, though that had never happened to him.

Then Fern told him about the vision she'd had when she fell down the stairs at the Underworld, and about the tempest stone and the effect it had on her. 'In broad daylight I was seeing things. I didn't understand at first, but now I'm pretty sure they were from the past. Scenes I'd experienced with him.'

'Him?'

'The thing that's after me … I don't know, but I think it's been after me for a long time. Shamesh said that in this lifetime it has incarnated as my father.'

Adam picked up a stick and started drawing lines in the sand, his name first, then circles, around and around. The thought of other lives stretching backwards and forwards in time made him dizzy. The stick snapped in his hand and he threw it away, then ran his fingers over his name in the sand.

'I've always had dreams,' said Fern. 'Anxious ones, the sort most people have. You know, being chased and not being able to move my legs, or trying to cross the road and the cars never stopping. But when I was in the psychiatric ward the dreams changed. Something started penetrating them. At first a hand grabbed my ankle, then I started to feel a terrifying presence or see a figure. And each time it appeared it was closer.' Fern paused, shivering at the memory. 'But there were other dreams too. Better ones. The Bear Handler came again and gave me a staff. He said to use it against the thing in my dreams but I was always too afraid. Then he came again and tried to teach me how to let go of my fear.' Fern glanced at Adam. His face was creased into a frown, not disbelieving, but not convinced either. She didn't blame him.

Adam looked at Fern sitting beside him, the gentle light illuminating her skin as she chewed nervously at a fingernail. For some reason he trusted her more than anyone he could remember. Even so, he felt uncomfortable: the world he believed in was unravelling with every word she spoke. He clasped the log beneath him, reassured by its solidity. 'Why does this thing want you?' he asked.

'I don't know. I don't really have any theories yet, apart from the fact that it's got something to do with my father. But whatever it is, it has wanted me for lifetimes. I'm not sure how or why it's found me now, though Shamesh said something about me beginning to open up. He said that three lifetimes ago I shut down and that meant giving away my power. Opening up means I can find that power again, but it also means this creature can find me.'

'What power?'

'I don't really know. I asked Shamesh once and he said it was the power to live well. To be free of bindings. He said that each of us has the potential to create miracles but few of us know how.' Fern stopped and looked at Adam resolutely. 'A month ago I would have thought this stuff was impossible. But now I have to believe it. And I have to see it through. I understand if you don't want to come with me.'

'I'll stick around,' said Adam, though he had no idea how to protect Fern from something he couldn't see.

'You don't think I'm mad?'

'Shit, the whole thing's bloody mad,' said Adam, trying to keep his tone light. 'I never told you, did I?'

'What?'

'That night, when you came for your bag, I went to the Underworld to see Shamesh and check up on you. Don't look at me like that - it was pretty obvious you were keeping stuff to yourself, so I was going to ask Shamesh.' Adam paused, not knowing quite how to explain what had happened. 'It wasn't there.'

'Shamesh had gone?'

'The whole bloody place had gone. I banged on the door, but no one answered. It wasn't locked so I went in. There was nothing there, just empty rooms, not a thing to say it had ever been a bar. It did my head in. I'd been drinking there the night before. Now who do you think is mad?'

Fern couldn't believe it. Shamesh gone, the whole place empty as if it had only been a figment of their imagination. Could it be possible for two people to imagine the same thing? Shamesh had introduced her to Adam at that bar. Fern reached out and touched Adam's arm. At least he was still there; *he* hadn't disappeared.

'Maybe we're both mad,' she said.

'Yeah, maybe we are.'

'But it's not fair on you,' said Fern. 'I've asked too much of you. I've even foisted myself on your family. There's no balance here – it's just you always helping me.'

She was wrong about that, Adam wanted to say, thinking about the dream that had haunted him for so long: the bloody hags hounding him, scratching at his eyes, pushing him further and further towards the edge; the nights he'd sat up staring at the television trying to hold sleep at bay; the amount he'd drunk, trying to knock himself into a state beyond dreaming. He shuddered at the memory. Then he'd met Fern and the dreams had stopped. He ought to tell her, but he couldn't because she'd want to know why he was haunted by these dreams, and if he told her that, he'd lose her.

'We're not negotiating a trade deal,' said Adam brusquely. 'Bloody hell, we're friends. At least I hope we are. You have no idea what you're giving me. I'd never have come back here without you. I'm not keeping tabs, so stop doing it yourself. Okay?'

As the sun finally slipped free of the horizon, Fern's eyes met Adam's. She saw the fire and the trust in him and she felt ashamed. No tabs, she'd thought. If he can do it, then so can I. 'Okay,' she said, kissing him on the lips. 'Oh, and by the way - Merry Christmas.'

Now here she was, back in the shack with Adam's family, surrounded by Christmas paper and kissing Adam again, as she slipped her new thermals on under her skirt.

'Cute,' said Adam.

'One more present,' shouted Michael excitedly.

'To Fern, from Adam.' Adam read out, blushing.

'Another one!' said Iris. 'You're doing well.'

Fern unwrapped the final present. It was a thick Polartec jacket in a rusty orange colour. 'It's lovely,' she said, putting it on and giving Adam a hug. 'Thank you.'

She felt overflowing with gratitude, to all of them. These people gave her strength; their goodwill was a counterforce to whatever malevolent thing was out there. She ran her fingers over the smooth wooden surface of Michael's present. 'A wise old owl,' he'd said when she opened it. 'Can see in the dark,' he'd added, looking at her intently as if there was something she needed to understand.

Adam had given his mother a food dehydrator and now she was making plans to sell fruit leather at the local shop, and looking for ideas in the book Fern had given her. 'Lovely,' she'd said when she'd opened it. 'Lovely, thank you.'

Michael was humming as he shaped a piece of wood with the carving tools Adam had bought him. And Adam was poring over the photographs in the book Fern had found him. Each picture drew him towards it, tugging at his heart, as if the wilderness itself was calling. When he was a boy, he'd played in the bush; just being out there had made his heart sing. But now these pictures hurt him in a way he'd never imagined would be possible.

He wasn't innocent anymore. He knew what was happening out there and instead of joy, he felt its agony.

Adam turned the page and gazed at a photograph of the Franklin River, the turmoil of its white water angrily splitting around boulders then reforming again, its furious eddies and calm respites reflecting the turmoil in his heart. It had been years since he'd rafted the Franklin but he could still feel the excitement of it, the surrender he'd made into its wildness. That kind of surrender is beyond me now, thought Adam. He was tainted and the wilderness would know it.

Fern could read what was going on inside him, the hurt and the love all bound up together. She watched nervously as Adam closed the book. 'Do you like it?' she asked.

'Yeah,' he said. 'It's great.'

As soon as lunch was over Michael stood up, gave everyone a wide smile and left the house, still wearing his pink paper hat. Adam managed to clear the table before collapsing onto the couch. Soon his snores were floating in from the lounge room and setting a rhythm to the chores; Iris was washing the dishes and Fern was drying.

'I never did understand why Adam went off to the army,' said Iris quietly. 'It just didn't seem right. His father served in Vietnam but he hardly ever talked about it - said some things are better left unspoken. When he died, Adam kept his medals. Maybe he thought he could get him back somehow if he followed in his father's footsteps? Or maybe he was angry with his dad for leaving him. Sometimes kids feel that, or they blame themselves. Adam always took too much on his shoulders. You can see it, can't you?'

Fern nodded and replaced her sodden tea towel with a fresh one. 'Yes,' she said, 'he's weighed down by the world, like Atlas.'

'Anyway, they sent him off to Iraq. I was beside myself. Can you imagine? We didn't believe in that war. Even Adam called it an invasion. But he went anyway. In the army you do as you're told.

'We exchanged letters for nearly a year, but then one of my letters was returned. I rang and asked where he was, but they said he'd been discharged. They wouldn't tell me anything more. When I rang again, begging for information, someone mentioned the discharge was on medical grounds. I was frantic, but what could I do? He just disappeared.' Her eyes filled with tears. 'It's horrible to feel so powerless.'

Fern watched Iris wiping her eyes with the back of her hand and thought of her own mother, waiting for word from her, distraught no doubt. She would be spending Christmas alone if Richard was still in hospital, or looking after him if he wasn't. Fern knew she should ring but there was no phone at the shack, so she'd have to walk all the way down to the shop to find a public one.

'Something must have happened to him in Iraq.' Iris looked at Fern hopefully. 'Has he ever mentioned anything?'

'No,' said Fern, wishing she could offer Iris more. 'He doesn't talk about it.'

Iris shook her head sadly. 'Just like his father … Anyway, he's here now.' She smiled through her tears. 'And you too. It's nice to have another woman around the house for a change.'

'It's good to be here,' said Fern, smiling at Iris, her heart warming to this woman who had opened her home to a stranger.

'There, that's done,' said Iris, taking the tea towel from Fern and hanging it up. 'Now I'm going to get my head down for an hour. Christmas is so exhausting.'

Fern followed the winding road for a few kilometres to Adventure Bay. It was good to be out alone like this, the wind in her face, the ocean stretching off into the distance, the sound of gulls and the rhythmic crash of the waves all easing the tension inside of her. But as Fern approached the public phone the tension returned. Steeling herself for her mother's questions, she put her money in and waited as the phone rang. It was a relief when the answer machine switched on. Perhaps her mother was at the hospital.

'Hi, it's me,' she said after the beep. 'I just wanted to tell you I'm …'

A panicked voice broke in. 'Fernanda! Is that you, Fernanda? Just wait while I turn off the machine … Hello? Are you there?'

Already Fern was regretting her decision to call. 'Yes Mum, I'm here.'

'Where are you? Oh Fernanda, I've been so worried. I didn't know what had happened. They just said that you'd gone.'

'I'm safe, Mum. I wanted to wish you a merry Christmas and tell you not to worry.'

'Where are you Fernanda? 'Why did you run away like that?'

'I didn't want to be there, Mum,' said Fern, her voice rising. 'So I left.'

'When are you coming home, dear?'

'I don't know. How's Dad? Is he out of hospital?'

'He's much better, they're discharging him next week. Where are *you*, Fernanda?'

'I'm running out of change, we'll be cut off in a minute. I'll ring again soon.' Fern pressed down the receiver and stood for a moment in the telephone box, wishing perversely she had given her mother more. She sighed and stepped out into the cold air, hugging her new jacket close to her, the silk scarf Iris had given her floating backwards in the wind. The conversation had left Fern with a feeling of unease. Her old life was intruding again and the sense of belonging Fern had felt here on Bruny was fading. She plodded back along the road, her chest heaving with the effort. The events of last night had left their mark on her.

Not ready to return to the shack, Fern decided instead to walk along the beach. She stepped out onto its southerly end and let her eyes feast on the long white stretch of sand, straight at first, then curving eventually into distant cliffs. She took off her sandals and let her feet sink into the soft sand, the grains squeaking as she walked. The wind was so strong it scooped up the sand and sent it whipping against her legs, fighting her at every step. But even so she felt better.

Further down the beach Fern could see something dark against the sand. At first she thought it was a piece of driftwood or a pile of seaweed, perhaps even a seal, but as she got closer she could see it was a crouching figure. It wasn't until Fern was really close that she recognised Michael. Curious, she walked towards him. He didn't look up but he must have noticed her because as she approached he put his finger to his lips. 'Shhh.'

Michael was sitting on the sand, bending over a tiny dead penguin, one hand hovering just above it. A moment later he gently picked up the bird and cradled its limp body in his hands. Fern watched him concentrating, his eyes closed as if in prayer. They stayed there like that for perhaps five minutes, the wind buffeting them, the sand whipping at their legs. Fern felt as though she was witnessing something private, perhaps a burial ritual Michael had concocted, some sort of blessing for the dead bird. She thought for a moment she saw its chest moving but that was impossible - it must have been just the wind ruffling its feathers. However, as she watched, riveted, these faint stirrings of life gradually strengthened into movement. Soon the penguin opened its eyes and Michael placed it back on the sand. It stood there for a few moments uncertainly then looked up at him as if to say thank you, and waddled towards the rocks.

Fern was astonished. 'What did you just do?'

'Sent it my life,' said Michael simply.

'Your life?'

Michael nodded as if already bored. But Fern needed to know more. She took his hand for a moment and inspected it, trying to see the force that must have moved through him and into the bird, but she could see nothing. She thought about the force that had stopped the clock in Iris's room the other night. Could it have been the same thing? Fern had used her fury on the clock, while Michael had used his love of living creatures to help the penguin. Perhaps that's what Shamesh had meant about finding your power. And once you did, there came a choice: to use it well or not.

'Fix you now,' said Michael.

'Me?'

Michael nodded.

'But I'm not dead.'

'Take out the bad things.'

'What bad things?'

'Inside.'

Fern didn't understand what Michael was talking about. 'Michael,' she said, trying to change the subject. 'I wanted to thank you for helping me last night. You saved me.'

Michael shook his head impatiently. 'Need to … need.' Frustrated, he hit his forehead with the palm of his hand, over and over. 'Make you strong,' he said. 'It wants you … wants to …' The effort was too much for him and he was trembling; specks of white froth forming at the corners of his mouth, as he rocked backwards and forwards on the sand.

Fern put her arms around him. 'It's okay,' she said. 'I'm sorry, I shouldn't have mentioned it.'

After a time the rocking subsided and Michael looked at her hopefully. 'Fix you now?'

Fern nodded. 'Okay, fix me.'

Smiling now, Michael sat Fern down on the sand in front of him, close but not touching. He reached out and closed her eyes with his fingers. 'Shh,' he said.

Fern waited quietly, listening to the sounds of the gulls and the waves. Soon she felt a strange wriggling inside her chest as if something was unravelling around her heart. There wasn't any pain, just a slight nausea. For a moment she felt lighter inside but then the wriggling began again. Something was being tugged from her. It felt as if Michael were hauling it out with a rope. There was a popping sensation and then a great vastness opened up inside her.

'Done,' said Michael, and Fern opened her eyes, dizzy now, the world spinning, her chest hurting, new pockets of air inside, her organs shifting… It felt as if there was suddenly a lot more room in her chest.

'What happened?' she asked.

'A snake,' he said. 'And a long black thing with lots of legs.'

'A millipede?'

He nodded, shuddering, and gestured as if he was pulling something long and heavy. 'And a grey lump, he said, shuddering again. 'Ugly.' Then he smiled. 'All gone now.'

'Where have they gone?' asked Fern.

Michael shrugged and gestured into the sky. 'Just gone.'

'Why were they there?'

He frowned and shook his head, then stood up, stretching his arms into the sky.

'Why, Michael?'

He stopped for a moment and looked back at her, his face set into a scowl. 'Dark things to close your heart.'

Fern watched Michael lumbering down the beach. He reminded her of a bear, huge, childlike and loyal. His moods were as changeable as Adam's but any anger he felt was fleeting and played about on the surface, whereas Adam's anger was deep-seated and not easily shifted. They both had a strong connection to nature, thought Fern, but Adam's was all mixed up with fury.

Michael had done something to Fern. There was a steadiness inside her chest that she'd never experienced before. She felt sturdier too, but there was also a new vulnerability, as if the shell had gone and her skin was fragile and sensitive, unused to the elements.

Fern found a peaceful spot in the sun and sat down on a rock, waves of fatigue washing over her as she relaxed. Close by a bird sang, a gull dipping and diving on the wind. Higher still a sea eagle hovered, gliding in wide circles above the ocean. In the distance Fern saw a lone surfer, out beyond the waves, moving up and down with the swell, waiting. She closed her eyes, trying to empty her mind of the thoughts that kept tumbling around, jostling for position. She was wearied by the need to unravel it all and understand. Perhaps she needed to do something else. Fern thought suddenly of her knitting: to simply unravel it would leave only a long, crinkled strand of wool waiting to be reshaped. That's what I should do, she thought, reshape it, create something from it, something useful and beautiful.

The wind found Fern again, sweeping and swirling around her. She thought of Kali, the Indian goddess, who embraced both destruction and creation, dark and light. One unable to exist without the other. With that thought, Fern's world righted itself and she could feel energy stirring inside her.

When she opened her eyes a man was walking towards her. It was the Bear Handler, his cloak shimmering too brightly in the sunlight, his long fair hair framing a narrow face. She couldn't fix on his features, couldn't say they were one thing or another. It was as if they were never quite still.

'How did you get here?' she asked. 'I thought you only appeared in my dreams.'

His smile was gentle. 'I am here but I am not here. Another paradox it seems. Like the creature of your nightmares, I too can step into your world, but only when the conditions are right.'

'What conditions?'

'Because you are relaxed. You are open. Not wanting. This creates a door between worlds.'

Fern thought about it, remembering how good she'd felt last night just before the thing had attacked her. 'So every time I let down my guard it can get me? Every time I feel good I let it in?'

He nodded. 'Yes. But it's fear that weakens you.'

'Well, that's ridiculous.'

'Perhaps.'

'So how can I beat it?'

'You must relax.'

Fern sighed; it felt as if they were going around in circles. And besides, she couldn't possibly relax when this creature was trying to kill her. 'Any more useful tips?' she asked wearily.

'You know already what you must do.'

Fern was about to emphatically deny this when she remembered the voice from the night before telling her to turn away. The creature had come unexpectedly and she should have turned her back immediately, before it got a hold on her.

The Bear Handler nodded. 'That's right. You must take the power into your own hands and allow your enemy to come only when you are ready.'

'Maybe it won't come anymore,' she said hopefully.

'It will come. Without realising it you have opened a part of yourself that has been closed for too long. You have lowered your defences, let the world, as you've known it, begin to unravel. As it should. But in doing so you have also given your enemy a ticket to come and go as he pleases, first in your sleep and now in your waking life. It is very important to have control of this opening. You need new defences, things of beauty and peace. Look for the paths that give you pleasure, things that take your mind from fear.'

'Who is my enemy?' asked Fern. 'Why are there so many manifestations?'

'He seeks to confuse you - and yet you already know his identity.'

As Fern pondered this, the wind whipped sand in Fern's face, stinging her skin, grit finding its way into her eyes. The Bear Handler was wrong, she had no idea, at least none beyond the obvious – her father.

'You will remember each manifestation,' he continued, 'yet in the end it does not matter. It is your task to make peace and sever the ties that bind you to him.'

'Why does he hate me?' asked Fern, realising as she spoke that it was not hate this creature felt, it was something else. Michael had been right. It wanted her.

The Bear Handler nodded again. 'Across time he has wanted you to surrender your power to him. To join forces with him.'

'Why?'

'Because together you could be monstrous in your intent.'

Fern flinched. 'Monstrous?'

The Bear Handler looked at Fern quizzically. 'Do you not feel its lure?'

Fern nodded reluctantly. She wanted to deny it, but in truth she could feel its draw, as if it were whispering promises in her ear. *Power.* How tempting it was: to slip into the minds of others, to move objects, stop clocks … And what else? She had a feeling there was so much more she could do, and the notion was both terrifying and tantalising. Was it true? Had she let the creature in of her own volition?

'That possibility is in you. It is in all of humanity. In the end it will be your choice. Once, long ago, you chose to surrender your power, but not to this demon. It hurt you and those you loved so much that you could not bear another lifetime fighting. So you closed yourself off, unaware that you would continue to live each life repeating the patterns that were already in place. To be free of these patterns you must reclaim that power. There is no other way.' He smiled gently at Fern, but his voice was stern. 'Reclaim it and use it well.'

Fern felt as if she were trapped in a dream and yet all her senses were awake and alert. She could see the waves, feel the wind on her skin, taste the salt on her lips, smell the seaweed, the freshness of the air. She was here, now, and so was the Bear Handler, though the edges of him were becoming less distinct. Worried that he might disappear before she could ask all her questions, she hurried on. 'What did Michael do to me?'

'What did it feel like to you?'

Fern reflected on the strange wriggling sensation and the vast expanse that had opened inside her. 'It was as if he were extracting something,' she said hesitantly. 'Unwinding chains around my heart.'

'Yes, they were fetters.'

'Who put them there?'

'Some were put there by you, as protection, but too easily they became prison guardians. The rest were chains put in place by that which hunts you. All its energy has gone into keeping your heart closed.'

'Why?' But Fern already knew the answer. The only way to access her power was by opening her heart.

The Bear Handler nodded once more.

'And yet it can't find me unless I open it,' said Fern, frowning.

He smiled apologetically. 'Yes, another paradox. Of course, there are degrees of opening. In the end the choice is yours. How do you want to live your life?'

'Well,' she said, without hesitation.

'Good. Michael has helped to unfetter your heart. Now you must find a way to fully open it.'

'Who are you?' Fern had asked this before, but she wanted a better answer.

'I am the Bear Handler,' he said, smiling. 'That is what you named me. It will do for now.'

'But *what* are you?' asked Fern, frustrated at his evasions.

He shrugged. 'It does not matter. I am here because you need me. Now, I have answered your questions; it is time for me to ask you a question.'

'Okay,' said Fern, cautiously.

'To whom are you bound?'

She frowned, puzzled by his question. The answer was obvious. She was alone, free of entanglements and obligations to others. 'No one,' said Fern.

He shook his head. 'You are wrong. Think about the promises you have made through this life and others. It is in releasing them that you will learn to fly.'

'Fly?'

But he was gone and Fern's question was carried away on the wind. As she sat listening to the roar of the waves and the cries of the gulls, the surfer who had been waiting out beyond the breakers, stood up and rode a wave, gracefully weaving one way and another, following lines only he could see, then slipped gently into the water before paddling back out again.

The Bear Handler's words had confused Fern and yet she felt them joining together like a mosaic to form a pattern she recognised, its perfection taking the breath from her. Her tiredness was overcome by elation and a sense of lightness, as if her bones were hollow and at any moment the wind could lift her into the air. For the briefest of moments Fern felt she was *seeing* the world, not just looking at it. Everything was clearer and yet not so certain, as if one form could easily slip into another. Bit by bit she was releasing all those certainties that had constructed a version of the world that was no longer useful to her.

A surge of joy rushed through Fern, joy and gratitude because she felt as if she'd been given a great gift; a new perspective from which she could truly see the patterns of life. She stood up and began dancing, a slow free-form dance, mimicking a bird spreading its wings and taking off, the dance becoming faster until she was almost flying, the wind lifting her skirt, her scarf, tugging at the rest of her as if it too wanted her to fly. She could feel her chest expanding and the muscles in her upper back twitching as if she really did have wings. She remembered the eagle, soaring up into the sky from the roof of her terrace house. Oh, to fly like that. As a child she'd sometimes flown through her dreams, but never soared. Later, the air in her dreams had become so thick she could hardly move in them, let alone fly.

Fern stopped her dance when she noticed the surfer paddling back into shore. She stood watching as he undid his ankle harness, picked up his board and began walking in her direction. It was only then that she was sure, recognising the confident stride, the slight angle of his head and the strength of his body. As Fern watched, she felt a stirring of desire. Last night's attack had drained all feeling from her and she'd become a body, uninhabited by a self. Now she was fused into one again and every nerve was reaching out to Adam.

'I saw you,' he said, stopping in front of her. 'What were you doing?'

'Dancing.'

She was smiling at him, a wild joy in her eyes, her cheeks flushed in the cold air, her hair standing on end in the wind, her skirt flapping, the goose bumps just starting on her legs. Her whole being made Adam desperate. He reached his arms out and she stepped inside them, snuggling up close to him, her face against the damp surface of his wetsuit. He bent to kiss her, sinking his lips into hers, then unzipped her jacket and slid his hands under her t-shirt onto her skin, bumpy with cold. She unzipped his wetsuit and helped him step out of it. Then they moved close together again, their skin touching, bodies pressing against each other. There was an urgency between them now, a need to complete the thing they'd been circling for days. She was stepping out of her underpants and he was lifting her skirt, lifting her whole body up to him as he pulled off his board shorts and she wrapped her legs around him, helping him to slide into her, their mouths, their tongues lost in each other as he pushed harder, desperate to do what he'd been wanting to do, since forever it seemed. She was gasping and he was coming and the sea pounding, the wind and the sand biting against their legs and backs.

Adam kissed her head, her nose, her cheeks, her lips. 'You're so beautiful,' he said, his voice almost a groan.

Fern ran her fingers along his skin, memorising as much as she could, so that she could feel him always. They stayed like this, Adam holding Fern, until the cold crept in and Fern shivered, bringing them back to themselves. Then they got dressed, pulling away from each other.

'Come on,' said Adam. 'You're cold. I'll race you home.'

So they ran, Adam carrying his board, Fern with her arms spread into the wind, whooping and winding their way down the beach.

That night Adam built a bonfire and cooked prawns on the barbecue. They all ate on the beach, sitting on logs, sucking the juice of prawns and crayfish from their fingers, the heat from the fire licking their faces as they sipped champagne. Mutt stayed at Fern's feet, munching prawn shells.

'That dog's really taken to you,' said Iris.

Fern patted Mutt, and Adam reached across and put his arm around Fern. She leaned into him, her hand resting on his leg. It was all perfectly natural, yet it felt strange. It wasn't just that they'd made love this afternoon, rather it was a surrendering to each other. An acceptance that yes, they were together. Fern wondered if she could bear to risk being hurt. She had always been so afraid of losing the people closest to her. This fear had made her push away Jeff and the others before him but now Fern made a vow to herself: she wouldn't let that happen again, no matter how vulnerable it left her.

Fern picked up a handful of sand, then let it trickle slowly through her fingers, a stream so fine it felt almost liquid as it caressed her skin. And yet there were thousands of separate grains in each handful. She looked up in wonder at the thick swirl of the Milky Way above them. How could it be that there were more stars in the universe than grains of sand? Then she looked at Adam staring solemnly into the fire, and wondered at the miracle of finding him. What has our lovemaking started? she asked herself, certain that it must have redirected their fates in some way, closed off some possibilities, opened others.

Iris started singing: 'Silent night, holy night, all is calm, all is bright', and one by one they joined in. Then they sang 'Rudolph the Red Nosed Reindeer', Michael enthusiastically doing all the actions, and then 'I'm Dreaming of a White Christmas', which made them laugh because even though Michael remembered only the one line, he sang it in a deep sexy voice that sounded just right.

Fern fetched her pipe and played along with the carols. Then when the others had finished singing she lapsed into a tune of her own, trusting her fingers, and sending the notes out to disperse into the night. Michael sat listening, a gentle smile on his face. Adam stared up at the stars, the notes finding their way past his defences, flowing through him, their purity bringing tears to his eyes

'That was beautiful,' said Iris when Fern had finished. In the firelight Iris looked younger, her face softened by the shadows and the yearning in her eyes, the grey in her hair replaced by a flaming orange that highlighted her cheekbones and strengthened her jaw.

Fern wondered if this was what the Bear Handler had meant when he'd told her to follow her pleasures. Making love, knitting, playing her pipe, talking and laughing with people she cared for. Sitting here with Adam's arm around her and the warm flames on her face, she could almost believe these things would be enough to shield her. Make beauty, she thought, seek harmony. That's what I should do. It would hate that.

Chapter Eighteen

'Shit, even a four-wheel drive couldn't get through this,' said Adam. 'We'll have to walk.'

On the detailed map Adam had brought, this was classed as an unsurfaced track, but in reality it was deeply rutted and almost completely overgrown. Adam had driven in as far as he could, but right in front of them was a ditch too deep for the station wagon.

Fern reluctantly laced up her walking boots and shouldered her pack. This had once been a thriving mining area, so the old track would have been a well-used road. Now it had an air of sadness and neglect, memories of better times still hovering nearby, while the wind and the rain and the bush slowly reclaimed it. According to the map, the track would once have taken them past the abandoned town, now in ruins, and past the remnants of the railway line until they came to her father's front door. But the track had not been maintained. As far as Fern was concerned the reason was clear: Eric didn't want any uninvited guests.

As they walked away, Fern kept glancing back at the car for reassurance. It felt like a lifeline to safety. The bush was alien to her. Even on the track she could feel its vastness and ponderous weight on either side of her. There were no houses, concrete footpaths, or cafes, just trees and dirt and sky. Fern felt a great loneliness, along with a sense of impending doom. She and Adam had disagreed about how to get to her father's place. Fern had wanted to fly in or take a boat. It made sense to her: the Pine House website said these were the only ways in. But Adam had objected.

'That's not so easy,' he'd said. 'First, we don't have a boat or a helicopter. Second, we can't afford to hire either. And even if we did, we'd only be announcing our arrival to your father. Unless of course that's what you want to do.'

The last point was the clincher for Fern, who wanted to sneak up on her father if she could, do something he didn't expect in the hope that this would give her the upper hand. Though, given his past ability to locate her, that might prove impossible.

'We'll follow the track in the car as best we can,' Adam had promised. 'But if it gets too rough we'll have to walk. After all,' he'd added, smiling, 'I promised to show you the wilderness.'

Fern had nervously agreed. She'd been on walks before but they were tame walks on good paths through pretty countryside, and only ever for a few hours. She had no idea what it would be like to immerse herself in the bush. The preparations alone had taken two days, during which Adam was withdrawn and focused, wanting only to talk about gaiters and sleeping bags, waterproof trousers and hats. He'd made Fern empty her bag out on the living room floor, then he sorted through it, a look of disgust on his face. 'None of this is any good … You haven't even got shoes. We'll have to start from scratch.' They'd gone into town and bought Fern walking boots in the sales, big heavy things that made her feel clumsy.

Then Adam had turned into a list fiend: compass, maps, bandaids ('You're sure to get blisters.', water bottles, cups, meths, trangia.('A cooker,' he explained when Fern asked), long trousers for the evenings, two t-shirts, a warm jacket, only one spare pair of undies ('We're going to stink,' said Fern, horrified.), sleeping bags, mats, tent, torch, spare batteries, a trowel ('For shitting,' he said. 'Oh great,' Fern responded.), gloves, rain jackets, beanies, quick-dry shorts…

And an PLB,' said Adam.

'A what?'

'A personal locator beacon. Just in case.'

And then there was all that high-energy, lightweight food. Using Iris's new dehydrator they'd dried their own vegetables and fruit, then prepared a dried fruit and nut mixture that Adam called scroggin. They'd also bought instant noodles and powdered milk, dried tofu and chocolate.

'Thank God for chocolate,' said Fern.

Iris made up some muesli: oats with cranberries, coconut, sunflower seeds and sultanas. Then she cooked oat bars heavy with seeds and honey. Adam made Fern measure out all the food into meal-size portions and put them in sealed plastic bags.

'They're tiny,' said Fern looking at the bags in horror. 'We'll starve.'

And all the time Michael was hovering. 'Take me,' he'd said, over and over.

'Not this time, Mike. Sorry.'

He'd hung his head and Adam had almost caved in but it would be hard enough taking Fern, and besides, they wouldn't have enough gear between them. As it was, Fern was borrowing Michael's gaiters, though they almost reached her thighs, and his sleeping mat, as well as Iris's rain jacket. Michael's backpack had been too big for Fern so they'd had to resort to Fern's day pack. Adam had converted it, strapping a sleeping mat on the bottom and a sleeping bag wrapped in plastic, on top. Then he'd attached side pockets so she could carry water, snacks and waterproofs. Even so, Adam was carrying much more.

When they were finally packed, Adam had gone through Fern's pack one more time. Scornfully he'd pulled out her knitting and her pipe, the pashmina shawl and a novel Iris had lent her. 'You can't take these. We're not going on holiday.'

In the end Fern had acquiesced on the knitting and the book but insisted on the pipe and the shawl, which hardly weighed a thing.

Now she was walking next to him, looking like a bumblebee, thought Adam, in her yellow and black striped thermal leggings under a pair of oversize silk shorts, a yellow thermal top under her t-shirt, and her pointy straw hat which she'd insisted on wearing even though they'd all told her it wasn't practical. Adam sighed; it was his fault, he'd jokingly told her that leeches jump out of trees onto people's heads, and that had done it.

Adam stopped and consulted the map, then took out the compass and did a reading. 'See,' he said. 'We're heading south-west.' He picked up a twig and used it to point out on the map, where they were. It meant nothing to Fern; all she could see were different shades of green and brown and an intricate pattern of lines. 'This track we're on goes practically all the way to your father's but it's a lot further than if we cut across. See here, there's another, smaller track heading off from this one, into the forest. That's what I've been looking for.' He walked over to the line of trees. 'I reckon this is the one, it looks pretty overgrown.'

'Where?' asked Fern, not seeing any sign of a path.

'See,' he said, pointing in further. 'These trees are a bit younger than the others and there's just a bit more space between them. This must have been well used once.'

'Why can't we stay on this road?' She shuddered, not wanting to go deeper into the dark, still forest, away from the light and the clear markers that told her where she was going.

'Like I said, it's much longer,' said Adam. 'And even walking, these ditches and fallen logs would slow us down. It would take days.' He glanced at Fern. 'Ready?'

No, she thought. I'm not. I can't do this. I want to go home.

'Sure,' she said and followed him into the bush.

Immediately the atmosphere changed. The air was damp and still but fresh too. Fern took a deep breath, feeling it cleanse her lungs. The smell was pungent: damp earth and rotting humus. It smelled of dead things but the effect was a concentration of life. Fern had to watch her feet, which kept catching on tree roots, sinking into thick boggy patches or slipping on the wet uneven surface.

They weren't walking on any path Fern could see; instead they were climbing over and under fallen trees and rocks, as well as pushing their way through bushes. After twenty minutes or so, Fern could feel the strain in her leg muscles. She was sweating and tired, her shoulders and back were aching where the straps of her pack tugged and she was out of breath. Carelessly she misjudged the height of a root and stumbled again, nearly falling.

Adam found a knotted stick and handed it to Fern. 'There,' he said. 'That should help you keep your balance.'

While he checked the map and took another compass bearing, Fern pulled out her water bottle and drank greedily. When they were walking, the forest was filled with the sound of their boots, the rustle of leaves and snapping twigs. But standing still, leaning on her stick, the silence descended on Fern. It felt heavy and unbreakable. There was a stillness, too, as if the forest was waiting.

Fern jumped as the harsh shriek of a cockatoo tore through the silence. Another joined in and then another, until the forest was ringing with their noise. Searching among the treetops, Fern could see a black silhouette here and there, and the very tips of the trees illuminated by bright white sunlight. The trees were incredibly tall, their smooth trunks stretching upwards to the heavens. The branches began high above her head and only the tops had leaves.

'These ones are mainly stringy barks,' said Adam, following Fern's gaze. 'They grow pretty big.'

Swathes of bark were peeling off some of the trees, and hanging down like Hawaiian skirts. The bark was piled up on the ground, curling like snakes. Fern picked up a long piece, surprised at how soft and pliable it was. The colours were exquisite, a deep burning orange, fading to cream in the drier places.

'This is a mixture of wet sclerophyll and rainforest,' said Adam. 'It's got a eucalyptus canopy, but there are still heaps of rainforest trees: sassafras, myrtle, King Billy Pine, man ferns…'

Giant ferns were scattered among the tall trees, their fronds towering over her head, a soft dappled sunlight filtering through them. Luminescent green moss grew underfoot and on the trees, wet and soft to the touch. Moisture dripped down the tree trunks, and delicate golden toadstools were growing in rings among the moss and jutting elegantly from the trunks of trees. Rocks too, were covered in moss and textured patches of white. Fern reached down and ran her finger across the rough whiteness.

'Lichen,' said Adam. 'It's two plants together. They have a symbiotic relationship. And get this,' he said, patting a rock. 'They draw their nourishment from these.'

'They eat rocks?' Fern was puzzled. It was hard to imagine a rock being nourishing.

'Yeah, it's amazing, isn't it? Everything's alive. Everything on this planet. Even the planet itself. A living, breathing organism. And we're just a tiny part of it … Except we've turned into parasites,' he added, feeling his mood change as if a shadow had settled on him. Here he was in the forest, so beautiful it broke his heart. That was the problem: every time he thought about its beauty, he worried about losing it. 'Come on,' he said and strode ahead, surprising Fern with his sudden anger.

For a time they walked more easily, their feet squelching in the soft ground littered with roots and leaves. They heard the stream before they reached it; a babbling, as if they had stumbled on a gathering of people all talking at once.

It was lighter here, the sun finding its way through the trees, sending dappled patches of light and dark onto the water, highlighting a moss-covered boulder, a gleaming ripple, the smooth rounded rocks under the water. The banks of the stream were lined with man ferns, their fronds filtering the sunlight.

'It's so beautiful,' she said, running her fingers along a giant frond that arched over her head. 'Like I always imagined Fairyland would look.'

Adam stood gazing at it too, its beauty tearing at him. Fern leaned over and cupped her hands in the water.

'Don't drink it,' warned Adam. 'We're in forestry territory, so there are probably clear fells around here and plantations. It'll be full of chemicals.'

'But it looks so pure,' said Fern, jerking her hands out of the water.

'Yeah,' he said sarcastically. Then he stopped himself, swallowing back the bitterness inside him. His anger would only confuse Fern and it didn't change anything. There would still be chemicals in the water. 'When we get in further the water should be cleaner,' he said, bending over and undoing his laces. 'Take your shoes off, we're going to have to wade through.'

When Fern stepped into the stream the water was icy cold on her bare skin. It reached only up to her mid-calves, but it was running quickly and she could feel its tug. The rocks were slippery and uneven and she had to concentrate to stay upright. The stick helped her keep her balance, but even so, when she was halfway across, her feet slid from under her and she fell backwards, landing on her pack, her arms and legs waving like an overturned beetle.

Adam wasn't impressed. He took off his pack and left it on the other side, then waded back for Fern, hauling her out by one arm. 'You should be more careful. What if you'd hurt yourself? We're in survival mode out here. No one knows where we are. If something goes wrong, we're stuffed.'

'Sorry,' muttered Fern, feeling stupid as she pulled on her wet socks.

'You can't wear them, you'll get blisters. Get some dry socks out of your pack.' Adam sighed, hating the carping sound of his own voice. Every word was pushing Fern further away, yet he couldn't stop himself. This place was getting to him.

'Lighten up,' said Fern. Angrily she reached for her pack. 'This isn't the army. I'm not some new recruit you can bully.'

Adam clenched his teeth. 'Don't talk about the army,' he said.

'Well stop treating me like an idiot then,' said Fern. She was surprised at her reaction. Once she would have swallowed back her anger and meekly taken what she was dealt. But something was changing within her and she found herself no longer willing to let anyone walk over her.

As Adam looked at her standing there, her hands on her hips, her eyes flashing, her hair dripping and her lips blue with cold, his anger switched to concern. 'Okay, okay - truce?'

Fern didn't answer.

'Look, you're freezing. You'd better get changed.' He paused, then rolled his eyes.

'Okay, let's try it another way … Would you mind, if it's not too much trouble, putting some dry clothes on?'

Fern still didn't move, though the corners of her lips were twitching.

'Okay, here goes … I'm going to say it … I'm sorry.'

'That's okay,' said Fern, smiling now. They'd had disagreements before, but this was their first argument. It could have been a lot worse, she thought.

'We may as well have a break,' said Adam. 'I'll boil up some tea while you get changed.'

Fern peeled off her wet clothes and put on her only dry set. 'I'm stuffed if it rains,' she said, warming one hand on her mug and popping chocolate into her mouth with the other. 'God, chocolate tastes even better out here.'

After a short rest they packed everything up and walked on. The chocolate had given Fern a boost and for a while she kept up with Adam. But gradually her energy drained away and she slipped behind, Adam stopping occasionally to let her catch up.

Suddenly, at a point where Adam had drawn ahead of her, a twig unrolled itself in front of Fern and lifted its head, transforming into a snake. Heart pounding, she froze. She could see its flickering tongue and the black depths of its eyes. One lunge of its head and it would bite her. She wanted to call Adam but she couldn't speak. She wanted to run but she couldn't move. It seemed forever that they faced each other like this: Fern poised to run, the snake poised to lunge.

'Fern?' called Adam, appearing up ahead.

'Snake.' It was almost a whisper, but he heard.

'Don't move,' he said.

She nodded, unable to tear her eyes away from the snake's hypnotic gaze while Adam stamped his feet. Then, after what seemed like hours, the snake lowered its head and slid silently away.

Shakily, Fern followed Adam again, her eyes scanning the ground for any movement. Every twig, every curled-up piece of bark now looked like a snake. Up ahead, Adam had stopped once more. Fern could read the tension in his stance, and even before she reached him, she could see something of what he was seeing, flashes of the images in his mind and flashes too, of the stabbing pain he was feeling. Hurrying, she drew level with him and gaped at the devastation before her. The scene had an aura of immense loss and violence, like the site of a mass murder.

Adam jumped onto the stump of an enormous tree and pulled Fern up next to him. There was still plenty of room. It could fit twenty people in its radius, she thought. At least.

'Jesus, look at this.' His words were forced through gritted teeth. 'It takes hundreds of years to grow a tree this fucking big and minutes to cut it down.'

'Is this a clear fell?' asked Fern, already knowing the answer.

Adam nodded, his fists clenched as he stepped off the stump and paced around it.

'They come in with their bulldozers and cut the lot, then take out the useful ones, the ones they want to turn into woodchips. Most of the really valuable ones, like the Blackwood, get left behind.' He walked over to a tower of broken trees, their limbs sticking out in all directions. Fern followed him.

'See,' he said. 'There's a myrtle and a sassafras. There's blackwood too. These are the hardwoods, you can make furniture out of them, musical instruments, beautiful things.'

All at once a memory came to Adam. His father had been a mild man, but Adam remembered the shocking force of his fury when he'd found Adam tearing fronds off a giant man fern. 'For the roof of our cubby,' Adam had explained, but his father hadn't been moved. 'Give the forest its due,' he'd told Adam. 'If you love it you should look after it.' After that he'd started teaching Adam the lore of the bush and slowly the love Adam had always felt for the wilderness had broadened to include respect.

'What will they do with this?' asked Fern, fingering a dead myrtle branch.

'Burn it. They use stuff that burns like napalm. You can see the mushroom clouds from miles away.' Furious, Adam kicked a stone, sending it thudding across the devastation. 'The fire burns so hot it kills all the seeds so nothing will regrow. Then they put down poison to kill off any creatures that survived the bulldozers and the chemicals. At least they do in the private clear-fells. The government supposedly only uses it to poison foxes – thing is there aren't any foxes in Tassie.' He stopped suddenly, grief catching the words in his throat.

Fern was filled with the horror of what she was hearing. The insanity of it was beyond comprehension. 'Why would they want to destroy it?' she asked.

'Plantations. They're easier to manage. They'll replant all this with genetically modified seeds that grow quickly and produce a soft wood that's easy to chip. Trouble is they have to keep spraying it with pesticides to keep it safe. Then the pesticide runs into the waterways and we all drink it.'

'It's horrible.'

'Yeah.' Adam turned away abruptly as if eager to distance himself from this place. Fern followed as best she could. She was hungry now and despite all precautions, her feet were beginning to blister and her ankle was sore again. She needed to stop and rest and eat. But Adam was unreachable. She could see him ahead but even if she called him, she doubted he would hear.

It seemed like hours before Adam finally stopped in a small clearing and took off his pack. 'We can camp here,' he said.

It was still early but already the light was dimming in the forest, and they needed to put up the tent and cook a meal before dark. Fern peered in the bag at the noodles, dried vegetables and tofu; the predominant smell was onions, while the orange stuff might be carrot but she couldn't be sure. It looked totally unappetising yet when Adam soaked the vegetables and cooked them up with the noodles, the smell became tantalising.

'This is great,' said Fern, swallowing her first mouthful, then looking up, startled, as a bird landed on a branch just above their heads. Kookaburras always made her smile. Lighten up, they seemed to be saying with their throaty laugh. But this one was not laughing. It had something in its mouth.

'Look,' whispered Fern, nudging Adam and pointing.

It was a frog, its two back legs dangling out of the bird's beak. The kookaburra looked at them for a moment. 'Take note,' it seemed to be saying, before it set about bashing the struggling frog against the branch with its beak. Then it paused to look at them again, and flew off, the frog still in its mouth.

'It's strange seeing a kookaburra deep in a forest like this,' said Adam. 'They're not native to Tassie you know.'

Neither are we, thought Fern but decided against pointing that out because Adam still seemed edgy.

'At least there are frogs around. That's a good sign.' He scraped his bowl with his spoon, then rinsed them out and packed them back in with the trangia. 'If the frogs die it means we've polluted the waterways,' he said, pulling a ball of string out of the front pocket of his pack and tying it around a tree next to the tent. 'One thing dies out and we get a plague of something else. Now the bees are dying. If the bees die, so do we. You'd think that would be enough to ring alarm bells, wouldn't you?'

'Yeah, I guess you would,' said Fern, as Adam tied the other end of the string to a different tree. 'What are you doing?' she asked as he hung the food bags from the string.

'Keeping the food safe from rodents. The little buggers get into everything. They'll eat through the tent if we leave the food in there or right through the pack if they get a chance.'

Great, thought Fern, rodents too. Suddenly the tent didn't feel so safe. If a mouse could nibble its way in, then maybe other creatures could too.

'Shhh,' said Adam as something moved in the shadow of a tree. They both froze and waited. Soon a strange spotted cat-like creature stepped cautiously out of the shadows and sniffed around, apparently unaware they were even there. Fern had never seen anything like it.

'A quoll,' whispered Adam. 'Look,' he added, shining his torch up into a tree. 'We're being watched.'

The torch beam revealed a pair of disembodied red eyes glinting at them. Fern shuddered. What was behind those eyes?

'Just a possum,' said Adam, but it was little comfort to Fern, who was feeling increasingly oppressed by the night settling in around her. The forest was coming alive in another way as if, like a city, it housed different worlds. The birds were quiet now; instead the night was filled with scuttling noises, the buzz of insects and the rustle of prowling creatures.

Fern stood up, sending the quoll scuttling into the bushes. 'I'm going to bed,' she said.

Filled with desolation, Adam lay rigid in his sleeping bag. The memory of the clear-fell had imprinted itself on his mind, affecting him more than he'd expected. He thought of Matt, his old school friend, who'd been camping out in the forests, living in the trees and chaining himself to bulldozers, while Adam had been hiding in his basement flat in Sydney and drinking. The thought filled him with guilt.

Lying next to Adam, Fern could feel the barrier he was building between them. The anger in him was so strong. When she concentrated, she got flashes of images: bodies and blood, confused with the barren starkness of a clear-fell, broken trees piled high, fire and the flash of a face. Images she couldn't make any sense of. Adam felt the bush inside him; every hurt it sustained was his too. She understood that, but still his reaction that day had seemed excessive. It was almost as if there were something else at work here, casting shadows over them and between them. Fern knew she should resist whatever force was pushing them apart, but she was exhausted, every muscle in her body aching and tight. Her blisters had burst, leaving her with a stinging, burning patch on each ankle. She wanted to reach out to Adam but instead, weary to the bone, she fell asleep.

In her dream, Fern was lying on a bed in a darkened room with a large wooden-shuttered window. She was alert, waiting for something and sure enough, a shadow soon crossed the window sending alarm signals through her body. Perhaps a second passed before the shutters burst open and something hurled itself through the window, a dark mass, inhuman, yet human shaped, surging at her without hesitation, its intent clear. Fern felt a great swell of terror, along with the knowledge that she couldn't escape. But in that split second something in her understood that she could turn away from it, and with a great effort, she did.

'No!' She woke, terrified that it had stepped out of her dreams and found its way into the tent

Adam reached out and wrapped his arms around her. 'It's okay,' he said. 'I'm here. It can't get you.' But he'd felt the flash of terror, a flicker of a shadow, and knew that he too was helpless, unless he found a way of following Fern into her dreams. And that was beyond him.

Fern knew it too, but even so Adam's words comforted her. She tried to remember details of the figure that had lunged at her tonight, but the room in her dream had been dark and the figure featureless. It had a masculine energy to it, direct and certain. And hungry. But it was not the same figure as the cloaked priest who had walked through her dreams. The man who had given the order to slice the head from the child in her vision and who had looked at her with triumph in his eyes as the spear plunged into her chest. His was a crafty, underhand energy. They had different forms but the same intent. She had managed to turn away from its force tonight and that was a triumph of sorts. The next step would be to seek it out in her dreams but that would take a courage she wasn't sure she could muster.

Think beauty, she reminded herself. If she could deposit enough beauty within her it might act as a shield. Adam was the most beautiful thing she could imagine. 'I want to see you,' she said, switching on the torch. Its light threw shadows across him, highlighting a shoulder, a nipple, the curve of Adam's calf, his ear. Fern kissed the places where light fell, her fingers roving over the rest of his body. They made love, slower this time, without the ferocious urgency that had consumed them before. Now in the dim light they explored each other's bodies, finding secret places: a birthmark on Fern's foot, the soft hair on Adam's ear lobes, a mole on his lower back. When they were finished, Fern lay sheltered in Adam's arms and slept a deep and dreamless sleep.

Chapter Nineteen

The next day Fern's teeth were furry and her hair greasy. She wanted a shower but all she could manage were fresh undies and a splash of water on her face. She'd forgotten to stir the porridge and now it was burnt and stodgy; it would have been inedible except that she was so hungry. And to make it worse Adam was in a foul mood again. Thank God they were in a conservation area now, she thought. Though even this was under threat, according to Adam.

'Nothing's sacred in Tasmania,' he said. 'Only world heritage listing is enough to stop the bastards sticking their greedy noses into it.'

His fury was wearing Fern down. The devastation that people had wrought on the trees and the wildlife was heartbreaking but there was no point in Adam re-creating it in his own heart.

Fern watched uneasily as Adam stomped on ahead. Unable to keep up with him, she went at her own pace, doing her best to follow his tracks. They were winding further and further into the bush, following the easiest paths towards their destination, sometimes one way, then back the other. As far as Fern was concerned they could have been walking round in circles. She felt lost and afraid. Perhaps it was Adam's mood that had changed things, but today the forest seemed to barely tolerate her presence.

Adam was leading her through this maze with his life-saving gadgets: a map, a compass and an PLB. Without him, Fern would be lost. It was a labyrinth, she realised, as they penetrated deeper into the bush. There was no clear path, no easy way through, only her father waiting for them in the centre. Fern shuddered. She had a sudden urge to leave a trail behind her, something she could follow back out again.

Adam was no longer in sight and the atmosphere was thickening into the slow dense stuff of Fern's nightmares. She felt something watching her from behind - or was it to her left? There were voices, too, murmurings at first, then becoming louder and clearer so she could catch the odd word or phrase. *Beware*, said one, followed by the cackling wild laughter of an old woman. *Mother*; it was a child's voice, laced with panic. Fern turned quickly, trying to find its source but there were only trees and shadows. *Help me.* Fern felt helpless despair fall on her. She had failed her daughter. Centuries ago probably, but the despair was fresh. The Bear Handler had said this creature had got to her through those she loved. Perhaps it would try to hurt Adam next.

'Adam,' she called. 'Adam!'

Fern felt her feet tense up with fear. They wanted to run, but that would be madness. She'd be lost in seconds. With an effort she focused her will and resisted the urge, waiting instead for Adam to retrace his steps and find her..

The sound of a man's mocking voice made her jump. *You are mine.* The words sent a chill down Fern's spine and she turned, trying to locate this new voice. Hearing a noise behind her, she whipped around and caught a fleeting movement before the stillness descended again. Had the thing stepped through again or was it just her over active imagination?

'Adam!' she called again but the sound could no longer penetrate the density of the atmosphere.

Fern began to wonder if Adam would come back. Perhaps she had been wrong to trust him after all. She could feel the doubts increasing alongside her panic and with an effort she pushed them away, remembering instead the intensity of their lovemaking, their laughter, the tears he'd let her see. With this, a calm descended on Fern and the atmosphere around her lightened a little. Adam would come for her. Of course he would. That faith was the thread that would help her find her way out of this maze.

With a surge of relief, Fern saw Adam crashing through the undergrowth towards her. 'Fern! Are you okay?'

She smiled. He'd come back. He'd found her. Of course he had. I'm sorry,' she said. 'I couldn't keep up with you.'

Adam took her in his arms, furious at himself. 'No, I'm sorry. It was stupid of me. I should never have gone ahead like that. I don't know what came over me. All the time in the back of my head I was worried about you, but I couldn't bring myself to stop or turn around. Then suddenly I was free of it. I raced back, but I couldn't see you. Oh shit, Fern, I nearly lost you.'

'It's okay,' said Fern, but Adam knew it wasn't. He didn't have any excuses. Everything in his army training and his experience in the bush, told him you stick together. It was the golden rule.

'Do you think he knows we're coming?' asked Fern, reading the bewilderment and self-condemnation in Adam's mind.

'What?'

'My father. It's as if he knows and he's trying to stop us.'

Adam was uneasy with this idea. Sure, he'd felt as if something had taken him over but that was just a bad mood. The clearfell had got to him. 'It's just the place, Fern. Your father's not some wizard in a castle throwing spells at us.'

Fern nodded, wanting to believe him. They walked on, staying close together now, Adam adjusting his pace to Fern's. If there'd been a clearer track, he'd have made her walk ahead of him but he had to navigate their way along this overgrown path, so he went slowly, fighting back the negative thoughts that kept trying to take him over. The idea of Fern's father somehow influencing their progress was ridiculous but he couldn't shake it - the friction, the anger, the stupid mistakes, the slow pace … It was as if there was a force here that was driving a wedge between them. Between them and within them.

As they walked, Fern could still hear the distant echo of the voices. *We have her.* She steeled herself to ignore the creeping shadows, the inexplicable voices, but terror and despair were slinking back again. *I was innocent.* A shocked bewilderment rose in Fern as she listened to those words because this voice was unmistakably her own. *I was innocent.* Then came another voice. *No one is innocent.*

'Let's talk,' Fern said to Adam, desperate to distract herself from these messages intruding from a past she didn't recall or understand.

'What do you want to talk about?' Despite his efforts, Adam too was withdrawing into himself, feeling the anger rise in him once more.

'I don't know, anything.'

'Okay,' he said. 'Tell me about your parents.'

'Which ones?'

'The real ones,' he said. 'The ones who brought you up.'

Fern thought about Grace and Richard. Were they her real parents? They certainly knew her better than her birth parents. And yet they were so different from her. 'My mother loves me,' she said. 'I'm grateful to her for that.'

'You're not supposed to be grateful for love.'

'I didn't get a lot of it as a kid. At least not from Dad. Everything had a clause. You know, if you do this then I'll love you, kind of thing. But Mum loved me unconditionally … I guess it's what saved me.'

'What about your dad?' asked Adam.

Fern stepped carefully over a fallen log, instinctively scanning the ground on the other side for snakes. 'I hated him for a long time. And I was afraid of him. Did I tell you he's in hospital? He had a heart attack a couple of weeks ago. His sixth, I think.

'You don't sound too worried.'

'He always recovers. Then he blames me. I'm used to it now,' she said, then paused, wondering if that was true. 'Once, when I was fifteen, something burst in his brain. An aneurism, I think they call it. He was put in intensive care. When Mum and I visited, the doctors warned us that he needed to stay calm. We went into this darkened room and he was lying there attached to wires and machines. He looked shrunken and afraid, and I felt sorry for him, but then he turned his head and looked at me. You know what he said?'

'What?'

'You tried to kill me.'

'Shit,' said Adam, stopping in his tracks and turning to look at Fern. 'That's a lot to lay on a kid. Why did he do that?'

Fern remembered how the words had struck her like a punch in the stomach. She'd known instinctively that it was vital to hand those words back at him, but Richard had cursed her with them and curses aren't so easy to break. Why did he curse her? She didn't really know the answer to Adam's question. 'I guess I wasn't doing what he wanted,' she said. 'Nothing I did was right, at least not in his eyes.'

'So what happened?' asked Adam.

Fern smiled bitterly at the memory. 'I shouted FUCK OFF as loudly as I could, and then I ran.'

She remembered the emergency bell ringing, the sound of her feet pounding along the hospital corridor towards the exit and the sound of doctors running. She'd found her own way home, coming back to the empty house, certain she'd killed him. Certain that those two angry words had sent him to his grave. Knowing she should never have uttered them. When she discovered he was still alive, the relief she felt was entirely selfish: she didn't have to carry his death on her shoulders. She'd promised herself then that she would never use words powerfully again. That she would never again lose herself in anger. But the accusation was still there, impossible to erase. It wasn't even the first time she'd become aware of the power of words, both good and bad. No, that had come much earlier; in her father's dismissive labelling, the cruel teasing of the kids at school and in the library where she'd borrowed book after book, the stories transporting her somewhere else for a time.

'Isn't it strange,' she said, 'how words can change the direction you go in life. We use them without thinking most of the time, yet they're really powerful.' Fern took a swig from her water bottle. 'Do you think it's possible to heal someone with words?' She recalled reading passages in books that conveyed a truth that hit her like an epiphany, a warming compliment given generously: surely these had as much power as an insult?

'Maybe,' said Adam, setting off again. 'I don't know. You can sure as hell hurt someone with them.'

Fern remembered again how a word that was well timed and sent with intent, could feel worse than a slap. And the pain lasted longer. Then there were the promises, formed and kept like spells, good promises and bad ones. She thought about the Bear Handler's question: who was she bound to? Now wherever she looked Fern could see bindings, like the promise she'd made the day her father had accused her. There were other promises too - *I will never let myself be hurt again ... I will always be nice, even at my own expense ...* each promise clamping another lock on her heart and sucking away her power until she was an empty shell with nothing left to give. No wonder she had withdrawn into her white attic room.

To be free of these bindings she would have to sever the emotional connections between herself and those she'd given her power to, and then she would have to reclaim the fragments of herself that had been left behind, in a place, or with another person, in another time. Shamesh had told her that she was almost empty, she'd lost so much of herself. But she felt less transparent now. Already she was reclaiming some of those lost pieces.

Fern looked at Adam walking just in front of her, his head at a slight angle as if he were bemused by the world. His blond hair was longer than hers, rough and unkempt after a day and a half in the wilderness. She longed to run her fingers through it, teasing out the tangles, feeling the roundness of his skull below. Each time Fern looked at him she memorised his features, the tilt of his nose, his certain chin, the cut of his ears, the way his hair framed his forehead. She held these memories close, along with the delicious smell of him and the taste of his skin. Yet when he was out of sight, or even with his back turned, the images fled, leaving her with an intense but unfocused yearning. The thought of losing Adam was becoming unbearable, creating an ache inside of her that was so strong she had to steer her mind around it. Already she couldn't bear to contemplate the possibility.

'Let's eat,' said Adam, eventually stopping in a small clearing. 'I'm starving.'

They sat on a log, in a patch of warm sunlight and ate chunks of cheese, slices of salami, dried fruit and some nuts. This was better than burnt porridge. For the first time that day, Fern felt good. 'Do you like being alive?' she asked between mouthfuls.

'What sort of question is that?'

'Sometimes you say stuff that makes me think you'd rather be dead.'

Adam's instinct was to tell Fern to back off, but he knew that if he didn't want to lose her, he had to let her in. 'Sometimes everything hurts so much, you just want it to stop,' he said hesitantly.

'Like your dad dying?'

'Yeah, like that,' said Adam, looking away.

'I don't think I've ever been too keen on living,' said Fern when it became clear that Adam was not going to continue the conversation. 'Otherwise I would have done it better.' She took another bite of her cheese and smiled. 'Though today just the taste of this makes me want to live forever.'

Adam laughed. 'I reckon you've got a healthy appetite for life,' he said, taking Fern in his arms and pressing his mouth down on hers.

She pushed him away. 'I haven't brushed my teeth.'

'Neither have I.'

'I can tell.'

Then they were peeling off each other's clothes, laughing and impatient as they fumbled with straps and zips. They clung together, shivering in the cold forest air, Adam's hands running along Fern's body, her nipples were hard against his tongue. Fern lay back on the soft mossy ground, savouring the cool dampness as Adam pushed into her. She looked up into the treetops at the tiny patches of vivid blue sky visible through the canopy, then back at Adam moving above her, his muscles taut, his eyes looking through her. He pushed harder and harder, and she gasped, thrusting her body up towards him again and again, wanting him so much. Then, caught up in the ecstasy of orgasm, it seemed for a moment that there was no distinction between her and Adam and the forest or the sky.

Afterwards they lay still, their bodies warming each other as the cold seeped into their backs. There was something exquisite about making love outside. Fern could feel everything acutely: the roughness of the bark digging into her back, the damp moss under her, the softness of Adam's skin, the tightness of his muscles.

'There's only one thing that makes me want to stay alive,' Adam said, his voice almost a sob.

'What's that?'

'You.'

Fern felt her heart lurch in surprise. Speechless, she licked the salty tears off his cheeks. He had given her a beautiful gift but she didn't know what to do with the responsibility that came with it.

Something was tickling her thigh, distracting her. She looked down and saw a black slimy thing attaching itself to her skin. 'Oh my God, a leech,' she shouted, pushing Adam away, jumping up and frantically trying to brush it off with her hands.

'Turn around,' said Adam. 'They're all over your butt.'

'Get them off, get them off,' screamed Fern, blind with panic.

Adam laughed, but his hands were working quickly. 'I wish I had a camera. Calm down. Keep still, will you, I can't get them off if you jump around like that … There, that's most of them, just a couple of hangers-on.' He dabbed some meths onto them and they dropped away. Then he checked his own legs. 'I only got two. Your blood must be sweeter.'

Fern's skin was crawling at the thought of them sucking her blood. 'That's it, no more sex outside. Ever again,' she said, reaching for her clothes.

'Ow, shit, I've been bitten,' said Adam, rubbing his hand.

Heart pounding, Fern scanned the ground for the snake.

'Bloody jack jumpers. I'd forgotten how much they hurt.'

'Jack jumpers?'

'Yeah, ants. See those black ones with the red legs? They've got a hell of a bite.'

'Thank God for that,' said Fern, relief flooding through her. 'I thought it was a snake.'

They got dressed, pulling on thermals and gaiters and boots. Adam was cradling his hand so Fern did up his laces for him. Then she took his hand in hers to get a closer look. 'It's swelling,' she said.

'Yeah, I always used to swell up with ant bites,' said Adam. 'There's some bite cream in the medical kit. Pity I didn't bring any antihistamines.' He dug out the cream, smeared some onto the bite, then stood up and swung the pack onto his back. 'We'd better get going.'

As they set off, Adam was overtaken by a sense of urgency. He would have run if he could, away from the pain increasing in his hand, but he contented himself with a fast walk. Puzzled, Fern followed as best she could. Even with fresh bandaids on her feet, her shoes were rubbing and taking up all her attention, so it was a while before she noticed that Adam was breathing heavily.

'Are you okay?' she asked.

'I can't get my breath,' said Adam. 'My throat's too tight.'

The swelling had spread all the way up his arm and now his face was puffing up too. Fern remembered a girl at school having a reaction like that when she'd eaten a nut. She'd been rushed to hospital, but even so she'd nearly died.

'Sit down,' she said, pulling the pack off his back, her voice urgent.

Adam sank to the ground and leaned against a tree. 'I can't breathe,' he gasped, clutching his throat.

Fern could see the fear in Adam's eyes and knew it was mirrored in her own. The bite cream wasn't going to help a serious allergic reaction and there was only one other thing she could think of. Hands shaking, she dug frantically through her bag for the little velvet pouch that Cassie had given her. Adam hadn't wanted Fern to bring it, telling her he had all the medical stuff they needed, but she'd slipped it in at the last minute, mainly in case she had another one of those night attacks. What was it that Cassie had recommended for bites? Apis had something to do with bees, so it had to be that one. There was no time for doubts.

'Here,' she said, opening Adam's mouth and squeezing four drops in, a part of her hoping for a miracle, another part sensing it was too little too late.

'I'm sorry,' said Adam, looking at her without recognition. 'I didn't mean it.'

It was happening too quickly. Adam was gasping for breath, the swelling on his face was getting worse and now it was starting on his neck. Already he was practically unconscious, his eyes rolling back, his eyelids closing. Instinctively Fern knew she had to keep him awake. She shook him gently, then patted his cheeks. 'Stay awake, Adam, please stay with me.'

He opened his eyes, looked wildly around and then shut them again. Desperately Fern grabbed her water bottle and poured some of it onto his face.

'No, no.' His voice was a hoarse whisper. Then he opened his eyes and stared at something Fern couldn't see. 'Go away. Leave me alone,' he rasped, waving his arms as if fending someone off, and almost knocking the water bottle out of her hand. 'Why don't they kill me?' he whimpered, folding over as Fern held him, his neck going limp, his head heavy in her hands.

Desperately Fern squeezed more apis into his mouth. It was all she could think to do. 'Stay here, Adam. I love you, don't leave me.' She kept talking and shaking him but his eyes stayed shut. Thirty seconds later she gave him some more drops, not knowing what else to do. He was pale now, his body clearly shutting down. Fern checked for a pulse; at first she felt nothing and then she got it, such a feeble rhythm. She couldn't bear it if it stopped. Perhaps she should try mouth to mouth, but she'd never been shown how and it wouldn't help if his airway was closed. The only other thing she could do was pray.

'Please,' she begged. 'Please help him.'

Suddenly out of nowhere she remembered Michael giving the penguin his life. She would try to do the same for Adam.

'Please help me,' she prayed again, not to any god she knew of, but to the life-giving force that had flowed through Michael.

Fern forced herself to stop panicking and as soon as she did, the knowing came into her. She put one hand on the bite and placed the other lightly on his neck. Then she waited. Innately she knew that the energy would only flow through her heart, but her heart was still closed. Despairing, she tried to open it, imagined it wide and vulnerable. However, it was only when she let her mind touch on Adam that Fern felt her love welling up and overflowing. She had the sense of the crown of her head opening and felt an immense pressure as light flowed through her head and into her heart, then down her arms and into her hands. Fern could feel her hands throbbing, the energy pumping through her and flowing into Adam. Never had she felt more certain. There was no room for fear or panic, just the certainty that Adam would live.

Fern didn't know how long she sat there bathed in the light as it poured through her and into Adam. Nothing mattered except that connection. There were flickers of visions, shrieking bird-like women with red-painted claws. And the word *guilty,* over and over. But this was different from the voices she'd heard as they walked through the forest. Now she was picking up the thoughts in Adam's mind. These creatures weren't here for her; they wanted Adam. She could feel the battle raging in him, one part of Adam submitting to them and another part fighting for life. Fern stayed focused. She felt a steady determination inside her. I know who you are, she thought, and you're not going to win.

Suddenly she was certain that she'd done this before, in another life, another time and place, using her hands, letting the energy flow, feeling her heart open and trusting. It was a beautiful certainty, a gift after all the horror. Fern wondered if this was what Shamesh and Cassie had meant when they'd told her she needed to remember who she was.

After a time the swelling began to subside further and Fern saw that the danger was over. 'Thank you,' she whispered, her heart filled with gratitude to whatever had allowed her to channel the life force.

Adam moved his head, then opened his eyes and gazed up at Fern. She smiled, feeling an immense happiness washing through her as the energy stopped its flow. The pressure in her head and the throbbing in her hands receded, leaving her dizzy and light and clean inside, as if the flowing energy had washed her out.

Adam smiled back. Their eyes locked for a moment in a gaze that held no defences. Fern felt herself falling into Adam as though they were one and the same person. It frightened her and she blinked, then blushed, overcome by shyness, as if Adam were a stranger she'd stumbled across in the forest.

As Fern moved out of his line of sight, Adam looked around him: at the trees, their trunks driving upwards towards the light; the sky, its blue offset by the clouds racing through the gaps in the trees; the fungi, glowing shades of orange and yellow and cream; and the dazzling iridescent green of the moss. He could have been seeing it all for the very first time. I'm alive, he thought, his reaction a cocktail of relief and surprise, with just a tinge of regret.

'Thanks,' he said, taking Fern's hand. 'What did you do?'

'I gave you apis, a homeopathic remedy,' she said, showing Adam the bottle. 'But it wasn't enough on its own, so I copied Michael. I sent you my life.' That was how Michael had described it, though Fern realised it wasn't her life she'd sent. She'd been only a conduit. It was life itself that had flowed into Adam, through her.

Adam smiled. 'He's always fixing things - animals, tractors, cars - he's great at it but I never thought there was any magic in it … Though Mum used to say he had healing hands.' Adam's voice was still weak and hoarse. 'I've always underestimated my little brother,' he added.

'He's pretty special. You're lucky to have a brother like him.'

Adam thought about all the times he'd hated his little brother. The way Michael had smiled as he trashed Adam's toys then looked at him as if he expected a pat on the back, until Adam had bashed the smile off his face. Even then he'd come back, following Adam around adoringly. So many times Adam had wished his brother away.

'Yeah, maybe I am lucky. I've never thought of it like that.' He smiled at Fern. 'Looks like I'm safe then. A brother and a lover, both healers.'

A healer. The title felt strange to Fern, yet Shamesh had said she would become a healer, Cassie had given her the potions and Michael had showed her the way. Together they'd made it possible for Fern to save Adam. One part of Fern resisted the idea that everyone had a predestined path in life but another part of her felt excited by the notion that each person's life was like a mystery in a detective story, laden with clues: their task, to inhabit the mystery and solve it. It seemed that the clues lay in asking the right questions, in understanding one's passions and desires, and the patterns behind them. Fern felt as if something askew had clicked into place within her. Perhaps she *was* supposed to be a healer. After all, it had felt so normal, as if she'd been doing it forever. Is this what I've been looking for? she asked herself, remembering how lost she'd felt and depressed, locked inside her attic. She shuddered at the memory, surprised that so little time had passed since then. How different she felt now.

Adam was shivering, so Fern pulled out his sleeping bag and wrapped it around him. 'I'll make some tea,' she said, and began setting up the trangia the way she'd seen Adam do it.

'You know, I felt the energy,' said Adam. 'It was strange. Your hands were warm and there was a light in me, I could feel it pulling me back.' He didn't add that something in him had wanted to let go; he didn't need to because Fern already knew.

'Here,' she said, handing him a mug of strong tea, sweetened with sugar.

'Thanks,' said Adam, the warmth of the tea thawing his frozen fingers. He wanted to hold onto his sense of wonder, to keep feeling the vibrancy of life around him and his connection with it.

'What happened in Iraq?' asked Fern.

Adam looked at her quickly, suspicion in his eyes. 'Did I say something?'

'You were shouting, "Get away, leave me alone," as if something was tormenting you. I got a picture of the things. I know what they are, Adam. They're Furies. You know, from Greek mythology. They're the voice of your conscience. They latch onto people who have committed a crime and they drive them mad.'

Adam looked away, his heart thudding. He'd never told anyone about the hags in his dreams, had even refused to discuss it with the army psychiatrist.

'You should talk about it,' said Fern, sitting down next to Adam and slipping her arm around him.

Adam pushed her arm away. He didn't want to go back there, to that hell on earth. The dust in his mouth, up his nose, in his eyes, the cracks in his lips, the blood, and the heat beating down on him so hard he couldn't think. And never knowing who was who, just shooting. 'Kill 'em all,' one of his mates had said. 'Don't be an idiot,' he'd retorted, but he'd known what Fin meant. When he looked around again, he saw Fin go down, a bullet in his face and another in his neck. He'd tried to help, but it was too late and Fin had died in the dust, his blood drying almost as it dripped onto the ground.

Fern still sat next to him with her knees tucked up under her chin, waiting. Her hair was sticking up all over the place but it made her even more beautiful. He didn't want to tell her what had happened, see her close off from him, but he knew he couldn't run from the truth forever. She'd trusted him, telling him things that left her vulnerable. She wanted to be with him, maybe even loved him. He owed Fern the truth. He had to give her the chance to leave.

Deliberately he sent his mind back to that afternoon: one o'clock, pretty much the hottest time of the day. He'd been exhausted and so thirsty there was no moisture left in his throat. His voice was hoarse, the way it was now.

'We were in Basra. There were snipers everywhere - us and them. It wasn't straightforward fighting, not the stuff we'd been trained for. It never was over there. I was getting spooked. Couldn't tell what was friendly fire and what wasn't. I shot a guy – he wasn't in uniform, but that was the problem, most of them weren't.' Adam stopped and took a gulp of his tea, not caring that it was too hot, wanting to feel it scorching his throat. 'He was lying there and I was about to move on but then this kid stepped out of the shadows and walked over to the dead guy. I called out for him to stop, told him to move away.' Adam paused, his voice strained, almost a whisper. 'The kid looked up, but he didn't stop. I called out again but he ignored me and slipped his hand into the dead guy's jacket. He could've been pulling out a grenade or a gun, it could've been anything. Why didn't he stop? Jesus, I didn't know what to do. I was scared.' Adam was crying now, bent and broken. Helplessly, Fern watched him. 'I killed him,' he sobbed. 'I shot him in the chest.' He groaned. 'He was nine or ten. Only a kid. And his sister was watching.

'I see it all the time, the boy looking at me, knowing what I was about to do. Knowing even before I knew. And the girl … there was no expression on her face. She gave one cry but then her face set. She just looked at me with those beautiful eyes and I knew what I'd done.' Adam was rocking back and forth now, trying to escape the ugliness of the truth. 'If I shut my eyes they come. These fucking old crones. It's like they're wearing me down, like they want me to kill myself. A life for a life, that's the law.'

'No, it isn't,' said Fern, reaching out for his hand. Impatiently Adam shook it away.

'They're illusions,' she said. 'They only have power if you give it to them. It's just your guilt talking.'

'Just!' said Adam. 'What do you mean, *just*? They're right. I don't deserve to live. You shouldn't have saved me.'

Fern was getting angry now. She was shocked by what Adam had done, shocked and disappointed, but it didn't change the way she felt towards him. 'For God's sake, stop wallowing in self-pity. Yes, it's bad what you did. Really bad, but how much worse would it be if you die too? That would be another life wasted. So do something special with your life. Make up for it by living well, not by refusing to live.'

Abruptly Fern turned away and started packing up the trangia. Adam felt as if he'd been slapped. He didn't know what to say. She was right. He'd been wallowing in self-pity but he didn't know how to pull himself out of it. He stood up slowly, his legs trembling with fatigue.

'Shouldn't we wait for a while until you get your strength back?' asked Fern.

'We can't. We're already behind. I packed six days of food, three in and three out - and that's assuming your father will feed us while we're there. We have to keep moving.'

Fern watched Adam hoist his bag onto his back. 'You know, since we got to Tasmania you've been different,' she said. 'Stronger somehow, as if the earth is feeding you. Or maybe it's in the way you love the wilderness. It's what gives you strength … Maybe this is where you'll find your redemption.'

'Maybe,' said Adam, the flatness in his voice belying the fact that her words had excited something within him. It was as if Fern had handed him a piece of a jigsaw puzzle, though he didn't know where it fitted yet. Yeah, he thought, I love the bush and that's what Tassie's all about. But it's completely polarised. One battle after another. It would be impossible for him to live here and not take sides. And Adam didn't want to be part of another war. He stood for a moment gathering in his energy and then set off again. He looked terrible: his face was pale and he walked stiffly as if each step was a great effort. Yet as they walked, Adam felt a growing sense of relief. He could stop running now. He'd told his story and Fern hadn't turned away from him. With the relief came a new sense of resolve. She was right, instead of destroying himself he needed to find a way to live well.

Adam looked at his watch but it was only just after three, too early to set up camp. The afternoon's walk had been gruelling, and he was hungry and needed to rest. He considered stopping a bit earlier than planned and making up for it tomorrow but quickly dismissed the idea. They needed to keep on schedule. If his calculations were right, they should reach the river in the morning and then it would be a direct line to Eric's house.

'Why don't we stop for a bit?' asked Fern, sensing his exhaustion. 'You need to rest.'

'No.'

'It doesn't matter if we're a bit behind.'

'Not yet.'

'God, you're stubborn. What star sign are you?'

'Taurus,' said Adam.

'That figures. What year were you born?' she asked, wondering that she didn't know, that they still had so much to find out about each other.

'Nineteen eighty-five. Why?'

'Let's see, what happened in that year? That's right, they found the *Titanic*. And the French government sunk the *Rainbow Warrior* in Auckland. Remember, the Greenpeace boat?'

'How do you know that?'

'There was a serious shortage of books in our house when I was a kid, but I had two; an encyclopaedia of mythology and an almanac. I got it for my eleventh birthday and read it over and over. Now the whole thing's stuck in my head.' She laughed. 'Dates and the gods, that's all I know.'

'Anything else happen?'

'There was a cyclone in Bangladesh that killed ten thousand people, and it was the year of the first Live Aid concert … Maybe that's why you're like that.'

'Like what?'

'A fighter, an activist. Always pushing against things. It's like you were born for it.'

'There's plenty of things to push against,' said Adam.

'There are, but you're so angry about everything, you want to hurt yourself. What good will that do? Maybe if you gave something back …'

'Will you quit having a go at me?'

'I'm not.'

'You are.'

'Okay, okay, I'll shut up,' said Fern.

They walked on, Fern limping slightly, her ankle throbbing, her blisters rubbing, but compared with Adam she felt fresh. Willpower was the only thing keeping him going.

'When were *you* born?' asked Adam.

'Nineteen eighty-nine,' said Fern. 'The Chinese army killed thousands of students in Tienanmen Square, the Berlin Wall came down, the Dalai Lama won the Nobel Peace Prize, Salman Rushdie was condemned to death for being rude about Mohammad, and the communist regimes in Czechoslovakia and Romania were overthrown.'

'A busy year,' said Adam.

'Yeah.'

A year of contradictions, thought Fern: free speech for some and not for others, the scales of justice squeaking into a new but not very different position. But maybe it had been the beginning of something bigger that, like most change, was a blend of the gradual and the cataclysmic and only noticed in retrospect.

'Anything happen in Australia?' asked Adam, his muscles straining under the weight of his pack. He couldn't go on much longer.

'Not much. An earthquake in Newcastle, Bob Hawke crying on television because he'd been caught cheating on his wife, university fees reintroduced … Pretty boring really.'

Fern didn't add that in the Adelaide Botanic Gardens, Simple Simon had uttered a prophecy that set in motion a series of events, nor that she was born on the footpath while her mother waited for the lights to change and her father waited for his next opportunity to kill her. If it hadn't been for that prophecy she wouldn't be hiking through this forest on her way to visit her father. She wouldn't have met Adam either, thought Fern, so there was no point wishing Simple Simon had kept his mouth shut.

Chapter Twenty

Fern was in two places at once. The gentle rise and fall of Adam's breath and the rustle of the night outside were welcome intruders in this dream, grounding her when every instinct was telling her to fly, her senses screaming DANGER as she cautiously peered into a small room. A place of worship, she thought, seeing flashes of a curved doorway, the intricate inlays on the walls. The room was empty except for a man sitting on a long bench. A man exuding power. He was a wealthy merchant, but there was more to him than that. She sensed some secret lying within him.

'You must go up and touch it,' Shamesh had told her but Fern's terror was so strong it almost overwhelmed her. Seeking to control her fear she took one silent step and then another, hearing a strange rhythmic gusting sound that she soon realised was her own breath. Instinctively she was using it to keep her fear down, the way the Bear Handler had shown her. Forcing her way through the dense atmosphere of her dream, she took another step, her breathing so loud she was sure the man would hear. Fern suddenly remembered the staff and instantly found herself clasping its rough-hewn surface, its solidity giving her the strength to go on. She was almost level with him now. Mustering all her courage she reached out with the staff and touched it to his shoulder.

'Sattar,' she whispered, as she woke. 'Sattar.'

Fern opened her eyes to the darkness and in a sudden flash realised what had just happened. She had turned everything around, become the hunter and sought him out. You were hidden, she thought, and I found you. She had no idea who this man was or how he related to her. Another manifestation, she guessed. From the same being, incarnating in different forms for God only knew how many lifetimes.

Since they'd entered the forest, Fern's waking life and her dreams had become increasingly indistinguishable and the visions and voices were coming thick and fast, like a volley of arrows. It seemed likely that her father was sending some of these dreams and visions, but this one couldn't have been from him. Fern herself had looked for Sattar, drawn him to her from memories that were stored deep in her unconscious. She was learning and becoming stronger. Each memory she faced and released solidified her in some way, planting her feet more firmly on the ground. And she could still feel the memory of the healing energy flowing through her hands and into Adam that afternoon; an act that had connected her even further to her potential self and in so doing, strengthened her. But even with all these changes, Fern was in no doubt that her father was far stronger than she.

Outside the tent, the night was noisy: the loud humming of insects, the crackle of twigs, a creak of a branch, the ghostly cry of a possum, and in the distance the constant roll of thunder. The tent was lit up with stark and eerie flashes of lightning. Through the thin layer of plastic that divided them from the forest, Fern could make out the silhouetted shadows of the trees as lightning pierced the darkness.

Lying in the tent, snuggled close to Adam, she felt vulnerable but also inexplicably safe. Knowing just how much darkness she carried within her, Fern had always feared and avoided the cracks in her life, suspecting that if she slipped down one, she'd fall forever into an inescapable darkness. Lately though, the cracks were widening so much that she could no longer avoid them. But instead of darkness, the light was finding its way through the cracks and Fern was beginning to realise that it was only her fear feeding the shadows within her.

In the distance Fern heard a roar, like a truck or an aeroplane. It was coming closer, the roar filling her ears until she was certain she and Adam and their tiny tent would be destroyed. When it hit, Fern realised it was the wind, gusting mightily above. She could hear the creaking and swaying of the trees and the rustle of the leaves, but no breeze touched the sides of the tents.

When the wind had blown itself out, the rain arrived, gathering first in the forest canopy, before large drops found their way through, thudding loudly onto the tent. Inside the tent, however, it remained dry and still. With her eyes closed, the sound of the rain was like a crackling fire, broken only by Adam's snores. As dawn approached, Fern finally dozed off, only to be woken shortly after by the sound of the zip opening.

'Shit, it's raining.' Adam fumbled around with his pack, and set up the trangia in the tiny annexe where they kept their boots. Fern sat up to watch him making the coffee, and gratefully accepted a cup. She sipped it, feeling groggy from lack of sleep. But alongside her tiredness was a new sense of clarity and even optimism. Unless they got ridiculously lost, they would arrive at her father's place today. On his website she'd seen pictures of the house and grounds. It was impossibly luxurious: gleaming marble, polished wood and velvet-draped four-poster beds. Six star accommodation he called it. Perhaps this was a category for the super rich. She didn't imagine she and Adam would be welcome but a part of her was secretly looking forward to using a six star bathroom.

As the morning passed, Fern felt her optimism slowly diminishing, replaced by a familiar sense of despair. It flickered to life as she dressed awkwardly in the cramped confines of the tent, then when she stepped out into the rain her sense of hopelessness deepened. As they trudged along, her feet squelched on the forest floor, the rain seeping through her rain jacket, sending shivers down her spine. It was not long before they were completely soaked and chilled to the bone. They walked for a couple of hours like this, without talking. Their faces were angled down, away from the rain, but it still poured off Fern's eyelashes, slipping into her eyes and making them sting.

It's just rain, she told herself. But irrationally she felt it was personal, that her father was sending the rain, the visions, the dark moods, deliberately wearing them down. He's winning, she thought, as they plodded miserably through the rain, all too aware that every step she took brought her closer to a confrontation she now felt too weak to face.

'Adam?'

'Yeah.'

'Maybe we should turn around.'

Adam stopped. 'You're kidding.'

'Please. I can't do this. I can't face him.'

'Course you can,' said Adam. 'Look, we're coming up to the bit I can handle. I can't help you fight this thing in your dreams but I sure as hell can manage your dad. He's flesh and blood.'

Fern sighed and followed Adam as he strode off again, her feet squelching through soaking moss and muddy puddles, the water seeping in over the tops of her boots and numbing her feet. Her bones were aching with the cold. It feeds on my fear, she reminded herself. I have to find a way to stop being afraid.

The answer came in the sound of birdsong, the rain washing the notes clean so that each one hovered clear and strong. *Beauty*, she thought. Fern took her pipe out from a side pocket, put it to her lips and played. At first she drew tunes from her memory, playing with difficulty, her fingers numb and slow from the cold, the notes sounding tentative and mournful. But soon she lost herself in the music, letting her fingers choose the notes, allowing the tunes to form and pierce through the dense atmosphere, resounding among the trees.

As Fern played, Adam felt his step lighten. The rain didn't matter so much now, or the mud. They walked alongside a creek for a while, the water running wild, bubbling and frothing merrily. Then they heard the murmur of a waterfall and for a time the water and the pipe sang together in harmony.

Suddenly the rain stopped and the sun appeared, filtering through the canopy and lighting their path. Fern looked up and saw drops of water suspended and glowing under a patch of blue sky. We're fighting back, she thought, regaining ground. With that she played on, a happier tune now, the rhythm faster, the notes tripping over each other joyfully. The forest wasn't so dense here, and more sun found its way through the trees. She even felt a breeze caressing her skin.

As they walked past a pile of rocks, Fern heard a rustling sound and looked up in time to see a snake hurl itself off the top of the rocks. Then, still attached to the top of the rocks by its tail, it dangled precariously, a mouse clasped in its jaws. Fern stopped abruptly, watching the snake, absorbing its power, its intent, its patience. She could feel these qualities inside herself, the awakening of a latent force, a strength she needed to say yes to in order to live her life fully.

Up ahead, Adam had paused, waiting for her in a patch of sunlight. 'Look,' he said as she caught up with him.

Fern gasped at the sudden explosion of space in front of them. They were standing above a wide river or bay, she wasn't sure which, but for the first time in three days she could feel the full strength of the wind on her face and see further than a few metres ahead of her. She stared at the sky, amazed at its vastness. There was a break in the clouds just above them, but beyond that the rain was falling in a heavy sheet, so thick she could see where it began and ended.

'Macquarie Harbour,' said Adam. He consulted the map. 'It looks like we've come out too far up but that's not a problem. We'll follow this track round the edge for a while, then maybe cut back inland to your father's house.'

Stopping for lunch, they sat gazing out over the water, sipping miso soup and finishing off the last of the chocolate. Then they set off once more, following the contours of the harbour. The rain began again in surging gusts, and the track wound down, almost to the shore, then up again before disappearing altogether. This forced them to a standstill.

Fern waited while Adam looked for a path. They were high up, not exactly on the edge of a cliff but higher than Fern was comfortable with. She could feel a familiar vertigo setting in, paralysing her legs.

'This way,' called Adam, who had climbed a bit higher. 'There's a good path here.'

Fern looked up in the direction of Adam's voice but couldn't see him. Dizziness descended on her and she felt as if she was falling, her body tumbling through the air, every ounce of her being anticipating the impact.

'Come on,' said Adam impatiently. 'It's not far up.'

'I can't do it,' she said, feeling another voice rising within her: a howl, a wail, hardly human and heavy with grief.

'It's okay, just give me your hand,' said Adam, reaching down. He was baffled. The height wasn't that great and the way up was easy.

'Keep away.'

'What?'

'Don't come near me,' Fern said in a voice that wasn't hers. Waves of vertigo washed through her, forcing her onto her hands and knees. She clung to a shrub, but the drop was suddenly vertical and she found herself perched on the edge of a tall cliff. From far below came the crash of waves against rocks. Terrified, she felt herself slipping, could feel her fingers loosen, her body slide. She was going to die, her body pulverised on the rocks below.

As she clung there, Adam reached down further to help her. She tried to say no but her mouth couldn't formulate the words, so she just shook her head. The wind was picking up, blasting into her back and soon the rain would wash away her handhold. She realised now that she was stuck somewhere between the present and a distant past that was coming at her in glimpses of terror. This is Adam, she told herself. Only Adam. He won't hurt me.

'Calm down,' said Adam. 'You're not going to fall.'

She was about to reach out to him but his suddenly face changed into another's; her husband or lover, she couldn't remember, but the face was so familiar. He was a lord, she knew that much. Handsome but cruel, his mouth like the slash of a sword, blood-red and sharp. She was afraid of him. And so was his horse, who was standing behind him, fretful and uneasy. He'd taken off one of his riding gloves and she found her eyes riveted by its elaborate design, deep red, with an embroidered golden dragon on the back.

Help me. The words sounded over and over in her head, but she couldn't speak them. She was mute. Literally tongueless, she realised with horror. Tongueless, by his hand. What had she been to him? The answer came unbidden: *an acquisition*, one that he was now discarding. Her gaze leaped unwillingly from his glove to his face. Their eyes locked and with a feeling of helpless dread she watched him smile as he reached down and stroked her hand before unpeeling her fingers from the edge. She remembered it all: the certain knowledge of death, the dreadful dizziness, the sun flashing in her eyes, and him standing at the top of that cliff, a triumphant smile on his face. I was innocent, she thought. Innocent.

'Fern! Take my hand.'

She looked up and saw Adam's face again, his strong square hand, his kindness, his good intentions. She reached her hand out and took his, forcing herself to trust him as he hauled her up to where he was standing.

'What was that all about?' asked Adam.

Fern shook her head helplessly. Her throat was closed, still muted.

'We'd better get moving then,' he said, giving her an anxious look.

Tears were streaming down Fern's face as she followed Adam along this new track he'd found. Still soaked through, she was chilled by the wind, her body shaking, her teeth chattering, as she cried out her grief over the tragic end of another woman's life.

Adam glanced back to check that Fern was still behind. 'Shit, your lips are blue. We'll have to stop and get you a warm drink.'

'I'm fine,' she said, wanting to keep moving. 'How long until we get there?'

'I reckon it'll take about another hour. That's if the track stays good. I wanted to double back and come in from the bush but this weather's crap. Maybe we just have to front up at the main gate.'

Fern nodded. It was pointless trying to sneak into her father's domain: he knew they were coming. He was playing with them, unearthing their fears and their deepest secrets, throwing stumbling blocks in their way. Every time she began to feel strong, something else would arise to crush her. Fern didn't know how long she could keep treading the line between the physical world and this other, metaphysical world, both of them throwing up one challenge after another. It was taking all her strength. The sooner they got there the better, but the thought of meeting her father was terrifying.

'Let's keep going,' she said.

'No. You're getting hypothermia. We have to stop.' Adam lifted the pack off Fern's back, then rummaged about in his own for the trangia. While the water boiled he wrapped Fern up in her sleeping bag.

'What happened back there?' he asked finally, when Fern was sipping her tea.

She shrugged, so tired she couldn't find the words for what she'd seen. It was more intuition than knowledge. 'I think it was a memory of a past life. I saw myself falling and you were someone else.' She shuddered, clasping her mug in both hands and letting the heat thaw her fingers. 'I think my father's taking images and memories from inside my mind, some that I wasn't even aware of. And he's using them against me.'

'The attack on Bruny wasn't a memory.'

'No,' she said, shivering anew. 'Michael could see it too. I don't know what that was. It wasn't my father though, at least not any version of him I'd seen before. It was something formless but powerful.' Fern put her face close to the cup, letting its steam warm and tickle her face. 'It could only find me when I was relaxed. But then my fear gave it power.'

Adam groaned. 'I can't believe we're even discussing this. Two weeks ago I would have put you in a loony bin. Now, I don't know. One minute I think it's crazy and the next I'm not so sure.' He stood up. 'I guess there's only one way to find out.'

Fern followed him stiffly, her muscles aching even more after the brief rest.

Half an hour later, Adam stopped abruptly. 'That looks like it,' he said, pointing at a pier up ahead where four boats were moored, three giant motor boats and a yacht. He whistled. 'There's a lot of money in those boats.' He looked at Fern.

'Okay, how do we approach this? Are we sticking with the lost bush walker thing?'

'I don't think there's any point,' said Fern. 'He knows. Let's just walk in and see what happens.'

'What if he's not there?' Adam asked.

Fern looked at him, surprised. The possibility hadn't even crossed her mind. 'He's there.'

There was no one at the pier, just the boats bobbing gently in the water. A gravel road led into the forest. They turned their back on the water and followed the road for ten minutes or so, the forest drawing in closer and closer around them as they walked.

Turning a corner, they found themselves standing before tall wrought-iron gates flanked by two ornate stone pillars, each bearing a statue of a lion. Behind the gates the gravel driveway continued between perfectly manicured lawns. Despite having already seen pictures of her father's property, Fern was taken aback by her first glimpse of Pine House. It stood solemnly, not attractive but solid, a pocket of order and control amid an untamed wilderness. On first sight it seemed audacious and wrong, out of tune with the environment, but Fern was tired, cold and dirty, and quickly its misplaced notes became intriguing, a promise of luxury and comfort, its pure cream walls seeming to defy the existence of mud and leeches. A two-storey square, with windows punched regularly in its walls, there was little that was soft about this building, except perhaps the delicate ironwork of the balcony that framed the second level of the house like an observation deck. Next to the house stood a helicopter, its gleaming metal looking out of place next to the historical building.

The gates were locked. As Fern studied their ironwork she realised with a shock that each gate was formed in the shape of a dragon; the design identical to the embroidered glove she'd seen only an hour ago. Around the dragons were snakes, pointing up or down alternately, their tails or tongues becoming sharp spikes that made climbing over the gate an impossibility.

'We're not getting past that,' said Adam. He walked around to the side of the pillars and inspected the tall fence. 'No chance of climbing this either.' He pointed at a bird lying dead on the ground at his feet. 'It's electrified. This guy's really into security.'

Frustrated, he kicked at the pillar and then noticed the intercom attached to the side. 'We could always announce ourselves,' he said dryly.

'No need,' said Fern, as the gates slid silently open in front of them.

Chapter Twenty-One

A man was walking along the gravel driveway towards Fern and Adam. He was carrying a large black umbrella with a curved wooden handle and he wore a formal suit which complemented perfectly the house behind him and its grounds, but was incongruous in relation to the wildness of the bush surrounding them. Fern watched him strolling through an arbour of massive oaks. He didn't look like the monster she'd imagined or even much like the photograph she'd seen which must have been taken some years ago. His walk was catlike and leisurely, certain of itself. And of its prey, Fern thought with a shudder. The silk scarf around his neck made him look softer, camouflaging the steel in him, though Fern felt the glint of it more and more strongly as he approached. She had no doubt this was her father.

'Hello,' he called. 'I'm so pleased you could make it.'

It was a normal voice, friendly enough, though Fern thought she could detect a hint of sarcasm. Not only did Eric know who they were but he was behaving as if he'd invited them.

'My daughter,' he said, as if her coming was a great relief to him, though Fern sensed there was something artificial about this display of emotion. 'Fernanda.' He held out his hand. 'Though I understand you prefer Fern.'

Fern was puzzled. She had imagined a number of possible receptions but this was not one of them. He was taking control, acting as if everything that was happening was his doing. His sense of certainty was frightening. But his hand was still poised in mid-air, waiting to be shaken. Trying to control the tell-tale tremor in her own hand, Fern reached out and clasped his, noting the long slender fingers, so like her own, and his smooth, pampered skin.

At the touch of his hand Fern felt a jolt of recognition, followed by a shockingly vivid image of him as a younger man, his face grim as he picked her up by the ankle and slammed her against a wall. She a tiny baby, dangling helplessly in his hand. It felt so real that Fern instinctively recoiled, snatching her hand away as if it had been burnt. It took all of her willpower to restrain herself from reaching up and cradling her head. She could feel the jolts of pain at the point of impact, the intense shock and the blood rushing to her head as she dangled there. She could hear her mother's cry of anguish, the worried footsteps of an approaching nurse and then his silky voice, smoothing everything over as he cradled her, rubbing her head gently with his devious hands. 'I almost dropped her. My God, they're so fragile.'

I was innocent. There were those words again, thought Fern. They were becoming a refrain, the phrase echoing down the corridors of time and space, through lifetimes.

'No one is innocent,' said her father, watching her carefully. 'Though most are too cowardly to face what they have been.'

Fern was surprised. He'd read her thoughts so easily and hadn't even bothered to pretend otherwise. Suddenly she had a glimpse of something else; a panicked sense that there was a memory inside her she must avoid at all costs. Then fragments: a horse, a sharp curved blade, the crunch of bones under the horse's hooves, the smell of blood …

'Oh yes,' said Eric, looking at her intently. 'We are all capable of anything.'

Fern was confused. It was as if she'd wielded that blade, felt it cutting through human flesh. Could this have been one of her own memories, or her father's? She hoped it was not her own, but she'd felt it so clearly.

Fern desperately tried to send her thoughts elsewhere, concentrating instead on the grandeur of the house, so different from her birth mother's dark, sad house in Katoomba, or Grace and Richard's tidy home in suburban Adelaide. For a moment she wanted it for herself and had to fight back a surge of resentment that she'd never partaken in this wealth.

'Yes,' Eric said, smiling and glancing behind him at the house. 'It is magnificent.'

Fern glared at him. He was playing with her, entering her mind without permission, showing off. But she could play the same game. Emptying her own mind, she concentrated on Eric, searching for his thoughts.

She had no idea that someone might actually feel their mind being probed, but Eric must have seen it coming because all she encountered was his own fierce will pushing her out. Remembering what her mother had said about the way he bent people to his will, Fern retreated. Immediately he counterattacked, forcing his way through into her mind. His immense power was almost irresistible. Fern tried instinctively to build barriers against him, but despite her efforts her defences were crumbling.

Adam looked from one to the other, not understanding what was going on. It was as if he wasn't there, the way they focused on each other like this. He felt a twinge of jealousy. There was something between them, something he couldn't penetrate. But he also felt a growing concern.

He stepped forward and held out his hand towards Eric. 'Hi,' he said. 'I'm Adam.'

In an instant the spell was broken and Fern's mind was free again.

Eric laughed. 'You truly are my daughter,' he said, a note of fatherly pride in his voice. Then he turned to Adam. 'And my name is Eric,' he said, taking Adam's hand and looking hard into him, making Adam feel as if his insides were being ripped out and inspected.

'You sure make it difficult to visit,' said Adam, extracting his hand and gesturing at his muddy legs.

'I value my privacy,' said Eric. 'Now to practicalities. Come and get some dry clothes on before you both catch pneumonia.'

They followed Eric back along the gravel driveway towards the house, which seemed to grow larger in stature as they approached. As did the helicopter perched at its side.

'My preferred means of transport,' said Eric, motioning at it casually.

Passing a well-tended rose garden, Fern couldn't resist pausing to sniff the richly scented petals. Directly in front of the house stood a stone fountain. Its base was a half-open shell, and from it emerged a naked Venus surrounded by lichen-covered stone fish, water spurting from their mouths in graceful arcs.

The granite steps leading up to the front door had worn smooth with age and the tread of many feet. Standing on a wide, covered terrace lined with flagstones, Fern looked at the heavy cedar door and its giant brass door knocker in the form of a wolf's head, its mouth open and its sharp teeth bared.

'Not very welcoming,' whispered Adam to Fern.

'It's a warning,' said Eric, turning towards them. 'To those who are uninvited, or perhaps not ready for what they will find inside.' He smiled but his eyes were cold. 'Like those delightful demonic figures you find on cathedrals.'

Fern paused at the door, feeling like an impostor, heavy and uncultured in her big boots and dripping rain jacket. She and

Adam peeled off their wet jackets, their muddy gaiters and shoes, Fern's cold fingers fumbling uselessly with the laces, so that in the end Adam had to help.

'Leave them there,' said Eric. 'I'll get someone to attend to them.'

Nervously they followed him into a vast entrance hall. Even without her wet and muddy outers, Fern felt as if she were leaving a trail of grime in this house that gleamed with polish and care.

Eric stopped in the centre of the hall. 'Welcome to my humble abode,' he said proudly. 'The original owner had little taste and it's an odd mix of styles, though predominantly Victorian. I've kept as many features as possible - the original doors, brass chandeliers, marble mantelpieces - and the furnishings are in period style, though I couldn't resist mixing in a bit of modern here and there. I've played on the disconsonance and created something new, an exciting and eclectic mix.'

Fern's eyes followed her father's to a large abstract painting on the wall. Its colourful geometry should have been awkward, she thought, hanging there among traditional portraits and antique furniture, but it was perfect. 'It's beautiful,' she said feeling the lure of this house again.

'Yes,' he said glancing around him with pleasure and then looking directly at Fern, his eyes piercing her. 'I'm a collector.'

Fern suddenly pictured him as a child, stalking butterflies with his net and then sticking pins into them. She stifled a shudder.

'Come along,' he said, climbing a wide wooden staircase up to the first floor. The carved rail gleamed with polish and vases of roses stood on plinths, their scent mingling with the polish, their gentle yellow tones offset by the cream walls behind them. 'I saved you a room, of course. Not the grandest, mind you. But we have a number of guests at present and it was short notice.'

He opened a door and ushered them into a room. After the cold wind and rain outside, Fern noticed the heat first: a fire was raging in the grate, the walls were warm yellow ochre, and the furnishings were mainly dark wood or deep red. The furniture was too ornate for her liking: the side tables with their curved legs and carved handles were ugly, and the bed had too many cushions. Feeling a childish surge of pleasure at finding a flaw in her father's taste, Fern crossed over to the French doors which were framed by heavy gold drapes, and led out onto a small balcony. Immediately below was the rose garden and further out the oaks, followed by what looked like a golf course; and beyond that lay the rim of the forest, its canopy so thick it looked impenetrable.

'You're just in time for our New Year's Eve dinner,' said her father. 'It's formal,' he added, eyeing their clothes with a frown. 'I don't suppose you've got anything appropriate tucked away in those bags of yours.'

'Nothing,' said Adam quickly, hoping to be spared the torture of a formal dinner with strangers.

'Sorry,' said Fern, who had completely forgotten that it was the last day of the year.

'Never mind, I'll send up something.' He glanced at Adam disdainfully. 'It will be a bit small, but you'll have to make do. And for you?' he added, turning to Fern and running his eyes up and down her body as if she were a dummy in a clothes store. 'Mmm, I'm sure we can find something appropriate. I'll see you at six thirty sharp,' he said, closing the door behind him; then he opened it again immediately, making them jump. 'Leave your wet clothes outside the door, I'll have them laundered.'

'Thanks,' said Fern, feeling more and more like a character in a play for which she hadn't seen the script.

She locked the door and leaned against it, breathing a sigh of relief. Her head felt as if it were going to explode: a new father, a glamorous house, a battle of minds or wills that she couldn't begin to understand. But there was something else even more disturbing: Fern had felt the recognition between them in a way she hadn't with her birth mother. Joan was right, Fern and Eric were alike. She should hate him; she should be afraid; but instead she was excited.

Fern needed time to digest all this new information but Adam was sitting on the bed looking positively sour. 'What was all that about?' he asked sullenly.

'What do you mean?'

'You know, the weird way you looked at each other. Something was going on.'

'He was reading my mind,' said Fern, slipping off her heavy backpack and feeling instantly buoyant. 'I was trying to stop him.'

Adam could see the excitement in Fern's eyes and hear it in her voice but he didn't understand it. He could easily punch the guy in the face, but he wasn't built for mind games like that: he was out of his depth and he knew it. 'He's an arsehole. Don't trust him,' he said pleadingly.

Fern felt a strange desire to defend her father and a momentary urge to lash out at Adam. With an effort she stifled it, knowing Adam was right. The pain in her head was still there, a faint echo reminding her what her father was capable of. Eric had tried to kill her, she must remember that and possibly more than once. She bit her tongue and concentrated on that knowledge, letting it chase everything else from her mind. The excitement drained away, leaving her weary and suddenly her legs felt as if they would buckle underneath her. 'It's so confusing,' she said, sitting down heavily on the bed next to Adam. 'I'm scared.'

'Just don't trust him, not for a second. He's dangerous … ' Adam tried to pin down what Eric reminded him of. 'Like a cross between a viper and a fox.'

'I don't trust him. How could I?' said Fern. She smiled and changed the subject, 'Bags first shower.'

Despite Fern's reassurance, Adam still felt uneasy. Eric was clever and secretive but there was something else about him; he took people's energy, confused them, twisted them to his will, while all the time they felt privileged to be near him. Fern was his daughter. How could she resist it?

In the end they showered together, the steaming water stinging their cold skin as they soaped each other and made love slowly, lazily, almost asleep on their feet. Then, exhausted and still damp, they fell asleep, curled up together on the bed.

A knock on the door woke them. Fern threw on one of the thick white robes that lay on the end of the bed and opened the door. A maid was standing in the hallway next to a clothes rack, from which hung a suit, complete with a shirt and bow tie, and a long shimmering silver evening dress. There were shoes too: a pair of silver stilettos for Fern and glossy black pointed lace-ups for Adam.

'Thank you,' Fern said as the maid wheeled the clothes rack into the room and left, blank-faced. Fern felt stupid and embarrassed, wondering if she should have given a tip. She was sure the maid could see that Fern didn't belong here. This was the first time she'd stood on this side of the division between those who serve and those who are served.

But the dress was beautiful. Entranced, Fern lifted it up and ran her fingers along the slinky material.

'Where do you think he got this from?' she said, unable to hide the glee in her voice.

'God knows,' said Adam sourly. He disliked Fern's father intensely, hated the way he looked past Adam as if he weren't there, his eyes hooked greedily on Fern. Adam couldn't make him out. One minute he wanted his daughter dead, the next he was ingratiating himself with her, playing the prodigal father. 'Is there any way we can get out of this?' he asked.

Fern shook her head, still dazzled by the dress in front of her. 'No, we're on his turf, we'd better conform as best we can.'

Adam got up reluctantly, lifted the suit off the rack and inspected it. 'Shit, it's Armani.'

Fern threw off the robe, stepped into the dress and pulled it up, lifting the straps over her shoulders. It was too long, the hem trailed on the ground a little, but otherwise it fitted perfectly. Her father had chosen well.

'This looks ridiculous,' said Adam. The suit was obviously expensive and well cut, but far too small; Adam's wrists and ankles were comically exposed. The shoes would no doubt be too small as well, and pinch his toes. 'God, I feel like a fool,' he grumbled, a suspicion rising in him that this was exactly how Eric wanted him to feel.

Fern kissed him, trying not to laugh. 'It doesn't matter what you wear, Adam, you look handsome to me.'

There was a bottle of perfume on the dressing-table. Fern took off the lid and sniffed, then, seduced by its delicate musky scent, rubbed a few drops on her chest and her neck. She stood in front of the full-length mirror and contemplated herself, hardly believing that this elegant beauty was the same bedraggled person who had staggered into her father's house a few hours before. Fern thought of all the clothes she'd left hanging on the clothes rack in her old attic room, none of them as beautiful or as simple as this dress. She would never have chosen it for herself, and yet it suited her perfectly. She loved the tantalising way it clung to her slim figure, sending ripples of anticipation running up and down her body. She didn't have any makeup but that didn't matter. Her skin was pale and smooth, her cheeks lightly flushed from the fire and her lips were full and dark without the need for lipstick.

'You look gorgeous,' said Adam, coming up behind her and running his hands up and down her body. He nudged his face into her neck and nibbled at her, inhaling the strange unfamiliar scent until she pushed him away, worried that he would leave a mark.

The outfit needed something else, something to make it her own. Fern dug around in her backpack until she found Cassie's lapis lazuli necklace tucked right at the bottom of the front pocket. As she withdrew her hand her fingers touched the tempest stone and for a moment she was tempted to hold it again. But no, she didn't want to open herself up like that. It would make her vulnerable and she knew that her immediate challenge lay here with her father, in the physical world.

Fern hung the necklace around her neck, and the cool stone settled into place between her breasts. Then she threw her pashmina over the top. It was perfect for the dress, a mysterious midnight blue, with a silver streak running through it. *Something old, something new, something borrowed, something blue*. She paused, wondering if she had heard the words or if they had simply arisen in her mind; it was becoming difficult to distinguish. As the words suggested, suddenly and inexplicably Fern felt like a bride dressing for her wedding.

The shoes were just a fraction too big, so her feet slid around a little. She tightened the straps and stood up, wobbling dangerously on the stiletto heels. At least the added height lifted the dress so that it didn't sweep across the floor so much. Still, if anyone treads on it, she thought, I'll be down in a shot.

She looked at the clock. Twenty-five minutes past six. Her father had said six thirty sharp. 'Come on,' she said, her eyes sparkling as she linked arms with Adam. It hurt Adam to see Fern like this. Her father was making a bid for his daughter and Fern didn't seem aware of it. Adam had already imagined many ways in which he might lose Fern, but now, for the first time, he saw that he might lose her to Eric.

'If we must,' he said, sighing.

As they walked down the stairs, uncertainty swept over Fern and she tightened her grip on Adam's arm. Every step felt precarious; one false move and she'd sprain her ankle again. She couldn't possibly be dignified in such ridiculous shoes.

The other guests were milling in the bar, sipping drinks, their voices rising and falling confidently. There were only sixteen or so, though the noise would suggest more. The men wore identical dinner suits, while the women were draped in expensive evening gowns and eyed each other surreptitiously. As they stood uncertainly in the doorway, watching this strange scene, Fern found it hard to believe that only hours ago she and Adam had been tramping through the bush in the rain.

Fern's father was standing next to an elegant woman, her hair swept into a loose bun, her arm draped possessively through his. Frowning, he glanced at his watch then at the door, his frown disappearing when he saw Fern.

'Ah, there you are,' he called Extricating his arm from the woman, he walked towards them, glass in hand, looking elegant in his black evening suit and velvet bow tie. Abandoned, the woman scowled at Fern, who suddenly knew exactly whose dress she was wearing.

'Fern, you look positively beautiful.' He paused and glanced at Adam, one eyebrow slightly raised. 'And you've scrubbed up well. Let me get you both a drink.' He stepped over to the bar and handed them crystal flutes filled with champagne.

Still clinging to Adam's arm for balance, Fern took a sip, the bubbles tickling her nose. She looked around again, listening to the booming voices of the men and the strained, barking laughter of the women. Everyone seemed animated, yet their features were expressionless.

'Botox,' whispered Eric, seeing her staring. 'Turns them into dummies.' He laughed gleefully. 'These women will hate you, Fern. You're so - how do you say it? - fresh. And they'll want you,' he said, turning to Adam and squeezing his upper arm. 'All those "real man" muscles. You watch.'

Adam scowled.

'Are these your friends?' asked Fern incredulously.

'You're so innocent,' Eric said, smiling. 'I'm acquainted with them all. But friends? No, these people all occupy positions of influence. They are useful to me. That's why they're here.'

'And what use are we?' asked Adam.

Eric's smile turned to ice as he draped his arm around Fern. 'This beautiful young woman is my daughter,' he said proudly, adding scornfully. 'And you, I imagine, are her current boyfriend.'

Fern heard the sneer in her father's voice and wriggled out from his embrace, making it clear whose side she was on. But still, she was irritated with them both. The amused expression on her father's face was infuriating, but so was Adam's bad temper. He needs to lighten up, she thought.

A large, round-faced man approached them, sweating in the heated room. 'Eric,' he said, clapping her father on the back and not noticing him wince at the contact. 'I meant to ask, how are you going with the negotiations?'

'A few hitches, I'm afraid. You know how it is. So many committees … '

'Anything I can do?' asked the man, looking concerned.

'Very kind, Andrew. I'm sure there is - let's talk about it later. Dinner is about to be served and I have an announcement to make first.'

Eric picked up a bell and rang it, waiting patiently until the chatter died away and everyone was looking at him expectantly. 'As you all know we are here to see in the New Year together.

That in itself is worth celebrating. But for me this is a very special occasion.' Eric paused, savouring the moment. He was a man who relished surprises. 'I'd like you all to meet my daughter, Fern.'

Fern smiled nervously as everyone's eyes shot towards her. There were gasps of astonishment and raised eyebrows, while one or two of the women were clearly assessing how much of a threat Fern might be to them.

'They're so alike,' someone said.

'Yes, look at those eyes.'

'Pleased to meet you,' said Andrew, grasping Fern's hand in his sweaty palm.

An elderly man approached and nudged Eric in the ribs, laughing wickedly. 'You've been keeping her a secret, eh Eric?'

The elegant women sauntered up and kissed her on the cheek. 'You're a lucky girl,' she said in an American accent. 'Having a dad like that.'

Fern smiled, not knowing quite how to respond to that one. Feeling like a mouse in a room full of cats, she glanced desperately at Adam, who was still scowling behind her. In the end she was rescued by a waiter appearing in the doorway to announce dinner.

'Let's adjourn to the dining room, said Eric, ushering them into the next room.

The first thing Fern noticed was the crystal chandelier, casting its sparkling patterns around the room. One end of the dining room was almost all glass, with doors opening out onto the terrace. Here, Eric had obviously succumbed to a more modern style, though the furnishings were still Victorian. The walls were cream, but their coolness was offset by richly coloured paintings, dark wooden floorboards and a Persian rug in deep burgundy tones. Like the bar, this room was warm, with a fire crackling at one end. A long table stretched the length of the room, covered in a starched white cloth and lavishly set with glistening silver cutlery, elegant white crockery and more crystal glasses. In front of each setting was a place card, the names printed in ornate gold cursive.

Eric's place card was at the head of the table. 'You're sitting here, Fern, he said, pointing at the seat next to his.

Fern took a quick uncertain glance at Adam, before acquiescing. This was Eric's show and he was playing his role perfectly, taking her arm and helping her into the seat, then pushing it in for her. He lifted the shawl off her shoulders and placed it on the back of her chair. It was warm in the room, but without her shawl Fern felt exposed, almost naked.

The room was a feast for the senses and Fern felt almost blinded by the glitter and the sophistication around her, so distant from the suburbs where she'd spent her childhood. Eric's world made those suburbs seem even more like a wasteland, devoid of beauty or style.

'Do you like it?' asked Eric, leaning over, his mouth almost on her ear, one hand brushing her shoulder. She nodded and looked up at him, her eyes shining.

Adam found his own seat towards the other end of the table. Worried, he watched Fern sitting next to her father, laughing, excited and drinking too much. A woman sat down next to him; she was mid-thirties, he guessed, and beautiful in the way of the wealthy and sophisticated: plenty of make-up, and a shapely, worked-on body extensively revealed by her low-cut dress. Adam couldn't help glancing down. She had an amazing cleavage.

Noticing the direction of his eyes, she smiled. 'Well, baby,' she said, leaning in close to him and putting her hand on his thigh. 'Wasn't that nice of Eric to put us together?'

In front of Fern was a menu, a single sheet of paper with a gold embossed pattern around the edge. There was oyster chowder for starters, followed by a choice of entrees, all seafood.

'I recommend the abalone,' said Eric. 'They're fresh today and the recipe is simple but superb.

Fern had never tried abalone before and was grateful for the recommendation. There was also a choice of mains: pan-seared trevally with fine herbs and balsamic reduction; crayfish, cooked with chilli, lemon grass, kaffir limes and coconut cream; or sirloin steak in a mountain pepper sauce, with caramelised sweet potato and onion.

'That's the one,' said Eric, pointing at the trevally. 'Again, simple but cooked to perfection.'

Fern felt a flash of irritation at the way her father assumed her ignorance, taking over so smoothly and leaving no space for her to choose. 'The abalone,' she said, when the waiter took her order. 'And the crayfish.'

Only a small rebellion but it made her feel better.

Each table setting had three spoons, two forks and three knives, and when the soup arrived, Fern had to watch Eric to see which spoon to use. The soup was exquisite, as was the abalone when it came, melting magically in her mouth and washed down with a cool Riesling. The waiters kept hovering, filling up her glass, then whisking it away between courses and filling up a new one with a different wine. She hadn't realised what an art there was to matching food and wines.

After the entree came tiny bowls filled with something that looked like ice- cream. Fern looked at hers uncertainly.

'Lime sorbet, ' said Eric. 'It's a palette cleanser.'

Fern tasted it, loving its sweet tartness, and glanced contritely at Adam to check how he was managing with the cutlery. She'd assumed he would be out of his depth here but he looked quite comfortable, eating his sorbet with the right spoon and deep in conversation with the woman next to him. At least, she was talking and he was ogling her breasts, thought Fern with a flicker of jealousy. Then, perhaps drawn by her gaze, Adam looked up at Fern and their eyes met. She smiled, but he didn't return the smile. When her father leaned close to speak to her again, Fern turned away from Adam, relieved.

By the time the main courses arrived, the volume had risen substantially in the room. The wine was flowing quickly and people's faces were red and shiny, their laughter too loud.

Eric held up his glass. 'A toast,' he said, and everyone held up their glasses expectantly. 'To the bankers, the insurers, the heads of corporations, the movers and the shakers, here they all are, shaking in their boots.' He laughed a loud wild laugh and drained his drink. Obediently they drank, a few laughing along nervously, unsure how to react.

'We'd better watch out,' Eric added. 'The scum are rising. They want a better deal.'

'They want our arses,' said one man, prematurely bald with a shiny scalp.

'Pah,' said Eric, draining his glass. 'Easily fixed. Give them some scraps, then sit back while they kill each other for them.'

Everyone laughed this time, except Adam. And Fern. Thank God for that, thought Adam, seeing her shocked face. She didn't fit in here and the sooner she understood that the better. He wondered where they'd all learned to despise people without money. At their elite schools, possibly. More likely they'd simply moved so far away from the real world, and felt so safe in their prosperity and their exclusive clubs, that they'd begun to measure value purely by money.

Furious, Adam cut into his steak. It was too rare, and the blood flowing out onto the plate, made him nauseous. He put down his knife and fork, looking around in disgust. Every day these people were creating more and more wealth for themselves, greater inequity, destroying the earth and displacing the people, yet here they were scoffing at those who were suffering.

'People want everything for nothing,' said the elderly man. 'We had to work for what we got in my day, there was none of this social security propping up the lazy buggers.'

'Hear, hear,' said Eric. 'I'll drink to that.'

Fern looked at her father; his face was serious but his eyes were mischievous. She couldn't tell if he was playing some strange game or if he really believed all this.

'Look at Tassie,' said the prematurely bald man. 'Brought to its bloody knees by forest activists with nothing better to do. They're all living off us taxpayers and putting honest workers out of a job.'

Fern looked anxiously at Adam. His face was red, his eyes fiery and his jaw set. 'The forests are worth saving,' he said between gritted teeth.

'Ah, we have a conservationist in our midst!' said Eric. 'Now Adam, tell us what you do for a living?'

Flustered, Adam paused for a moment. 'I save forests,' he said eventually, surprised at his words but realising in that moment that a part of him had already made the decision to join the battle. Eric's derision had only helped him decide.

'Mmm, not too well paid, I imagine, but very worthy.'

Fern was horrified. Eric was enjoying this too much: she could feel the cruel streak in him, sharp and eager. She knew she should make a stand - say something, or at least walk out of this room with Adam by her side. She half rose, then sat down again quickly. Her mouth was clamped shut and it felt as if she were glued to her seat. Adam was such a great distance from her, too far for her to reach. She felt passive and helpless, drained of her will. She looked at Eric, begging him with her eyes to stop baiting Adam, but if he noticed, it had no effect.

'And where did you grow up?' Eric persisted, his voice smug.

'First the Midlands,' said Adam. 'Then in Kettering.'

'Ah, so you're a country boy from Tasmania. How wholesome.'

Adam nodded. 'My family's been here for six generations,' he said proudly. 'We owned a farming property in the Midlands. Until the drought … and Dad's death,' he added quietly.

'So you were landed gentry then.'

'You could call it that,' said Adam. 'We weren't convicts, if that's what you're asking.'

'Convicts! I'm sure you weren't, Adam. Though I understand they're all the rage these days. It seems everyone's related to one.' Bored now, Eric turned back to his dinner. But Adam wasn't finished with him.

'Where did you grow up, Eric?'

Fern saw a flicker of venomous anger in her father's eyes, rapidly replaced by a calm haughtiness. Adam had got to him but Fern didn't understand why her father was upset. His background was public knowledge, on the internet for anyone to read.

Only the tension in Adam's jaw revealed his fury. This was a different Adam, honing his anger into a weapon and hurling it back at her father. Fern was proud of him but afraid too because she had no doubt that Eric would make Adam pay for this. As she gazed at Adam, torn between pride and fear, the room seemed faded around her and she found herself in another time and place, watching a man tied to a rack, sweat pouring down his naked chest as his muscles were stretched beyond their natural capacity. Fern tried to block it out, tried to turn her face away but felt invisible hands holding her head in place, forcing her to witness her lover's torment. Dizzy, she closed her eyes against the memory but she couldn't block her ears to his cries. With an effort Fern brought herself back to the present, to the strained silence in the room as the guests watched Eric, waiting for his response to Adam's taunt.

When Eric spoke his voice was unexpectedly sweet. 'Unlike you, Adam, I had humble beginnings. I am a self-made man.' He gestured around the room. 'But everything you see here is mine. Everything.' The gesture had included his guests and at that there was the subtlest ripple of unease around the table.

Eric turned to Fern and smiled. 'And now my happiness is complete.'

Feeling everyone's eyes on her, Fern blushed, discomforted. Turning, she risked a glance into her father's eyes. Where she should have seen paternal love she could discern only incipient madness and a craze for power.

When the dinner was over, the guests retired to the bar, their voices more subdued as they drank strong coffees and brandy in balloon glasses or smaller glasses of port. After all that food, Fern felt incredibly tired. She'd used up her tiny vocabulary of small talk and wanted to slip upstairs and into bed. But it was New Year's Eve: she would have to make it through until at least midnight.

When Adam joined Fern he was still fuming. 'Divide and rule,' he said. 'It's a classic technique. Your father's trying to drive a wedge between us.'

'He just wanted to sit next to me at dinner,' Fern protested weakly.

Adam raised his eyebrows. 'How can you deny it? You're the one who told me that's what he was doing. Out there in the bush. They're your words, Fern.'

Adam was right. She'd almost forgotten. Fern stifled a yawn. The forest seemed so far away now.

'I'm not denying it, Adam,' she said. 'But he can only drive a wedge between us if we let him.'

'You're being seduced by it all. The sparkling crystal and the costumes.'

'I am not.'

'You are.'

'When I was a kid,' Fern recalled, 'I imagined it was all a mistake, that somehow I'd been mislaid and the wrong family had taken me home.' She paused and looked around her. 'Now here I am, practically a princess.'

'Yeah, and that makes Eric the king,' said Adam. 'Just remember that kings are ruthless. Watch your step.'

'I will.'

'He's playing games with us. Don't you get it?'

'I know he is, Adam, but he's also my father.'

'Some father! He had you followed, remember, Fern? He tried to scare you half to death.'

'But he didn't hurt me.'

'I thought you said it was him attacking you, or something he sent … You nearly died on Bruny.'

Fern looked away, not wanting Adam to see the uncertainty in her eyes. Walking through the forest she'd been so certain of what she felt but now she was here, she couldn't remember the connections. Her mind was fuddled. 'I feel safe here,' she said.

'Safe! He's looking at you like a viper, tongue flickering, getting ready to lunge. God, Fern, can't you see it?'

Fern turned to look at her father, still immaculate in his formal suit, as he strolled over to them, glass in hand. Adam was right, he was a viper. She didn't trust him but she believed she could handle him.

'Come,' he said, taking Fern's arm. 'I'll show you some more of my domain.'

Adam made to follow them but Eric stopped him.

'Excuse us, will you,' he said, the smile warm but his words unbending. 'I would like a private word with my newly acquired daughter.'

'It's okay, Adam,' said Fern. This would be a good chance to talk to her father and she was certain she could protect herself. Wobbling a little from the wine and the high heels, she climbed the stairs after Eric, all the time feeling Adam's eyes on her back. Upstairs, the air was still warm but despite this there was a chill in the atmosphere. Fern shivered, wondering if the place was haunted.

'These places are always haunted,' said Eric. 'It's convict built, you see. They were treated with extreme cruelty and that generally leaves an impression on a place. We've had sightings: a servant woman on the stairs, a strange rattling in one of the bedroom windows, a depression that keeps appearing on a bed, as if someone is sitting there, strange smells … It's all part of an old house.'

They walked past a number of closed doors, their footsteps muted by thick carpet. 'These are the guest rooms. All taken at the moment, I'm afraid, so I can't show you inside.'

'What do you charge?' Fern asked curiously.

'We start at four thousand dollars a night.'

Fern gasped. 'That's so much!'

'It's loose change for these people,' Eric said dismissively. 'But of course, there are many ways of paying.'

Fern thought of the round-faced man who had offered to help Eric with his negotiations. Perhaps this group weren't paying at all, at least not in hard cash. She wondered briefly what form of payment Eric would want from her, then dismissed the thought. He was her father. She did not owe him anything. 'What do they get for their four grand?'

Eric laughed. 'Style and good taste, the best of everything, silk-stuffed mattresses, designer furniture, good food and privacy. That's what they want - especially the privacy. And they want to feel special.'

'But why here?' asked Fern. 'Why wouldn't they take off for a tropical island or something?'

'They like it that I'm one of them. They can pretend we're all friends. I know their needs. I don't care who they bring, what they wear or what they do, here or anywhere else. I don't make judgements, I don't ask questions and I don't let the media in.'

'Do you take them bush walking?' she asked, finding it hard to imagine her father in hiking boots.

'Me! Heavens no. They come here because they like the idea of the wilderness. Some of them take a stroll or a short hike, but mostly they don't want to get their feet dirty.' Eric stopped outside a door at the end of the hallway. 'And here are my chambers,' he said, ushering Fern into a large sitting room adjoining a master bedroom.

The subtle lighting shrouded the sitting room in mysterious shadows. It had an oppressive masculine feel, with dark burgundy walls, dark wood furniture, a deep brown leather couch and heavy velvet curtains. The room smelled strongly of spices and cigars, as if it hadn't been aired for a long time.

'Here, let me get you a drink,' said Eric, picking up a bottle of champagne that had been chilling in an ice bucket on the bar.

Fern watched him expertly twist the bottle and take out the cork. It reminded her of that strange first evening with Shamesh, the way he'd clinked glasses with her; 'Cheers,' he'd said. 'It's not every day you embark on a journey.' Her life had changed so much since then. Only a few weeks ago she'd been trapped in her attic room with not even an inkling that she would soon meet her birth mother and Adam. And now here she was clinking glasses with her father.

'Cheers,' said Eric. 'To my daughter whom I have waited so long to meet.'

'Cheers,' said Fern. She looked up and noticed the king-sized bed through the doorway, then stupidly felt herself blushing. To cover her confusion she took a gulp of champagne. Adam was right, she was quickly forgetting her reasons for coming here. And forgetting how dangerous her father was. The champagne, the lighting, the door closed behind them … it all felt planned. She needed to be careful.

'Why are you so pleased to see me?' she asked, struggling to clear her head.

Eric looked shocked at her question. 'You're my daughter,' he said, as if that explained everything.

'You had someone follow me. You wanted to scare me. You wanted me … ' She stopped, biting her tongue. She had no proof that he'd tried to kill her. How could she accuse him of attacking her in her dreams or even in the womb? It would sound ridiculous.

'Yes, I admit that at first I thought the best thing would be to have you …' he paused, looking for the right word, 'terminated. Now don't look at me like that. It's only natural. After all, who wouldn't want to rid themselves of a dangerous opponent?'

'Me?' asked Fern in surprise.

'Yes. I assume you know about the prophecy; your foolish mother would have told you. I thought you would fulfil it one way or the other. That is the way of fate. But now, I wonder … Perhaps there's another way.' He let his eyes wander over Fern's body, making her squirm. 'And I admit, you intrigue me. I hadn't expected paternal feelings, but it moves me to see someone of my own blood - my creation, if you like. And what a fine woman you have turned out to be.'

Fern felt herself growing angry. 'Your creation? Where have you been for the past twenty years?'

'Ah, my dear, perhaps I was mistaken to abandon you like that. I had ambitions. Wealth to amass. Back then I had nothing for you.' He gestured around the room. 'But now - now I can give you anything you want.'

'So why *don't* you want to kill me?' she said.

'As I said, there may be other ways. And recently I discovered something else: it seems that you are not simply my daughter. You are also someone very dear to me. How could I miss the opportunity of reacquainting myself with you?'

Fern nodded. The events of the past few weeks had forced her to accept that there were depths to life she had never imagined. Now she had no doubt that they had met many times before but she also knew that each time it had ended badly for her. It struck her as absurd that he expected her to believe he didn't want her dead when he had clearly already tried to kill her.

'You were much stronger than I imagined,' he said, answering her unspoken question. 'You, how shall I say, survived certain challenges or tests.'

'Attacks, more like it.'

'Call them what you will. But you have proved your strength and that is enough for me.'

Fern was astonished. Once again he was acting as if everything she did was part of his plan. 'What do you want from me?' she asked.

Impatiently he refilled her glass. 'Don't you see? I want nothing for myself.' He motioned around the room again. 'You are my daughter. All this is yours.' He leaned closer to her. 'And you have no idea how wealthy I am. If you stay, you could be rich beyond your wildest dreams.'

Fern sipped her champagne. She was really drunk now, her mind fuzzy and the room spinning ever so slightly. She couldn't credit her father's selflessness. It was obvious that he was a man who wanted something from everyone. Yet she was tempted. She'd never had money. She'd never had the choices money could buy.

'This house is only one of many,' he said, his voice as smooth and sticky as honey. 'I have a penthouse in New York, a Regency house in London, a harbour-side apartment in Sydney, an island in northern Queensland and more. I own a computer company as well as restaurants, luxury hotels. I am wealthy beyond your imagination - so wealthy the last recession only touched the very edges of my interests.'

Their eyes met; Fern felt his searching hers, then going deeper, looking inside her. She shivered, feeling his magnetism. And the lure of his money. She could do so much with it; there would be choices she'd never imagined possible. Fern felt herself melting into his eyes. This was her father. She was like him, so very, very similar.

'You are beautiful,' he said, reaching out his hand and stroking her cheek.

Fern felt the shock of his touch surge through her body. She turned her face away, the blood rushing to her cheeks.

'You could have anyone,' he continued. 'Do you understand? A man who can satisfy you in every way.'

'And who might that be?' asked Fern, trying to inject a scathing sarcasm into her voice, trying to bring the conversation back to solid ground. 'Not Adam, I imagine.'

Eric sighed. 'It is the plight of fathers all over the world, that no man is good enough for their daughters … No, not Adam, but I have someone in mind.'

She realised with a shock that he was acting like royalty, selling off his daughter, matchmaking for power. Even his own child was an asset to be bought and sold. It was outrageous, yet there was something tantalising about it. He was pampering Fern and making her passive, a tool for his negotiations.

'But would he love me?' she asked, maintaining her sarcasm.

'Ah, love! There are other things more valuable than love.' His fingers stroked her neck as he stepped closer to her. Fern wanted to push his hand away but found she couldn't move. Her feet were glued to the spot, one hand gripping her drink, the other stuck by her side.

'Like what?' she whispered.

'Power,' he said, his mouth tickling her ear, sending shivers down her spine. 'I could show you how to use yours. Imagine, a father and daughter team. We would be formidable.'

Fern couldn't think straight. What was he saying? She couldn't remember. Couldn't think of anything except his fingers on her skin. His mouth closed on hers and she felt her lips respond, her body arching towards him as he kissed her.

'Power,' he whispered, pulling back slightly. 'I will show you how.'

He took the glass from Fern's hand and placed it on the table next to them, then took her in his arms, his lips crushing hers, one hand on the small of her back, the other running over her dress, tracing the contours of her body.

'You are beautiful,' he said, kissing her again. 'My daughter. My lover.'

Fern stirred for a moment. An image of Adam flashed into her mind: his worried face. 'Don't trust him.' But Eric's hands were running all over her and she could feel herself softening, opening to him. His fingers were silken smooth, so different from Adam's … The thought of Adam made her pause again. Struggling to regain some lucidity, Fern instinctively grasped the stone around her neck. As she held onto the lapis lazuli, she felt an energy flowing into her and her mind cleared. She saw the lust in her father's eyes and felt a surge of revulsion.

'How dare you,' Fern hissed, pushing him away. There was nothing seductive about him now, only a leering ugly willpower that was concentrated on wrong ends.

'Dare!' he said, his voice as cold as ice, his face drawn into a disdainful sneer. 'You wanted it.'

Fern fought the impulse to race to her room and scrub herself, washing every last vestige of this man off her. Instead she faced him, her heart pounding, her body still trembling. She had already known that her father was using his power for gain, that he didn't hesitate to hurt others for his own purposes, but now, as her fingers reached again for the stone hanging around her neck, she could see much more. There were glimpses of his other faces - the handsome lord, the hooded priest, the Persian merchant, a creature of the dark - all leering at her, the same greedy expression in their eyes. But these incarnations were just transitory costumes. It was his constant spirit that was a force against compassion, a force that had been working against the waking of humankind for aeons and aeons, she had no idea how long. And he was immensely strong, though she sensed that his choices eroded and weakened him.

'Who are you?' she asked.

'Your father,' he said and she caught a flicker of uncertainty in his face before he was back in control. 'That's all.'

'You told me yourself there was something else.' Fern stared into his face, trying to see past the facade again, but now he was blocking her. Still she tried, testing her will against his in a battle that she had no hope of winning. It felt interminable. He was wearing her down, she didn't have the strength to hold out, felt a sinking of her willpower, a surrendering, and then suddenly he was inside her head. She could feel him penetrate her mind, searching for something. Desperately she tried to empty her mind but he was deep inside, violently forcing his way into her memories. A confusion of images flashed past Fern: a toddler sitting in a paddling pool sucking her thumb, a classroom and her ten-year-old self copying something down in her exercise book. Then a hospital waiting room. Fern shouting, *Let me go*, as they injected her with something. A flicker of a different hospital bed and the words of her adopted father. *You tried to kill me*. His hand clutching his chest … And then Grace's voice. *Your father's had another heart attack.*

Eric withdrew so suddenly that Fern lost her balance and almost fell. Her mind felt violated, traces of him still polluting its corridors. When she steadied herself, her father was staring at her coldly but there was a triumph in his eyes that filled her with suspicion and dread.

'Don't try to play mind games with me again,' he said, his voice filled with a mixture of malice and contempt. Taking up his glass he dismissed her with a wave of his hand. 'Go back to your coarse boyfriend. I'm disappointed in you.'

Feeling dizzy and sick inside, Fern stumbled out of the room. Her father had tried to seduce her and she had come close to letting him. It was disgusting. Completely unforgivable. She paused on the landing, not sure whether she could bear to join the others again but afraid to go back to her room alone and risk another encounter with her father. In the end she made her way down the stairs, tottering on another woman's crippling heels. Halfway down she stopped and pulled them off in a fury, discarding them on a step. Holding her dress up off the ground she managed the last steps more confidently. The sight of Adam in the entrance hall sent her body into a confusing combination of dread and relief.

'Fern! Are you okay? Has he hurt you?'

Fern wanted to sob on Adam's shoulder, but she had to pull herself together. If she told Adam what had happened, he'd attack her father. And he'd lose. She couldn't bear that. 'He didn't do anything,' she said. 'He just showed me around. He wanted me to go into business with him.' Fern reached up and kissed Adam, hoping he couldn't taste her father on her lips, hoping that in Adam she could forget Eric's touch. But her father's fingers still burnt into her, his lips still burned her own.

'Business?'

'Yes.' Fern laughed loudly. She felt reckless now, as if she'd survived a massive challenge. In her own way she'd won. 'He said we would make a formidable team.' She kissed Adam again, rubbing herself against him until he was hard and breathless. She knew she was using him, trying to erase her memories in Adam's body. But for the moment Fern didn't care. She was drunk and wild and angry.

'Let's go outside,' she whispered, almost groaning with desire. It was Adam she wanted. Adam's body she remembered. Adam, she thought, astounded that she could have forgotten even momentarily. This is the man I love.

Hand in hand they crept out through the front door and then around the back of the house where it was darker.

'Here,' said Fern, leaning against the wall and drawing Adam to her. It wasn't making love: Adam knew it as he pounded into her and she pulled him in harder. No, Fern was spurred on by a strange angry urgency. What had happened back there with her father?

Afterwards Fern was relieved to feel the fire and the anger abating. She'd survived her first encounter with her father and the pain of the memory was already receding, though not the wariness. He would never succeed in seducing her.

'I always wanted to make love to a man in a suit,' she said, playfully pulling at Adam's bow tie.

'And I always wanted to make love to a barefoot woman in an evening dress.'

Arm in arm they walked back to the front of the house and into the bright light of a noisy party.

It was almost midnight. The music was loud and jarring. People shouted over it, others danced, spinning each other from partner to partner. They were all laughing, their faces grotesque, red with heat and alcohol and exertion. Only Eric was calm and unruffled, standing next to the fireplace with a glass in his hand.

He was smiling but his eyes fastened on Fern and Adam as they entered the room.

'Come on, join in, said the elderly man, drawing Fern and Adam in among the dancers. Fern was soon enjoying herself for the first time that evening. She was drunk on expensive champagne, she was barefoot, Adam was with her and her father's spell was broken. He looks harmless, she thought as she twirled past him again and again. He can't hurt me now.

As Fern danced she found herself blocking out the ugly rhythm of Eric's music and the noise of his shouting guests; instead she began moving her body to a tune of its own. She imagined playing her pipe, remembered dancing on the beach, feeling the movement of wings on her back, the muscles tugging one way and another. Her notes wove their spell and lifted her so that she was in two places at once, spinning and weaving among the guests in Eric's house and at the same time soaring over and above the crowd, the house, the grounds and the forest, her eyes scanning the land, searching, seeing, wondering. *I am a patterner ... I am a patterner ...* The words repeating themselves in her mind, while Eric stood watching, unaware of the power that was growing in Fern as she danced.

A giant clock on the mantelpiece began chiming. At the same time waiters popped bottles of champagne and people cried out, kissing and hugging and clinking glasses.

Adam took Fern in his arms and kissed her. A long sensuous kiss. 'Happy New Year,' he said.

'Our first one together,' said Fern.

'The first of many,' said Adam, scowling again as Eric approached and grasped Fern's arm.

'Happy New Year,' he said, giving her a chaste kiss on the cheek. 'Any resolutions?'

Fern hadn't even considered it. 'No,' she said. 'And you?'

'Just one.'

Chapter Twenty-Two

Fern woke from a deep drunken sleep into a foul hangover. She lay still, listening to Adam snoring by her side and a chorus of birdsong outside. The rest of the house was quiet. She checked the time. It was still early, only seven, but she was restless. The events of the previous evening played over and over in her head, making her squirm, wanting to get away from herself.

She slid quietly out of bed and peered through a crack in the curtains at a perfect morning, the sun already sending steam rising from the wet grass. She'd always preferred the first day of the year to the last. New Year's Eve was a time for retrospection, New Year's Day for fresh beginnings. But this morning her hangover dragged at her, along with the knowledge that her father had almost drawn her over a line from which she would not have been able to return. She felt another wave of shame wash through her. In the light of the morning it was even harder to believe that she'd let it go as far as it did.

Fern went into the bathroom and turned the shower on hard so it sent jets of water at her. First cold, to jolt her out of her morning stupor, then hot, to comfort her. When she emerged, Adam was still asleep on his back, legs and arms splayed, his mouth wide open and trusting. She sat watching him for a few minutes, wondering if she should wake him. He looked so relaxed that in the end Fern decided against it, though she couldn't resist reaching down and kissing him on the lips. He responded briefly, then spluttered and rolled over.

Stepping out into the hallway, Fern walked quietly towards the stairs. Last night the house had been noisy and a little malevolent, but this morning, filled with sleeping guests, it was surprisingly peaceful. Downstairs the kitchen door was shut, but she could hear noises inside: the staff preparing for the day. She stepped into the empty dining room, looking for a kettle. The large table around which they'd sat the previous evening had disappeared, and now the room was furnished with smaller tables, each one set for breakfast. On the sideboard sat a steaming hot urn and all the paraphernalia she needed to make coffee.

'Ah, Fern, you're an early riser, like me.'

Fern jumped as if she'd been caught doing something criminal. How could Eric's voice sound so fresh and hearty? She'd watched him drink copious amounts last night.

Turning to greet him, she was surprised to see he was dressed in running gear. His trainers were wet, but that was the only sign that he'd already been out. There was no sweat, no messy hair, nothing to say that this man had exerted himself. In contrast she was blushing like a schoolgirl, only this time it wasn't embarrassment, it was anger. Impossible to believe that she'd let him touch her. Impossible to believe that he'd tried.

'I always have a morning run,' he said, answering her unspoken question. 'It's vital to keep oneself fit.'

Fern studied her father. Here was another persona he was presenting to her. He was a shape shifter, she decided, seamlessly moving from one role to another. She couldn't trust anything about him. She shouldn't. But she also couldn't forget that he was her father. Once again she could feel herself being drawn to him, her anger beginning to dissipate in his presence.

'Come, have breakfast with me,' he said.

Suddenly, Fern's stomach was churning with hunger. 'Okay,' she said suspiciously.

He smiled. 'Don't worry, I won't poison you.'

Scowling, Fern pushed down the plunger and poured herself a coffee, then added cream and sugar, making it as unhealthy as possible. She always craved sugar and greasy foods when she was hung-over. Now she wanted bacon and eggs and fried mushrooms and lots of slices of hot toast with too much butter.

'One moment, I'll let the staff know.'

Fern moved to the window and stood in the sunlight, letting it warm her as she sipped the coffee, feeling clarity return with the caffeine. She sifted through the few clues she had about this man. There was so little to draw on; instead she was relying on the hints that Shamesh, Cassie and the Bear Handler had given her, as well as impressions from the few short hours she had known her father - in this life. That was the key. If only she could remember more, not just fragments, but whole lives. If only she could see the patterns more clearly.

Fern was beginning to understand what the Bear Handler had meant when he'd told her that the stories weren't important but the patterns were. Like a stuck record, she had kept coming up against the same forces, life after life, year after year. In this life, injustice and terror at birth, abandonment and closing down. In other lives it seemed that events had inevitably forced her to an early and violent death: that push off the cliff, the spear in her chest, a burning at the stake. All were linked to the same person. Still, she couldn't shake the feeling that there was something eluding her. Fear wasn't enough to establish a pattern like that. There had to be more: injustice, betrayal, guilt, grief and finally, terror. A combination that had scarred her so deeply she couldn't break free of it.

'You have an individual style, like myself.'

Fern jumped, spilling some coffee onto her hand and scalding herself. She hadn't heard Eric return. Self-conscious, she looked at herself in the mirror over the mantelpiece. Her hair, roughly towel dried, was sticking out in a number of directions, her feet were bare and she wore baggy silk shorts with leggings underneath and a *Where the Wild Things Are* t-shirt over a long-sleeved thermal top. Individual? Suddenly she felt stupid. 'I didn't expect anyone to be up so early.'

'It wasn't a criticism.' He poured himself a coffee. 'To be successful in anything, to be truly creative, one must be an individual. If you run with the pack, you will never produce anything original in life, only reproduce what has already been.'

'And you call yourself a creative person?' asked Fern, thinking that everything he did was destructive.

'The two go together,' said Eric. 'Creation, destruction - they are not so different.'

'It takes centuries to grow a tree,' said Fern, remembering what Adam had said, 'and only minutes to chop it down.'

'Ah, but that is not the point,' he said dismissively. 'The question is, what will you create from that tree?'

Fern shrugged. 'Woodchips?'

'Don't be so predictable,' said Eric, scowling briefly. 'Use your imagination, that's where creativity lies.'

They were interrupted by a waiter pushing in a trolley laden with food: a jug of freshly squeezed orange juice, a rack with slices of toast, steaming croissants and tiny bowls of butter, jam and honey. Fern's plate was piled with bacon, poached eggs, fried tomatoes and mushrooms – exactly what sh'd been craving. Her father's mind reading didn't even seem strange anymore; it was quite practical really, saving unnecessary words. No wonder he did well in business; he would have the upper hand every time.

'A traditional English breakfast,' said Eric, 'though here we would call it something else, and charge accordingly: sauteed field mushrooms, roasted baby potatoes with rosemary, traditional free-range smoked bacon and crispy caramelised onions. Much more appealing, don't you think?'

Ignoring him, Fern took a mouthful of fried mushroom. She didn't care how it was described, she just wanted to eat it.

Her father had a bowl of muesli and fresh fruit. 'I am watching my weight, while you could do with a little more,' he said, pouring them both an orange juice. 'You're too pale. You need to look after yourself.' He paused. 'Especially now.'

Puzzled, Fern glanced quickly at him, then frowned; the fatherly role didn't suit him. 'I think I can manage without your concern,' she said pointedly.

'Have it your way,' he said. 'Now, what more do you want to know of my affairs?'

'Why would I want to know anything?'

'If you haven't forgotten, tomorrow you will be turning twenty-one. Officially you will be of age. You are my daughter. As I said, much of this will be yours if you so wish.'

Fern had forgotten. All her life she'd planned to have a big party for her twenty-first, and now it was here it didn't mean anything. Most likely she'd be back in the bush eating dried vegetables and noodles with Adam. Suddenly, she couldn't think of anything nicer.

'Something had been nagging her. 'If you're so rich, then why do you run a guest house in the middle of nowhere?'

'I spend very little time here,' he said. 'For the most part it runs without me. Personally I prefer New York. However, I wanted to meet you, and I'm developing a number of business interests in this state.'

'Such as?'

'You're curious. That's a good sign, perhaps you will be tempted yet to follow me into business.'

'But then I would only be copying you,' said Fern. 'I wouldn't be *truly creative*.'

'Touche.' He smiled, but as always his eyes were dangerous. 'Let me put it differently. Together we could create untold wealth and business interests.' He paused and slid a slice of mango into his mouth. 'Mmm, mango is such a delicious fruit, isn't it?'

'You haven't answered my question.'

'No, but I will. Tasmania has a great many natural resources.'

'The forests?'

'That's small fry,' he said dismissively. 'Wood and water, it's all anyone talks about in this state. No, it's what's under the ground that interests me. Oil and uranium.' His eyes gleamed as he leaned towards Fern. 'There are billions of dollars to be made here.'

Fern chewed on her bacon and studied him closely. In the cold light of day she could see lines on his face and grey hair creeping out from his temples. All that power and wealth wasn't stopping the onslaught of age. He was fallible after all. She had to concentrate on that, not lose herself in fear or admiration. Alarmingly there was still a part of her that wanted what he had: money, power, but most of all, choices.

'You are like me,' he said.

Fern paused, fork in mid-air, shocked again by his assumptions. His mind was blinkered by greed. He couldn't understand internal conflict or the layering of personality. Of course she wanted his wealth and power - who wouldn't? - but she couldn't do what her father was doing, couldn't mine for oil or uranium without regard for people or the environment, couldn't scoff at the forests or refer to ordinary people as scum. She would rather walk away from it all.

'I am not like you,' she said and took a mouthful of egg and toast, wondering that she could eat so calmly in front of this man.

He sighed. 'Have it your way.'

'I still don't understand. Why haven't you killed me?'

'You are far more interesting to me alive.'

'But aren't you afraid of the prophecy?'

He smiled. 'I admit it did concern me for a time, but there's no need to worry now.'

Fern felt a surge of alarm, as the sense that something had gone terribly wrong descended on her. 'What do you mean?'

He took a croissant, tore off a piece and dipped it in his coffee. 'Mmm, this is the perfect way, don't you think? Just like the French. So civilised, those people.'

'I asked what you meant,' Fern said, more forcibly.

'It's simple really. I changed the prophecy.'

'That's not possible,' said Fern, wondering at her certainty. Only weeks ago she would have dismissed prophecies as nonsense, yet now she was convinced they were immutable, carved in stone.

'Of course it is. It has always been possible. One powerful person can change the future for many others. It happens rarely, because there are so few people with that sort of strength. I have it, Fern, and so do you.'

'How have you changed it?'

'You will find that out in your own time.'

Fern was puzzled. He seemed so complacent, sitting opposite her, delicately eating his soggy croissant and drinking his coffee with skim milk. She didn't understand how Eric could be so sure that he'd changed a prophecy he'd believed in enough to want her dead.

'So you were studying fashion design,' said Eric, dabbing his lips with his napkin. 'It's a strong industry. I could perhaps invest in a label, if that would give you a leg-up.'

Feeling the tug of temptation, Fern hesitated. With money came opportunities. She could slip into the industry at the top. Once again Eric was trying to buy her, she realised, and he would most certainly expect something for his money. She shook her head. 'I don't know what I want to do,' she said. 'I'm still working it out.'

'Just say the word. Any university, any career, I'm sure I can help you.'

But Fern was no longer listening, the pieces were coming together: last night the look of triumph in her father's eyes after he'd probed inside her mind; now she remembered what her last memory had been, Grace's words: *Your father's had another heart attack.* Simple Simon had said she would bring about the death of her father - but which father?

'My God!' Abruptly Fern stood up and pushed back her chair. She didn't care that Eric could see the shock on her face, or read the thoughts in her mind. It was too late. She knew that with a dull certainty. Even so, she had to talk to her mother, just to be sure.

Fern raced up the stairs and back to her room. Desperately she picked up the telephone and dialled out. Her hands were shaking as she tried unsuccessfully to convince herself she was imagining it all. Surely her father would be at home reading the newspaper and drinking his first cup of tea for the day.

Her mother answered on almost the first ring.

'Mum,' said Fern, then stopped, not knowing what to say next, but her mother said it for her.

'He's dead, Fernanda. He died a few hours ago. They were going to let him out of hospital tomorrow. No one understands it. His organs just stopped working.'

Even though Fern had expected this, the shock still left her struggling for words. 'Oh Mum,' she said, finally. 'I'm sorry.'

There was a long pause while her mother cried into the phone and Fern sat silently listening and trying to digest this new information. Her father was dead and she had practically signed his death warrant.

'Where are you, Fernanda?' asked Grace.

'I'm in Tasmania, Mum, with a friend. I'm okay.'

'Please come to the funeral, dear. I don't know when it will be. I can't think straight. Oh Fernanda, I need you here.'

'I'll be there, Mum,' said Fern. The bathroom door opened and Adam came out rubbing his hair dry. 'I have to go now. It will take a few days but I'll be there. I promise.'

'Who was that?' asked Adam, when Fern put down the phone.

'My mother.' Fern's voice was flat, her face blank as the familiar, heavy weight of guilt settled inside her.

'Hey, what's wrong?'

'My father's dead. Richard, my adopted father. I killed him, or I may as well have.' Fern's voice was so bleak it reached in to Adam's heart as he sat down next to her on the bed. 'Remember what the prophecy said - that I'd bring about the death of my father.' Fern looked at Adam. 'Don't you see? We all thought it was my birth father; I think it was meant to be. But somehow he shifted it. Eric did what he's no doubt best at, finding loopholes in contracts. And now my father's dead.' She sat on the bed, waiting for the grief to flood into her, but there was only a numb shock. It was all too simple. Last night, Eric had found the information he needed inside her mind, and he'd acted on it.

'How do you know all this?' asked Adam, confused.

'I just had breakfast with Eric. He was gloating over something. He said I wasn't a threat to him anymore.'

'We should get out of here,' said Adam.

'No, I have to talk to him.'

'He's dangerous, Fern.'

'I don't care.'

'Then I'll come with you.'

'No, Adam, please. I have to do this myself.'

Adam was torn. This wasn't his battle, he knew, but Fern was dealing with something so much stronger than herself. And he didn't want to leave her alone with this man for a third time. Last night he'd acted like a servant boy, doing everything he was told. Then this morning he'd slept through Fern's meeting with Eric. He should be there this time. He was supposed to be protecting her.

'I have to, Adam,' said Fern.

'Okay,' he said reluctantly. 'I'll give you five minutes, no more, then I'm coming down.'

Fern found her father downstairs in his office, working on a laptop that looked incongruous in the old-fashioned room. The giant mahogany desk was illuminated by a brass lamp, the walls were lined with dark wooden bookcases, and on a sideboard sat a crystal decanter and glasses. Overnight, though, the house had lost its seductive power. Now it seemed nothing more than a cliched replica of another time.

Fern paused at the door and looked at her father. He'd changed again, into casual trousers with an ironed pleat down the front, and an open-necked shirt. 'Do come in,' he said, looking up as she entered. He shut the lid of his laptop. 'Isn't it a tragedy. I have to work, even on New Year's Day.'

He poured himself a coffee from a steaming silver pot on his desk. 'Would you like one?'

Fern shook her head, her face steely.

'Come, come, don't look so upset.' He took a sip of his coffee then leaned towards Fern. 'Good riddance, I say. He was a weak man: frightened and cruel, a dreadful combination.'

'He was my father.'

'I am your father,' said Eric, his face twisting into sudden anger. 'He was an impostor.'

'He brought me up. He looked after me.'

'Come now. How many times did you wish the man dead?'

Fern recoiled in shock. 'Never,' she said.

'Don't lie to me, Fern. I have no patience with dishonest people.'

Fern shook her head stubbornly. She hadn't liked Richard but she hadn't killed him or even wanted him dead. Eric was twisting everything around the wrong way.

'Oh, for God's sake, Fern, why was he in hospital in the first place? It was you. Your behaviour. Do me a favour and at least shoulder the responsibility.' Eric sighed. 'I thought better of you.'

Fern felt her fists clenching. She wouldn't take responsibility for Richard, not for his heart attacks, nor for his death. She was fed up with shouldering the blame for other people's incapacities, fed up with tiptoeing through life weighed down with guilt and afraid of the consequences of every action. 'No,' she said. 'Richard made himself sick and you finished him off.'

The anger was rising inside her, but she tried to subdue it. Anger would make her want to fight Eric and she couldn't win on his terms. She'd learned that already. Anger was dangerous too, uncontrollable. But despite her efforts, she could feel it growing until finally she could contain it no longer. First one book slid off the bookcase, and another. Then it seemed as if they all came at once, hurling themselves at Eric, who deflected them with hardly a glance. Fern wanted to stop but she couldn't. The anger was unleashed and had taken on a life of its own. She was astonished by it, excited and horrified by the power she'd tapped into.

At some point she realised Adam was standing next to her, watching, his mouth wide open in shock. Fern knew she needed to regain control and put a stop to this, but there was so much hate inside her. More than anything she wanted Eric dead. She wanted to pull the walls down, smash them onto her father. She imagined the way it would cave in and bury him among the dust and rubble of other people's dreams. The hate she felt was palpable, drawing itself together from a lifetime of buried fury, forming its own shadowy shape, its lines and contours telling the story of lifetimes of darkness and hatred. *No.* The word appeared in Fern's head but she wasn't listening. She felt hatred growing steadily, her own creation, a creature of destruction, a weapon she could unleash on her father. *Stop.* Fern could hear the walls creaking around her as her fury moved beyond the books and attacked the fabric of the house. *This is not the way.*

All at once Fern knew what she had already suspected. The shadowy figure that had attacked her on Bruny was her father's servant, constructed from the foulness inside him but feeding off the darkness and fear inside her. Fern knew too that she must rein in her anger before her own shadow creature became an autonomous and destructive thing that would control her because she didn't have enough power to command it. She reached out for Adam's hand, feeling his earth energy begin to steady her. Then she breathed deeply, letting her out-breath dispel her anger, the way it had with her fear, and feeling herself deflate as the fury dissipated. But still the books came and the walls creaked and Fern couldn't understand why it wasn't stopping. She felt her residual anger turning into fear as she realised this was already beyond her control.

'You're playing children's games in a dangerous world,' Eric said, his voice steeped with contempt.

The books stopped immediately, some falling heavily to the floor, and to her dismay, Fern realised that Eric had indulged her, let her make a mess of his office, then switched it off when he'd had enough.

'You have the talent for it, of course,' said Eric, more softly. 'But you need someone to show you the rules.'

'No,' said Fern, her voice sounding strangely distant and uncertain, as if it had fled into the room's shadows and now didn't trust even itself. She was spent, exhausted by her own fury, her knees buckling under her, but certainty was returning quickly, along with a new resolve. She'd used her power in anger and it had been destructive. Her will had been misdirected, drawn from a wrong source. In doing so she'd somehow joined forces with her father and let him dictate the terms. There was another way, she was certain of that. But she didn't know what it was.

'Come on, Fern,' said Adam, grasping her shoulders. 'It's time to go.'

'That's right, run away,' said her father mockingly.

'No,' said Fern again, determined not to leave until she'd achieved what she'd come here to do. She grasped the lapis lazuli around her neck and waited while it cleared her mind. The anger had been replaced by a cold clarity. She stared at her father, seeing him properly once more. Last night she'd been trapped by whatever spell he had cast, the desire she'd felt for what he'd offered her. Today she was free. Or she would be yet. He was a sorcerer, a wizard, an occultist: the label didn't matter. And he was a businessman. That was all. The pieces were falling into place. He might be stronger than she, he might know the rules of his power and the extent of it, but his heart was closed and because of this his power would turn against him eventually. He relied on illusions and fear to bully and win. Shamesh and Cassie and the Bear Handler had all been right: hunt the hunter and you take away his strength.

The connection Fern had with him was strong. Doubly so. He was her father and she even looked like him. Then there was the other relationship, the one she'd never understood, that had carried across lifetimes: each time he'd wanted her and each time she'd resisted. This partnership he talked of would work only if she came to it of her own choice. And she never would. She never had. She might have died many times because of her refusal, but she'd never yet succumbed.

'Yes,' said Eric. 'Your own free will, that's what I need.' He glanced slyly at Adam, then back to Fern. 'You gave me your body so beautifully last night, Fern. Will you give me your partnership today?'

'I did not,' said Fern.

Eric smiled, a slow, corrupt smile. 'Whatever you say, my dear.'

Adam's confusion was growing and with it a sense of alarm. 'Fern?' he asked, searching her eyes for the truth.

Fern met his gaze. 'He tried to seduce me. And he failed. Don't you understand? He's trying to drive a wedge between us. We've known that all along. I said it in the forest and you did last night. He's divisive, that's how he works.'

Eric smiled and waited, looking from one to the other. Adam was confused. He believed Fern, of course he did, but already the questions were entering his head, little barbs of distrust. Her strange mood after she'd met Eric, the way she had thrown herself on him. 'Then why…?'

'I was trying to get rid of the memory of him. He kissed me, Adam; and he touched me, but I stopped him.'

'Why didn't you tell me?'

'Because you would have hit him.'

'Maybe I should,' he said, clenching his fists as the anger surged through him.

'Don't,' Fern said. 'That's what he wants.'

For a moment more, Adam hesitated. Then he took a deep breath and unclenched his fists.

'How sweet,' said Eric.

Fern looked at her father's leering face and felt cold hatred once more. If she only knew in which life she had been forced to close her heart, then perhaps she could break free of whatever lay between them. She needed to peer into the stormy centre of the tempest stone and locate that life, but the stone was upstairs, tucked safely in her pack. Fern sent her need out to it now, imagining, remembering its contours, the liquid patterns within it … and then had to steady herself as she slipped suddenly back into another time and place. She felt the chill first and the aching discomfort, then realised she was chained to a stone slab, the sharp metal cutting into her wrists and ankles, the cold creeping through her back. There was a shuffle of feet outside the door, as the blue-and-white uniformed guards stood to attention, then the creak of metal as the door opened and the hooded man stepped into the dungeon, his face in shadow, his arms folded, his hands tucked into sleeves. In the midst of her fear, she saw clearly the role he was playing in this life – a religious figure exuding piety and power.

'You may go,' he said, dismissing the soldiers, who backed out obsequiously, closing the door behind them. He turned to her, his prisoner, and lifted the hood away from his face to reveal a hooked nose, a narrow face and an ugly crooked mouth. He stood for a moment before her, gloating, then stepped forward and tore her gown away, leaving her naked and shivering. A whimper escaped involuntarily from her mouth before she set her face again, steeling herself for the worst. As he took her there on the slab, coldly and efficiently, almost as if it were a duty, she sent herself out of her body, watching as if she were elsewhere, a great distance away in time and space.

Fern fought to bring herself back to the present, to this warm study with Eric safely on the other side of his desk, but she could still feel the cold and her hands felt numb where the bindings had cut off her circulation. Shivering at the memory she rubbed her wrists, trying to bring some life into her hands. Then she spoke his name. 'Porteus.'

Eric looked up briefly, answering her summons and reading the knowledge in her eyes. 'Not my finest moment,' he said, his mouth twitching into a smile. 'Still, one can only work with what one has.'

But Fern remembered. And she knew that the remembering weakened him somehow, if only by giving her the power to resist him. Porteus, the priest man taking her against her will - though that wasn't what had broken her. The vision had faded, both too late and too soon, but she already knew the rest. There'd been a baby and might easily have been again, Fern thought with a shiver, if she had succumbed to her father's seduction the previous night. Then there were the fragments the tempest stone had shown her that day on the train: the soldiers and Porteus and the young girl beheaded in front of her. Her daughter and Porteus's, but even so he'd coldly ordered the soldier to strike off the child's head. The image was still caught in Fern's memory, playing over and over, twisting her stomach and her heart. She couldn't believe that he would be so cruel, to kill his own daughter like that, without a backward glance. And all the time watching her, knowing it would destroy her. He'd waited until the knowledge and the grief had settled inside her and she'd felt her heart slam shut. Then, in triumph, he'd had her killed, letting her die slowly, in an agony of grief and guilt, all the time aware that she had failed to keep her daughter safe.

'Why did you have us killed?'

A look of distaste settled on Eric's face. 'You used your powers to mock me. '

'Mock you? ' Fern paused, as an image flooded into her. A woman in a long robe, her hair covered with a veil, sitting on the edge of a bed, her little daughter standing beside her watching as the life force found its way through this woman who was Fern and not Fern, and entered into the injured man lying on the bed, pulsing gently, without urgency until a little colour returned to his cheeks. At this the girl glanced triumphantly at her mother, who smiled. 'He'll live to see another day. Pass me that salve.'

She'd escaped from that dungeon and taking her tiny daughter with her, fled into obscurity, sheltering in a convent and using her power to heal the sick. Until one day, drawn by rumours of a healing woman, Porteus had found them both.

'Why did you kill us?' she asked again.

'You were no longer of use to me in that life, ' said Eric matter-of-factly. 'And you have to admit, it was an effective measure.'

Fern looked at Eric, sitting there behind his giant desk, his open-necked shirt perfectly pressed. Her father and her enemy. Life after life he'd reduced her to poverty, destroyed the people around her and eventually murdered her for refusing to submit. All this and her will had never broken. In the end, though, he had succeeded in breaking her heart and once broken she'd lost her ability to channel the life force. Now it was beginning to mend. Once again Fern felt the tingling in her hands that had come only two days earlier in the forest with Adam, the same tingling she'd felt in that woman's hands as she healed the injured man so long ago. Her heart had been open fully then and soon it would be again. That was the only thing her father feared.

'Oh yes, your heart. We'll keep it broken, shall we?' The menace in Eric's voice was so strong that Fern had to force herself not to shrink from it.

She studied him, trying again to see past the monster she feared so much. He was a small man, slender and without a great deal of physical strength. The power he talked of was vast in some ways but limited in others. He had money and connections, he had charisma and the courage to take risks, and he had psychic powers; there was plenty he could do to hurt her, but there was one thing he couldn't do: make her his.

It was beginning to make sense to her now. It was Fern's chosen path to oppose his spirit. Life after life she had done this but then, broken-hearted after her daughter's death, she'd closed herself down. It was time to change that. She wouldn't allow it to happen again. She wouldn't run and she wouldn't fight. She would simply be herself.

'I want you to understand something,' Fern said, leaning over the desk towards her father so that their faces were almost touching. 'No matter what you do, you no longer have the power to break my heart. I am the only person who can do that.'

Fern had a New Year's resolution after all. It would be difficult to achieve, but nevertheless she would try. From now on, Fern told herself, she would let herself feel everything: love and grief, joy and sorrow. Anything that arose she would feel. Never again would she close herself off. Never again would she live in fear. 'It's my choice,' she said to her father. 'You will never break my heart again.'

He shrugged. 'You may go now; I have work to do.'

Fern turned her back on her father and walked towards the door, then spun around to face him again. 'You're right,' she said. 'I've been trying to deny it, but I am like you. Which is why I won't hate you. Hating you means I hate a part of myself. And I won't do that anymore.'

'Good,' said her father. 'You're one step closer to joining me.'

Fern shook her head. 'No. There's one important difference between us. Your heart is shrivelled inside your chest. It's all dried out.' She paused, remembering the dried vegetables Adam had cooked in the forest and how perfectly they had returned to their original form. Even the taste and the smell of them had reappeared. 'Why don't you try reconstituting it?' she suggested. 'See what happens.'

'That is not my path.'

'You choose your path.'

'No,' he said and for a moment Fern thought she saw a hint of sadness in his face. 'It chooses you.'

'You're afraid,' said Fern, in a moment of clarity, seeing for the first time how small he was inside as well as out. She'd been wrong again: the shadow creature that had attacked her on Bruny wasn't Eric's servant it was his master. Her father had lost control long ago.

Eric stood up, suddenly and alarmingly looming much larger than before. Fern stepped back involuntarily and banged into Adam.

'You are trying my patience,' Eric boomed. 'I am not afraid. Though *you* have every reason to be.'

Suddenly Fern felt him inside her mind again, probing, striding the corridors, turning over her memories, violating her. She pushed back at him, furious at this intrusion. Images flashed at her: Grace pushing her on a swing; her grandmother slapping her face; the minister at church talking about the sheep and the goats and her sinking certainty that she was a goat; the swish of muslin curtains in her attic; and Eric, his fingers stroking her. Fern shivered and tried to push him out again, but without warning a part of him lunged at her. She felt his intention and the familiar terror and swayed back, as the power of his shadow engulfed her.

At first Adam noticed only that Eric and Fern were staring at each other. He almost laughed, remembering the game he used to play with Michael as a kid, seeing who blinked first. Then Adam felt the terror of the thing that had thrown itself on Fern. He could see more of it now than he had on Christmas Eve, as if it were solidifying. It's gaining power, he thought, racking his brain for a way to break Fern free of it. He tried turning her away from Eric but her body was too rigid. It was tempting to punch Eric in the face, but he resisted the impulse, knowing that Fern wouldn't thank him for it. So, in the absence of any better idea, he reached out and placed his hand on her back. There was nothing more he could do for her. It was clear that Fern and Eric were fighting in a place he couldn't go. This was Fern's battle, not his.

He had guided her into this house of Eric's and he would guide her out. In the meantime, all he could do was wait and hope that his touch would give her strength.

Fern felt the reassuring warmth of Adam's hand and his regular breath on her neck, felt it grounding her. With the comfort that it brought, new images began flashing at her: Shamesh, his eyes pouring energy into her; and the feel of the bear's fur in Fern's fingers. She felt a surge of gratitude for their help and almost immediately her father receded a little, only to return again stronger than before. But this time she was holding the staff the Bear Handler had given her. Instinctively she held it up and her breathing changed as she let her fear dissipate and the bear take over, sending its strength into Fern.

The triumph was already evident in Eric's eyes. Too early, she thought and threw the thought at him, watching him flinch just a little. Almost instantly he was back, his mind trespassing in hers, trying to engulf and consume her. Fern struggled again, trying to use her will and her anger to push him away, but she was weakening. Something was missing, tantalisingly just out of reach and she strained towards it.

Surrender. The word came from nowhere, surprising her by its simplicity. *Surrender.* Against her instincts, Fern stopped struggling. She let herself relax, then as the last of her fear and hatred diminished and then died, she reached out with the staff and gently touched the surging intent that was consuming her. 'Eric,' she said, in a tone that was almost loving.

In that moment everything changed. Fern's mind was released, the atmosphere cleared and Eric slumped onto his chair in a crumpled heap as if someone had extracted his spine. Fern felt herself sagging, the last of her energy draining away. She would have fallen if Adam hadn't caught her.

'Do you think he's okay?' asked Fern, looking at Eric. 'Maybe he's had a heart attack,' she added, thinking how ironic that would be.

'Too much to hope for,' said Adam.

'What if he's dead?'

'Good riddance,' said Adam, though he was getting worried too. If Eric was dead, they would have to stay and answer questions, which would be awkward. Adam picked his away among the books littering the floor and felt Eric's wrist for a pulse. 'He's alive.'

Adam jumped as Eric moved his arm and then, with an immense effort, lifted his head. He looked old suddenly, and powerless, all the facades gone.

Watching her father use all his will to force himself upright, Fern could hardly believe it was the same man. He looked beaten and small and she found herself feeling sorry for him.

Eric held up his hand as if to stop her. 'Don't,' he said. 'Pity is such a revolting emotion. It doesn't suit either of us.'

He stood up, leaning on the desk, the effort it was costing him showing in his face. 'You have performed better than I expected, but that is all. It would be dangerous to bask in your triumph.'

Already he was issuing threats and trying to take control again. Fern backed away, too exhausted to fight him once more.

'Don't worry, I won't hurt you. I have no desire to harm my granddaughter,' said her father, his face twisted into an expression she couldn't read. Was it a smile or a grimace? 'Yet,' he added, before abruptly turning away as Adam half carried Fern out of the study and up the stairs into their room.

Shocked by Eric's statement, Fern tried to look inside herself, to see if she could sense another living presence, but she could sense nothing. Somehow she'd managed to reconfigure the pattern of events. In another life, Porteus had tied her to him with a baby. And last night Eric had tried to do it again. But he'd failed. If she was pregnant, it would be Adam's child.

Back in their room Adam started throwing things into his pack. 'Come on,' he said, 'we're going.'

'Now?'

'It'll be safer out there than in here.'

Fern lay down on the bed. She was so tired. Too tired to move, let alone pack or walk. She just wanted to sleep.

'Come on, Fern,' said Adam.

'I can't. I'm exhausted.'

Adam sat down on the bed next to Fern and gently brushed her cheek with his fingers. 'I reckon you're the bravest person I know.'

'Me? '

'Yeah. You've faced down your fears. Not many people do that. Believe me, I should know.'

'But I didn't stop him killing Dad. '

'Look Fern, you've got to let that one go. It wasn't your fault. Your father was already sick. ' Adam stood up. 'Come on then. We're getting out of here even if I have to carry you.'

'Okay. ' Fern sat up reluctantly and began pulling on her boots.

Adam thought it was over, she could see that. But Fern knew better: she could feel the lingering malice, much weakened, but still there. Something was still troubling her. Fern knew what had caused her to shut herself down; but weary as she was, she needed to know more, needed to truly understand the source of the conflict that had re-surfaced in this lifetime with her father. Otherwise she would never be free of it.

She reached into her pack and retrieved the tempest stone, hoping to find the answers in there. The stone looked different: it was cracked in places, while other patches had turned a dusky blue. It was as if each retrieved memory had depleted it in some way. She peered into its depths, searching for the memory she needed, but nothing came. It was just a stone, sitting cold in her hand, heavy and closed to her. There was more in there, she could sense it, but it wasn't ready to emerge. Not yet.

'Here, let me help you,' said Adam.

'It's okay, I can manage.' Fern leaned over to tie her laces, but the lump in her throat made her helpless as the tears overflowed and she cried for her dad and the child she'd lost and the lives she'd wasted, shut down and hiding from Eric.

Adam wrapped his arms around Fern, and drew her to him, letting her sob on his shoulder, her tears soaking through his t-shirt. 'You've done it,' he said. 'It's over.'

'No,' said Fern, wiping her eyes. 'We did it together.' She thought back to that first meeting with Shamesh. How she'd shrunk from the idea of taking a journey and shrunk from Adam too. And yet in such a short time she'd grown so much. Somehow the dark places inside her had opened to let in the light and now Fern recognised the need in her that was drawing her towards a path already there, not visible yet, but sensed. For that she was immensely grateful.

For now at least it was enough. She didn't know all the answers yet, she might never know them, but she knew enough. That life with Porteus was the one that had shut down her heart but now she was breaking free and not even Eric could stop her finding a better way to live.

She stood up and heaved her pack onto her shoulders, feeling herself bend under its weight. It seemed so much heavier than she remembered. Was it only yesterday they'd walked into this strange house? It had felt like an oasis of comfort then, but now it was more like the sticky centre of a spider's web. Adam was right, they needed to get out of here while they could. Fern was no longer afraid of Eric but she still wanted to put some distance between them. She had no idea how far his power stretched in the physical world but she already knew how easily he could hurt the people she loved.

Fern took one last look at the room filled with the trappings of luxury. She picked up the perfume on the dressing table and put it down, then looked longingly at the evening dress. It was tempting to take something as a keepsake, but this house had woven its dangerous spells around her once and she'd nearly allowed herself to be seduced; she wouldn't let that happen again. She would prefer a tent to this, any day.

Fern followed Adam out the door and closed it firmly behind her. Together they walked down the hallway and then down the ornate staircase. The atmosphere in the house had completely changed again. Guests were emerging from their rooms, casting strange looks at Fern and Adam with their heavy packs and grubby walking boots. How long, she wondered, since any of these people had carried anything heavier than a cocktail glass?

Fern glanced into the dining room as they passed. People were sitting at the tables, their noisy chatter accompanied by the clattering of spoons and cups, and the squeak of knives on plates. It was so different from an hour or two earlier when Fern had sat there with her father. How long ago it already seemed. She looked around the room, half hoping for one last glimpse of him making inconsequential small talk with his guests, something to remind her that he was just a man playing a role and no longer the monster that inhabited her dreams. But he was nowhere to be seen.

Near the front door Adam picked up a pamphlet addressed to 'Intrepid Walkers' and studied the simple map. It showed a path leading out to the north east through a small gate in the fence. The walk was only a few kilometres long before it looped back to the harbour, making a circular trip. Still, at least they could follow it for a while before cutting off into the bush.

They stepped outside into a perfect day, hotter than any Fern had yet experienced in Tasmania, the sun so fierce she could immediately feel it burning her. For once she didn't put her hat on. The heat felt good on her skin, as if she'd been caught in a long dark night and now the sun was burning away its lingering traces. This was real, she told herself, the heat of the sun on her face, the gravel crunching underfoot as they walked together along the drive, the solidity of the oak trees they passed, her hand caressing their rough trunks. These trees would have been there as long as the house, over a hundred and thirty years. And yet they were young compared to the forests around them.

Adam paused and half turned.

'Don't look back,' said Fern urgently.

Startled, he looked at her, a question in his eyes. But Fern had no idea why she'd said that. The certainty had arrived in her mind, unheralded, unexpected. *Don't look back.* What would happen, she wondered, if they did? She shuddered, suddenly afraid that what she and Adam had together was too tenuous, a fine thread that could be severed in a moment. Perhaps her father would simply bide his time before trying to break her again, and the easiest way would be to hurt Adam, she thought, or their child if they were to have one. At the thought of that she felt a cold fear wash through her.

Don't look back. The very thought of turning for one last glimpse was a temptation, tugging at her head. But she had willpower. She could resist.

'Come on,' she said. 'Let's get out of here.' They crossed the lawn, their footfalls suddenly muted as they headed towards the forest.

In the end it was Adam who looked. Fern watched him taking it all in, committing it to memory; perhaps suspecting, as she did, that it wasn't over yet. That maybe it would never be over and that they would have to live with that uncertainty. Fern saw it then, a part of Adam left behind, a bond between Adam and that place, between Adam and her father. She wanted to take a knife and slice through it. But it was not for her to own Adam's choices. And she had no power to halt their unfinished business, for if Adam had known her in previous lives, she had little doubt that he'd also known Eric.

Adam felt something too, a draining of his strength, a deep foreboding and a shuddering fear. He'd wanted to take one last look at the house, standing there defiantly, he thought, in the middle of the wilderness, money and staff all employed to fight off the creep of the wild, to maintain the property's manicured lawns, to cultivate order. For Adam it had none of the beauty of the forests; its very existence was a denial of nature. And yet it was beautiful too, in its own way.

He shielded his eyes against the sun, trying to see past the reflections in the windows. From here it looked as if the house was a shell, that the forest existed both within and without. There was a figure on the top verandah. Was it Eric watching them leave? Adam dragged his eyes away from the house and looked at Fern, standing before him, her back turned squarely on her father's house. There were dark rings under her eyes and her shoulders were tensed as if she was holding herself together but she seemed taller somehow and more solid. He'd been proud of her in there, standing up to her father. That took real courage. That was what they had come for.

Adam had changed too, could feel himself turning towards life once again. He had a direction now, he'd made a decision. And if Eric was right, he had a daughter on the way. Adam felt a thrill of excitement at the prospect. He'd better get organised.

Resolute, he turned his back on the house and took Fern's hand. Then together they stepped through the gate and into the cool twilight of the forest.

Within seconds it was as if the house had never been.

Epilogue

I am becoming a patterner. It is a strange title but I'm not alone in this role. There are many patterners in this world, though most do not call themselves by that name and many would not perceive that this is what they do. There are other titles for this role, words loaded with the weight of history, prejudice and expectations: shaman, clairvoyant, magician, artist, story teller, musician, politician, prophet, orator, historian, scientist - names that close the hearer's mind. A patterner is a name that does not cause discomfort. It's open not closed, broad not narrow. A name that crosses boundaries.

Labels are dangerous. They are binding and most often not self-applied. In truth they only reveal something about their creator. Definitions are dangerous too; like labels, they create boundaries, fix identity and work against change, which is part of the natural flow of life. Nevertheless there are times when it is useful to understand a word. In doing so, one must always remember that words carry power. In their interpretation, context must be taken into account, as well as gestures and intent. Literal readings cause misunderstandings and ultimately war. Destruction arises from the fixing of words, from the turning of transparent to opaque. Now, in this shifting time of endings and beginnings, it is more vital than ever that we learn once again to see beneath words to their deeper meanings.

For the sake of those who seek clarity, I will attempt to describe without definition. A patterner is simply someone who understands the shape of things and the relationships they bear to each other. Someone who can distance themselves from the everyday and move far enough away to see clearly, in the way perhaps that an eagle or hawk might circle higher and higher in the sky, ever broadening their view, seeking the movement of creatures below. For a patterner the motive is not to hunt, but to perceive. Perhaps at times to unravel a pattern and weave a new one, though this is a dangerous act and must not be carried out impulsively, for the changing of one thing is the changing of another and consequences cannot always be anticipated.

From the outside it may appear that a patterner does little, but that is not the case. They see and hold the patterns of life. There are patterns in everything: in the events of this world; the cycles of the seasons; and in the behaviour of individuals, families and societies. There are patterns in communications and in the shapes of cells and shells. And there are patterns in words. Words that are woven into stories, whose meanings will shift and change over time and according to the ears of their audience.

I spend a lot of time in my garden, seeing the larger patterns reflected in the smaller patterns that I, in my small way, help to sustain. There are ponds with lilies, and tadpoles which drop their tails, grow legs and eventually emerge as frogs. There are tall ferns in the shadows, arching their fronds across the sky like wings, and trees that drop their leaves in winter, carpeting the ground and protecting it from frosts. There are bulbs that lie dormant through autumn and winter, then in spring, at some mysterious signal, push their way through the hard ground towards the light. There are flowers that bare their heart to the sun each day, following its path, their petals closing each night to embrace the darkness. There are trees whose blossoms become fruit that ripens and weighs down the branches, sending summer scents into the hot, still air. There are bees that lift pollen from the flowers, winds that lift seeds from their source, worms that labour underground, enriching the earth, food scraps that become soil. Everywhere in my garden are the patterns of life. I have only to use all my senses, to watch and listen, smell and touch, to taste, and to intuit. I have only to do this and I know what I need to know.

We will not live here forever but for now it is the right place. Freya doesn't need much. At eighteen months she's bewitched by the wonders of nature. For now, the boundaries of our garden are enough, along with our regular excursions down to the beach. Here we walk along the white sand, Freya picking up shells and seaweed, a piece of broken glass worn smooth and round-edged by the sea, treasures she fills my pockets with and then later arranges on the verandah, all the time talking to herself and to the objects as if they were friends, which I suppose they are. I think about her childhood and how different mine was. Then I'm glad. Glad that my childhood forged me and sent me on this path so that I can stand here now with Freya, and feel content.

Sometimes when I look at Freya, I see myself, but more often I can see Adam, in a gesture, a brash smile, a sudden laugh, the line of her chin, a tilt of her head. And in her eyes. They are Adam's, dark, deep and unreadable. Adam has become a forest track worker and an activist. He spends weeks at a time in the forests, trying to save them. Like me, Adam has found his path, followed the clues: a nudge from Matt, Eric's scoffing voice at a New Year's Eve dinner party, a challenge from me.

I have not heard from my father, though I have heard of him. Not long after we left Pine House, a flash of lightning ignited the forest around it and a wild wind lashed the fire into a fury that consumed the house in minutes. Poetic justice, Adam called it, nature taking its revenge. My father was not consumed in that fire. He was already lying in hospital, weakened by a stroke that came only days after our confrontation. He had tried to outwit the prophecy and, in doing so, nearly brought about its fulfilment. Now his life hangs in the balance. Even so I prefer not to think of him. I don't want to tempt the fates, or to lose the tenuous equilibrium I have found.

My father is not a reflective man. If he were he might realise his own madness, perhaps even perceive the limits of his power. He's not reflective, but he reflects the worst in others, mirroring back to them their desires, their fears and their greed, using them to achieve his own desires. I don't believe he's evil, only that he works against compassion. But he is greedy, seeking worldly power, commercialism, materialism, endless consumption. He has powers that are beyond the five senses, and with them he wants to control all worlds.

I do not often leave the safety of our home, only making the occasional and necessary foray into the outer world. Sometimes we go with Adam into the forest. Like her father, Freya loves the wilderness, but there's anger and unnecessary violence between the protesters and the forest workers, so we stay only for a short time. We visit the local shop for mail and small groceries. Otherwise, if Adam's away, I rely on Iris for the shopping she brings over weekly, as well as the produce from the garden that Michael helps me with. We go to the city once a month or so, always unwilling, and always pleased to return.

In the cities, people, for the most part, are carrying on as if nothing has changed, pretending they can't feel the energy shifts or the pervading panic that makes them hurry, faster and faster, checking watches, talking on mobile phones, reassuring themselves that all is normal, that time hasn't sped up after all. All they can feel is the fear, heralded and amplified on television, in the news and the dramas that feed them. Cassie was right, this is the ending of an empire, but it is also the beginning of something new. The world is changing and we are changing with it. It's too soon perhaps to see how.

I have become so sensitive that when I return home after one of my forays my head is buzzing, my heart palpitating, the things that I have seen and heard imprinted on the back of my eyelids so that they accompany me even when I close my eyes and slip into sleep, forming maddening and surreal composite dreams that force me to toss and turn all night. Freya is sensitive too. After an outing, her sleep isn't peaceful. Instead she walks the rooms of the house, her eyes wide open and not seeing, calling for me and not hearing my voice, holding her arms out to be hugged, but not feeling my own arms enfold her tiny body.

On those nights, if Adam is away, I gently wake her. Then we lie down together and I tell her stories about her father. I tell her of his courage and his passion. I tell her that he was there when she was born and that he carried her into the forest proudly, his eyes shining with love. I tell her that he has a path to tread, that he makes a difference. The world is changing, I say, and the time has come to let go of the old ways, the ones that ensure the repetitions of history. Peace is a gentle thing that can no longer be fought for. Instead it will enter our hearts and spread from there like the ripples of a pebble dropped into our pond.

Freya watches me and listens. I don't know how much she understands of my words, but she hears my intent and is comforted. As Freya's eyes close sleepily, I tell her that the universe is filled with the beauty of paradox. We do not live in a world of black and white, but a world that comprises a multitude of colours and shades. It is for us to embrace them all.

When Freya sleeps, I pick up my books again and read, learning all that I had forgotten. I have been studying homeopathy and the way of herbs, trying to understand the patterns of illness, trying to see its source which so often lies far beyond the physical. I've understood that true healing is not something you can do with a closed heart. It must reach deep into the spirit and work its magic from within. True healing changes a person, clears scar tissue and the patterns of reaction that have formed their character. It is not an easy path to choose.

Sometimes Michael shows me his own way of healing, though he has no knowledge of how he does it. Since that time in the forest when Adam was bitten, I have not felt the flow of energy that Michael uses. I place my hands on Freya's feverish head and it cools a little, or I gently kiss a bruise and the pain eases. I don't know if that is healing or simply the love of a mother for her daughter. Perhaps the two are not so different.

My mother is coming to stay and Freya is excited. We pick parsley and basil for the pasta, then courgettes, beans and fresh cherry tomatoes, the sweetest sort that Freya can't resist. I will fry them lightly in garlic, then throw in the herbs and some rich Greek feta, before tossing it all in the pasta spirals. I watch Freya feasting on our garden, her face dripping with sticky juices, tomato pips running in a line down her shirt. I watch her and laugh as joy surges through me. A joy that comes with the knowledge that I am exactly where I should be, that Grace is coming today and that tomorrow Adam will be here. Then, still laughing, I hold Freya up high so she can pick apricots and nectarines, gently placing each one in the basket for her grandmother.

In the kitchen, I finely chop the garlic and parsley, then put the basil and olive oil in a pestle and mortar and let Freya work them into a paste. Occasionally I look out through the windows at the ocean in front of us. Today is warm, the air is still, the sky free of clouds and the water a rich turquoise that suggests a tropical paradise, not the cold waters of southern Tasmania.

My eyes scan the road below for any sign of a car. It's good to have company, though I am rarely lonely here. When Adam is away, Iris comes often and so does Michael. They love me as if I were their own and they love Freya. Especially Freya.

'Grace here,' says Freya, tugging on my skirt impatiently as a car pulls up.

My feet feel firm and steady on the ground as I watch Grace step out of the car. Freya takes my hand and we walk towards my mother, the one who took me into her home and nurtured me with all the love she could, the one who now accepts me as I am, and who I have learned to love without fear or guilt, without anger or resentment.

'Fern,' she says, reaching out to me and I feel her stiff body soften in my embrace, feel the warmth of her tears on my face, see the joy in her smile.

'And Freya! Look at you, so very, very tall,' she says, bending over to let her granddaughter plant wet kisses on her cheek.

My mother is here and I am happy. We walk up to the house together, three generations bound by love and shared experience. I have learned so much in such a short time. That blood is not thicker than water. That love comes as a gift and should not be turned away. That fences divide, and divisions kill. And most importantly of all, I am learning to fly.

I am truly blessed.

Acknowledgements

First I would like to thank Teresita White for her generosity and patience in working with me on the early drafts of this novel. Our lifelong friendship is so precious to me.

Flight was originally published by HarperCollins and I would like to thank Anna Valdinger who supported this novel so enthusiastically. I am grateful too for the assistance of the Australia Council Literature Board, as well as Arts Tasmania; without this support my writing journey would have been a good deal bumpier.

I am deeply grateful to my beautiful children, Nikita, Freda and Harry, who have taught me so much and believed in me always. And to my husband, Tim, for his patience, his trust and his love, as well as all those coffee-fueled plot discussions.

And finally, my gratitude goes to the mystery behind inspiration. My thanks as always, to the giver.

Between Worlds

(standalone sequel to Flight)

'A compelling and powerful story of how past lives can shape and shadow the present.'
Kate Forsyth

Fern lives on Bruny Island, with her partner, Adam and their young daughter, Freya. Adam has dedicated his life to protecting the old-growth forests in Tasmania, while herbalist Fern has become a healer who no longer heals. Instead she is filled with a growing sense of foreboding.

When a stranger tells Fern she must resolve the divide that is growing between herself and her daughter, she is dismissive, but then a tragedy occurs and in its aftermath Fern is forced to reconsider the stranger's advice. Fern travels with Freya to the home of a renowned therapist in Southern France, who agrees to help, and invites them to stay in his villa. It is here that Fern begins delving into the past and is drawn deep into an historic tragedy which threatens once more to possess her.

An unforgettable journey through the illusions of time and space that separate one life from another. *Between worlds* is a compelling ghost story, an exploration of grief and the complications of love, particularly between mothers and daughters. It is at once a metaphysical story and a celebration of the magic of everyday life.

Gathering Storm

'You'll be swept a long by this journey of discovery. A great road movie of a novel.
Katherine Scholes

English artist Storm Cizekova grew up believing that her mother died when she was born. But then Storm finds a photo of herself in the heart of the Australian desert – and in her mother's arms.

Haunted by unanswered questions, Storm embarks on a journey of self-discovery that will challenge everything she holds dear: her family history, her art, even her relationship with her partner Max. Who is she really, and where does she belong?

Her search will take her from the snow-covered Malvern Hills in England to the rich red heart of the Australian outback. Retracing her mother's footsteps through the stark beauty of the desert landscape, Storm hopes to find the courage to confront some shocking truths from her past and the strength to face her future.

Gathering Storm is an exploration of identity and dislocation in a personal sense, through family history and genetic inheritance, but also from a broader cultural perspective, in relation to nationhood and citizenship. It explores the nature of truth, the power of lies and the damage they leave in their wake. But probably, most importantly, Gathering Storm is about identifying and breaking free of negative patterns, by turning around and facing the monsters in one's life and taking the journey from anger to forgiveness and compassion – it's about becoming oneself and living one's life in relation to that, instead of through the wounds that can be inherited from one's ancestors, from one's culture, and created through the experience of living.

'… A bit of a Heart of Darkness Apocalypse Now tale. It is part thriller, part hippie road story and part rite-of-passage trip in search of identity. Above all it is a compelling, stylish and well-paced read. Frightening at times and searching in its awareness of landscape and family secrets, this is a fine debut.'

Weekend Australian

'A deeply moving fiction debut in which Dub examines the virtue of truth, the harm of lies, the pain of secrets, the desire for belonging and the difficulty of confronting ones past to ensure the future.'

Weekend Gold Coast Bulletin

'A gritty sandblown kind of story that once begun gets into your consciousness with compelling insistence. Yes, it's a page-turner and yes, it's a thriller-cum-rite-of-passage tale… The strength of Dub's ability to tell a story and hold an audience is clear in this first novel of hopefully many more. It is a book of many pathways to the heart and soul, of not only a country but families who deny the truth of who they are and what they strive to protect…'

Sunday Tasmanian

'Here we have a Tasmanian writer with a first novel that grabs you from the very first page. Well written, it is a compelling story that takes the protagonist on a journey of self discovery… We will hear more from Rosie Dub; well done.'

Tasmanian Life

www.ingramcontent.com/pod-product-compliance
Lightning Source LLC
Chambersburg PA
CBHW030516120726
47904CB00005B/1484

* 9 7 8 0 6 4 8 1 2 2 7 2 2 *